About the Author

An adventurer all his life, Stephen Harris brings his extensive experiences to the pages of his work. He loves to garden, cook, play golf and listen to the waves of the ocean while not working to offer his imaginations to the world.

Shooter Marble

Stephen Harris

Shooter Marble

Olympia Publishers
London

www.olympiapublishers.com
OLYMPIA PAPERBACK EDITION

A CIP catalogue record for this title is
available from the British Library.

ISBN: 978-1-80439-241-6

First Published in 2023

Olympia Publishers
Tallis House
2 Tallis Street
London
EC4Y 0AB

Printed in Great Britain

Dedication

I dedicate this novel to my dog, Casey, who sat by my side during its creation. You'll always be missed, Casey girl. And huge thanks go to Kathryne, for your love and support to bring this book to life.

Acknowledgements

Thank you to the team at Olympia for gently treating me to their professional guidance.

PROLOGUE

September 5, Assawoman Bay, Maryland

Sheets of mist floated above the water as if they hung from invisible clotheslines. At seven a.m., the sun not yet high enough to burn off the low-hanging condensation, it should have been the promise of a beautiful day. But the unease was so thick Doc Gilbert could cut it with a rusty scaling knife. Normally rich with the sounds of feeding birds, the bay barely whispered, a quiet more in tune with a funeral home. Doc whistled a ragged rendition of "Oh, Suzanna" as he guided his gunner boat, roughly hewed of white oak and coated with enough paint for an authentic old-school look. He skillfully manned a fifteen-foot-long wooden rod that propelled the craft through the grass-topped shallows. He was in a crouch, the stooped posture of a bay man, on the bend to retrieve the morning's bounty from his blue crab traps. A deeply tanned arm wiped away the salty mist from deep crevasses around his eyes. It was going to be hot, he knew, as soon as the sun burnt off the mist. *The Old Farmer's Almanac* dubbed it Indian summer. That periodical first appeared in 1818 and it claimed to be eighty percent accurate since its debut, but Doc knew it couldn't foretell or solve the mysteries of Assawoman. He trailed a grizzled right hand into the water, causing a mini wake.

"Got some gunk in yer gumption, I know, what's ailing ya, girl?"

He propelled the boat toward the whelk and crab trap buoys. The gunner boat rocked slightly to the starboard when a salty zephyr kicked up, an easterly Atlantic breeze, good to keep the stinging no-see-ums inland. A welcome draft on most days, it was typically an omen for a peaceful, bite-free twenty, maybe thirty hours. The sheets of mist bowed gracefully before disappearing. Still, the silence began to stink. Doc cocked his head to the side. "Peace doesn't always walk hand-in-hand with quiet," his mother used to say. He looked to the sky where segments of blue peeked through higher fog. It was autumnal migratory season, and the sky should have brimmed with birds, especially in the bountiful marshes that buttressed Assawoman Bay, a food court smorgasbord of bird treats. "What by Jupiter is this shit?"

The answer came from the sky, and Doc was so startled he almost fell overboard. Mangled, bloody remains of a gaggle of Canada geese noisily splashed into the water off the starboard bow. Downy feathers soon followed, rocking like a cradle on a grisly path to the bay. Doc Gilbert scratched his grizzled chin. He dragged a tattooed forearm across his brow while he scanned the world above. *Niente*, he saw nothing.

He poked a carcass with his pole; the geese were in shreds, as if they had flown into a giant meat grinder. The tiny hamlet of Clydesdale, Maryland had a major league problem on their hands. He nodded his head in solemn confirmation. Similar savagery had turned up over the past several weeks in town: all species of birds, all sizes, their decimated carcasses splayed throughout the tiny hamlet and its surrounding marshes.

***

Twenty feet off the starboard bow, hidden by the Salicornia grass, another life struggled with a more deadly conundrum.

Silas battled to keep his head above water. His right wing was broken. He was certain because he couldn't lift it high enough to maintain his balance. A busted wing was a death sentence for a Canada goose, making it easy target for predators. He had been a proud number three in the highflying chevron, and now this nightmare.

The attack had come from *invisible* predators. The assault, the shock, was so sudden and brutal. He knew of nothing that could inflict this type of mid-air damage. Only carnivores attacked Canada geese and unless wolves, coyotes, foxes, or bobcats sprouted wings, he was at a complete loss.

Silas eyed the ground bounder's boat as it slipped through the reeds. Major league predators, these ground bounders, but they only harvested one, maybe two geese at a time, and never in this fashion. Survival instinct hammered his heart as the brackish water began to tug him down. He struggled to release enough air through his vocal cords, his long, beautiful neck undulating with the effort.

***

Doc heard the weak honk, and he steered in that direction. Easing the skiff through the marsh grasses, he spotted the still whole goose as it battled to stay afloat.

"Well, will ya lookee here, Mr. Molson! Easy now… looks like ya got a lucky break today, yep. You must be the warrior of your clan, the only surviving soldier. War sure ain't pretty, no denying that, I seen it before, back in the day." Doc used a long-handled net and gingerly scooped up the goose, saving one of the last living birds in the bay.

"Ouch, looks like ya got a bum wing. Not to worry, I'll get ya to Ismelda, don't be concerned none, she's a good witch, you'll see. She'll fix ya up all ducky in no time at all."

Doc gingerly lifted the bird from the netting and laid him on his oilskin haversack. The crab and whelk pots could wait. Again, he examined the sky before he gassed the old Evinrude's throttle and steered toward shore.

"I ain't seen this type of predator before, fella. Even when we attacked the Huns, I ain't ever seen a campaign like this. Gonna need some powerful magic here about, yesiree.

"Back in the day I seen elephants in battle with armor that glistened in the sun; the reflection almost blinded us. Big shiny shields hung off of them huge white tusks. The armor was some kind of metal, I'll tell ya, no shit, all glittery and bright. That's when they'd fire their crossbows. Had to keep our shields high above the head, ya see, them arrows was near done invisible in that glare, just like what you must have been through. Them Huns thought they was gonna end the grand Roman Empire then and there but no sir, me and a few others figured a few well-placed arrows in them shiny beasts' eyes would send them all a rage…"

Silas had no clue what would happen, nor did he even care anymore. Shock assumed command as he lowered his head and released himself to whatever fate the babbling ground bounder held for him.

1

Delmarva Peninsula

Two weeks later

The rain mercilessly pounded the windshield and Larry Marble struggled to focus on the road. He couldn't recall if rain was a good or bad omen when beginning a new adventure. Either way, he was committed to follow through with his Grand Plan, sink or swim.

He and his Ford were southbound in lower Delaware, only miles from the Maryland state line, when the torrential rains hit. His cell had warned of the storm, and it pissed him off that he didn't make it to his destination before it hit. The storm had a name, some obscure Swahili grouping of letters that made absolutely no sense. In actual damage, it is currently dumped upon the Delmarva Peninsula, the north/south finger of land trisected by state borders from Delaware, Maryland, and Virginia. Streams and marshes swelled, flood sirens wailed, and instant ponds appeared at every swale, not a great night to be outside. Marble flicked the window defogger on high. He cocked his head to the right until his vertebrae cracked. His fingers nervously tapped the steering wheel, a staccato accompaniment with the battering rain.

A quick glance in the rearview mirror revealed no other cars in his wake, so he eased off the accelerator. There was no longer a need to hurry; for the first time in years, he had no agenda other than reaching Ocean City, Maryland. He checked his anger at not beating the storm and, in the process, renegotiated his Grand Plan mantra. No timetable, no scheduled appointments to keep, no plans beyond taking each moment as it arrived. It scared the living daylights out of him, sure, but the unbridled surge of energy it delivered far outweighed the negatives.

A duet of lightning and thunder rattled his attention, followed by two huge yawns. Maybe it was time to find a place to stay the night and recharge that unbridled energy. The Maryland state line flew by, and he dismissed the last thought. If it weren't for the rain, he might be close enough to roll down a window and smell the ocean. Perfect time for a smoke, the devil on his shoulder whispered.

He changed the radio to the AM band while his brain rumbled, rumbled, rumbled with nicotine *feed me, feed me, feed me* hunger. With a move born from habit, he stuffed his fingers into his left shirt pocket in search of the phantom pack of smokes. All he grabbed though was a sore pec muscle underneath the cotton and rayon blend eggshell-white oxford adorned with an amoeba patterned tie, the formal duds worn for Deelah and the divorce papers. He yanked on the Windsor knot and released the pressure around his neck. You won't choke me anymore, Deelah, no more.

The radio scan landed on "George Noori's Coast to Coast," a nationally syndicated radio show. A caller claimed to know the reason behind the mysterious disappearance of all the birds centered around Clydesdale, Maryland.

"Global warming is diabolically controlled by an alien mother ship disguised as an asteroid and hidden in the shadows of the moon. I know because I've intercepted their

communications with my Tesla tower. They've concentrated a million ultraviolet rays into a laser beam that refracts off the junkyard of satellite debris in orbit and they've redirected this beam towards Clydesdale, Maryland, simply crisp-frying every bird in the sky. It's a manufactured, controlled solar flare, boo-yah! The same alien mother ship influence caused the disappearance of the honeybees, another mystery I've also solved."

George Noori asked, "Why have the aliens chosen Clydesdale, Maryland of all places? Why not Washington, D.C? New York City? London?"

The caller never hesitated in his reply. "They are targeting another alien force sequestered in a hidden base beneath the bay; take off your aluminum foil hat and you'll be able to figure this out too, George."

Marble chuckled at the kookiness – *just another crazy whacko*, he thought. Crazy was a word that also reminded him of his ex-wife, Deelah, now officially an 'ex' for the past five hours. Marble laughed out loud, and it surprised him. He should have been angry. Weren't all divorcees angry, bitter people? Try as he might, the only emotion he could muster was laughter. Deelah despised any AM band station. It had always been a tug of war to agree on anything of mutual listening appeal with her in the car. One of the many little hairballs that make up a shit pillow's worth of stuffing in a relationship. He turned up the radio's volume and laughed so heartily it hurt his ribs. If this is how good divorce felt, he was in for a real hoot on his Grand Plan.

Deelah had wanted to end the marriage. Marble never put up too much of an argument. He figured when someone says they no longer love you, the only honorable response is to walk away. Marble's few friends offered encouragement and advice. One path he chose led to a health club in Middletown where he met Samuel, the trainer with a five-foot-three, three-foot-wide, not an ounce of body fat, rock-hard physique. Marble hated the workout regimen Samuel assigned, not so much because of the sore muscles, but his true dislike for the trainer. Samuel reminded Marble of a troll. He had been deathly afraid of trolls as a kid, and Samuel looked like a pumped-up abomination. Marble's lower lip began to quiver as he recalled the memory. Recollections of his childhood were a rare occurrence.

His tires hit the rumble strips on the road's shoulder, and he turned the steering wheel to the left. Nope, death is not a diet, he yelled in his head, the only place on his body that wasn't sore from the troll's exercise/torture regimen.

"Mr. Marble, you'll drop ten pounds in one week. How, Mr. Marble? Stomach crunches… calorie-munching, ball-busting, gut-tearing stomach crunches. You ain't ever seen a fat guy with rock-hard abs, have you, Mr. Marble?"

For the life of him, Marble couldn't deduce how even his toe muscles were sore from all the crunches, burpee mashers and, the troll called this one his specialty, bridge busters. His body was about to experience a new form of tension.

A pair of headlights blasted onto his rearview mirror as a tractor-trailer emerged in his wake like a phantom leviathan booted out of hell. The truck passed on the left and sent a blinding tsunami of water onto Marble's Ford.

He yelled every four-letter word he knew. Then he saw his speedometer. He was only traveling at thirty-five miles per hour, a violation of the holy rules of the road.

It was an urban myth among the road warriors of the world that whether or not you earned the right to drive in Heaven depended on the asphalt angel's evaluation of your road skills on

Earth. Marble wanted to put the pedal to the metal in the next life, especially if Deelah miraculously managed to make it there.

The tractor-trailer breast stroked into the lane in front of him as his radio provided further entertainment. George Noori feigned enthusiasm for a nut case Texan who claimed to have invented the time machine from an ingenious assortment of rubber bands and paper clips a person could easily hide in one's pant pockets.

Marble couldn't resist the humor while he squeezed the steering wheel tighter and hoped he wouldn't miss his exit. He checked his trip meter – he had to be nearing his goal, although it didn't help his wounded road ego that the ass end of the tractor-trailer had a painted Mr. Gobble potato chip bag that mocked him with a toothy grin.

The observations almost made him miss a green road sign with reflective white lettering. When it came into focus, *US 90 Ocean City* was all he spied as he sped by at a more respectable fifty miles per hour. That was his turn-off, the first step of his Grand Plan, to the ocean. Once upon a time, he had spent a weekend in his youth at the shore. Two big-haired sisters from New Jersey had taken him on a carnal roller-coaster ride that had spanned two days, a recently surfaced memory that served as added motivation to his Grand Plan.

A second green sign blipped by, and he coiled his head around to look as if the message was printed on the back for daydreamers who didn't pay attention. He faced the front again, only to see the bright brake lights of the tractor-trailer. Marble slammed his brakes and almost French kissed the potato chip mouth with the shit-eating grin. He cursed again his bad luck. This must be the exit. Now he would have to follow the eighteen-wheel rainstorm all the way into Ocean City. He snapped his turn signal while George Noori's whacky time traveler stonewalled about exactly how any moron could simply use paper clips and rubber bands to visit the ancient Roman Empire.

***

Willem Clydesdale IV was in a proverbial putrid pickle. One ball-busting quandary after another had piled up all day at his feet like a smelly mound of two-day-old chicken shit from Tommie's Chicken Farm out on Peppertick Road.

His old Chevy pickup drifted along the exit ramp leading to town. The vehicle sputtered to a stop, tilted to starboard on the shoulder as the rain played "Wipeout" on his roof. The vehicle had run out of gas and his cell phone had lost power. To add seasoning to his shit sandwich, it was black as hell outside with a storm that seemed far too angry. Willem's gut churned a dangerous brew of his dinner of IHOP pancakes, coffee, and tons of maple syrup, an acidic belch that made the skeletons in his closet gag.

He was on the last stretch from a desperate mission to Seaford, Delaware that had turned out to be a complete shit parfait. A bogus shaman had assured him that his mysterious cargo, wrapped in a blotched oilcloth on the passenger floor of his truck, was easily controlled. It had been total bullshit. All Willem had obtained from his quest was a nose that still stung from the heavily perfumed blend of wannabe shaman incense.

"I should have known better. Fucking fake, that's all he was, should have practiced his magic on a Slurpee machine."

A clap of thunder dangerously close caused Willem to flinch. He stared at the pond that rapidly formed at the bottom of the ramp. Rain kept insects undercover, but he still grabbed a can of

Cutter insect repellent because it paid to be cautious. Most of the town's residents braved the recent onslaught of winged bloodsuckers by drinking a specially concocted tea brewed by local witches. Willem grunted with disgust at the smell of the bug spray as he smeared it on his skin.

"This is still better than a dapple with witch's magic. Especially since I got my own version of hocus pocus."

A gust of wind rocked the pickup and he looked at his watch while he fired up a Lucky Strike. Ten p.m. His options were slim. No one, not even flounder-faced Carl Heffley, town sheriff, would venture out to the highway on a night like this. He'd have to sleep in his vehicle. "Shit happens, deal with it." That was the only worthwhile advice his dead father had ever shared.

A muddled movement on the passenger floor caught his eye. A vibration from a world unlike anything on this planet caused the oilcloth to pulse with energy and he reluctantly reached out. He pulled back the cloth slowly and exposed the eerie magic in his life: a wonderfully strange and haunted pile of black, gnarled twigs beneath. He gingerly lifted the cargo and opened it like a book. It burped and Willem smelled shaman.

A flash of lightning illuminated the interior of the car and, for a second, Willem thought he saw a black smile on the surface of the twigs. He placed the cargo gingerly back on the passenger floor and blanketed it with the oilcloth.

For thirty years, the package had remained quiet in the footlocker in his bedroom. He had originally found it in the burnt out remains of the family mansion. It was the only relic he bothered saving. Not quite three weeks ago, he had awakened in the middle of the night to a nightmarish sound that would have turned his hair gray if he had any. The wail emanated from his footlocker. The package awakened and ensnared Willem. And now it had killed, or "at least disappeared a man right in front of my eyes," mumbled Willem.

Bright lights splashed off his side-view mirror and the action released his mind's lock on his spooky passenger. Midweek evening traffic in September was usually light to non-existent for this exit. Recently, though, the town had received an unhealthy influx of state and national attention because of *a few dead birds*.

"Damn nothing lessness scientists sticking their noses where they don't belong. Ain't a thing nature can't handle on her own."

Willem considered himself an original. He conjured up his own vocabulary and *nothing lessness* was the current Clydesdale word of the month. He rolled down his window, stuck a meaty arm into the downpour, and waved his snot rag at the oncoming lights.

***

The tractor-trailer's brake lights flashed but the smiling potato chip bag didn't slow down. It surfed past the pickup sitting on the shoulder of the exit ramp and splashed it with a ten-foot wall of water.

Marble eased off the gas as he neared the stranded pickup. Movement in the front seat caught his attention. His headlights illuminated the animated baldhead of a fat guy who punched both fists with the middle finger raised in the direction of the smiling potato chip truck.

As if pummeled in the head with a 2x4 baseball bat, Marble's head jolted with a new vision's impact. He now saw the same man at the helm of a large boat, baying at the moon. Marble shook his head to free the sight. Reality greeted him with another shocker. This time he didn't pump the brakes – he slammed them hard. His Ford slid into a pond that still rippled with the tractor-trailer's wake. The impetus plowed a second wave of puddle into the open-windowed truck. A couple of three-sixties later, Marble found himself pointed in the direction of Clydesdale, MD, unbeknownst to him because his whirly-dos in the small lake had flown him right past the sign that read:

Welcome!
Clydesdale, Maryland
Pop. 8,877
The Mid-Atlantic Bird Watchers Paradise
The Honorable E. Willem Clydesdale IV, Mayor

Marble hit the gas as he coughed up the tongue he had just swallowed. The whirly-do with hydroplaning had superseded contemplation on his first clairvoyant vision in over three decades. Now free from the pond, he navigated the narrow two-lane road, surprised how much smaller the path to Ocean City seemed after eighteen years.

***

Willem rolled up his window and tossed the soaked snot rag into the back of the cab. He yanked his stretched to the limit shirt out from behind his suspenders and dried his glasses. *Mayor* was more titular than operational, but still, he steamed, it should earn some more respect.

The Peterbilt tractor-trailer he recognized. It was Popeye Worthington, the devil black nothinglessness down from Milford, making his bimonthly stop in Clydesdale to deliver potato products to a few businesses and poke his nose into the widow Anna Smythe's affairs.

The Peterbilt nothinglessness would have his day soon

enough, that was for sure. The Ford with Pennsylvania plates was another matter, an outsider, a carpetbagger. Willem got a funny feeling; in his experience, nothing good ever came out of Pennsylvania. In addition, it was the middle of the week, ten days after the Labor Day weekend. Tourist traffic had dried up. Visitors were rare, even rarer than good Samaritans, which meant his chance at rescue was slim to none.

Willem shrugged, so be it, a night in the car would have to do. *I'm the fucking mayor; you'd think someone would actually give a shit.* He settled into the rigid vinyl bench seat and resigned himself to his fate. The sign of a healthy mind is the ability to fall asleep easily. Willem believed his mind soared above all his peers. He quickly snored his way into a dream where the pretty widow Smythe lifted her skirt as she begged him to give it to her hard and deep. The mysterious passenger in Willem's car didn't join its host in carnal slumber. It pulsed with a blood-red light that emanated eerily in a spidery web across the floorboard and out into the night, for it too sensed something ominous in the car from Pennsylvania.

The same eerie light caught the attention of hidden eyes deep within a copse of loblolly pine and the twitters of delight cackled like cicadas. A hundred set of yellow orbs blinked back through the tree limbs, joining the wind in shaking off the warm September rain.

2

Streetlights, blackjack oaks and sycamores cast macabre shadows, devilish dervishes danced across the wet macadam, and imps swirled through the air as the road into town beckoned caution to all who dared enter.

Marble slowed to twenty-five miles per hour and allowed the tractor-trailer to move well ahead. Plus, he was careful not to run afoul of the law on his first night's foray into his Grand Plan. He eased the Ford through an intersection cornered on four sides by closed businesses and lit in the center by a blinking yellow caution light that shook violently on its cable.

The windswept crossroads revealed vendor signs draped in shadows, a 1930s film noir snippet of a shuttered ghost town. Every shadow whispered peril, every airborne vessel a mischievous ghoul.

A childhood memory bobbed to the surface like a fishing line float. He recalled his Boy Scout days when scary stories about witches, trolls, and headless axmen had kept him awake many a night after the campfires died. Martin, his older brother, had been the one to comfort him, to tell him to buck up and not be afraid, that bad monsters weren't real, just imagination. The recollection shook him to his core as his eyes welled. "Marty, you were so wrong; sorry, I haven't thought of you in so damn long."

The storm rocked his car and whatever memory had surfaced about his brother retreated into the background. The line of buildings to his left ended, now replaced by a deep blackness that held a sultry allure. He succumbed to the temptation and gazed out the driver's window, into the tired eyes of his reflection.

Forty years on life's treadmill had gouged a toll on his once chiseled lines. Now he just resembled a pouty everyman, nondescript features, a flabby excuse for a divorced guy. The early signs of permanent bags and the hint of swollen jowls reminded him of his late father, a man who on the eve of his forty-eighth birthday had met a massive coronary. Marble grasped for the comforted beat of his own heart and wondered how many paternal genes he had inherited.

Thank God I quit smoking, he thought, even though the weak praise ignited his end of the day tobacco crave. Once again, he pawed at his shirt pocket. The big buttski bear passed, followed by a heavy sigh that reminded him of how desperately he craved sleep. Then it hit him: the recollection of his father. An anvil lifted off of a dusty steamer chest of memories. Cloudy ghosts filled his thoughts, so distant yet so eerily familiar; he couldn't recall how long they had lain silent.

He refocused on the road ahead and then screamed to high heaven. The Ford rapidly approached a dark, cloaked figure that stood in the middle of the street. There was no time for the horn. He slammed on his brakes, squeezed his eyes shut and skidded to a stop on the rain-slicked macadam. There was no bump, no thump, no scream, and no contact. He checked his mirrors, twisted round in his seat, and scanned the street behind.

"What the, where in the hell…" The moment was eerily familiar. Hollywood portrayed it in countless horror flicks. Marble imagined his own audience screaming, "Don't get out of the car!"

Three rapid bursts of lightning saved him the debate. To his left, he earned a glimpse of a large expanse of water but no dead body. Mother Nature aided his vision again as he looked to his right. A small business sign hung in the front yard of a large Victorian home.

He eased the car onto the graveled shoulder. He retrieved a Maglite flashlight from beneath his seat, put a tweed beret on his head, and then grabbed his raincoat. He stepped out into the storm and thought, let the theater patrons scream all they want, the wusses.

A gust of wind tried to smack him with a flurry of punches, but he held firm and shone the light across the road. A search of the far shoulder's marsh grass revealed no body.

"What the hell was someone doing in the middle of the road in the pouring rain?"

The flashlight's powerful beam cut through the haze that hugged the pavement behind the Ford. There was no body, no sign of any human.

"Maybe I am beat tired. I'm beginning to see things." *What a shock that is, now that old memories show up after thirty years,* he thought, *and to top it off, I'm getting soaked looking for an imaginary body, this is so not funny.*

He circled the car and examined the front bumper and grill. No dents, clumps, or humps of hair, no discernible blood, *all good, all good,* and a soft sigh whooshed out of his mouth; the theater patrons sat back in their chairs with sweaty palmed relief. Marble turned toward the building.

The Ford's headlights captured a wooden sign made of pine with burnt lettering beneath a lacquered patina. A ground-anchored spotlight splayed a weak beam on the placard as it rocked violently in the breeze, so it took a couple of swings through the light before Marble could read the engraving: Ismelda's Paradise Bed & Breakfast.

"A B&B," he said out loud while looking at the Victorian. "Interesting coincidence, spooky on a stormy night. Now all we need is a…" Thunder clapped so close it made his knees shake. "What the hell, it'll have to do."

He chuckled nervously. His Grand Plan skipped onward to the unexpected; it fed on coincidence and thrived on surprises. Marble returned to the car, eased it past the B&B's driveway, and parked beneath the branches of an enormous old blackjack oak. Another flash of lightning blazed much too close, and he thought he spied a pair of yellow eyes staring down at him from within the massive tree's bark. He blinked a few times before looking again at the tree. Only the dark giant loomed back.

"This place will do just fine. Spooky maybe, a little Adams Familyish, but still, it will do. One, maybe two nights here, and by then I should already have found a cheap apartment with a view of the ocean." It had to be a view of the ocean, too, he reminded himself. That was, after all, part of his Grand Plan. "And I really have to stop talking out loud to myself, or else somebody is gonna lock me up and throw away the key."

A gust of wind and rain rocked the car so violently that Marble stayed put until the fury passed. He used the moment to rehash his long, long day.

***

"Stop acting like a crazy man, Marble, what if I need to get a hold of you?" Deelah adjusted a fake eyelash while the ink dried on their mutually agreeable, irretrievably broken, uncontested, irreconcilable differences divorce papers at her pig-faced lawyer's office.

"What do you need my number for? You wanted this

divorce, now you want to call me too?"

"You are such a bumbling idiot, Marble. Our accountant will need it for next year's tax preparations. Your friends will need it whenever they sober up enough to realize you're gone. Personally, I could give a rat's ass about it, I'm just taking the high road in this unfortunate situation."

"This unfortunate situation? Give me a break, Deelah, don't patronize me. It's over; this paper means we don't have to contact each other ever again. Fuck the taxes, I'm filing single." Marble wanted to remain cool as ice, so he employed his best Clint Eastwood bravado. He was six feet tall, two hundred and thirty pounds, proportioned throughout his frame to give him the look of a barrel-chested middle-aged man.

Deelah was shocked, her mouth hung open but silent, as rare as Saharan rain. Marble snapped a mental picture. This one was a keeper. Her Jimmy Choo pumps, and a tight Liz Claiborne navy-blue dress revealed most of her size 4 assets, which included her new and improved 36Cs. Her sculpted blond hair was molded into a tight bun atop her head. Her makeup heavy but proportioned evenly, highlighted by ruby-red lipstick that had evolved into an oral chastity belt over the years.

They had met eight years earlier on a Thursday, Lady's Night at Maxie's, the townie hot spot not far from Agricultural Hall. He and his pals had camped out in front of the DJ booth, a strategic position for snakedom. It bordered both the dance floor and the entrance to the ladies' room. Deelah had brushed by him three times – deliberately, she later admitted. Marble took the bait on the third pass, complimenting her tan. The rest, as they say, was history.

He stared at her cleavage. He remembered thinking that she still had a great tan. *All the quicker to wrinkle you with, my pretty.*

The pig-faced lawyer dryly bid them adieu as Marble checked his own torso for signs of open wounds. Deelah addressed him. As with most of their conversations, Marble again noticed she never once made direct eye contact.

"Since when did tough-guy talk become part of your repertoire, Marble? It's not you. Don't look for the macho inside because it doesn't exist. Now, seriously, what if somebody calls for you? You just got that new cell phone; no one has the number, including me. What should I tell them, Marble?"

It sounded funny to him for the first time, even though she had always called him by his last name. He forced down an urge to giggle.

"Screw 'em. Anybody that I want to know what's happened already knows. Get that through your pretty head, cupcakes." Michael Madsen was a rebel and Larry Marble always wanted to be a tough guy, a Reservoir Dogs' Mr. Blonde badass rebel tough guy. It was his version of divorce therapy, walk the walk.

Deelah acknowledged the act with a sudden glint in her eye but soon the vacuum behind her colored-lensed vision reappeared.

"Knock off the false bravado, Marble. You watch far too much TV, no wait, my bad… watch whatever you want, OK? I'm not your mommy anymore." She made the 'L' shape with her fingers over her forehead. Marble thought at this point Michael Madsen would have brought out the .357 Smith & Wesson.

"I gotta go, Dee." She hated that nickname.

"What if it's an emergency and I can't reach you? You don't have a job anymore." She wouldn't admit it, but Marble could tell she relished jabbing that dagger into him one more time. "So I can't call you at *work*. Just give your damn number…"

He wanted to mess up her five o'clock anchor hairdo but his

hands might have become permanently stuck in her super-hold gel vise, an awkward arrangement for a divorced couple. Instead, he opted to stay with the verbal repartee. Mr. Blonde would be disappointed.

"Deelah, try and understand. For once in your life, listen to me. You wanted this divorce. I'm a pitiful loser, remember? I'm too much like a little boy, always having to be babysat. Remember? You didn't want to be married to me any longer. Remember? Well, I obliged. So, I'm starting a new life. You are not part of this new world. You're not part of Larry Marble's Grand Plan. Period."

He had just referred to himself in the third person. It felt like trying to squeeze into three sizes too small spandex bicycle pants. The sweat poured down his armpits and a thousand tingled needles pricked him in the halupkis.

Deelah laughed belittlingly. "Memories mold the future, so I will always be part of your life, whether you like it or not."

Now it was Marble's turn to snicker at her Hallmark philosophy. When she tried to sound smart, her south Jersey accent resurfaced magnificently. *It's just what the blue-collars of central Pennsylvania wanted to hear when they turned on their boob tubes for a little prejudiced local yokel news reporting*, he thought smugly. Deelah cut him off at the pass.

"What are you smiling about? You look like a little boy with a hand caught in the cookie jar. This is serious. What if I come across something of yours in the condo?"

"Nothing of mine is left in the townhouse. Everything I want is either in storage or in the Ford." Here it came, the big aloha, the grand adios, the fond farewell, the final kiss-off, the whole enchilada of "here's looking at you, kid". Maybe he would ask for one final sloppy kiss that would smear the sticky red lipstick all over her face.

She had been a good kisser at one point of their relationship, mostly when drunk and lipstick free. But two years prior to the divorce, she had given up alcohol for Lent and it had been one long Lenten sacrifice for Marble. Abstinence really sucked when force-fed. He decided to keep it cordial and summoned forth the master, his best Humphrey Bogart oomph.

"Goodbye, Dee. We had fun but now we closed the joint for good." He twirled round and sauntered down the granite-floored hallway, his greatcoat bucked, his back stuck straight, and his chin pointed at the ceiling – the John Wayne strut – and he wondered if his final words had been a hand around the throat moment, one of those last a lifetime, tear-choked memories. He had been up most of the previous evening rehearsing them, after all.

She quickly shot his hopes down and did her best to get in the last word, a cowardly six-gun blast to the back. "What's this Great Plot bullshit, anyway? Sounds like something a twelve-year-old would come up with. Oh, that's right. You just got in touch again with that little boy living in you. Well, guess what? I knew he's been there all along. I feel like I've been fucking babysitting for the past eight years. Do you hear me? Marble? Eight years of changing your diapers. And another thing…"

The spinning vacuum door of city hall drowned her out. He walked the free man strut down Front Street, a spark in his step, a weight off his back, a whistle on his lips. He reached his Ford, the back seat piled high with his meager baggage of life. Once on the freeway, he powered down the windows and let the early fall air swirl all the dust from his interior. The highway ran parallel to the Susquehanna River, and he glanced at the trees in the throes of color change that lined the mighty waterway. As he passed the

Loganville exit, his demeanor improved. He flashed the bird in the direction of the Cheek Tool and Die Company billboard that stood high above the manufacturing plant below.

"Those British consulting firm bastards with ugly teeth are downsizing the sales department into a room of cubicles, we're doomed, all of us doomed." Those had been the fateful words of his sales manager. Outside salesmen who'd spent a good part of their adult lives making their own hours, seeing movie matinees during the week, sleeping under the shade of willow trees in parks that lined the Susquehanna River, were now reduced to clock punching robots with headpiece telephone tiaras.

"Telemarketing, the wave of the future" – his Cheek sales manager had bravely pitched a week later, towing the company line, two days before he stuck a pistol in his mouth in the garage of his suburban Camp Hills rancher. Marble had taken the loss of his boss hard. On the fateful morning that would decide the rest of his life, he recalled his words to Deelah after she had bailed him out of jail. "I burst in on a closed-door upper-level management meeting and dumped a bucket full of cow shit right on top of the faggot Englishmen."

Deelah hadn't laughed. Regrets ruled Marble all his life yet losing his job in a handcuffed parade out the Cheek's offices didn't even rank in his top ten. It had been worth it, even if it was the final unravel of a marriage never tied too tight in the first place.

His sore shoulders felt surprisingly light. The weight of a job he had never wanted was finally gone. The burden of a bush-league news talent like Deelah, constantly whining about her unlucky breaks, and how, with the right agent, she could anchor network news, was also gone. All that lay ahead was Ocean City, Maryland, and his light-as-a-feather Grand Plan.

He would relocate there for a couple of months, then maybe Ft. Lauderdale, and then, after selling the rights to his novel to a major film studio, he would kick up his wealthy heels in a Santa Barbara beachfront home. First, he had to write the book, a task also of the Grand Plan.

An angel's bowling tournament of rolling thunder rocked Marble back to the present. He was surprised by the daydreaming because that was something not done since he was a— wait a second. Deelah's earlier words hit him hard. He *was* in touch with the little boy inside his head and the dusty memories hidden for so many years now slowly crept forth, at least until a thud on his car's hood made him flinch.

The enormous eyes of a barn owl's severed head stared back at him before it slipped slowly off to the side. He sat still for a moment, not sure if it was real or a hallucination. A light turned on at the front porch of the B&B. He grabbed his duffel bag out of the back seat and stepped out of the car. The owl's head wasn't a hallucination because it sat against his front tire. Must have flown into a power line or something, he thought. Omen or sheer coincidence or spooky doings, none of them mattered as the rain renewed in earnest.

With a quick glance over his shoulder for the cloaked phantom, he sprinted up the sidewalk, underneath the ancient oak and onto the covered wooden porch. To his right, an empty lover's swing rocked in the wind, almost in measured time with the two Boston rockers that swayed to his left. He turned the knob on the stained-glass front door and walked into a musty hallway. It was lit by turn of the twentieth century wall-mounted oil lamps. Déjà vu flashed in his noggin. It all looked vaguely familiar. He shook his head and chalked it up to fatigue. To his left, an antique country bench extended all the way to the foot of a long stairway, lit to the second level by another row of wall lamps. Tony Bennett and Lady Gaga made him look to his right.

Music emerged from behind closed French doors. The scent of sauteed onion and garlic lingered in the hallway and his stomach growled. *Shit*, he thought, *I haven't eaten anything in over twelve hours.* A laminated post-it read Manager/Owner. Marble knocked and the doors rattled in their tracks. Furniture creaked, floorboards squealed, and then the wooden doors slowly slid open, emitting a breath of tangerine and vanilla. Five oil lamps lit the room and an eerie luminescence danced around the innkeeper's visage.

"Good evening, whew, some weather. Um, any vacancies?"

"Welcome, stranger this stormy night, shelter your power with gentle might, or beware the inn keep with the sharpened knife, makes no difference be it black or white." Thunder crashed and Marble briefly recalled a scene from Mel Brooks' *Young Frankenstein.*

"Uh, excuse me?"

"A Celtic welcoming to a weary soul. I'm Ismelda, welcome to the Paradise. Fifty bucks a night, no booze, partying, no American Express, Discover, or checks, the other credit cards, OK, but I prefer cash. No AAA discount bullshit, either. Breakfast is from seven to nine. Since you're my only guest, I don't eat anything after seven forty-five and I hate to eat alone, so breakfast is at seven fifteen. East room has the best view of the water. South room has leaks. North room is a bit girly for the likes of you. West room has bats. You game, mister?"

Marble was amazed at her lungpower. All of it delivered in one breath. As his eyes adjusted to the light, he noticed she was in the fifty-to-death range. Her hair might have been gray, but Marble couldn't tell because of the large, lumpy, purple-flowered nightcap she wore over curlers. A faded pink Annapolis sweatshirt covered her petite torso all the way down to her knees where her bare legs disappeared into a pair of pink, fuzzy slippers.

"Hey, Gilligan, anybody home in there?"

"Uh, oh, sorry, but I'm pretty tired. Sleep, that's what I need; it's been a long day. Do you accept cash?"

"In a heartbeat. You're lucky my light was still on. Won't find too much more open this time a night. Especially in a pickle like this." As if for emphasis, a gust of wind cold-cocked the front door. It banged open into the bench and staggered the stained-glass panes into a standing eight count.

Marble jumped like a goosed Girl Scout, still a bit freaked from the close call on the road and the owl head. Ismelda glided by and firmly shut the door and locked it tight.

"Here you go, fifty bucks, breakfast at seven fifteen." He handed her the cash and tried to remember. "Um, east room?" She cast him a thumbs-up over her shoulder as she snapped open a cash box and inserted his payment. He cast a glance into her room. The flickering glow reflected off a huge oil canvas of a snowy egret hung above a bricked-in fireplace. His eyes centered on the painted orbs of the bird. He could have sworn the creature turned its head and looked at him. In fact, the bird flapped its wings…

"Just go up this staircase and turn to the right at the top of the steps. Straight down the hallway is your room." Ismelda began to close the sliding door and the painting from his view. "Houston, we have a problem. Hey, are you listening? Hard of hearing, mister?"

"What's that again?"

"The room, mister, at the top of the stairs, east room will be dead ahead. You don't need a key. I don't lock them anyway.

Bathroom is in the middle of the hallway on your right. Towels are hanging on the wall. Oh, and you might want to make sure everything important is out of your car, you know. Can never be too certain these days.”

“My car? No, uh, I’m fine. All I need is in here.” He hoisted the duffel bag’s strap over his shoulder.

“Suit yourself. Sleep tight.” With that, she, Tony Bennett and Lady Gaga disappeared behind the French doors.

“Uh, miss, I mean, Ismelda, does the front room have a view of the ocean?”

Marble could swear he heard a surprised reaction before calmer words ensued.

“Sure, it does, that view will be anything you want it to be. Have a ball.”

He sloshed up creaking steps lined with carpet worn so thin that just a ghost of its original pattern remained. Once at the top, he turned toward the front of the house. There was a closed door on the left, one at the end of the hallway, and the bathroom on the right. The portal straight ahead was the only one wide open and he surmised it was his rental. He looked over his shoulder. At the far end of the hallway, a huge cedar chest blocked another doorway. *Must be the one with the bats*, he thought.

He made a pit stop in the bathroom and relieved himself into an authentic porcelain bowl with a wrought-iron base. Ornamental porcelain faucets lined the claw-foot tub and sink. He was in a turn of the century water closet that had just entered the world of flushing toilets and pressurized water. *Geez, Deelah would love this place.* He stared in the mirror. “Stop it, Marble. You’re not supposed to think like that anymore.”

He trudged down the hallway and entered his room. With each step, the floorboards squeaked hello. The room had a calming scent of lavender and rosemary. The bed was canopied – a warm invitation. The room had two tall inset windows and two cherrywood night tables. To the right, an old armoire sat with open doors – it had swallowed a small TV. His duffel thudded to the floor and the wet raincoat flew off and draped itself over the back of an upholstered sitting chair. His amoeba patterned tie was removed, and the shirt unbuttoned when the fatigue of the day hit him like a sledgehammer. Barely free of wet shoes, he flopped onto the cushioned mattress and found sleep before the bedsprings stopped their squeaks.

Moments later, outside his window, gnarled roots exploded, globs of mud shot-gunned into the air, and the massive blackjack oak leaned into a fateful fall, drooping further downward, its two-hundred-year-old roots about to take their first steps. Gravity said, "Come on babe, that's it, yeah, come to mama". Slowly, the giant bowed to the earth and crushed everything in its path. The Ford disappeared beneath ten tons of wood. Out on the street, a dark, hooded figure appeared from the shadows and watched the old tree gracefully succumb. A second later, lightning flashed above Assawoman Bay, and just as quickly, the specter vanished.

Marble missed it all. As he snored softly, Ismelda tiptoed into the room and draped an antique quilt over his body. She peeked out the front window and the demise of the old oak brought a smile to her lips. She closed her eyes and thanked the Good Mother because the prophecy had come to be. *The one who sees will request a view of the sea.*

Ismelda turned out the lights and left his room as the wind and rain continued to lash away at the slatted wooden shutters. Salvation is near, she thought, as she crossed to the western room, stepped over the chest, and entered its dark domain. From a bed of hay and moss nestled in a dormer's small alcove, with bandaged wing and healthier prospects, Silas, the rescued goose, weakly honked agreement.

It had begun.

3

It was a postcard sunny day and the rented Schwinn felt good beneath his chiseled glutes. He glided down the boardwalk with nary an effort, perfect speed for absorbing the full effect of the scenery. Women in thong bikinis blew kisses, flashed their breasts and tongue-in-cheek blow jobbed him as he drifted by, his bronze, tanned Adonis body glistening with silver perspiration. It was a by-the-seashore confectionery store: a tempting nibble here, a sultry licking there, sweetness everywhere. He wove through the young, firm bodies, their manicured nails teasingly stroking his skin.

A plop of bird shit splashed off his handlebars and Marble angrily looked up. Hundreds of birds watched his progress and the vista put a strain on the credibility of the day. Perched on both sides of his parade route were gulls, terns, plovers, kingfishers, swallows, geese, egrets, herons, owls, hawks, and pelicans. He pondered his newfound mental capacity that enabled him to identify each species of his winged admirers.

In the blink of an astral eye, the birds and bikinis took flight, a great whoosh of wings, thongs, and tramp stamp oriental tattoos. His postcard vista now replaced by hoary solitude, aching with loneliness, there was not a breathing soul on the boardwalk but he and the Schwinn. A dark, thunderous cloud tumbled in, a churning black cumulus that funneled down from above and spit a ragged-haired Deelah onto the boardwalk, followed quickly by a dumpster worth of dead, mangled birds.

Deelah stared at him with crazed, bloodshot eyes, and he

slammed on the Schwinn's brakes, his flip-flops tearing apart in the process. Deelah's red-lipped mouth, with a clownish smirk, opened to speak, but what issued forth was more chainsaw gnash and snarl than words. Her anger erupted in jagged sparks that sprang from her wild hair when she saw his bike with the manufacturer's gold embossed model name *Ye Grande Planne* sashayed on the handlebar. She bent over and began to chew the wooden boardwalk.

Plank after plank burst into puffs of splinters and sawdust as she sawed and churned her way toward him. He tried to turn the bike around but now it wasn't there. Neither was his tan, svelte, rippled, chiseled body. He was outside and naked. Panic engulfed him as a terrible, wrenched, unearthly noise made him look up. His ex-wife was no longer doing the chewing. She had been replaced by a hideous beast unlike any nightmare had ever produced. Train whistle decibels rocked his eardrums and great cloudy, sulfur-yellow eyes bore into Marble as the beast sawed faster, faster, closer, closer—

"Halloo in there, Mr. Sleepyhead. Hey. It's seven fifteen, mister, reveille, reveille, morning chow time."

…The beast stopped chewing and now spoke, although it didn't sound so ominous any longer…

"Say hello to the morning, Gilligan. Jeez, you think you'd have a little more respect for my quilt, sleeping on it with wet clothes. Any damage and it goes on your bill. Hey, are you alive in there?"

Definitely not the beast, or Deelah. In fact, the picture changed channels. He now swam through a waterless lake and sought a place to pee while the voice followed him—

"Fine, ignore me, I been eating alone for more than twenty years, no sweat off of my back. Wahoo, get a gander of that.

Whaddoyou know! Some view of the bay. I could probably get seventy, maybe a hundred a night off-season for this room, now. A buck fifty in the summer. Too bad about that car, though. Hey, mister, you own a Ford?"

There it was. Hallelujah! the men's lavatory, right outside the pig-faced divorce lawyer's office. He breast-stroked feverishly, his bladder on the verge of explosion. He opened the bathroom door and climbed into his Ford and hold on, he couldn't pee in his…Ford…*Ford…*

Marble's eyes snapped open, and his first view was of a petite woman who stood at the window next to his bed. It took a second, but he acknowledged his environment, although a landlady in his bedroom reeked of improprieties. Marble smiled a tight-lipped morning breath smile. She wore the same grossly oversized pink baseball hat as the night before, with her hair and some other kind of rollers pushed up underneath. He liked women that didn't give a hoot about their hair twenty-four hours a day.

Deelah would spend an hour and a half each morning, primping, pumping, spraying, gelling, teasing, blow-drying, hot curling and cursing at hair that wound up in a sculpture as high as her ever-present south Jersey accent. Marble would tell his buddies – never to Deelah's face – that you could take the girl out of New Jersey, but you could never take the high hair out of the Jersey girl. God forbid, if he, a breeze, or a sprinkle of rain got in her way after her morning molding.

The woman in his room was *familiar* though, definitely not New Jersey. Her name, what was it… *Ismelda… The Paradise B&B… Ocean City… day two… bingo!* Ismelda turned and he noticed a pink Bloomingdale sweatshirt, matching designer sweatpants, and white-and-pink Nikes. He smelled spearmint.

The voice of his dreams returned.

"Morning, sunshine; storm washed away all the crap that floats over here from D.C. Sucker also knocked over the old blackjack; took the power lines with it, too. Can't cook worth a lick if there ain't no power cuz my wagon train days are way behind me. Thought we'd take a stroll down to Callie's, today is crab n' eggs day. Four bucks ninety-nine includes coffee, my treat. I do owe you breakfast, after all. Heck, why else do you think I call it Paradise?"

Marble tried to respond but his mouth felt like he'd just eaten a handful of sawdust. Only a grunt escaped as he sat up, immediately followed by a groan. *Too many years of living the wrong life aching through my bones,* he thought. It was mostly Samuel the Troll's handiwork, but he liked the first reference better.

"A Ford. You said something about a Ford?"

"Yeah, flat as a pancake. Some poor sucker parked right underneath the old blackjack oak last night." She saw the color fade from Marble's face. "Guess you might be that guy, huh? Well, don't worry. Most insurance covers acts of nature. Nothing that a good hot breakfast of crab n' eggs can't fix, that's for sure."

My car, my car, my car, the voice repeated in his head, followed by a hearty *what the fuck?* He paused a second or two to allow his heart to return to a normal rhythm. "No, no, no, not my car. This isn't supposed to happen like this." He mumbled the last sentence, not certain he wanted to share his Grand Plan with the innkeeper. He stood and his back cracked loudly. Biceps, triceps, lats, pecs, glutes, and all the other assorted muscle masses screamed in protest. He sucked in his gut and his obliques stabbed him for the effort.

Forty and falling apart, though, was not on the Grand Plan's agenda either. He was a combatant in the battle because old age lurked just around the corner. He tried his best to wake his body quietly because nausea crept into his belly as he crossed to the window. *There are no problems, just solutions, no problems, just solutions,* his former sales manager's mantra resurfaced in his mind.

He opened his eyes and discovered a view of Assawoman Bay, which was somewhat of a shock since he expected to see the Atlantic Ocean. He stared out the thick-paned glass window forged at the turn of the twentieth century. He tried to swallow away the fear to focus on street level.

"Jesus. My car…" *No problems, just solutions,* a tiny voice drilled it into his thoughts.

Only crumpled bumpers were visible, fore and aft, splayed out from under the fallen tree like a squashed beetle. Three men in yellow hard hats, goggles, and earmuffs methodically carved the branches off with chainsaws and fed them into a giant wood chipper. Sunlight reflected off a pool of the Ford's blood and guts: a mixture of oil, gasoline, antifreeze, and brake and transmission fluids. Most of his mobile belongings had been stored inside the car, and he did a quick inventory in his head. Laptop, cell phone, Wii, iPod, Xbox, CDs, DVDs were toast – it was an assassination of electronics.

"Shake it off, mister. We'll call your insurance agent after breakfast. There's plenty of car dealers across the bay, no worries, cuz a new car smell is on my top ten list of scents. Let's hit the road. No day has hope without a good hot breakfast, plus, moss won't grow on a rolling stone. Hear that growl? The lioness, my stomach, won't deal with anymore delays."

He looked at Ismelda. Hazel-green eyes, lightly marked with liner, surrounded by gentle starbursts of crow's feet, stared back.

"Um, bathroom first, um, ma'am, I mean, Ismelda. Bathroom, then we can do breakfast, then insurance agent. It's a plan." *No, it's a solution.*

He grabbed his toiletry bag from his duffel and staggered out of the room slightly dazed as thoughts jumbled for attention. *My Ford crushed... I'm out of wheels... I didn't see the Atlantic Ocean... What was Ismelda doing in my room... I wish Deelah was here... no, no I do not.* It hurt his head to think too hard. A loud grumble in his stomach won first prize for attention. He was famished. There had been no food now for two days. How "mutually agreeable" divorce may read on paper, was the ideal dietary supplement. It tasted like shit-on-shingles, the military version.

*****

Willem's salvation arrived by way of a *Delmarva Gazette* van, the weekly fish wrap that claimed most of the rural communities of the Eastern Shore as readership. The driver wasn't about to stop, but Willem had stood in the middle of the exit ramp while he peed on the white lettering sign that said STOP AHEAD. The driver recognized hizzoner and intuition told him loudly not to ignore the man. It was either that or drive right over him. The driver reluctantly called Lou's Repair Shop on his way into town.

Now with a fresh tank of gas, Willem was good to go. A few miles toward town, he waited for the oncoming traffic to clear before he swung his pickup past the orange cones at Ismelda's fallen oak.

He was ornery, more so than usual, but the sight of the crumpled Pennsylvania license plate that hung off the smashed Ford made him feel giddy. It was the same number he had memorized from the nothinglessness prick who had left him stranded the night before.

"Evil spirits got you back, boy," he cackled out loud.

City employees dismantled the tree, and he made a mental note to make sure that Ismelda received a bill for the labor. Nobody in his town was gonna get more than what their measly taxes paid for, that was a certainty.

Clydesdale was a sleepy little town. During the Civil War, it had neither sided with the South nor the North, not because of its concurrence or abhorrence with slavery, but because the then mayor and town founder, Ezekiel Willem Clydesdale, decreed the town would be a haven for the civilized families that neither cared for, nor participated in the war, as all others were scalawags.

A single road led from the high ground of the interior through the marshes and into Clydesdale. For one-hundred-and-fifty years, the town's leaders had continued to do their best to dissuade subversives from entering.

A good number still made it in, though, either by mistake, like Marble, or by the express desire to vacation "off the beaten track". That was a slogan Ismelda Cooper and Callie Bergeman had advertised in travel magazines during the eighties, a time when Clydesdale made its mark as a quaint and beautiful vacation spot, close enough to the night life of Ocean City yet right on top of some of the world's healthiest estuaries. Tourism had increased, dollars had perked the local economy, and Willem's marina business prospered through it at all.

The recent influx of scientists, news media, and remora whackos from all over the country had been disturbing though, the attraction of all the dead birds and the fact that no one had spotted any living ones recently. *Shit, I've lived here all my life and I never looked for a fucking bird; another waste of our tax bucks if you ask me.* Willem tended to neglect most of the reports that languished in his inbox. He couldn't ignore the carnage though. Even he was alarmed at the mangled avian remains that turned up all over town, even on his own boat. "This too will run its own course, probably avian flu or some bird Ebola shit," had been his canned reply to the townsfolk; for not even Willem knew the real demons that lurked in the shadows.

***

"This old guy was a blackjack oak, *Quercus marilandica*. Shaded me and my guests through many a hot summer day, that's for sure. I stole my first kiss under its shade way back when. Memories, more joyful than not. I skip down that path right regular. Morning, Danny; morning, boys."

One of the three sawdust-covered park employees, now on a ten-minute morning break with Tastykake pastries and thermos-fed Yoohoo, turned to look at Ismelda as she and Marble approached.

She treated them like old friends. "If you don't mind, sure would appreciate it if you and the boys piled up the fireplace sized logs 'round back for me, near the wood shed. Oh, and see that burl on the trunk? Careful when you cut there, boys. I want it removed in one piece, gonna make some fine wooden bowls with that beauty. Treat it right and there'll be some of my world-famous lemonade for you 'round lunch."

Danny smiled at her with a wide, gap-toothed grin and gave a wave of acknowledgment before he turned his limited attention back to his butterscotch Krimpets.

Marble's shoulders stooped as he approached the remains of

his Ford. "My car, my poor, poor car." The closer view was a slap-in-the-face shock.

The loss of the vehicle was another door slammed shut from his life with Deelah. That realization was crystal clear as he shaded his eyes from the rising sun – it was time to move on. A red plastic piece of his taillight was on the sidewalk, and he nudged it with his right wingtip, afraid to cause the broken car anymore pain.

It had been a company car, and when Cheeks management had eliminated the outside sales force, Deelah had insisted he buy his former ride. It was cheaper than a new one and besides, she was due to get her new BMW. A small-town part-time news anchor, full-time weather person needed to travel in class, after all – even if it was only in Harrisburg, Pa.

Now his former company car was destined for the recycling plant. He booted the piece of plastic out into the street and searched for a metaphor. Zip, nada, nothing. His literary block moved aside for the rumble-grumble in his gut and the tug on his elbow from Ismelda.

"Kamikaze skeeters are on the attack today. A moving target is harder to hit, stand still for too long and you turn into a human bullseye. Besides, ain't no use paying respects to the death of an inanimate object, unless, of course, you're one of them pathological types, the same as on *Law and Order*. In that case, hang out with crushed metal all you want, just leave little old me to scurry on ahead by her lonesome. Lordy, what a bungle that storm done to our pretty little town, the bay is screaming with insults."

Marble's arm was still in Ismelda's grasp as she dragged him across the macadam and up a water-soaked sand dune. "Did you say bay?"

"Insects might not be too bad once the sun warms things up. Smell that, biscuits and gravy calling my name, whoo-eee. Nothing good can come of a day without breakfast. Callie's ain't far. Five minutes, tops. We'll walk along the water, always good to be close to the power of nature. Ah, ozone cleaned, thank you all."

"Who are you talking to?"

"Why, the bay, silly."

"Uh, sure, why not, my car is gone, I'm not in Ocean City, let's all talk to the water."

They meandered through a narrow swath of assorted marsh grass, and onto the ribbon of sand and gravel that lined the western side of the bay, now speckled with tiny islands of foam, seaweed, and flotsam.

"Storm churned up a mighty cycle of life, all right. Watch your step; don't wanna get those fancy-schmancy shoes ruined now, do we?"

Marble stopped in his tracks and looked down at his wingtips. He had only bothered to change his shirt and tie, part of the duffel bag supply. The shoes were remnants of the Deelah era. "The Grand Plan era doesn't allow wingtips." The words were an intended whisper, but Ismelda raised one eyebrow. He bent over, yanked them off without untying the lashes, and heaved them into the bay, and his right rib cage instantly ached from the baseball-style motion. "There. Hated the way they made my feet look, anyway. Hah!"

Ismelda stared expressionless at him for a moment. His stocking feet were now covered in sand. He proceeded down the beach as if his behavior was right as rain. After a few more steps, a pair of smelly black socks soon found a new home afloat in the bay. He gazed across the expanse and filled his lungs. A junky old diesel tug spewed dark exhaust on its southward jaunt towards the open sea and Marble watched the spiral of exhaust drift into the sky.

Ismelda turned to gaze back at Marble, who now began a whistle rendition of The Beatles' *Here Comes the Sun*. His pant legs were now rolled up to the knees, the dress shirt unbuttoned to a V, sleeves uncuffed, and his amoeba patterned tie a retro headband. She also noticed his belly, the faithful companion of middle-aged men.

Marble waved back and then diverted his attention to the grisly remains of a pair of plover ducks that lapped the shoreline. Before he could comment on the carnage, a kamikaze squadron of mosquitoes arrived, and he turned his attention to a double-handed swat fest.

"Better slow down with the undressing, mister. Callie won't let you eat if you're naked."

He jogged up to her, scratched a few new bites, and continued to ward off the aerial attacks.

"Wow, there sure are a ton of dead birds around here, and plenty of insects. That storm must have packed a wallop. I even had an owl's head plop on the hood of my car last night, must have flown into a transformer or something. Hey, what body of water is this? I seem to remember more of a beach and rolling waves. And a boardwalk... are we in the suburbs?"

With hardly a step lost, she bent over and picked up a piece of driftwood. "Assawoman is the bay, actually it's a lagoon, used to be called Assawoman Sound, back in the day. And a suburb, sure, of the marsh, no boardwalk though. Not in this town." She examined the wood in her hands. "Hardwood, probably mahogany, Meliaceae, this guy traveled a way." She tossed it back into the water next to a group of dead gulls, their torn remains tangled in a maze of seaweed and driftwood.

"What do you mean no boardwalk? I thought Ocean City had a big one."

"Yep, they sure do, about fifteen miles that way, as the crow flies." She pointed southeast across the bay. "All kinds of tourists, noise and cash. We only wanna piece of that pie here. No drunk-as-a-skunk college kids, no DC-ites, no gangs, just bird watchers and fishermen. It helped put our little town on the map as the bird watching capital of the Mid-Atlantic States."

"Fifteen miles, you mean, I'm… I'm… not in Ocean City?"

The question was rhetorical but also upsetting. Marble had to calm his breathing as it galloped toward hyperventilation. *Breathe slowly. He thought about marijuana and how long it had been since he took a few hits… he thought of a Tracy Chapman song, but he couldn't remember the name… he squished his toes into the gravelly sand and let the bay lick him lightly… the air felt like fresh laundry still wet on the line… he sensed an Indian summer heat on the horizon, and he wondered why it was called that. Whew, there, that's better.*

"Ever wonder how our ancestors survived without electricity? Shoot, a storm like last eve can rip a hole in modern amenities. I'm darn near a happy dance we didn't lose our grid, sure would have been tough for you to spot my porch light. Here we are. Hope you brought your appetite." Callie's Bistro loomed above them, a two-story, red-shingled building with an open-aired deck patio that extended out over the bay, at rest on tree trunks sunk deep into the bedrock below.

Marble continued to swat the insect assault that now included voracious horseflies. "Damn, I must taste good today." He picked up the pace as Ismelda hiked up the steep bank. "You've got to be kidding me. I thought this was Ocean City. Shit, I must have made a wrong turn during that wicked storm."

"Your prospects will only improve, trust me. Look who you get to dine with? A good breakfast is the most important meal of the day, you know."

He struggled up the steep sand dune to Ismelda and his lungs wished he had done a bit more cardio with Samuel the Troll. They walked past an old Chevy pickup, parked directly in front of the restaurant, squeezed in between two news vans. Marble thought the truck looked vaguely familiar, but he didn't dwell on it. A familiar sight sat to the south, and the tractor-trailer with the smiling potato chip bag pissed him off even further. The big black Peterbilt sat between Callie's Bistro and Willem's marina, the same truck he had blindly followed down the wrong exit ramp.

Ismelda bent over to the side of the glass front door to retie her sneaker and Marble walked by her, always a gentleman, to get the door first. He looked down at the back of her pink hat and saw the hint of red hair beneath. Then he noticed something that looked like an egg. *What the…?* The side thought proved to be painful.

Callie's delivery guy, Pablo, backed out the front door at full speed, his arms loaded with a to-go order for Lou's garage. The glass door crashed into Marble's chin, knocked him backward, past Ismelda who vainly tried to stop his fall. His impetus landed him onto the mottled hood of the Chevy pickup, his head bouncing twice and neatly denting the thin metal with a few dingers.

The last thought that glass-jawed Marble had before he succumbed to the world of the unconscious was that he had yet to see or hear a living bird. He'd had such a wonderful time identifying them in his dream. That's what he had wanted to ask Ismelda. *Strange*, he thought, *for the shore to be without birds.*

<h1 style="text-align:center">4</h1>

"Maybe we should give him a Motrin."

"That's some bump. What if it's like, you know, a tumor?"

"They be treatin' tumors with aids now, go figure, cleans up that bad hombre lickety split."

"Motrin is for cramps, this here is a man, child, I guarantee he ain't got no hoo-haw."

"Aleve works for me, every time a migraine comes to party, knocks that sucker right off the front porch. Hey, you sure he's the one? He don't look so special to me."

"Give him space so he can revive first, don't you think? Can't force-feed an unconscious person, heck, he may be a Bufferin guy."

"Look at all them nose hairs, shit, he could braid a sweater with that farm."

"The man has no shoes, you sure he's not just some homeless drunk that washed in from Ocean City?"

"That's a pretty good knock on the head but I seen bigger."

"I heard that ibuprofen can damage the liver if you're a heavy drinker."

"How the hell does aids work on a tumor?"

"He don't look like a drunk. Is he a drunk, Ismelda?"

"Don't think so, he seemed sober enough to me last night. But the poor fella just got his car squashed by the old blackjack oak, front of my place. Going shoeless might be his way of coping."

"Yeah, now Pablo knocked him clear out of his shoes. Golly, was Clydesdale ever pissed when he saw that dent on his truck."

"He don't look like no prophet, but then, I ain't never seen a prophet before anyway. He's the one though, our bird man?"

"I seen tumors, big as golf balls, on the dorsal fin of fish after that chemical spill back in… aw shoot, when was that?"

"He is not a prophet, but he is touched, and yes, he is the answer to our prophecy. He is the one." Ismelda paused for maximum effect. "He asked for a view of the ocean." A chorus of *ooohhs* followed. "We need him healthy and nurtured, spread the word. Dear me, this isn't a pleasant welcoming, I'm afraid."

"He can solve the mystery, then. Show a little respect, will y'all?"

"For Clydesdale?"

"Nah, for this feller. Izzy, what's mystery man's name?"

"Don't rightly know, never got that far."

"A mystery man with no name who asks for a view of the ocean. Hot damn, I'm excited."

"Mysteries are always befuddling me, like when a sock goes missing from the dryer."

"I think he's kind of cute."

"Suck on an ice cube or two, you'll get over it."

"Or the mystery when your poop looks like corn but you ain't ate corn for over a month."

"You mean you let a guy sleep in your house without knowing his name?"

"Or like the mystery this morning. There was another flock of crows, all dead, right in town square. Me and the boys cleaned it up good afore any one's seen it. Yeah, now that's a mystery. We gotta get this fella on his feet and soon."

"I can see where he might clean up real nice. Muscular and

soft, a fine combo, if you ask me, and will you look at those calves. I do like a man with meat on the bone."

"You'd like a man with a wooden leg if he'd stay by your side more than a day."

"It's a murder of crows, not a flock, *Corvus brachyrhynchos*, sheesh."

"That's what I said, they been done murdered."

"Very good, Jackie, you've been studying, quite impressive."

"Maybe we should look in his wallet, you know, for a license or ID, in case he winds up in a coma or worse."

"Probably in his back pocket, under his butt."

"Ooh, let me, I'll get it. I can be a nurturer."

"No you don't, go on, get back to work, now, you hear? This is a grown woman's job. Oh my, he's got some junk in this trunk, mm, mm."

It wasn't really a dream because Marble wasn't asleep. Besides, his head ached too much for it to be the work of his subconscious. The skin on his temple stretched as taut as a trampoline. It throbbed in beat with the exterior chatter, but he didn't want to open his eyes – the voices frightened him. Apparently, the Grand Plan deposited him in a blender of *Mayberry, RFD,* meets *The Twilight Zone.* He smelled chewing gum, the spearmint variety. *They must all be chewing it like cows. I wonder if I stay quiet, they might return to their pastures.* He tuned to the throb in his head, but the voices wouldn't leave. *And they damn sure aren't going to get into my wallet.* He popped open his eyes just as a thick hand reached under him and roughly squeezed a butt cheek.

"Aah, sweet Jesus, he's alive."

Marble focused on Callie Bergeman as she pulled her hand

away as if caught in a forbidden cookie jar. Rich, vibrant laughter rolled from her as she patted her heart. She was a hearty black woman with a soiled apron, and a fishnet in her hair, and she smelled like fried shrimp.

"Hey, boss, you done give him CPR. Cool." This came from a pimple-faced person who Marble had difficulty pinning with a sex, scraggly red hair stuffed into a paper hat, baggy gray-and-white kitchen duds over a scrawny coat hanger body, bouncing like a jack-in-the-box next to Callie.

"That ain't CPR, Jackie." *Great, an androgynous name.* "CPR, you need a needle."

Spoken like an authority on the wrong side of the glass in an insane asylum. *Maybe this really is The Twilight Zone.* Marble turned his head to check out the medical moron. Doc Gilbert saluted Roman centurion style, forearm across the chest. He was older than dirt with skin wrinkled like a worn-out baseball glove. He wore a weather-stained captain's hat, and he sported a tank top, a violation of man law if you're over seventy. On his arms were tattooed naked women old enough to be Marble's grandmothers; they yawned and sagged where biceps once reigned. Doc Gilbert was the sperm daddy of Danny, one of the three toothless chain saw operators, a connection Marble had yet to make. All Marble could think about was the fact that he was glad he wasn't in real need of CPR.

Marble had heard enough. It was time to enter their world. "I'm Marble. Larry Marble, that's my name. And I would love an Aleve."

"I knew it. I knew it. I use 'em for my menstrual cramps. Be right back, Larry." *The androgynous one gets a period. Jackie is a girl, great, one riddle solved.* His head pounded louder as he propped to his elbows and looked around the joint. He was on a cream-colored linoleum table attached to a booth, the bench seats covered in cracked, burnt-orange vinyl.

"This isn't your day, is it Mr. Marble?" Ismelda placed a cool cloth on his forehead. Her eyes snagged him for a bit. He never gazed into somebody's soul before. He wasn't sure he was doing it now, either, but there was something powerful in the depth of those eyes. Deelah never kept her gaze steady long enough for him to check if she even had a soul.

"I'll be fine. This, ouch, this is just a bump. So, am I too late for breakfast?"

"You got yourself one nice-size egg on your noggin, that's for sure. But don't worry, honey, I won't use that one. Couple of scrambled and crab coming right up, sit yerself down in the booth, now, I ain't got bed trays." Callie laughed heartily as she bustled into the kitchen. A frantic Jackie passed her in the other lane.

"Here you go, Larry." The *Larry* came out in five or six syllables, the way a horny teenage girl might speak to a dude she wanted to rainbow in the back seat of a car at the cheesy drive-in. She handed him a stein of orange juice and two little blue pills and took her sweet time in pulling her hand away. "Fresh squeezed, Larry. I did it myself. Good for what ails you. Ooh, you're solid. Do you work out with weights?" She had her hands around his sore right bicep as he raised himself up to sit.

"Thanks. Jackie, is it?" Her lips turned into a shy smile and Marble was sure he'd see Danny-like dentures. Instead, two rows of straight and clean teeth smiled back, and he thought of the Peterbilt, a blushing Peterbilt. "I get to a gym, now and then, sure." Samuel the Troll would love to roast his cajones on a whittled hickory stick over a campfire below some old bridge for that comment. "Thanks for noticing." He smiled and she flushed cooked-lobster red. It wasn't often in Jackie's nineteen years that a man made her blush, so she twirled about and scurried back to the kitchen, her mannerisms a perfect match for flustered.

"Oh, you made her day. Come on, Mr. Marble, easy does it. Let's sit down like civilized folk." He didn't need Ismelda's aid, but the attention felt good, and he decided to milk it a little. He settled on the bench and quickly scanned the rest of the place, a Diver Dan meets Audubon motif.

Callie Bergeman obviously loved nature. Framed photographs, paintings, charcoals, and lithographs of marsh and shore birds indigenous to the Delmarva Peninsula plastered the walls. To his left, above the fifty's era mini-jukebox carousel that sat in each of the booths, was a photo of a Rufus-sided Towhee, *Pipilo erythrophthalmus*. To its right was a larger photo of two American Widgeons, *Anas Americana*. To him, they just looked like ducks. Marble had never heard of either bird.

Above the front door, a sign declared a seating capacity of ninety and he did a quick count of the patrons. The horde that had presided over his prone body had now dispersed back to their respective booths. Save for them and a smattering of others, the place was near empty.

The further walls had dark, stressed wood paneling that provided the backdrop for a montage of bird paintings. Fish netting, driftwood, and crab and whelk pots seasoned the remainder of the decor. Sliding glass doors led to an outdoor patio. Marble leaned back and tried to catch a glimpse of the bay. Not Ocean City; he was close, but now he was also without wheels. This was a less than auspicious start to the Grand Plan.

Marble felt the stare of Ismelda, and he returned her gaze.

"You gonna be OK?"

"Fabulous, always had a thick skull… genetics. A guy needs

a knock now and then to shake the dust loose. My car is another thing. I don't know how much I'll get for it so guess I'll have to wait and see. Aw, shit, my cell phone was in the car, this is a nightmare. Can I use your phone back at the inn?"

Callie swung through the kitchen doors and set two plates down. The aromas alone won his taste buds. "What do you need a phone for? You're not gonna sue me, now, are you?"

"Not unless I find shell in this crab. I hate lawyers. Trust me; you have nothing to worry about."

"Well, I guess it's a good thing I didn't poison your food then." She slapped him on the back and his sore lats bellowed a reminder of Samuel the Troll's punishments. She disappeared with a whirl into the kitchen and with a laugh that couldn't possibly be from an episode of *The Twilight Zone*.

"Phone your people when we return to Paradise. Right now, eat. Get your energy back. Your color is a little low." He looked across the linoleum table just as Ismelda's hand returned quickly to her side. *Did she just slip a mickey into my juice? Nah, must be this lump on mi cabeza, I'm seeing things.* He watched his landlord plunge into her breakfast and pause between mouthfuls to douse each bite with Tabasco. Marble popped the Aleve into his mouth and chugged from the cauldron of juice before he dove into his food.

He cleaned his own plate as well, also with a healthy dose of hot sauce. He had never eaten with a woman who liked Tabasco. Deelah couldn't even stand it if a dried flake red pepper came near her slices of pizza they had shared every Sunday night for the past seven years. Giamono's was something from his former life that he'd miss; they made the best pizza, strombolis, and hot grinders in central Pennsylvania.

"Hey, are you still with me?"

From Giamono's to Callie's in an instant. "Hmm? Yeah, sorry, lost in thought."

"You might have a slight concussion, Doc says, so I have to keep an eye on you. Looked like you sailed away there for a minute."

"Believe me, Ismelda. I'm definitely here." It felt good to eat. His Grand Plan needed him healthy. "There was actually a doctor here? How long was I out?"

"Not long, and Doc isn't exactly a medical doctor. We just call him that because he claims to be a reincarnation of a medic centuries ago from the ancient Roman Empire's legion of centurions, commanded by Mark Antony." Marble wasn't sure if he should act surprised at this revelation or sad for any ancient Romans who received CPR from Doc.

"You're heading for Ocean City, huh? What's there?"

"Don't really know. Hopefully, a job that gives me time to write my novel. Some place cheap to live. Stay for a bit and then move on south." The layman's version of a hobo lifestyle; somehow it didn't sound so enticing that way. "I just got divorced and the ink isn't even dry. Unloaded a lot of old baggage from my life, you might say."

"Amazing, isn't it? Words, I mean. A couple of sentences can sum up a person's life, just like that." She snapped her fingers and Marble noticed they had a fresh coat of polish. He was an expert at that kind of thing. *Deelah used to polish hers every night in bed. Way back when things were good, I got to blow them dry while she...* a burp worked its way up his esophagus and he struggled to mute it, only to have it jump out through his clenched teeth.

"Excuse me."

"Please, my late husband used belches as a way of saying

thanks for the chow. And eating was as important to him as breathing." That was quite a bit more than she cared to reveal about herself. She quickly refocused on her earlier line. "Guess you know all about words and all, being a writer, I mean."

"Well, sure, I guess I do. But I haven't started writing yet. I will soon, though. The ideas are ready to leap from my head. Getting crowded in here." He tapped his head and flinched as his fingers nicked the knot.

"We have a published writer here in Clydesdale. Anna Smythe, she wrote the *Bird Lovers Guide to Eastern Maryland Shore*, a Bible of sorts for those of us who love birds. And nature is a vitally important segment of Clydesdale's economy; we're all quite well versed on the subject, Anna being the cream of the crop." She pulled cash from her sweatshirt's pocket. "Breakfast is on me, part of Paradise."

"Thanks, it was delicious. Speaking of nature, birds seem to be a popular topic around here. How come so many are dead? Did the storm kill them?"

"Mr. Marble, birds are an integral cog in the way of life. We don't know what, but something terrible has upset that ecological cycle. We, all of us, are in harmony with the balance of nature. When one of the elements is disturbed, we all suffer." As if on cue, Doc Gilbert sprang to his feet and sang a rendition of an off-key *God Bless America* in Italian.

"I have a full day of chores awaiting me. And you've got a phone call or two. Let's get back before the sun gets too hot. Finish your juice, it's got healing powers."

Ismelda rose and briskly walked toward the door, oblivious to Doc's performance. Marble drained his glass as instructed, stood and, with a new wariness for Pablo the delivery guy, carefully followed her through the front door.

"Ismelda, speaking of birds, why haven't I seen any *living* ones this morning? Isn't this supposed to be a pretty popular spot for them?"

She stopped and turned to him, her eyes filled with tears. "We... need to get you some good insect repellent, Mr. Marble, especially if you plan on doing any outdoor exploring. I have just the thing for you back at the inn. We all take it, one hundred percent natural, works like a charm." With that, she strode off, her oversized, lumpy hat bobbing with each step.

Is she evading my questions? Marble sensed there was something more she wouldn't spill. The thought was set aside though as a new wave of winged bloodsuckers dive-bombed him. He swatted the air like a truly disturbed escapee from a mental institution and hurried after his mysterious landlady, his bare feet skipping over the hot macadam of Main Street.

5

Bud 'Popeye' Worthington thanked God several times each day for all the wonderful people in his life. It had been a darn good travel and he constantly reminded himself and anybody else who happened to sit next to him at the string of truck stop diners along Route 13.

After twenty years in the U.S. Navy, the former Master Chief Boatswain's Mate amassed a modest portfolio in investment bonds with his military earnings. His frugality paid off when he retired at the ripe old age of thirty-nine. His savings bought a brand new, jet-black Peterbilt, *finest piece of truck made.* His second life as a trucker got underway with nary a hitch and twice a day, he thanked the Man upstairs for that blessing. After the Navy, he worked for Gobble Potato Chip Company, a job earned as the result of a heroic act he had performed twelve years earlier.

Gobble's CEO had been a lieutenant JG based on the same destroyer as Popeye. While on a Mediterranean cruise, the officer's wife and young daughter visited from state side to pay a visit when the destroyer made Rota, Spain, a port of call. A large wave caused by a young Saudi prince revving every horsepower out of his new speedboat had capsized the dinghy that carried the officer's family out to the ship docked in Rota's harbor. Popeye had pulled officer-of-the-deck duty when the accident occurred. Fully clothed, he dove thirty feet before hitting the harbor and swam to the upside-down dinghy. The officer's wife and the piloting seamen held onto the capsized hull.

The three-year-old little girl was nowhere in sight though.

Popeye dove repeatedly beneath the surface. On the fourth dive, he found the little girl, near death, ten feet below the dinghy. He brought her to the surface, laid her on the hull, and performed CPR while still in the water. Too bad Doc Gilbert wasn't around to watch. The little girl lived, and Popeye was a hero. He also began a lifelong friendship with his lieutenant junior grade, the future president of Gobble Potato Chips.

Twelve years later, when Popeye's final tour of duty ended, the former lieutenant JG offered him a job. Popeye never let Gobble down, or they him. Sales of Gobble products grew so fast in Popeye's region that the company soon doubled his salary, an act that brought the big man to tears.

Despite his resemblance to a bear, he had the temper of a butterfly. In fact, only once in his life had he ever deliberately caused harm toward another. But he got over that one slip up quickly. The U.S.S. Gettysburg left Rota's port the same day a mysterious explosion ripped apart the Saudi prince's new speedboat. It helped having Navy Seals as friends.

Popeye prayed hard for years but never once felt an ounce of regret for his actions. That bothered him and he vowed never again to strike out at another person or their belongings. He would drive the highways, make friends, and spread his faith wherever he parked his rig.

Another lifelong friend from the Navy was at one time his former Commanding Officer. Captain Turner Smythe had been Popeye's favorite out of all the good souls he had met in the Navy. His recent death seriously challenged Popeye's pacifist beliefs and provided yet another reason to make tiny Clydesdale a regular stop, despite its off the beaten track reputation. Anna Smythe was the captain's widow – another reason he loved Clydesdale. When the ex-sailor had been lost at sea under extremely mysterious circumstances, Popeye had been devastated. He never displayed an ounce of shyness though when asked by Anna to offer the eulogy. He had also agreed to first visit Anna whenever, no matter what time of day, he arrived in Clydesdale. To her delight, Popeye kept his word.

The other reason he frequented Clydesdale was Callie's Bistro, or more precisely, Callie. He had it bad for the vivacious restaurant owner, so much so he could barely speak when he was in her presence. His physician had dubbed it situational stuttering. Popeye preferred to think of it as yummy-gooey-heebie-jeebies. Thoughts of Callie made him goofy-happy and occupied his fantasies throughout the long hours he spent on the road. But he was much too shy to ever let her know. When a man reaches forty still a bachelor, certain habits are hard to break. Popeye's bad habit was that he had never developed the social skills to speak to a woman he liked. If he wasn't attracted to them, he could gab all day. But as soon as someone as fine as Callie signed her first delivery slip for Gobble's frozen pre-cut curly fries, he could only blubber and drool, always followed by a quick retreat to the safety of his Peterbilt.

The same morning Marble discovered his smashed car, Popeye hugged Anna and promised her he would help in any way possible. Too many questions, he agreed, remained unanswered. With his heart beating a mile a minute from Anna's encouragement, he walked the mile-and-a-half back to his Peterbilt, splashed on some Clubman's cologne stashed in his truck's cabin and headed for Callie's Bistro.

***

Barely twenty-four hours had elapsed since signing the divorce papers and walking away from Deelah forever. Marble mentally kicked himself; the break should have been cleaner. His mind crept slowly toward clarity, and the years of Deelah's high-maintenance badgering and belittling were reasons enough not to miss her company. Now he had the rusty knife-in-the-gut burden of making a phone call to her. His head still throbbed as he fingered through his wallet.

It contained every bit of information he thought he needed: credit cards, his new checking account number, his buddies' telephone numbers, but no insurance agent number in sight and for the life of him, he couldn't remember the carrier company or the agent's name.

The Ford was the first car he had owned since college. Up until Cheeks took away the company vehicles, he had never concerned himself with insurance because it had always been under a company policy. When he'd purchased the car outright, Deelah had just added it to her policy. The only contact with the insurance agent he had made was to put the card in the glove compartment, where it still sat, crushed beneath the trunk of the old blackjack oak.

He glanced outside. The squashed car was far from tree removal. Danny and his two brothers were missing in action when he and Ismelda had arrived back at the B&B. They had finished pruning the biggest branches, but the main trunk still lay across the front yard, entombing the car.

Marble sat in a Windsor swivel chair at an antique cherrywood tambour desk in Ismelda's living room, behind the sliding wood doors. He sipped the slightly bitter tea, a medicinal herbal blend of yarrow, spearmint and elderberry flower, and other secret ingredients he wasn't sure he wanted to know. "Homemade tonic that's good for what ails you", she had purported, the second time that morning someone had handed him a beverage with that disclaimer. He needed all the help he could muster to swallow his pride and call Deelah.

He would never admit it publicly, but Deelah had spoiled him during their marriage. She was a control freak. All the bills, the worrisome paper trail that anchors itself to anyone who aspires for the false nirvana of middle class, all the banking, insurance, auto, home, and medical concerns had been under her strict control. He was accustomed to coddling, even if it came dressed as a strange tea blend.

The brew calmed the snare drum throbs in his head and Marble did what came naturally – just let the mind roll with the flow. He leaned back in the chair, and it creaked in compliance as he set the chair into a lazy twirl. The room was painted in a comfortable peach tone with a stained maple wood chair rail wrapped around the perimeter; it disappeared behind two large bookcases, then re-emerged on the other side, only to be blocked by another open doorway that led to an adjacent room. Marble picked the chair rail up again as it wound around the rest of the room, joined by an antique nineteenth century Shakeshaft of Preston grandfather clock, a large, bricked in, marble-mantled fireplace and a small table with a computer smothered by a purple afghan blanket.

From the center of the water-stained ceiling hung a six-bulb chandelier. An insulated wire ran from the light fixture, across to the wall, then down to the 1930s era push-button light switches next to the sliding doors. At his feet, a vibrant oriental rug lay atop a rough-surfaced oak floor. Marble followed the tail of an embroidered dragon up to its torso covered by a plump, mottle-colored couch, complete with lace doilies and assorted throw pillows never meant to complement the couch's colors. A multi-horned dragonhead appeared on the other side of the couch, where a short armoire doubled as an entertainment center. He recognized the garment cabinet as a twin of the one in his room.

Must have been a good yard sale. He guessed Tony Bennett and friends lived behind the armoire's closed doors. The furniture faced the fireplace crowned by a large painting that hung above the mantle.

The oil original was one of many around the room. Each one depicted wildlife of the Chesapeake Bay in rich, colorful strokes. They didn't remind him of the pictures he'd seen at Callie's; instead, he felt a strong attraction to the artwork and the room itself, especially to the beautiful snowy egret above the fireplace, its regal head poised above the marsh, forever poised for a fish to swim by. He chuckled to himself and recalled the previous evening's hallucination. *Just a painting, that's all, folks.*

He stared at the picture and tried to find the artist's signature, but his angle was too steep. He chuckled nervously as his line of sight seemed to pinpoint on the painted bird's eyes, and goosebumps popped up. It was if he could gaze into the soul of the snowy egret, *Egretta thula.* Marble triple blinked. It was just like his dream.

"Whoa, Nellie, where did that come from? Since when do I know the Latin name for birds?"

He drained the teacup just as a switch clicked in his brain and a very different vision unfolded: a vivid, sepia image leapt into his mind as if some unseen hand had changed the channel. He now watched as two men, clad in dirt-stained overalls atop ladders positioned the *Egretta thula* picture above the mantle and then turned to look in his direction for guidance as to proper alignment.

"Get a hold of your insurance guy?" Ismelda's voice spirited him back to the reality of present day.

"Hmm? Uh, no, not yet. Line was busy."

"Take your time, Mr. Marble. I'll be out back at the woodshed if you need anything. The boys removed a pristine burl, and it should produce three, maybe four, burl treens from this beauty. Praise the Good Mother, when one door slams closed, another window opens somewhere in the home." She winked.

"Yeah, that's how I got out of my old townhouse. Oh, Ismelda? Call me Larry, please."

She looked at him for a moment, gave a quick smile, and then left the room. Was her smile mischievous? It had a hint of something more than a casual it's-nice-to-be-on-a-first name-basis-with-you smile, he thought. The smile, not Ismelda, made him think of Deelah. The fateful day he had dumped the cow turds on the limey bastards and lost his job, she had initially reacted to the news with a smile similar to the one he had just seen, like he'd just supplied the answer to her prayers.

The tea mellowed his countenance and he decided to get the phone call to Deelah over with, but something strong nudged him back to his earlier vision. Or at least it's what he should call it since it was a new experience. Or was it? A childhood memory door creaked open, and the rush of old, dusty thoughts surged forward. The birth of a scream emerged but before it blossomed through his vocal chords, the door slammed shut once more.

The sound of chainsaws made him wheel toward the window. Danny and his cohorts had returned. They attacked the old oak's trunk nearest the road. A shadowy movement flashed by to his right, and he twisted toward the vestibule. He stared for a moment before he spoke.

"Ismelda? Is that you?" The ensuing silence made him question whether he had seen anything in the first place. After all, the shadow had been very quick and headed in the direction of the front door. But he hadn't heard the door open or close.

The chainsaws quieted and he gazed out front again. This time the view was bizarre. Just outside the bay window, a woman sat on the porch swing with a large black crow perched on her raised right arm. What made the sight bizarre was the fact that the woman was completely naked while she carried on an animated conversation with the bird. She was young, early twenties he guessed, with long ebony hair. He couldn't see her face but from the delicate shape of her shoulders and the unblemished softness of her milk-chocolate skin, he sensed a beauty. He quickly glanced down at the workers by the tree, but they were obviously unaware of her presence.

Doesn't mean I can't get a closer look, he thought as he unashamedly gave in to Neanderthal origins, pushed himself up from the squeaky Windsor to catch a clearer view of her breasts, stomach, thighs and…

"Whew, Indian summer today, that's for sure. Don't rightly know why we call it that though. Gauge out back already says eighty and it's not even ten a.m. ConEdison boys just fixed the power lines. Saw them down at the intersection, hallelujah for modern amenities, you know? My log splitter is gassed and ready to rock but before I worked my magic, I thought I'd come on in to the fridge and sure enough, lemonade is cold. Here, I brought you a glass. Did you finish your tea? You look a little flushed, is everything OK?"

A startled Marble stood up. "I'm not quite sure, is there another guest, um, out front?"

He pointed to the swing. The naked girl and the bird were gone. Danny and his mates were camped on the trunk of the oak, above his car, on another Tastykake break.

"Just a second ago, I swear, there was a woman sitting out there with a bird." The porch bench swing was now empty, no bird, no beauty and the absurdity of the moment made him chuckle. "This may sound crazy, but I think I just saw a naked woman talking to a crow." He was right, it did sound like he had a few screws loose. He wished he could rewind time a couple of seconds. *Heck, there are rubber bands and paper clips within reach.*

Ismelda stared at Marble with a blank expression as she

handed him a tall, sweating glass of lemonade.

"We figured you might hallucinate, pretty common with a bump on the head. It's nothing to get worked up over though. You're not even drinking one of my stronger blends. Give a yell if any pink elephants show up. Enjoy your lemonade, freshly squeezed with a hint of spearmint and other proprietary magic, good for keeping the bugs off. I'm going out front to check on the boys." She crossed to the vestibule and then turned back to Marble. "This woman you saw, you say it was a crow, *Corvus brachyrhynchos*, on her arm?"

"Um, what? Yeah, I think, sure, why not? Why, do you know her, the woman?"

"Know her? Now that's an interesting question. No. Don't *know* her. Well, see you in a bit. Oh, the door, do you mind?" He moved to open the front door for her since her hands held a tray of lemonade glasses.

Marble watched her move down the sidewalk, her large billowing hat bouncing with each step. His eyes then gravitated down to the swing outside the window. It still swayed as if… *No, it can't be*. A black crow's feather blew off the arm of the swing onto the seat. He rubbed his eyes. Something weird was going on and it was enjoying a coming-out party in his head. Two hallucinations in the matter of five minutes; they had looked so real though. Or had they?

The memory arrived slowly, as if the gentle massage he now gave his temples rubbed yesterdays onward. The picture was clear, black and white, a Phillies game in May, early seventies. A chill ran up his spine, not because of the dreadful play of that storied franchise prior to the twenty-first century, but instead because of a recollection of… the memory vanished quickly.

He shrugged and shook his head. Reality returned as he walked back to the desk and stared at the phone. Deelah would be at the studio by now, already with her pressing news assignments for the day. *Who knows what kind of cat-in-a-tree crises she may get to cover?* Grimacing, he dialed the number from memory.

***

Ismelda approached the boys. Danny perked up like it was Christmas morning.

"Hey, Miss Izzie, sure is hot. We done stack the wood for ya. Are we making too much noise with the saws? We can stop 'n come back tomorrow." Danny had an IQ of eighty, and he was the smart one of the group; a scary thought for men that wielded massive chainsaws with reckless abandon.

"Nah, boys, you'll need to cut up this old oak today. I want you to do me a favor though, Danny. On your lunch break go fetch your daddy for me. Bring him here right quick now, you hear?"

Danny, Ronnie, and Woody all flashed smiles that would make an orthodontist drool. "Sure 'nuff, Miss Izzie." The boys liked running errands for Ismelda. She always paid in Tastykakes.

"Thanks, fellas. Now get back to work before Clydesdale comes driving by. The Good Mother knows we don't need him meddling around here today."

Lou Ottney, owner of Lou's Auto Body, with obvious trepidation, mumbled it would cost upward of three hundred dollars to fix the dent in Willem's hood. Willem took the news poorly. Fortunately, Lou was lithe enough to duck away from the pipe wrench that Willem hurled at his head.

"You traitor, we're playing on the same fucking team, remember? Teammates are supposed to protect each other's asses. And not for three fucking hundred smackers." Willem picked up a crowbar and bounced it in his hands.

"Whoa, hold on there, Clydesdale. I don't give a rat's ass if you're the mayor or not; you don't have the right to throw my own tools at me. That's a fair estimate, at cost; I don't make a dime on this job. Shit, drive your piece of crap over to Ocean City and see what those shysters will try and get out of you. Teammates, my ass; I owed you one. One. My debt to you is paid. I kept my trap shut, just like you asked, so knock it off." Lou glanced nervously toward the passenger door of Willem's truck. "And don't even try to use that fucking bird's nest, or whatever you call that monster."

Willem watched Lou's face turn the color of chalk as a bloodcurdling cry rang out from the interior of the Chevy pickup. Lou backed away and banged into his workbench, waking every nut and bolt in their Gerber baby jars. "Th-th-th-this here," he waived the estimate at Willem while the pickup began to rock, "th-this here is business. I got bills to pay, asshole. Go ahead, try and throw something else at me and w-w-we'll see how fast I get Heffley down here to lock your ass up."

Willem laughed sloppily, spittle spraying in all directions. In his opinion, Sheriff Carl Heffley was a weak-willed pussy without a threatening bone in his body. Lou's attitude, on the other hand, was worrisome. *Time to take out the garbage, Lou old boy, nothing personal.*

Lou Ottney and he were the same age. They had grown up together as cautious friends and neither really trusted the other further than they could throw him. Willem just stared at the mechanic for a moment before he climbed into his dented pickup. There were bigger fish to fry before he could release his powers on Lou. After all, the Pennsylvania nothinglessness required dire attention before peace could reign once more; that's what the nest portal wanted, and the nest portal would not tolerate anything less.

He pulled out of Lou's Auto Body in a haze of blue smoke and onto Clydesdale Avenue, right across from Clydesdale public park, where a weather-beaten statue of his great-great granddaddy, Ezekiel Willem Clydesdale, covered in a summer's worth of seagull shit, stared wistfully off into Assawoman Bay.

The Clydesdale family had roots in Clydesdale as deep as the post-revolutionary war. At the height of the Civil War, they had reached their greatest wealth, attributed greatly by a fleet of fishing, and sailing ships that, some whispered, were a cover for slave trade. Ancient rumors still circulated to the present day that Ezekiel Clydesdale had tricked large numbers of slaves to hide on his farm during their northerly treks to freedom. The slaves that made it to Clydesdale though, never went any further north. Ezekiel developed a profitable side business of reselling the recaptured slaves in Havana.

By the turn of the century, most of the tainted Clydesdale money resided in land. The depression of 1929 forced Willem's grandfather to sell most of his assets, though. Being the only Clydesdale survivor, Willem inherited only a fraction of the once prominent holdings.

The pickup pulled into a parking space at his marina. Willem exited in a hurry, the nest portal clutched under a fat arm. Popeye's Peterbilt blocked some of the marina's parking spots and that was a mistake. The bile that had roiled in his gut since Lou's estimate now turned to acid reflux. He belched and spit into the harbor. Five baitfish turned silver bellies up, dead chum, a crab dinner bell.

"Oh yes, big mistake, mister, big mistake. Let's see how you like a nice hefty illegal parking ticket. I'll get Heffley to shove it up your potato chip black ass. And that, boy, is just the start of your troubles. You done stepped into a whole hive of army ants on this trip."

He waddled into the marina's office which also doubled as city hall, a wooden shack that would never earn an honorable mention in *Better Homes & Gardens* as a nouveau take on the nautical motif. It resembled more a mass of rotted driftwood held together by ambergris.

"Get that lazy ass Heffley on the horn, pronto." Willem directed the words to his secretary, Patti, his lap dog and periodic paramour for over twenty years.

Most of the Christmas bulbs on Patti King's tree had burnt out in her thirty-nine years. The cake of cheap foundation makeup on her face did little to hide the fact she looked closer to a hard fifty. Her body hadn't fared much better. Neglect, alcoholism, and depression had tag teamed with gravity to give her nursing home sag. On the rare occasion he noticed, Willem thought she resembled the cartoon character Underdog in drag.

Patti talked to all her friends most of the time while at work. She didn't even use the phone. Every table, wall, desk, chair, toilet, plastic *Dieffenbachia*, water bottle, key to the city, and copy machine had played a part in their sex life over the years. It wasn't just an office, it was a room filled with memories, her lovemaking arena. And memories were the only ones left since Willem lost his hard eight years earlier.

"And a good morning to you, too, boss. Somebody got up on the wrong side of the room today."

"Bed, somebody got up on the wrong side of the bed. Get Heffley on the horn." He yelled this close enough to her that she could smell the stale coffee and two-pack-of-cigarette-a-day stench of early emphysema on his breath.

"I think he's on the move, maybe over to Izzie's. Do ya know that old oak fell in last night's storm? Done crushed some feller's car she's got staying with her. Funny how if he'd a parked in the driveway—"

"Stuff a sock in it, call Heffley, now." Willem belched into his office, a garage-sized space with casement windows and a marina view. The digs also doubled as the mayor's office. He slammed shut the door and the reverberations rattled the filthy window behind Patti's head.

"All right, Mayor Prickface, right away Mayor Prickface." She tried to stifle the giggles. Her daughter, Jackie, had given Willem the name after she had seen him get so mad one time that his face blew up like the head of a swollen penis, all purple and red. Patti had never thought to ask Jackie how she knew what a swollen penis looked like. Instead, she had just laughed and laughed and laughed.

Patti had gone to work for Willem at the marina when she

was pretty as a peach nineteen. Her husband of two months had just been sentenced to life without parole for a triple-decker robbery, rape, and murder of two college co-eds on vacation at the Esmeralda in Ocean City. In a tragic turn that would imprison her in another manner, Willem had taken her in, and she him, on countless sweaty nights when he had asked her to work late. He had fathered Jackie, but she had never told him it was his seed. He had never asked either. Patti was afraid of Willem's bad temper, and she didn't want to lose her job. She had raised Jackie on her own, without even a "How's your kid doing?" from him in the past nineteen years.

"Right away, Mayor Prickface, coming right up Mayor Prickface." Her face turned redder than her clown-like rouge as the giggles wiggled out. She pressed the dispatch key on the microphone stand and barely kept the merriment down. "Hey Heff, come in, come in… do ya copy, baby?"

***

"Good morning, you have reached WTTE-TV, the Nose for News Station serving Dauphin, Cumberland, and Lancaster counties. If you know the extension of the person you would like to reach, please enter it now. If you would like to lodge a complaint, press one. If you don't have a push-button phone, please hold for the operator."

Marble was tempted to press "one" and tell them how much he hated automated voice messages. It sounded like a foreign language, a maze of chattering, tinny syllables that only became more indiscernible with each expletive-filled time he pressed redial. How hard could it be to have someone who speaks perfectly audible, precise English do the recording?

A whiny, nasally voice screeched. "This is Cheryl, how may I help you?" Marble pictured her, a bleached blonde with serious PFA – Pennsylvania Fat Ass – a dumpy, lumpy, wide-assed body built from halupkis, pierogies, and bratwurst, pressed into tight, short dresses and fishnet thigh highs.

"Hi, Cheryl, may I speak to Deelah Thayer, please?"

"Is this Brad?" *Brad? So Deelah is seeing someone else already.* The pain in his chest surprised Marble. He didn't think this type of news was supposed to hurt.

"No, this is…" now came the tricky part. He had yet to call himself the ex. "Her husband, I mean, former. You know." *There, that didn't twinge a bit.*

"Oh, you, uh, sure, let me see if I can find her." The chirpiness was long gone from her voice.

He kept the receiver pressed to his ear and hoped Deelah took his call. His gaze carried past the bay window and into the yard that now resembled a giant sawdust factory. Crappy muzak filtered into his head as he performed the waiting-on-the-phone pirouette in the swivel chair, returning once again to a view of the front yard.

Marble had an artistic mind that had mostly gone unused since childhood. The last time a creative idea slipped out had been when he had initiated a cow-tipping expedition at the county fair, during the blue-ribbon ceremony. His old high school chums still relived glory days over that episode at Maxie's Tavern. More inspirational ideas, however, just bounced around in his head with no hope of ever escaping. His Grand Plan was now the doorway for these thoughts, and they bunched up at the exit and tried to muscle their way out.

He whirled back around to face the snowy egret painting, a serious delayed reaction. It was still on the wall above the mantle, but the bird had vamoosed, replaced by empty marsh. He closed his eyes and rubbed away the altered vision. When he looked again, the painting was once again as before, but another nightmare entered through his ear.

"Let me guess, your soapbox car lost a wheel, and you need another one for your race downhill. Am I warm?" She wasn't prophetic, he thought, just evil. She used her anchorperson voice, an affected staccato that emphasized each verb and adjective as if she reported the Coming of the Messiah. "I know you're there, Marble, I can smell your sweat."

He sniffed his armpit. "Deelah, sorry to bother you but I need our car insurance agent's number." Keep it business-like, don't react to her smart-ass remarks, he mentally coached himself.

"It should be in your glove compartment, duh." Her tone of voice had idiot written all over it. "Honestly, Marble, are you capable of handling yourself in the big, bad world?"

Come on man, you have a spine. "The name, Deelah, please, agent and/or company. It's a simple request." *Atta boy, don't wallow at her level.*

"What's wrong, Marble? Did you get in an accident, Mr. Perfect Driver, Keeper of the Cardinal Rules of the Road?" The anchorperson voice smoothly transgressed to bitch. For her, it was like riding a bike.

"Deelah, can we just do this civily so I can get back to my life? Why give me bitch in the process?"

"Listen, you want to be a mystery writer rather than play by the rules, figure this mystery out yourself. We're not married any longer, remember? I don't have to watch over you anymore."

"Deelah, please, a simple phone number or name is all I want."

"What did I just do, stutter? Am... I... talking... too...

fast… for… you? English motherfucking language got you confused?"

"I don't need this crap. Thanks for nothing, Deelah. Sorry to bother you. Oh, and by the way, does Brad know that you fart in bed?" Click.

Oh, I am such a bad boy. Yeah, that was a total waste of time. Even worse, I hung up before I got a name. Outside, a police car parked next to his pancaked Ford. A creative light went on in his head: police, DMV records, registration, and insurance info. Sure, why hadn't he thought of that before? He crossed to the vestibule and quickly glanced over his shoulder at the picture above the mantel. Everything appeared to be normal. *Good, damn it, good.* He hurried out the front door, concerned about the visions he had experienced. Maybe Ismelda was right. The bump on his head was probably the cause of it all.

From a second-floor dormer, a jet-black *Corvus brachyrhynchos* preened her wings as she watched his every move.

***

Ismelda handled the introductions. "Hey, Mr. Marble. This here's Carl Heffley, town constable. Carl, Larry Marble, owner of the metal crepe."

Marble shook the sheriff's beefy hand. The rest of the officer's body resembled a bull, minus the tail and the horns. He reminded Marble of a taller version of Samuel the Troll.

"Tough luck you got on your side, Mr. Marble. That old tree has been around long as I can recall. Never shown any signs of weakening roots, did it, Izz? One might say its destiny y'all got stuck here in Clydesdale. Yep. The Good Lord works in mysterious ways." The sheriff's accent was a mixture of a southerner living too close to the Mason-Dixon Line. "Course, one Jehovah bucket of water got dumped last night. Never know about nature. Never know. Just when you think things are going smooth, she sneaks right up and bites you in the buttocks. God's way of saying, *don't forget about me*." From his belly came one of the heartiest laughs Marble had heard since, well, Callie's earlier that morning. He took an instant liking to Heffley.

"Yeah, it sucks all right. Do you think, officer Heffley…?"

"Call me Carl."

"Carl, right, um, could you run a check on my license and tap into Pennsylvania's DMV? I need to find out who my insurance carrier is."

A serious look appeared on the sheriff's face. "Can I call you Larry?" He produced a clipboard from behind his back and led Marble away from Ismelda. "Already ran a check on your plates. Car's registered to a Ms. Deelah Thayer. Seems she canceled insurance on it a couple of weeks ago; she familiar to you?"

For the first time in the eight years since he had first laid eyes on her, the bitter taste of hate dried up the saliva in his mouth. He decided to savor it awhile. "Yeah, I know her, my ex-wife."

"Anyways, I sort of figured such; you got that starting-a-new-life-smell-about you." Marble realized he was dressed in the same fashion as earlier that morning on the beach. A shower still awaited the heebie-jeebies on his skin. He adjusted his amoeba-patterned tie headband as casually as possible.

"So technically, according to PA's DMV, she still owns the car, and the canceled insurance is still covering said vehicle until the end of this month."

Marble tried a mental perusal of the divvied asset list from yesterday's divorce paperwork. That file was now part of the crushed Ford. He silently cursed. Despite every effort to make a clean getaway, Deelah had kept her web tangled around his ankles. She never transferred ownership of the Ford over to him. Of course, Marble had also been under the assumption that he had always owned the car anyway. There was nothing blissful about this ignorance, he thought. Deelah had known about it all along. *Why else would she cancel insurance and not tell me? Amiable divorce, my ass,* he fumed.

"Carl, thanks for the info. I gotta make another phone call. Excuse me."

He shook Heffley's huge paw and turned back towards the house. His legs froze in place as if he'd stepped into quick-drying concrete. Something was vastly different with the view up the sidewalk. The house was the same, but this view was shaded, provided by the huge blackjack oak tree, still standing, the whole picture colored in the sepia tones he had seen earlier with the workers and the painting.

OK, maybe I made that turn too fast. Maybe the blood from my damaged forehead couldn't catch up and it's still hanging back with the sheriff. Ismelda might have put something in the tea or the lemonade. No, you're just being paranoid; it's from the knock to your head. What if there was hallucinogenic herb in the tea? You're a nimrod; you're under a lot of stress, simple as that. How do you explain the naked girl with the crow, unresolved sexual urges?

His pro-and-con debate hit a concrete bridge abutment as the front door of the house opened.

A man emerged through the stained-glass doors, dressed in a white woolen greatcoat, high muddy boots, and a wide-brimmed straw hat, his one hand filled with the hair of a screaming young milk chocolate woman, his other clutching a Bible. Marble guessed that she screamed because all he heard was the sound of rushing wind. With arms and ankles bound together, she appeared terrified; spittle flew from the corners of her mouth as the long-bearded man roughly dragged her down the steps and across the lawn toward the oak.

She wore a necklace of bird feathers that came undone as he tossed her heavily into the tree; Marble watched the plumage dance away on the phantom breeze. The man casually walked behind the trunk and reappeared with a long length of rope, which he slung over a low branch. He deftly tied a hangman's noose, snapped the rope taut against the branch, and moved toward his prisoner. Marble's heart pounded against his chest as the noose cinched about her neck. The man then hoisted her to her feet, and she squirmed violently but he seemed oblivious to her struggles.

He opened the Bible and seemed to read a passage to the frantic woman. The doomed woman instantly ceased her struggles and snapped her eyes in Marble's direction, a passionate, desperate stare directly at him. Goosebumps the size of golf balls galloped up Marble's spine and arms. The bearded man then grabbed the other end of the hangman's rope and yanked her off the ground. At the same moment her bare feet left the earth, a hand grabbed Marble by the shoulder and he yelped. The vision vanished in a flash.

"Whoa, Larry, it's only me, Carl. You gonna make it OK? You passed out there for a sec, weird-like, eyes open and standing still and all. Thought it might be epilepsy, that's why I have my wallet out, was gonna, well, you see, my younger sis had it, uh, sweet Marylou... uh, want I should call the Doc? Izzie, what do you think?"

Ismelda's gentle touch wrapped around Marble's left arm.

"Thank you, Carl, I'll manage from here. Mr. Marble is my guest; it's my duty to keep a good eye on him."

"Well, if anybody can, it'd be you. Don't worry, Larry; Izz has a magic way with healing what ails you. Like I say, the Good Lord works in mysterious ways. Sweet Marylou… hey, Izz, why don't you give him one of those concoctions you…"

"Sheriff, that will be all, thanks." She fixed a shut-your-mouth-or-I'll-shut-it-for-you stare at the man who was roughly three times her size. His demeanor quickly changed.

"Right, OK, as you say, ma'am, as you say, just being neighborly; Marylou says it's a weakness of mine. Um, good luck, Mr. Marble, with your phone call and all. I best be going about my business, seeing's I'm on taxpayer time. See y'all around, folks." He bounded down the sidewalk, waved to the tree crew currently on a Tastykake cream-filled chocolate cupcake break, and squeezed behind the wheel of his patrol car.

Marble stared at the trunk of the massive oak. The vision he had just seen disturbed him deeply, more so than the fact that he now had experienced four visions within an hour's time. At least he was certain of one fact: the woman hung at the tree was the same person he'd just seen on the porch swing.

"Come on in outta the heat, Mr. Marble. We should talk. You've been seeing some things, visions maybe, around here. I can feel it, very real, vibrant, and powerful. And your aura, it's grown brighter since last night. Come on in, honey, I'll fix you another cup of tea. Everything is going to be all right."

The physical movement of walking jogged his recognition back to the moment as she led him up the porch stairs and into the vestibule. He glanced into the dining room as they passed its open doorway. A room of antique tables and China cabinets glanced back. At the end of the hallway, she led him into an airy kitchen, surrounded on three sides by an open-air greenhouse that fed into a large outdoor vegetable and herb garden.

Marble felt a warm blanket of comfort wrap around him as the pale-yellow kitchen walls welcomed him in. Hanging above the space were countless clusters of dried herbal cuttings, tied at the stems with string and hung from ceiling hooks. They extended to the main solid wall of the kitchen, lined with tall wooden and glass cabinetry that descended all the way to a stone counter.

Behind the leaden glass, he spied a cornucopia of mason jars, a colorful representation of home canned vegetables, fruits, sauces, oils, and powders. An island sat in the center of the kitchen, occupied by an open stove, range and grill attached to a double-sided sink. She led him to a tall stool at a high wooden table, next to the entrance to the greenhouse. Ismelda opened a canister she had removed from one of the cabinets and poured dried leaves into a steeping ball. As she set a copper kettle on the stove, Marble felt his head begin to swim. His vision began to blur as the echoes of the past marched through his mind.

A clap of thunder imploded in his head. *That word, that word.* It was a serious delayed reaction to Ismelda's comments. It leapt right up and demanded attention: the last time anyone had talked about his aura was the same day his older brother, Martin, had murdered his girlfriend and her family; and a young Larry Marble had seen it all unfold hours before a drop of blood spilled.

7

Larry Marble was born in Lancaster, Pennsylvania, ten years after his older brother, Martin. His parents had called him a blessed mistake, another term for an improperly placed IUD. His brother taught him how to hunt when he was seven but other than the occasional shared family meal, he had very little interaction with his sibling. It wasn't until he was in the fifth grade that events began to occur that would seal off a corner of his mind for the next thirty years.

Soon after his tenth birthday, he discovered his prescient talent. It had just arrived one night, unannounced and homeless. Marble granted it shelter and he immediately learned he could predict the final score of his beloved Phillies before the game even started. At first, he deemed it blind luck and kept it quiet. When he started correctly forecasting scores to other games in both the National and American Leagues, he did what every young boy does: he shared the news with his pals.

His buddies were amazed, and the news quickly spread in school. Mr. Erhardt, a kewpie-doll-shaped gym teacher who made a point of walking through the boy's shower to "ensure that everybody washes your family jewels thoroughly to keep from getting the dreaded crotch itch," had shown interest in the young Marble's cognitive ability. In the process, the fifth grader got his first bitter taste of the real world. After two weeks of relaying Marble's picks into big wins through his bookie, Mr. Erhardt mysteriously disappeared, only to turn up a week later, floating in the Susquehanna River just south of Three Mile Island, face down with a bookie's bullet hole in his brain.

Young Marble believed his own clairvoyance played a part in Erhardt's death. He wasn't sure exactly how, but his new mental capacities hinted at his involvement. The day the police found the gym teacher's body, Marble walked home from school along a familiar stretch of road. He was alone when the new vision hit him, so hard, in fact, that it knocked him to his knobby knees. Something had changed the channel in his head, and he now stared at the kind of grisly movie his parents would never let him watch.

Blood and brain matter splattered the walls and furniture of a stranger's living room. He thought the furniture would be OK because of the plastic covers that coated its upholstery. The carpet would not get off so lucky. Four bodies were on the floor, their faces grotesquely altered by the effects of close-ranged shotgun blasts. He knew it was a shotgun because his brother, Martin, walked into the picture, his weapon held across his body, the same way he had instructed young Marble on the many fall days they had gone pheasant hunting in the fields behind their house. He watched his older brother track bloody footprints all the way out the front door. A hand touched his shoulder, and a full body shiver removed the grisly picture.

"Sonny, are you all together? Smile it off, young Shooter, smile it off. Da tings your inner eye sees is not of your making, that's for sure. Go on now, young Shooter, smile it off."

Marble focused on the face of the first black person he had ever met. Her accent sang of Jamaican roots, a marvelous, wonderful lilting reggae. Her skin was crinkled old and her eyes black as onyx. Her dreadlocked hair was shiny black and gray, squeezed into a bun that sprouted shimmering black feathers. She wore a long, brightly flowered dress of orange, teal, and cinnamon, and used an emerald-green wooden cane to steady herself. With a wrinkled hand the color of coffee, she helped Marble to his feet and then stared at a spot above his head.

"Lord a mighty, sweet Mother, you blessed with one of the brightest and finest auras this ole bird ever done seen. Keep it polished good, young Shooter. Keep it polished now. You never know when the Mistress is gonna throw you in the ring." She laughed musically and then patted him lovingly on the head.

"Now you listen good to me, you hear? Go on and face the music, young Shooter. You don't need to see what's not happened yet, nnh-nnh. I'm gonna close that door, that third eye, close it now for your own good. This mess you be seeing may be bad but there be plenty of good dancing tunes for you down the road, oh Lordy, yes, that's a certainty."

She waved the cane above his head and young Marble heard a slamming vault between his ears. She then grabbed him by the shoulders and turned him facing the other direction. "You hurry off to home, now, Shooter. Be seeing you around one of these days, young Shooter, mon, you be splendid good, now, you hear?"

With that, she turned and limped off in the direction of Marble's school. He remembered how he had progressed only a few feet before he had turned back around to look for the old woman, but she had vanished. Only a large black crow stared back. It cawed menacingly, flapped its wings, and hopped toward Marble. He turned and ran home as if the devil was on his tail.

Young Marble blamed himself for the deaths. He never should have told anyone about his ability to forecast scores. He should have tried to stop his brother when he got home that afternoon. He remembered how Martin had walked out of the house with his shotgun, mumbling about how he was going hunting and how nobody was going to baby him into getting married. That same afternoon, his family lost their anonymity, just as he sealed tight the visions of his mind that had watched his brother leave bloody footprints down the sidewalk, and the baseball scores that had sent Mr. Erhardt to a greedy death.

Thirty years later that door had creaked open, and this time Marble heard the groans of hinges long unused between his ears. His aura leapt out, did a pirouette, and bowed deeply, gracious in its return.

***

"Don't go falling off that stool. You've had enough trouble for one day already. Now, some questions. Drink this first." Ismelda handed Marble a mug filled with a steaming brew, another liquid nudge.

"What is this?" Marble held the mug with both hands and let the steam swirl to his nose.

"The curious cat. It's just medicine for your soul, all natural herbs, a potion right from my garden."

"A potion? Come on, what is it really?"

"Oh, just a little of this and a pinch of that plus an elixir of skullcap, peppermint and rosemary with a smidgen of schisandra berry."

"Sounds French to me." Marble raised the mug to his lips and sipped. It had a funky, spicy berry taste but it felt good sliding down his esophagus. "Mmm, not bad. A magic potion, all-natural elixir, you say? Something like a witch's brew?"

Ismelda sat on a stool opposite him. "A witch, you ask? Because I brew my own herbal teas? You've watched far too many movies. The real magic is in the balance of the natural. That, I'm afraid, has been missing."

"Ismelda, it was a joke, it's a problem I have injecting a little levity into situations that look bleak. I was trying to…"

"Tell me about your visions. Are they bleak?"

She stared at him, and he felt like she had a view right inside his head. He met her gaze for a long moment but then returned his attention to the teacup in his hands.

The doomed woman hung on the tree jumped to the front of his memory queue. It was as if the woman had seen him watching from the future. She had revealed an eerie glint of recognition, and the time paradox conundrum made him ponder if he should call George Noori's radio show. Marble chuckled to himself and shifted his position on the stool while nervously sipping from the mug. The visions Ismelda referred to were not the same ones that danced about his head though. Something else was evident now in his mind… an old friend was back.

It has returned, he thought, covered up for close to thirty years, his talent to see the world as others couldn't. Maybe it was the knock on the head. Maybe it was the abrupt change in lifestyle. He balanced questions in his mind about the strange painting over the fireplace and the figure he almost ran over the previous night. *Or maybe I'm just losing my mind.* He'd read somewhere that it was an offshoot of divorce.

Marble returned Ismelda's gaze, and this time a warm breath of sensuality washed over him when they locked eyes. It took him by surprise, maybe the tea was liquid Viagra. He hadn't had spontaneous erections since high school. "Whoa, what is in this again?"

"My tea, that's all." A ghost of a smile washed over her face and then she asked again. Her tone seemed anxious. "Now, your visions, how many have you had?'

Marble's defenses went up. He recalled the ruddy jowls of Mr. Erhardt, asking him the same kind of questions. *"Well, let's have it, Marble. Steve Carlton's pitching tonight, what's the score gonna be? Let's have it, son."*

He sipped from the mug again and stared into its brown warmth. She had asked about plural visions, not just one. *How does she know there was more than one?*

"The woman with the crow on the porch swing. That one I know. What others?"

She was persistent but not enough for him to give in. "It... *they*, don't concern you, Ismelda. Probably just due to the knock on my head, that's all. I do know there are bigger fish to fry than dwelling, on, uh, hallucinations. My immediate future holds another glorious phone call to my ex and a visit to the guy whose truck I fell into. I think I'll do the latter first. A little air will do me good. Just point me in the right direction."

He stood slowly, drained his mug, and looked at Ismelda. "Thanks for the magic potion. No insect bites, huh? I'll give you a first hand report."

Ismelda noticed his reticence, but she didn't want to press. She chided herself to be patient. "Mr. Marble, about the missing birds, there are... powers in play that need attention, *your* attention, your abilities. Trust your inner eye, your sight. You may stay here free for a few days. My insurance probably doesn't cover the loss of your car, but, shoot, it was my tree."

"Well, thanks, that's mighty kind of you."

"Now, for your walk, I suggest you might want to shower first, no offense meant, our Indian summer temperatures are powerful ripeners. Then proceed south on Main, down to Callie's. The marina is next door. Willem Clydesdale is your man, the owner of the dented pickup. He's also town mayor. But be careful. He's a miserable coot, a real sonofabitch." She laughed but he could tell she didn't think it was funny.

He sniffed his armpits. *Yikes.* "Thanks. I'll be sure to watch my back. See you in a little while. Oh, and uh, you can call me Larry."

Twenty minutes later and after a soothing shower, he put on clean Dockers and a Polo shirt. The only other footwear he had in the duffel was a pair of flip-flops. They would have to do.

Something Ismelda had said stuck out in his mind. *There are powers in play here.* He chuckled to himself as he walked down Main Street, but the mirth soon skedaddled. The head of a pelican dropped from the sky and splotched before him on the sidewalk and his breath caught in his throat. The bird twitched its bucket beak a couple of times before it stilled.

Marble looked up and a glimpse of black wings, long talons, and yellow eyes slipped behind a line of loblolly pines. He jogged forward, hoping to catch a better glimpse of… again a series of shadows flitted beyond the tree line to the west before vanishing from his sight. "What the hell?"

Ismelda watched his progress from the bay window. The tea would open more doors, release more powers, and heighten passions, and her sisters would nurture his progress in whatever way they could.

***

Anna Smythe let the tears run down her cheeks. She was on her balcony that overlooked the bay and marshland to the south of Clydesdale. The quiet of the skies was tragic but her tears were for another soul. She raised her gaze upward. The hood of her cloak fell back, and long, brown and silver-streaked hair bounced free as she sat upon a redwood deck chair.

The September sun had not yet reached its mid-morning zenith as she opened her cloak to the sky. She was naked beneath; the soft, sultry curves, the velvet sensuality of a body just a tad shy of voluptuous. Slight crow's feet and the silver in her hair were the only evidence of forty years on earth. She leaned back and let the cool bay breeze tease her skin. This morning she had shaved herself for the first time in months, the lotion applied to her skin nurtured its suppleness. As her nipples stiffened, she remembered how incredibly satisfied she used to make her man. She arched her pelvis and allowed the salty breeze to lick her moistness, and the wind's tongue hungrily obliged. It had been so long without his warmth, so long without his kisses, his laughter, his manhood. Her stomach tightened as her hand moved lower. It didn't take long for the memories of him to bring her to a tearful quaking gasp. Closure complete, she thought, forgotten, never.

As her breathing returned to normal, she reopened moist eyes and wiped the tears from her cheeks. The morning should be rife with squawking gulls, playful bufflehead ducks returning to their winter nesting area, sandpipers darting above the reeds and a myriad of other winged life. The imbalance in the universe spread deep into her soul; things definitely were not as they should be.

Her earlier conversation with Popeye hadn't helped. The death of a soulmate can lead to depression. Anna was careful not to let the numbing intoxicant rule her life. Although her writing had suffered, the passion to uncover the truth about her husband's death had occupied her daily.

It had been four months since Captain Turner Smythe had

disappeared at sea and, despite her exhaustive efforts, authorities initiated no renewed inquiries into his mysterious demise. Willem Clydesdale had covered all the bases neatly, with any incriminating evidence swept far out to sea. It didn't help her distress either that Ismelda Cooper had yet to contact anyone in the spirit world who had seen her husband. Ismelda's earlier phone call gave her hope though. Perhaps the new visitor to town was the answer, perhaps not. Either way, she was going to get some answers.

****

"Eight hundred dollars?" Marble wanted to add, "for that piece of shit?" But he remained civil. "That's a lot of money for knocking a dent out of the hood of a rusty pickup. You could find a hood in a junk yard for fifty bucks and pay some kid to spray paint it whatever color you want. Three hundred tops, that's all it's worth."

Marble calmly stared across the desk at hizzoner Willem Clydesdale. He tried to place the mayor's age, but Willem had the broad look of a middle-age mismanaged body, somewhere between a spark still in the step and ears that grow as big as zucchinis. It came complete with sagging eyelids and jowls, layered bags under the eyes and flab abundant. Marble tried not to look too surprised because Willem was also the same man he'd seen the night before at the exit ramp. He was sure of it. There was something else too, not as clear as the visions he'd been having all day, no picture in his mind. Just a scent, not discernible to his nose, but one his mind detected. A wave of memories surfaced, and he remembered his dad's warnings of a bad storm, a vision of Willem baying at the moon, the thought of Mr.

Erhardt's body bloated by the murky Susquehanna, his brother's grisly crime – they all smelled the same as the marina office: rotten clam bad.

"What are you, some kind of nothinglessness expert on insurance?" Willem smiled like a snake about to attack.

Marble blurted out a short laugh. "Excuse me? What kind of word is nothinglessness? You've got to be kidding me. You make up your own words? Oh, that's priceless. No, I'm not an expert about insurance but I do know when someone's trying to rip me off."

Marble stared at the manatee of a man behind the heavy, wooden desk. Willem's eyes were glassy bloodshot, and blotches of purple and red splotched his scalp. A thick, bulbous nose was pockmarked from ancient bouts with acne. Marble coiled back each time Willem spoke because of the spittle that flew forth from the gap between his tar-tanned teeth. *And this guy holds a public office?*

"Eight hundred is what my mechanic quoted me for your handiwork, stranger. So that's what your insurance is gonna pay. You do have coverage, don't you?"

Marble wasn't sure anymore what he had. Did he even have any health coverage? A small panic flag went up with the thought of anything that might land him in a hospital. Deelah had also taken control of that area during their time together. He looked at the estimate with Lou's Auto Body boldly typed across the top. Willem had fudged Lou's 3 into an 8 but Marble missed the deception.

"Listen, I have to make some phone calls."

"Who's your insurance company? What's your policy number?"

"You can rest assured, restitution will be made. It's just not going to be $800. My fair guess is $300 but that's up to the claims adjuster. I just wanted to stop by as a gentlemanly courtesy. Now we'll let the insurance adjusters settle on the amount, that's their job."

"You can bet your sweet gentleman's ass retribution will be had. And don't go trying to skip out of town before it is either. Where you staying?"

"At the Paradise B&B up the road." The news had an interesting effect on Willem's face. It reminded Marble of an old MTV video where Peter Gabriel changed expressions at lightning speed. Willem's final face was bright red and his mood morphed right along with the color.

"So, you're the motherfucking nothinglessness who splashed me last night, the same fuck wad who had his car smashed to shit. Ha! Ha! Ha! Serves you right, asshole. Welcome to Clydesdale, Maryland. Just our friendly way of saying howdy doody to our town, you dumb peckerhead."

The outburst struck Marble silent as he watched the hundreds of tiny blood vessels that seemed ready to burst out of the mayor's pasty scalp. The image morphed to indignation. *What the hell did he just call me?*

"That was you? Look, I'm sorry. Hey, I didn't see you until too late. Wait a sec… what did you just call me?"

"You selfish prick. Evil spirits are paying you back for your failure to help a stranded motorist. You're the poster child for the dead Samaritan. Ha! Ha! Ha! Double whammy got you back for damaging my truck. That's what that is, a healthy dose of evil spirits getting you back, you stupid fuck. Sure sucks to be you, you sorry looking dog turd."

Marble glanced down at the whale-shaped paperweight that read "Mayor". *How the hell did this asshole win this office? And how long am I going to stand here and take this crap?* Another childhood memory popped to the surface. Prior to his development of cognitive powers, Marble had gone to grade school with a smart-ass kid named Billy Krilly who had a habit of always saying evil spirits got you back whenever somebody screwed up. It didn't matter what the screw up was, Billy would always add his two cents. Marble remembered that he never liked Billy.

"Excuse me, Mr. Clydesdale, I came here in good faith to offer to pay for the damage I inflicted on *your* piece of shit truck." *Ah, that felt good.* "I don't appreciate being harassed about my misgivings, especially from a civil servant. Well, there is nothing civil about you sir. And I don't appreciate your taunts. I endured enough name-calling from my ex-wife. If you have a problem with my—"

"Get your insurance number to me pronto. Now I'm done with you. Go on, get your sorry-smelling nothinglessness Pennsylvania carpetbagger ass outta my office. And get your pancaked Ford out of my street before I cite you for littering, you pansy ass cocksucker."

Marble felt his blood begin to boil. *What the hell is the problem with this dude? What happened to the Golden Rule?* The comebacks started to pile up at his interior door, begging for release. *OK, you cut me off. I used to have a customer who would do that to me constantly. And I hated his guts. But nobody except Deelah ever called me a motherfucker and cocksucker to my face more than once in a span of sixty seconds.* Marble had built up enough steam.

"Hey, dick face. Call me a motherfucker one more time and I'll shove this down your throat." Marble the Crazed held the whale-shaped paperweight above his head in a Conan the Barbarian pose. "I came here in good faith. And you're treating me like crap. You are not a nice man. And you know what? I don't think you care. And that makes you a pitiful-not-nice man. Here. Sue me." Marble dropped the nameplate, and it broke in half. Unfazed, he then ripped up the estimate and threw the pieces into the air. He twirled to leave but a loud THWACK made him wheel back around.

Willem stood at his desk and cackled like a mad man. The thwack, Marble guessed, had come from the rusty grappling hook that Willem had just imbedded into the top of his desk.

"Yeah, you betcha, I'll definitely be seeing you around, boy. All kinds of evil spirits are gonna get you back. That's for sure. Now run on home to your witch landlady."

Marble couldn't resist. "How old are you? That evil spirit thing went out the door with elementary school, wedgies, and spitballs. What are you, some kind of dinosaur? First, I could have you thrown in jail for threatening me. Is this your first day on this planet?"

Willem didn't get a chance for a comeback. His desk spoke. Deep within a center drawer, the nest portal came alive. Marble watched in horror as the heavy desk rose from the floor and began to spin. *OK, this is definitely not like any of the visions I've been having. This one is live and in color.* Willem stood back against the window and howled with deranged delight. Marble had seen enough.

He backed towards the door, raised a double bird toward the mayor, and bid a silent yet swift farewell to the mayhem. As soon as Willem's door closed behind him, Marble heard another thwack that sounded just like the previous one. Only this time the grappling hook was impaled on the other side of the door exactly where Marble had stood. In front of him, Patti feigned slumber and he didn't even pause for formality's sake.

Once outside, he inhaled a deep I'm-alive breath. Willem was whacked, but the twirling desk pegged up a few notches on the crazy as a loon stick. Marble concentrated his inner eye on something more, but he sensed an alien block, a foreign stop, a smell of bad clams that sent shiver me timbers along his spine. The heads of six seagulls bounced off the macadam and he jumped back, tearing a stupid flip-flop in the process. Again, he shot a look skyward but this time no hint of spooky winged shadow beasts.

A scream erupted from the marina office and that was enough motivation to keep moving. Rather than Ismelda's Paradise B&B and a phone call to Deelah, he turned left. *Did that lunatic mayor really just call Ismelda a witch?* He had to admit upon reflection that his landlady was a bit peculiar. But witchcraft was a concept as foreign to him as country music. Neither ever occupied an ounce of cerebral time in his life.

Deep in thought about the physics-challenged spinning desk, he never even noticed the Fish and Wildlife rangers who pulled up in a government van and scooped up the seagull heads into plastic baggies. A gaggle of news folk, cameras, boom mikes, and hairspray galore quickly surrounded them. The media swarm had emerged from a series of news vans parked near Ezekiel Clydesdale's bird shit coated statue. Marble missed it all, intent on avoiding any sharp objects that might impale the tender pink of his one bare foot.

Behind him, Willem charged out of his office with the grappling hook. The nothinglessness smart-ass had pushed the wrong button and he wanted to make sure he got in another zinger. He was fuming and Marble was in for a lot more verbal whoop ass. He turned toward Callie's and swallowed his tongue. The approaching hulk of Popeye Worthington made him dart back inside the shack, manatee tail tucked between his legs.

8

The tarmac sizzled his bare foot like bacon on a hot skittle and Marble cursed his broken flip-flop. His uneven gait was even more annoying, so he threw the other foam plastic noisemaker into a trash canister and darted on tiptoes to a swath of shade provided by a storefront's awning to allow his dogs to cool in the shadows. A few quick glances in either direction aided his appraisal of the environs. North and south along the block were a series of businesses, hardware, real estate, insurance, attorney, food mart and his own shaded awning, a drug store. It was eerily quiet for a commercial center and Marble guessed one of the reasons might be the grisly battlefield of torn bird bodies that littered the gutters.

"Dear God, what in the world?" As he leaned over to examine the remains of a blue heron, he felt eyes upon him, and he stepped from beneath the awning and scanned the skyline. A cloud of dark shadows sailed by overhead and darted quickly behind the A&P. Marble squinted and tried to make some sense of the image. A red flag began to flap in his head. Those flying shadows held the secret, he was certain and yet none of his awakened senses "saw" anything further. His baby-pink bare feet began to scream in pain, so he skipped into the shade once again. He now faced the pharmacy store's front window banner that read "End of Summer Clearance Sale, Great Deals"

Aware his feet needed better protection; he dipped in for an air-conditioned peek. A cylindrical wire bin just inside the door held a mishmash of flip-flops, each for a buck ninety-nine. Marble passed on the bargain. He hated the feeling of that little rubber stub wedged between his toes, anyway. Almost as much as he hated the sound that flip-flops made when you walked. Deelah had a closet full of flip-flops. His last pair had just died and there was no turning back.

Added to his fantasy of things he would change if ever elected king of the universe was the banishment of sculpting hairspray, flip-flops worn anywhere outside of a beach, and making sure that no minion of his ever, ever had to endure the pain of a pig-faced divorce lawyer. The daydream brought a needed smile to his lips, the perfect shopping guise.

Along the southern wall, a display of injection-molded boat shoes caught his attention. He picked out a pair born in Taiwan and barefooted it to the register where a cute, pudgy-cheeked clerk arose from behind the counter. Her name tag read Jasmine. Marble was pleased to see her body held none of the pudginess her cheeks belied. She smiled warmly and his body shimmied with the yummies. *What was in that tea?* His forty-year-old conscience slapped him alongside his head. *What the hell is wrong with you? You're hornier than an eighteen-year-old who just got his first smell of forbidden fruit on his fingers.*

"That'll be $4.99, sir, a stupendous bargain, congratulations. Would you like a bag?"

No, but I would like… "No thanks, I'll be wearing them." His mind locked for a second. *Small talk, doofus. You haven't been out of circulation that long.* "Oh, uh, any place around here that sells books?" *Books? How about cars? And why are there so many dead birds outside? Why did I say "books"?* He opened his mouth, his mind had picked a question, the synapses fired, his vocal chords responded and instead of "dead birds" the word "books" came out – *weird*.

"You mean like a Barnes and Noble? Closest is Ocean City. There is a little shop just outside of town though that sells some books. It's called Anna's Nest, kind of quirky in a 60s hippy way but cute. Not much of a mainstream selection though. A lot of nature, spiritual, and new wave if you're into that kind of tree-hugging stuff but no Stephen King, Dean Koontz, or Tom Clancy. She also sells incense and candles, you know, metaphysical trappings if you want to take a trip down memory lane or any astral plane. Some books claim you can burn a certain candle and the smell will reduce stress. She also has these funky aromatherapy vials that can turn a woman into a nympho. Tried it once but it was kind of blah, especially after B.O.B. died, aka my battery-operated boyfriend. But it's not too far a walk, especially now that you have covers. Look. I'm wearing a pair too, bitching comfortable for the price."

Marble was amazed at her lungpower because she'd said it all without taking a breath. Jasmine inhaled deeply and propped a nicely muscled, smooth leg onto the counter.

"See? Same color as yours. I was a gymnast in college that's why I'm so limber. Helps to keep my legs toned too. What do you think? Do I have good legs or what?" His eyes crept up toward her skirt hiked almost up to her hips.

"Yes, you have great legs. Very presentable, very, um, good muscle tone, smooth and… Wow. It's warm in here all of a sudden. Boy, I'm hungry for lunch. Do you eat?" Maybe Anna's Nest had a book on the Dummy's Guide to the art of conversation with a woman. Marble felt like a ninth grader stumbling through his first request for a dance.

"My, aren't you the bold one. I am duly charmed. Yes, I eat; it's a weakness of mine. But I don't get off until five, no relief for poor old Jasmine today. That's me, Jasmine Culpepper, twenty-four, single, no kids, live on my own in an efficiency upstairs waiting for a chance to use my degree for something more than selling condoms to pimply faced kids. So, if you can extend the invitation another five hours, I would be more than pleased to dine with you. You're cute, in a bohemian kind of way. I like that. You look a little reckless, carefree, fun. I'm good with first impressions. Honest. Can always put a finger on a person's pulse if you know what I mean." Her index finger playfully poked his sternum, and Marble instinctively sucked in his gut. "There's this great little place called Callie's that makes the best crab cakes. I figure you're a tourist cuz I've never seen you before, so I figure I should probably recommend the place we go to eat, seeing how I've lived here for almost a whole year."

Marble smiled sheepishly and prayed that he didn't have anything stuck in his teeth.

Jasmine took a breath, only one. "Marine biology, that's my major, was my major. The state wants to create a wildlife observatory in the south marshes, but it's still caught up in red tape because of that wahoo psychopath they call a mayor. Do you know how he won? Nobody else ran for the office. It pays squat, but still, you'd think somebody would challenge the asshole. I mean, he gets a powerful vote on this town's future, and he pisses it away. Apathy runneth amok in these parts. You heard it here first, loud and clear, Jasmine Culpepper clanging the alarm."

Marble was stuck with the realization that he'd just landed the Grand Plan's first date. He hoped she was as talkative then as now. Most of the dinners he remembered from marriage took place in front of the TV, a tough way to improve one's dinner conversation skills. "Dinner is fine. Callie's, it is. I'll meet you back here at five. I promise to dress a little better for the occasion."

"You want some pain reliever for that bump on your head?"

"This? No ma'am, no pain coming from this little accident anymore. I'm fine, thanks. See you later." He had to get outside to breathe. He'd been holding in his gut for far too long now.

"Oh, wait, what's your name? I don't date a man until I know his name."

"Shooter, just call me Shooter." *Shit, there it is again.* "Larry" was the word his brain sent down to his vocal chords, but "Shooter" came out instead. *Wait a second, that's the same name that black lady with crow feathers in her hair called me thirty years ago.*

Jasmine laughed and her mirth sent Marble's brain on recess. "Shooter, you have yourself a date. Now don't be late. Oh yeah, this is dinner only, no funny business, not unless you get me drunk." That said, she pulled her leg down from the counter and hopped in place.

He smiled and gave a weak wrist wave before skipping back into the sunlight. Before the hot pavement scalded his feet further though, he bent over to put on his new shoes. Now safely shod, a very fine mood should have joined his brisk walk down Main Street toward Anna's Nest. He didn't question himself why he had asked Jasmine about a bookstore. He didn't contemplate why he was on his way for the bookstore. He didn't care that he had used the name Shooter, something the strange Jamaican lady had called him in his youth. Instead, his attention refocused on the grisly battlefield of bird remains methodically scooped up with long-handled dog pooper shovels by a gang of hooded and gloved dudes from the National Wildlife Agency.

Marble looked up to the deep blue sky. The channel changed again in his mind and a vision of cloud-yellow eyes hidden in thick fog popped into his head and rattled his mind.

***

Popeye Worthington swallowed his ire and followed it up with a prayer to God Almighty for strength. He was tempted to wake Patti with a loud noise. He was mad. It wasn't a bad mad, though, not one that could inflict harm on others. There would be no more of that kind of cow's crap in his life, even though he was sorely tested. His anger fermented upon the sight of Willem's hasty withdrawal back into the marina shack. He was mad at Willem, not the napping Patti. The one-hundred-and-fifty-dollar parking ticket in his hand had just brought him in the door.

"Ahem. Ahem. Excuse me, miss. Miss." Patti finally opened her eyes, well, one of them. The other had difficulty because a false eyelash had slipped during slumber and pinned itself to her cheek. "Sorry to wake you, but I would like to file a complaint. This is city hall, isn't it?"

Now with both eyes free, she focused in on the hulk of the man who had it bad for Callie. It was no secret that Popeye was interested, as affairs of the heart and other organs were free banter for Clydesdale's women folk. This, however, was her first chance to speak with the shy hunk in person. The only problem was that her brain had not yet caught up to her eyes. Whiskey sours for breakfast had a way of delaying the old synapse connections. "You betcha. City Hall. Grand trappings, ain't it?"

"This ticket. It's absurd. I park in the delivery zone every time and never before a ticket. This must be a mistake. I was legally parked. Could you please void it?"

Patti whirled in her chair and peeked out the 1945 vintage metal venetian blinds. The turn made her dizzy though, so she took her time facing back. "Seems to me like you look just fine. I mean, your truck. I seen ya there before plenty of times. Give me that." She grabbed the ticket from his hand.

Popeye kept his body open to Willem's office. He sorely fought the temptation to bash down the closed door. His talk with Anna that morning had riled him in a manner that he hadn't felt since the Med cruise many years before. But the sound of ripping paper directed his attention back to Patti.

"There, just like that." She leaned in and whispered conspiratorially. "I'll make sure I nab Heffley's copy when it comes by my desk and make confetti of that one too. Whee." She threw her arms up in the air and the ticket pieces took flight.

Something roared from behind closed doors and Popeye whipped around to face the rage. The beast, he hath awakened, he grimly thought. "Thank you, miss, I'm much obliged. One doesn't find such kindness in public officials very often. Seems most of them forget about what they're supposed to be governing soon as the power hits their heads. I've seen it all over the peninsula. Heck, even across the bay. Makes no sense. No sense. Think they're above the law. But they'll get theirs soon enough. The good Lord will see to that, oh yes, He will, praise be His name. 'Let him that hath understanding count the number of the beast: for it is the number of a man, and his number is Six hundred three score and six.' The bad eggs will be expelled, tossed out of the nest to die. And we'll find him. Oh, yes, we'll find that bad egg. Good day, miss."

Popeye briskly walked out of the marina and then paused to calm his breathing. That was the first time he had ever quoted Revelations out loud. He took another deep breath, and he knew the spirit of God inhaled with him.

The outside door closed, and Patti quickly checked her

compact's mirror. Maybe something was on her face. Or maybe he really was as shy as people said. Because most of the last words he had spoken were directed straight at Willem's door.

The same door creaked open, and Willem sheepishly stuck out his head. "Is he gone?"

She nodded and her compact fell to the floor as the trembling shakes came out to play. She had seen that look a hundred and one times from Willem – even when things had been physically good between them – she whimpered a feral mewl.

Willem stalked back into his office and set the nest portal gingerly on the table, out of Patti's view. It pulsed with hunger, and he knew from experience that he didn't dare cover it just yet. Besides, another matter was at hand.

He stalked back to the main office, quickly closed the gap to Patti and punched her hard in the arm. And again. And again. And again. Each time with a labored "oomph."

She knew better than to shout or yell or fight back or run. She'd tried all of them before and the additional bruises had looked like tattoos because they lasted so long. So, she took her punishment, silently twirling in her chair with each pummel only to have him whirl her back into position for another. And despite the pain, it wasn't all that bad. The bruises were easy to cover up. Willem was kind about avoiding her face.

Willem quickly winded from the pugilistic abuse. He stormed back into his office and slammed the door behind. No words spoken and none needed.

Patti knew what she had done wrong. She had thwarted his evil little scheme to make the trucker pay for being different than him. And she would do it again and again and again. She wiped away the tears, picked up her thermos, and poured herself a luncheon cocktail. For the second time that day, as the whiskey

sour worked its magic, she succumbed to the Mayor Prickface
giggles.

***

Doc Gilbert smelled like the bay. Crab shell and guts covered his
overalls, fresh from a crab cleaning committee in Callie's
kitchen, so Ismelda made him stay outside on the porch. Callie
needed him less now because the tourist season had wound down,
so he could dare to dally longer than in full season. Besides, his
hammer, pliers, and crab knife were due for sharpening, and
Ismelda had the best electric grinder in Clydesdale. After he had
eaten most of his peanut butter and banana sandwich, she decided
to speak.

"I need your help. Do you remember Mr. Marble, the
gentleman from breakfast this morning?"

He nodded while his tongue worked feverishly to clean the
ample gaps between his remaining teeth.

"Well, he's had some pretty bad luck since getting into
town," she said.

Gilbert smiled a peanut butter-toothed grin thinking of the
knock to the noggin Marble had sauntered into earlier that day,
not to mention the pancaked Ford.

"I want you to keep an eye out for him, Doc. Don't let
anything bad happen."

"Can't you, you know, give him some kind of rabbit's foot
or something?"

Ismelda smiled. "Now, Doc Gilbert, we've had this
discussion before, remember? I don't have powers like that.
Remember? I am a healer. A provider. All else is beyond my
control. You're one of the protectors. Remember? So please,

please keep an eye out for him, you and the boys." She glanced at the three park employees who had restarted their chainsaws, about to effectively quiet their conversation.

Doc Gilbert actually looked a bit wiser. "Yeah, I remember now. You're sure he's the one who can help us, eh? We got you. Nothing will happen if we keep a watch. Me and the boys. The protectors. Ol' Clydesdale won't get his hook in this one. Oh hey, how's our goose feller doing?"

"He is recuperating nicely though I'm certain he'd much rather be among his own. Soon, several more days and, well, I can't release him yet, can I?" Her eyes filled with tears.

The roar of the saws prevented any further conversation. Doc simply nodded and turned away and began singing "Volare" at the top of his lungs. She watched as he limped down the walkway, turned to the right, and headed toward the restaurant. The limp, so he claimed, was a lingering injury from his former life when he'd taken a Germanic spear in the hip while he protected the personage of Marc Antony.

Ismelda watched the former centurion until he disappeared from sight at the row of bayberry and forsythias that lined the southern boundary of her property. It was all coming to fruition now, she thought. It had to be. All her powers exhausted, the entire coven had attempted to thwart the demons without success. She leaned her forehead against the doorframe of the house. The building was soothingly cool to touch yet troubled in spirit.

Ismelda knew all too well of the home's history. To her, the building was alive; she even felt its breath at times. For, indeed, within its walls, it held energy of the *samanth* who had died in the front yard a hundred and thirty-eight years before. The diary of Clydesdale's ancestor told in specific detail of the sacrifice made by the slave who impudently claimed to be a high priestess.

Ismelda had never discovered her name though. She had found the book within a false drawer of the armoire in the west room back in 1985.

She allowed her gaze to fall upon the gnarled bark of the dead oak. The tree had now been trimmed enough for her to see the green hood of the smashed Ford. A smile formed on her lips just as her hat began to bulge outward upon her head. The felling of the oak had been a trick that even she had been surprised with. The Shooter had arrived as foretold, and now he had been captured by the town at the sacrifice of the old giant.

She lifted her eyes to the sky, then walked back into the house just as a large black crow landed on the porch railing. Ismelda knew it was there, but she continued into the hallway without a glance backward. The bird's song was not for her. The crow would stay until Shooter returned. And besides, Ismelda had plenty to keep her busy. Mother finch's eggs beneath her cap were about to hatch.

***

Caught within the web of confusion, Marble heard the anguish of the birds. Shock, dismay, horror, terror, all bounced off his mind. Invisible predators, why were those words emblazoned in his thoughts? He looked to the sky and scanned each horizon, first the east, then north, west, and south. Nothing, the air was void save the clouds and wind.

When he refocused back to earth, he found himself in front of Anna's Nest. He still hadn't given any thought to why exactly he was there. Nor did he waste time crossing to the entrance. It was a one-story clapboard cottage backed up to the bay. Marble smelled burning incense as he opened the stained-glass door. It

109

was dark inside and it took a moment for his eyes to adjust to the sudden contrast.

"Please close the door if you will. The harvest sun likes to sneak an early peek or two inside my emporium when the portal is left open this time of the cycle." A female's voice, seductive, warm, challenging, came from the shadows.

"Hmm? Oh, sure, no problem." Marble closed the door behind, sending its rattan horizontal blinds into a clattered frenzy. "Um, that's incense you're burning, right?" The woman's voice had come from his left, so he directed his words there. *I haven't smelled incense since… college. There had been a girl I had dated… Maryanne Santangelo… she had been a fan of incense. Wow, it's been… how long?* He inhaled deeply as the memory shook off its dust, but he set it aside and concentrated on the present.

"Yes. I find the aroma very soothing and sensual. Is there something I can help you find, Mr. …"

"Marble, Larry, but you can call me Shooter." He still was not consciously aware of the new name declaration until the word leapt from his lips and any chance of correcting it went by as Anna Smythe came into focus, the ribbed-light pattern from the rattan blinds displaying her movements in kaleidoscope fashion. Gliding with feline grace and stealth, she slipped closer.

"Anna Smythe, Mr. Shooter. I am quite pleased to make your acquaintance."

He took her offered hand and an electric jolt shot up his arm, through the shoulder, scaled the neck, and entered his brain, scrambling the sensual picture before his eyes and instead, splashing a vision far from incense.

Marble now stared at the hairy, sweaty back of Willem as he struggled to lift a heavy bundle over the side of his boat. The boat rocked upward on a swell and revealed the object to be the body of a young black man, with two large cinder blocks tied to his chest. Just as quickly, the picture changed back to a very concerned Anna.

Her eyes were wide, her voice a moist whisper. "You're the one. We've been waiting for you. Thank you, Mr. Shooter. May I inquire, what is it you just saw?"

Marble suddenly felt lightheaded. "I… could I… do you have any water?" *Time to settle down a little bit, old man. Now, what the hell does she mean by all that we've been waiting for you bullshit? Hell, I didn't even know I was coming here. How could she be waiting for me then? And how did she know I had a vision? Maybe she's one of them, she's like Ismelda.*

His eyes had adjusted to the lower light levels, and he watched her return with a bottle of Evian. Her sexy blue sundress aligned his focus. But it didn't do squat for his weak conversational skills.

"Do you have a book on birds? You know, um, the local birds?" It was a crappy segue, but what the hell, he'd just seen a vision of a black guy thrown overboard for crab food.

"Certainly, but first, please forgive my impudence, Mr. Shooter. It's just that you possess powers that can help a great many souls in Clydesdale. I… oh my, I may have spoken out of turn once more."

She playfully tossed her auburn hair back over her shoulder and revealed a neck Marble could only describe as luscious.

"What the heavens, the spirits abound anyway, I must confess. Sooner or later, you'll find out from someone, I'm sure. Willem Clydesdale, you see, killed my husband, Captain Turner Smythe – at least that's what I believe – on a chartered fishing trip. The boat returned without my man and without answers. You may have a power within you to help me find those answers."

Marble listened to her as he chugged the *agua*. It was all weird, he had to admit. *Should I tell her what the vision portrayed? Was the husband the black man thrown overboard? No, no, no, I better wait. How do I even know the vision is real? I mean, is it something that already happened or is it something that's about to take place? And how can my visions help the birds?* He decided to play it cool.

"I'm sorry for your loss. I had a chance to meet your infamous mayor this morning. I must say he's a real piece of work. In fact, I think he's a bit shy of a full deck. But I don't know what I can do to help. Just passing through, you see. I'm on my way to Ocean City. Soon as my… my car situation is taken care of, I'm outta here." He took a long swig. "How about that book on birds?" *A book on birds? What the hell do I want with that?*

Anna moved in close and invaded his personal space. She was intimate enough that he could smell the lavender in her hair. Her eyes bored deep into his and for a second he felt himself weakening. She stepped closer, pressed her breasts into his chest and energy surged through his body that he hadn't felt in a long, long time. She leaned up and kissed him gently on the lips.

"Mr. Shooter, if you're only passing through, it is my humble responsibility to make sure your stay in Clydesdale an enjoyable one."

This time her mouth parted slightly as she again pressed against his. Marble couldn't recall if that was a signal to thrust his tongue or not. What was the first kiss etiquette? He searched his memory. First kiss, first kiss, first kiss… for some reason the search engine failed.

His tongue got tired of waiting for him to decide and joined the party anyway. Angelic chants sang hallelujahs through his body as she responded for what seemed an eternity of shared passion. They finally parted lips, and she leaned up to his ear. Her hot breath earned a couple of wows from the peanut gallery in his head.

"I have not been with a man since my late husband. My request is not frivolous, Mr. Shooter. I want you. Right here, right now."

He heard the distinct click of the lock on the front door as she once again brought her mouth to his. Were they standing that close? Had she even taken her hands off of him? Again, his tongue left him behind, never hesitating to proceed. His hands followed suit and acted without waiting for permission. He reached down and lifted up her sundress, bunching the fabric until he felt skin.

She hungrily responded to his touch and wrapped a leg high around his waist. He lifted her free from the floor, evoking a gasp of awe from Anna. Actually, it was more of a moan since she was still suction-cupped to his face. He knelt with her in his arms down onto the floor, never once breaking kiss. Samuel the Troll would have been very impressed, shouting in his steroid-altered voice, *"Good flexibility, Mr. Marble,"* It was the last non-sexual thought he would have for the next ten minutes.

She continued to kiss him gently as he lay drooling on his back. God, I could use a cigarette right now, he thought. She propped up on an elbow and looked him in the eyes.

"No smoking allowed in here, Shooter. I think we've generated enough heat for one afternoon, don't you?"

Marble just stared back goofily. The endorphins that coursed through his bloodstream sapped him of the ability to communicate. They also put a hold on his cognitive powers. He hadn't even noticed that she had read his mind.

"Come on, big man; let's reassemble ourselves for the public. I have to get you back to the Paradise. Not my wish, you see, for I would more than love to take advantage of you all afternoon, but you have other tasks waiting. And sharing is a virtue."

To Marble, what seemed like only dreamy moments later, Anna pulled up in front of the Paradise B&B, parking her black BMW behind his flattened car. She leaned over and kissed him on the lips, and then handed him her book on birds. Without a word, he exited the car and walked toward the Paradise, never once looking at his smashed car.

It hadn't yet occurred to him how Anna had known where he was staying. Or the query as to what exactly had been in that water she handed him. He even missed the large black crow that sat on the porch railing, keenly watching him as he passed by. All he could think about was how badly he needed to take a nap.

Anna watched her new lover open the front door. She then looked at her reflection in the mirror. Marble had not been a mistake, nor was he regret. Her task was that of nurturer. If experiencing intense sexual pleasure in the process was a result of that comfort, then so be it. After all, it had been very good for her too. With a sly smile, she looked back at the house and watched as the crow followed Marble into the hallway.

"Sleep now, lover man, sleep now. Energy will find thee, threefold three. The spirits be, the spirits be. Energy will find thee, threefold three. The spirits be, the spirits be. Energy will find thee, threefold three. The spirits be, the spirits be."

***

Willem watched Anna Smythe's black BMW 535i pull away from the Paradise B&B. He rolled down his window to let out the steam that shot from his nostrils. *That motherfucking nothinglessness Pennsylvania prick has just been dropped off by the future Mrs. Willem Clydesdale. And the sonofabitch actually kissed my bride to be.*

"Looks like you gotta take your nothinglessness ass on a fishing trip, Mr. Pennsylvania plate. Oh yeah, they be a biting this time of year. They especially like dirty nothinglessness dicks that stick their ugly head in a place they shouldn't be." He lit a cigarette before pulling out from behind the mulberry bushes that had concealed the pickup's lurking presence. Drifting in front of the house, he stared up at the second floor.

"I knew it. You've gone and sealed your fate. I knew nothing good comes out of Pennsylvania." He pulled away, cackling like he belonged in a Looney Tune.

9

Marble drifted effortlessly to the right and earned a clearer view of the woman who knelt in front of him. The only illumination of the area came from two crude-pillared white candles that cast enough glow for him to discern that the woman was the same person he had seen lynched in front of the B&B. This image, though, was far less traumatic, and the fact that it appeared in a dream was ethereally hypnotic.

A movement of air from an unknown source tousled her hair. Marble now noticed the gloriously hued bird feathers that sprang from her long ebony locks, cascading down over smooth bare shoulders. A subtle shift again and he could now see her breasts, firm and supple, mocha areolas and nipples hungry for the light of the candles' flame.

Her woolen smock crumpled at her waist and as her hair swayed, Marble noticed the myriad of black welts that lined her back, like earthworms disjected haphazardly across a pavement after a rain. He wanted to lash out at the monster that had inflicted them on such a beautiful creature.

Marble leaned to the right and noticed her attention was on a large dark object that sat in the shadows before the candles. The woman began to chant and rock back and forth, but he could only guess at the sounds. She stretched out her arms and opened closed fists to reveal two beautiful-hued egg-sized stones; perfectly smooth and clear, they shined with a kaleidoscope of colors, swirling at the speed of clouds floating overhead on a summer's day.

The splash of light that erupted next from the dark void between the candles made Marble's dream goosebumps stand at attention. A blood-red mass of glowing veins now pulsed within the encasement constructed in the same manner as a bird's nest, an architectural marvel of intricately arranged twigs, rock, and mud. But this was not a normal nest as the top gaped open, four gnarled sides parting wide. His heart jumped in his chest as the portal exposed a vista unlike any he had ever seen. The gaping, toothless maw revealed a gullet of barren wasteland, whitewashed sand pricked randomly with bleached bones, some in shapes that Marble didn't even want to guess their origin. It was a nest portal to an alien world, a land of the heebie-jeebies, boogeymen, and trolls… or worse.

He glanced to his left and the mind-boggling sight invoked a dream gasp. Soft downy feathers now sprouted from her skin, blanketing every exposed inch save her face. Her mouth again opened, and this time Marble heard an audible raptor screech. He reached to cover his ears and just as quickly the picture snapped off, replaced by the afternoon sun that peeked through his room's beveled glass window. Now awake with very conscious throbbing eardrums, he stared at the bed's lacy canopy and tried to make some sense of the vivid pictures he had just witnessed in dreamland.

"The forties is the time when the body needs extra sleep, sometimes in the middle of the day. Don't make it a habit though, nosiree, you see. Important things might pass you by if you do."

Marble quickly lifted his head to stare in the voice's direction. He uttered a girly scream. Perched on the foot of the bed's brass railing was the same Jamaican woman he had met thirty years before on a street in Lancaster, PA. She even wore the same flowered dress he recalled now so vividly and the black, shiny feathers in her gray hair were sticking out in the same manner as before.

She laughed heartily. "Now that's an interesting way to say hello there, Mister Shooter. Birds be talking about you funny like if you make that a habit."

Marble stopped screaming and searched for breath, any breath. He began to hyperventilate. The emotions that ran through his body in tsunami fashion made it feel like even his heart had taken a sabbatical from pumping blood.

"You done grown up strong, that's for sure. And it's been essential for you to keep your gift quiet all these years, the Good Mother knows. That inner eye has come alive again, eh? That ol' door done creaked open, hmm, and now you be seeing some things again, ain't you?"

Marble just stared back at her with the look of a freshly sliced lobotomy patient.

"Yesiree, I thought so. Hmm, that's a mighty powerful gift you has there, Mister Shooter. No telling what level it grew to over these thirty years. It's time I opened them doors all the way. But you got to be careful. You remember that teacher man o' your youth, eh? Well, now you know. You can use your gift for splendid good though. And the heavens and the Mother Earth know they need you big right now in this town, Mister Shooter. For be good. For be good. Mmm-hmm, for be good." She lifted an ebony cane, stretched an arm in his direction, and neatly tapped him on the top of his head.

Somewhere in the room, the sound of a vault door sealed by vacuum swung open. Marble's brain belched and the pressure escaped through his ears, nose, and mouth in a stale mist. Next, he felt the clamminess of dizziness on his skin and he sensed his conscious moments numbered in seconds. He blinked his eyes rapidly to try and make sense of the peculiar gurgles emanating from his body.

The proverbial straw that broke the camel's back was the fact that this overly plump woman stood perfectly still on the very thin brass railing at the foot of his canopied bed. Where her feet should have been, in fact, were a pair of very real crow's talons. Marble's eyes rolled back in the sockets on sensory overload and his head soon followed as it plumped heavily back onto the goose down pillows.

***

Willem sensed the nest portal leering at him. There had been many times in his life that he had run from a room after feeling like the eyes in a picture or a painting tracked his every move. It had always unnerved him. Flight at this moment wasn't a wise choice though. The nest portal had no eyes that he could discern, but that painting on the wall sensation made his skin crawl. His guest sat still, deadly silent, perched before him on his massive desktop but he knew that the beast within was far from unaware.

Ever since the day he pulled it from his footlocker, nothing but a mixed bag of problems had come from inside its gnarly cover, and most of them had erupted without warning. Of course, he never saw anything erupt from the demon, it was just more than strange coincidence that the very day the portal awoke, birds started falling from the sky. Sure, he thought, the nest portal was a powerful tool in eradicating nothinglessnesses like Capt. Turner Smythe, and the dot-head false shaman up in Seaford.

But Willem had begun to suspect his guest had something to do with the bird disappearances that had upset the balance of

119

nature in his beloved Clydesdale. Despite Willem's abrasive, narrow-minded approach to the world, he was still an Eastern shore man, a tough, salt-stained sonofabitch who knew his livelihood depended on the bounties of a healthy land and sea.

He rubbed a meaty palm across his mouth. A cigarette joined the lips next, and a match flashed in a mini cloud of sulfur, all in the same movement, a well-rehearsed ballet toward lung cancer. As the first exhale of smoke filled the room, he noticed movement in the nest portal. He wheeled his chair closer and reluctantly peered into the cover. He didn't want to get nearer; hell, he wanted to run far away. Despite his fears, he still inched his sweaty nose downward, breathing heavier as if he were a peeping Tom. Theirs was a mating of strange bedfellows. This partner wasn't about to give him his walking papers.

***

Bobby Kaster was at a professional plateau in life that many men eventually attain. Mid-fifties and their battle cry of "I coulda been a contender" their new mantra. In Bobby's case, this phenomenon was partly due to his ineffective choice of allies to venture into battle with in the never-ending political wars of middle news management. It was also partly due to his never dropping the nickname of "Bobby" from his first post-graduate resume, the same resume that forever aligns one's professional career with whatever faux pas are committed. The "Bobbys" of the news world never seemed to garner respect when sporting a playground moniker. To say he had a chip on his shoulder was an understatement.

As with most narcissistic, irrational, immature men mired in midlife depression, he blamed women for his failings. Three divorces had earned him a healthy distaste of the *conniving, manipulative, cheating witch sex.* He did not believe all the fairer sex fit that bill, just the ones he had chosen to climb into bed with. When the same type of vixen entered his workspace, his teeth sharpened. Two years earlier, a Boston affiliate banished him to the paltry backwater news team in Harrisburg, PA. That is where he began a silent oath to bring down the resident queen of bitch, one Deelah Thayer-Marble.

When Deelah began her affair with the station owner's son, Bradley Thigbottom Jr., it had been virtually impossible for Bobby to assign her the shitty assignments she so richly deserved. Especially ones that matched her personality: like the annual Harrisburg Farm Show. Ever since Deelah had jettisoned her spineless husband and dipped into the weak-chinned Bradley's pants, Bradley thwarted Bobby's every attempt to stick it to Deelah.

Thursday mornings were like most other mornings – they sucked. This Thursday though showed promise; in fact, it was particularly ripe with revenge. Bobby could taste it in his 20 oz. Wawa caramel blend coffee.

The real clincher for his mood came in the form of a company email. It seemed the entire Thigbottom clan had hastily shuffled off to Buffalo in the middle of the night for a viewing/funeral of a deceased blue-blood family member. Bobby's first reaction scanned the wire for that juicy piece of turd assignment usually reserved for news rookies. He found it within three minutes, a simple three-line blurb from some late night AP lackey that had Deelah written all over it:

AP—Scientists are baffled by the sudden disappearance of migratory birds within a ten-square-mile area encompassing

the tiny Chesapeake Basin hamlet of Clydesdale, MD. Speculations range from crop circles, West Nile virus, avian flu, Al-Qaeda, UFO interference, overzealous hunters, or military intervention. To this date, no local solutions have arisen.

Quackery, he giggled to himself, just the ticket for Ms. Missy. Outside his office window, the perfectly coiffed Deelah held court around the coffee machine. She shook her head back in feigned laughter and turned her head in his direction. The deer caught in headlights look flashed in her eyes as she caught the leering gaze of General Manager Bobby Kaster as he pulled the assignment out of the AP printer. With her protection out of town, she knew she was deadly vulnerable.

As if a starter's pistol had ignited them, the sprint began. Bobby's fireplug body barreled through his office door, nearly decapitating a ruddy-cheeked intern from Shippensburg University with a hearty shove. Other newsroom lackeys dove out of his way, his path intent on hindering Deelah's escape route to the hallway.

Deelah executed a clean hurdle over the receptionist's desk, a remarkable display of agility considering she wore a tight skirt and pumps. Mid-flight, she even made a Jordan-esque adjustment and switched directions when she noticed that Bobby would reach the hallway before her. She landed without fault and then bolted for the perceived security of the lady's room. As she was soon to discover, Bobby Kaster held no illusions of vaginal sanctuary as he burst in behind her. He caught Deelah by the arm, just as she passed the bidet.

The irony of the moment escaped Deelah since the bidet had been installed after a calculated series of mind-blowing zipper favors for Bradley. Deelah had never really used one before, nor had this urinal seen action other than snickers and gabbery from the station's other womenfolk. It was, after all, the only bidet they had seen anywhere in Central Pennsylvania where clapboard outhouses still held chic nouveau.

"Deelah, glad I caught you." Bobby made a mental note to cut back to maybe two packs of Camels a day as he waited impatiently for his lungs to return to normal. "Finish your business in here and then report immediately to dispatch. I'm sending you and Iguana down to Maryland to cover a breaking blockbuster of a story. This has top three network splash material written all over it so move your butt. I'll have the skinny waiting for you in the van."

Top three was insider industry jargon for the three lead stories of nightly network news, the big break, the step on the golden ladder that led to a choice network assignment. Bobby knew she'd bite hook, line, and sinker. He gave Deelah his best *I wish you the worst fucking nightmare imaginable* smile. Not wanting to offer her a chance of rebuttal, he abruptly turned toward the door and banged his left kneecap into the pale-yellow porcelain trough of the bidet. "What the… what the fuck is this thing?" It was a rhetorical question since he didn't wait for Deelah's reply.

"It's French, a *jaune pâle* bidet. For the sophisticated woman's hygiene…" her Martha Stewart voice trailed off. The door swung shut as Bobby exited. It took another second before her next question flew towards the door.

"Iguana? Why the fuck do I get stuck with that degenerate reptile?"

10

Ammonia inhaled through the nostrils and the resultant million tiny needles stabbing your sinuses is less messy but just as effective as an ice-cold bucket of water dumped onto the face. Marble sat up so fast he knocked the tiny gauze encased vial from Ismelda's hand.

"OK, we have to stop meeting like this. People will begin to talk." He reached up to wipe the tears from his cheeks.

"You're right. I prefer a man who doesn't need constant resuscitation." She handed him a box of tissues with a mischievous laugh.

Marble focused more closely on her; the large oversized hat was now gone, revealing beautiful coiffed auburn tresses that cascaded over her freckled shoulders. Again, with the pink color captivating her appearance, this time in a tasteful sundress imprinted with large yellow sunflowers.

"Yep, this is what an old lady can look like if she exercises regularly and watches her diet. It also helps not to sport a bird's nest in your hair."

Marble honked a blow into a tissue, and he swore part of his cerebellum joined the snot-exit parade. He then made a quick word association, the ammonia vapors now at a more tolerable level of *motherfucking-it-still-burns* in his brain. Bird's nest… Anna's Nest… Great sex… hot author… hot woman… Jasmine…

"Oh, my God, what time is it?"

"Four forty-five. I hope you clean up quickly. I ran a bath for you. Fresh towels are on the hamper. Please also take a few moments to run a razor over that stubble. Chop, chop. It isn't proper keep a lady waiting on the first date."

Marble swung his legs off the bed and grabbed his duffel bag while he passed by a coyly smiling Ismelda. As he turned toward the door, an observation thwarted his haste. Lying on the floor at the foot of the bed were two large, shiny black crow's feathers. He slowly turned back to face the innkeeper.

"This may sound crazy. Damn, it is crazy. Jesus, what is happening to me?" His heart rate escalated to Samuel the Troll happy levels. "Has there… was there… uh, you know, anyone else… did you see anyone else, a black woman perhaps… wandering about here not long ago?"

"Did I see anyone wandering about? No, Shooter, but you really should keep the windows closed. One never knows what the wind could carry in… or out."

Behind her, Marble noticed, the double hung window was open fully. He knew one certainty – he'd never opened it.

"Yeah sure, never mind. Like I said, sounds crazy. That seems to be my new middle name."

***

It was a command decision, easy to reach. Popeye Worthington decided his Gobble Potato Chip truck and trailer would stay parked exactly where it currently was for as long as he gosh darned wished. He stared at Willem's office with a steely air of defiance and wished that the murdering son of a gun would show his cowardly face. The blood that had slowly boiled all afternoon had now reached a blowing point. Popeye knew this feeling and he did his best to defuse it. A nice long walk would help. He looked back towardsCallie's. He would love to have her join him, but she was busy preparing for that evening's dinner rush. Maybe later, he thought. Maybe later he'd get up enough gumption to talk to her without reverting to a stuttering fool.

He walked toward the marina and its moorings. *You can take the sailor away from the sea, but you can never take the sea out of the sailor*. It was a saying that the late Captain Turner Smythe would throw at Popeye every time he felt a need to justify living in a shoreside town. Popeye repeated it softly now as he strolled down the planked boardwalk. The pier creaked with old wood arthritis, now weathered the hue of mussel shells from years of exposure to salt and Mother Nature.

The skin began to tickle on the back of his neck as if someone watched from behind. He didn't need to turn around to know that Willem stared at him from the marina office window. Popeye didn't care; let the murderer stare. This was open to the public, and he could do as he pleased. Part of him wanted the mayor to engage in a confrontation. *Oh, that would be so sweet, Lord, so sweet.*

Popeye scolded himself for being so selfish. He walked this pier because it was the last place anyone beside the seedy mayor had seen the late Captain alive. Like the widow, Anna, he too sought closure, answers to the riddle of his disappearance.

He reached a T in the wooden-planked walkway, which spread out on either side of him in goalpost fashion. To his left, the northern arm was virtually empty, most of its moorings leased to inlanders who now had their vessels dry-docked for the winter. The southern arm still had boats at moor. Popeye turned in that direction, the outrigging of his intended search standing high above all the other occupied slips.

It was evident this was the high-rent district. Each slip had its own fire hose, electrical and fresh water receptacles, blazoned in taxicab yellow. Popeye passed a potpourri of the wealthy elite's toys. There were vessels from Horizon, Bertram, and Hatteras mixed in with forty-foot sailing yachts. There was a *Honey Bunch*, a *Sailor's Dream*, a *Bambooshay* and a *Papillon*. But the real jewel of the neighborhood sat moored at the end of the pier.

His pulse quickened like a child's does on Christmas morning. He executed a right-hand turn, and he now faced the object of his quest, Willem's sixty-foot, custom-built Rybovich. Per the perks of owning the marina, it was moored in the optimal slip for bay navigation. Adjacent to its own gas pump, the boat rocked dreamily from the diurnal tidal swells of Assawoman Bay.

Popeye's heart jumped into fourth gear as he readily found the emotion, and he instantly knew why Captain Smythe had been so captivated by the vessel. This was Popeye's first Rybovich experience and the loss of virginity was exhilarating. Custom built by the Rybovich Spencer Company in West Palm Beach, Florida, the vessel was indeed a sight to behold.

North Carolinian teak elegantly displayed its rich patterns along the toe rails, deck transoms, and interior. Willem's Rybovich appeared to have all the toys. Popeye gazed up toward the cockpit and spied a gleaming 6-inch copper fog bell that reflected itself off the tinted glass of the helm 13 feet above the deck. He strained up on his toes to try and see inside the helm area, but his vision was limited.

The real treat of the vessel, though, was underneath the teak deck. He'd read about this boat, the way some men gaze longingly at Porsche spec books, Legacy stereo speakers, or thoroughbred horses. Popeye was a boat nerd. He reeled off the engine specifications in his head from memory.

Beneath the Rybovich proprietary insulated sound shield slumbered twin Detroit Diesel DDEC Series 2000s, 1480 hp each, mounted on powder-coated steel stringer caps with appropriate ZF transmissions, rock 'em, sock 'em power that could push the ship up to 43 knots. His hands perspired so heavily that he wiped them on his shirt, already drenched with sweat.

Popeye took a deep breath for composure. He wiped the smile from his face and the Christmas morning glee of *mama, mama, look what Santa brought me* feeling from his heart. Despite the marine engineering beauty in front of him, it still smelled of evil doings. For this was the last place anyone had seen Captain Turner Smythe alive. Dubbed 'Hizzoner,' Willem obviously spared no cost in his ocean transportation. Willem may have driven an old clunker of a truck and lived in a trailer, but he owned the crème de la crème of the ocean, the Rolls Royce, the Bentley, the Lear Jet of boats.

Popeye lovingly glided his hand along the recently polished copper railing that ran along the circumference of the ship and wished for the power to derive some psychic message from its soul. Nothing reached out to him except a growing suspicion that somehow, someway, Willem had been less than truthful about the disappearance of one Captain Turner Smythe. Anna told him earlier of the arrival of a man who had such powers, but so far, he had yet to meet the one the coven called the Shooter.

He heard a splash in the water to the aft of the Rybovich, and he noticed the torn torso of an egret, its body clawed through with deep cuts that let the bay seep in and claim it for a grave. This too was a major concern of the town, and Anna had wondered if Willem also had a hand in these strange experiences. Popeye looked to the sky. Maybe this stranger could help with this problem too; awful lot to ask of a man, he thought. So he said a prayer in the hopes that if God knew what was going on, maybe He'd send some help.

"Shiver me timbers, matey. Red sky at night, sailor's delight, red sky at morning, sailor's warning. I wonder what color the sky was the day Captain Smythe boarded you. I wonder."

He now understood another piece of the puzzle, for he too found the Rybovich to be a compelling piece of beauty. He put on his deductive detective hat. The vessel could not sail safely without an additional deckhand on board. This meant if Captain Smythe received an invitation to board as reported at the last moment, another mate would have already been on board. Someone else may know what happened.

Popeye turned and headed back up the walkway, all the while glaring at the horizontal blinds on Willem's office window. There was a flurry of activity as they bent to a V in the center and then snapped back to form.

"Let him spy on me," Popeye prayed as he walked. "And please, dear Jesus, let him squirm. Because the Good Lord willing, if it be Your will, aid this town's well-intentioned witches solve this devil's curse." Popeye had never prayed with his eyes open, and he had a feeling this time that God didn't mind one bit.

***

Rich with urban myth lore, written down somewhere, probably on the back of a Jägermeister label, in the one-page manual of *The Dummy's Guide to Hiring a Cameraman*, all prospective employees must have a nickname of a non-human creature. And the more the cameraman's features appear like his animal spirit, the more effective his or her karma would reign, game on, god

129

warrior, ancient samurai, demon-slayer dude.

Deelah loathed Iguana. She silently steamed because, without failure, every cameraman she had ever worked with had shared in some state the characteristics of their moniker. There had been a hairy-necked Gorilla, a long-necked Mongoose, a serious over-bitten Walrus, an interminably slow Turtle, and even the downright smelly Animal. But none of them measured up to the detest she felt for Iguana.

He ignored her stares as he stroked his platinum-blond goatee while he darted his tongue in and out of his mouth, unconsciously tasting the stale air of the van. Dressed in a 60s era bomber jacket and sporting a raggedy excuse of a beret, he flicked his purple ponytail as if swatting at flies. Bobby Kaster knew she couldn't stand Iguana too, the bastard. She was accustomed to having her way. Just wait until I tell Bradley, she fumed.

A pothole jarred the van and Deelah felt a bang of hair free itself from her carefully sculpted forehead. She made an entry into her iPhone to remind herself to stop at the first drugstore for Bare All's Super Vise Monster Hold-It-In-A-Hurricane Gel. In the haste to cover this "blockbuster of a story," she had only been given time to grab her daypack which carried only one bottle of sculpting-spray. Enough to carry me through the night, she silently panicked.

Speaking of night, she thought, where the hell are we going? She opened the manila envelope that sat on the dash. Her name scrawled across the front in Bobby's inimitable style. She extracted the work order and, five seconds later, exploded.

"Stop the fucking van. Iguana, stop this van right fucking now."

Iguana had been happily head banging to his iPod sounds of

Rusted Root when the shrill banshee screams interrupted a bitchin' drum solo. He slowly looked at his passenger as she seethed. He pulled his Bose earphones out to rest around his neck and reached into the center console as if searching for something.

"We're on the interstate, Dee, ain't safe to pull over unless it's an emergency. And even then, with no shoulder, no can do. Besides, we're juiced with cellular signal right here in the van so if you feel like yelling at anybody besides me, go for it, dude. Yet another miracle of modern technology if you ask me, Dee."

She abhorred the nickname Dee and Iguana knew it. It was obvious that there was mutual distaste. He wasn't alone in that sentiment. Every single other employee at WTTE-TV felt the same way. Deelah just had a knack for belittling anyone she perceived as a little person. Translated, it meant anyone making less than her "paltry, embarrassing, insulting" 60K per year.

"This *is* an emergency, you reptile. There is no way on God's green earth that I will step one foot into some hick town. This is a junior-grade, first-year virgin news rookie assignment. Not me. Not me. Not me. We've got a whole pool of snot-nosed hos who'd cream themselves to land this gig. But not me. I deserve so much more respect than to chase after a story about some fucking missing birds. Now pull over."

Iguana smiled and his two gold-capped incisors sparkled. "Bobby thought you might balk a bit when you found out. He gave me strict orders not to turn around for any reason. It looks like it's you and me on the way to the shore, Dee."

A wave of repulsion washed over her and coated her tongue with the taste of sand. "Listen, asshole, you turn around or I'll have your sorry ass fired so fast you'll be fortunate to get a job slinging slop at Denny's."

Iguana glanced at the rearview mirror and then slammed on

the brakes so hard that a trailing truck trumpeted its air horn as it passed. The news van screeched to a stop on an available shoulder just wide enough for them to squeeze out of traffic.

"Hey, Dee, I got news for you. You ain't my boss. And remember that miracle of modern technology I just talked about? Well, here, say hello to Mr. Bobby Kaster." He pulled the cellular from the console and handed it to Deelah. "The boss has been listening to your ranting and raving on Nextel. Freaking modern miracle of our day, I tell ya."

Deelah's cheeks lost all color. She held the phone out away from her as if it had the plague. She glared daggers at Iguana and whispered, "You set me up, motherfucker, you'll die for this."

"Thayer? This is Bobby. Do you kiss your mama with that mouth? Interesting timing you have because we're now on a three way with Mr. Thigbottom… Mr. Thigbottom *Sr.*" Bobby's dramatic pauses would have won praise from Captain Kirk.

"I wish I could say I was charmed, Ms. Thayer."

Deelah's cheeks went from raging red to ghostly pale in a split second. Somebody call the Discovery Channel. Spreading her legs for Bradley Thigbottom Jr. had been a calculated attempt to garner a glowing resume referral from Bradley Thigbottom Sr. in her ongoing attempt to land a major market anchor's desk.

"Yes, sir, Mr. Thigbottom, sir, um… how are you?" The sand taste had now turned into a nasty fairway bunker in her mouth. "Once again, sir, I am very sorry for your family's loss." She had no idea which relative had died so she kept it generic. Blowjobs didn't offer too much time for small talk.

"Thank you, Deelah. Fortunately, it wasn't one from my side of the family; now, on to more pressing matters.

"This junket has not been all gloom and doom for I've also concluded a delectable business venture and in the process, have expanded my empire." Alexander the Great would have been proud of Bradley Thigbottom Sr. and his strategic military prowess to divide, conquer, and multiply.

"In front of me now are signed and notarized documents of sale entitling me to new ownership of an independent radio and TV station in Rochester, New York. Bradley Jr. is general manager effective immediately. Now, Deelah, I'm aware of your ambitions and unless you have a desire for a transfer to this independent satellite, I suggest you begin to adhere to the merits of the chain of command within your own posting. Threats toward fellow employees are also an unacceptable ingredient in my recipe for success. Do I make myself clear, Ms. Thayer?"

Deelah forgot how to breathe. "Rochester" and "independent" were two words that could initiate hyperventilation in news people, almost as bad as Madison and Wisconsin. When used together in the same sentence, it constituted an inescapable Siberian death camp. She wondered how she could have screwed up so badly. It wasn't in her character to make poorly calculated errors, especially one as titanic as this: she had dropped to her knees for the wrong Thigbottom.

"Thayer? You still there? We still live, Iguana?" It was an obviously gleeful Bobby.

"Uh, boss… and, uh Mr. Boss… Dee seems to be having some kind of conniption…"

Deelah sucked it up and gave Iguana a look that could kill, an act she was fully capable of now. Timing, however, called for extreme tactfulness and Deelah put on her best professional face. Using the bravest of anchor voices, she straightened her spine and lifted the handset to her mouth.

"Congratulations are in order, sir. Please convey the same

sentiments to Bradley Jr. on this exciting news." She knew the weak-chinned lap boy would be eaten alive by winters that buried homes in snow for six months every year. "And, sir, Bobby, and I are on the same page. You can expect full compliance from me." Her agent was going to get the first phone call.

"Yeah, we're on the same page, Thayer. I want updates every six hours. Do you have anything else to add Mr. Thigbottom, sir?"

"Not at all, Bobby, you're in command of that legion. Carry on. Ms. Thayer, we shall conference together upon my return. Carry on."

Deelah dropped the receiver to the floor of the van and just stared ahead. There was no way that Iguana would see her cry, not a chance. She looked to her right and hid her face from Iguana. *Carry on.* She was shocked that Marble's gentle smile came to mind. She thought of her ex and before her heart could thaw, she quickly slammed the freezer door shut.

Now, things couldn't get any worse but a tiny yet boisterous foghorn at the back of her mind warned that a whole boatload of bat guano might be waiting at her next horizon. Her stomach quadrupled into a boatswain's knot.

Without another word, Iguana flicked the turn signal, checked his side mirror for oncoming traffic and then eased the van southbound onto Interstate 83 while Rusted Root once again rocked him on toward tiny Clydesdale, MD. And for added panache, he farted.

*****

The Tastykake company of Philadelphia started baking treats for mass consumption in 1914, and kids, both big and little, have gladly gobbled their pastries for several generations. Arguably, the best Tastykakes made are either the peanut butter or chocolate Kandy Kake. One could challenge that the jelly or butterscotch Krimpets deserve the same lofty status.

Danny, Ron, and Woody didn't give a hoot which brand sold the most. All they cared was that Tastykake kept their ovens busy, and that the local Wawa kept them plentifully in stock. To the boys, each bite of any Tastykake was as close as one could get to mouth heaven. This might explain the drool that seeped from Woody's jack-o'-lantern smile as he and the boys packed up their chainsaws, anticipating their end of the workday snack. Danny popped open his Styrofoam ice chest just as a frenzied Marble sprinted from the house, sporting a wrinkled yet clean eggshell oxford cotton rayon blend, gray Dockers, and his new injection-molded sneaks, putting on his belt as he ran.

"Hop in the truck, man. Looks like ya need a lift and we're the best taxi you can get this time of the day. Ain't that so, boys?" Danny worked expertly at freeing a jelly Krimpet from its wrapper and then offered it to Marble. "OK? OK? OK?"

Marble didn't have to weigh his options long since it was already 5.02 p.m.

"That would be great, guys. I'm just heading to the drugstore. Have a date that I'm already late for." Marble grabbed the offered Krimpet and stuffed its sugary sponginess into his mouth.

"Yup, we know. Hop in." Danny ran around to the driver's side while Ron and Woody climbed into the bed with their gear. "It's just a mile or so but we can git ya there in a jiff."

The cab of the old Ford 150 reeked of chainsaw oil, sweat, and stale pastry crumbs. Numerous mystery items clamored for attention underneath the vinyl bench seat as Danny squealed the tires in acceleration. As Marble finished the last of his Krimpet, he had an urge for a large glass of milk. Odd, he thought, I haven't had a glass of milk since I was a teenager. The next batch of memories arrived in staccato flashes, causing the color to fade from his face: his brother Martin, the shotgun, the mass murders, the bloody footprints, his clairvoyant vision of the atrocities, his brother's Gratersford prison garb.

Marble lurched toward the dash as Danny skidded to a sloppy stop in front of the drugstore. His little soiree down memory lane also came to a screeching halt. The deceleration had noisily sent all the gear, including Ron and Woody, slamming into the rear window of the cab. Marble did a quick glance over his shoulder and saw their faces and assorted Tandy Cakes smashed against the glass as if they were a modern-day Picasso. Marble hastily said his thanks while he composed himself quickly in the cracked side-door mirror. He jumped out of the truck and scurried to the drugstore's front door with a flattened cream-filled chocolate cupcake on his right butt cheek, a regular guerilla-warfare-grass-roots advertisement for Tastykake.

11

"My, my, my, you sure clean up nice. But you're seven minutes late, Mr. Shooter. Didn't your mother ever tell you it's not nice to keep a lady waiting?"

"Sorry I'm late but it took me a little longer to scrub away all the dirt. My mother never wanted me to be dirty in public."

"I so enjoy a man who keeps his momma in his heart."

Jasmine emerged from behind a cardboard Texas display stand that promoted suntan lotion at an obscene seventy percent discount. Marble got an eyeful. She wore a skintight, spaghetti strapped black dress with a neckline and hemline that seemed anxious to meet each other. Her shapely legs earned the added enticement by two-inch heeled, open-toed pumps. Marble spotted silver toe rings on the second toes of both feet that seemed to complement perfectly with her ruby painted toenails.

"You like?" She said this with just the right blend of a Shirley Temple innocence spiced with a smidgen of tempered naughtiness. Marble took the bait, hook, line, and sinker.

"Wow, I mean, yes, you look great, um, is it always this warm in September?"

"Oh, it can get much hotter than this. Indian summer sometimes absolutely sizzles." She moved in close enough for him to smell the captivating scents of cinnamon and honey flowing from her hair. She took both his hands and caressed them gently. "Let me see, here we go, oh yes, a very strong lifeline. I read palms on the side, you see," she playfully teased. "Ooh, and this one here is your psychic line. Very, very powerful, I can feel the energy emanating from you." She traced a painted fingernail along the inner part of his thumb and then pulled both of his hands closer to her bosom.

Ta-tas, tits, melons, boobs, the girls, mountains, hooters, knockers, mamasitas, yodelers, wahoos, yippie-kai-ohs, every breast slang name ran ape-shit through his mind. Victoria's Secret enhanced gorgeous breasts were within fingers' reach and he wondered if he dared take a chance to touch. He frantically searched his ever-expanding memory banks for a sexy, witty reply but his mouth had enough trouble avoiding the dreaded drool. Instead, she handled the transition like a pro.

"I'm famished; how about you?" She brushed his freshly shaven cheek with her hand and then bopped over to the sales counter. "But first, we need to free you of the markings of a certain thoroughly disgusting yet refreshingly charming traveling band of cavity hoarders." She returned with a roll of paper napkins.

"Turn around, mister. I'm about to get this evening going with a booty call on your buns."

Marble blushed with embarrassment. Human beings spend their lives occupied by fears and frightful nightmares of horrendous situations that could cause them discomforting moments in front of others. She assuaged his discomfort with a laugh, and he found her removal of the smashed cream-filled cupcake from his butt far from abashment. In fact, it was somewhat fun.

"Mmm, mmm, and I don't mean the pastry. That's a hint of a massage, but I can do much better." She teasingly patted him on the butt, cheerleader patting football player style. "OK, let's rock and roll, Shooter, I'm starving." She grabbed a small black handbag with one hand while she discarded the paper towels with another. She then led him out of the store, locked it behind, and then entwined an arm through his.

"There is definitely not enough published or talked about concerning the merits of massage. I believe that more marriages would survive if lazy, fat-assed couch potatoes took an interest in this amazingly rewarding therapy. Are you aware how many nerve endings there are just beneath the surface of the epidermis? Not to mention it's the body's largest organ, the skin, and the benefits it reaps from massage. Oh, and what luscious benefits those are. Have you ever had a massage with hot oil? Anna Smythe from Anna's Nest sells a light juniper and rose petal oil that is heavenly. Do you mind if we hold hands?"

Marble flinched at the mention of Anna, but he didn't have time to reply because she never gave him a chance. She interlocked fingers with his, and he marveled at how well they fit together. Not unnoticed by him was the fact that for the first time in his Grand Plan, he was now on an official first date, boldly strolling down Main Street with a beautiful young woman clutching his hand. *Oh, if only Deelah could get a look at me now.*

"I have a craving for a margarita. Maybe we could drive across the bay to OC after dinner and have a nightcap or two… or three. I must warn you though, tequila and I are old friends, and I get all warm and fuzzy around old friends. I prefer an old friend to Achilles' heel, anyway, don't you? There's a club across the bay called Seacrets, that's the bomb. Have you ever been? It's probably the most popular spot in OC. We'll take my Jeep since you're out of wheels for the moment."

Marble didn't remember talking about his smashed Ford but then, this was a small town. "Yeah, that sounds like fun. But let's see how dinner goes first, you may get your fill of me by then."

"Oh, I don't think so, Shooter. It's a beautiful fall evening and I plan on seeing that you enjoy every bit of it with me."

The stroll to Callie's was painless as Marble enjoyed Jasmine's endless chatter. He was so engrossed in the moment that he didn't even notice the six network news vans illegally parked on city square across from Callie's restaurant.

When they entered the restaurant, a visibly blushing Jackie, now clad in a cute pair of mini shorts and a Hooters style halter top, led them to the same booth that Marble visited earlier that day. Then she disappeared without a word into the kitchen.

The joint had a buzz, much busier than normal and Jasmine turned to appraise the situation. "Oh great, the circus is in town. U.S. Fish and Wildlife Service out of DC, a regular picnic basket filled with Ranger Smiths. Any day now, we'll see National Marine Fisheries Service. I wouldn't be surprised if there are some retreads from Fish and Wildlife posing now as agents from the National Resources Conservation Services. No doubt, some fly farmers up from Chincoteague, some oceanographers up from Woods Hole, some geeks from the Audubon Society, yadda, yadda, yadda. And to top it off, media hounds. Just what we didn't want, our dirty laundry aired in public."

Marble stared at his pretty date. About thirty questions battled for attention but once again, his mouth wasn't quite in sync with his brain and she rattled on, deftly changing the subject with nary a segue.

"Crab cakes are to die for; Callie spanks them with her own blend of spices and then broils them. Heavenly, heavenly, heavenly. The best you'll ever have."

His mouth caught up to speed. "Jasmine." He reached across the linoleum table and grasped her hands. Now with them immobilized, she was temporarily unable to speak. "What's going on? Why are all these scientists here?"

Jasmine asked seriously, "You mean, no one has told you yet? From any dimension?" Marble shook his head no, but he wasn't sure what he was supposed to be denying.

She whispered dramatically. "The birds, haven't you noticed? They're gone, all gone; every single one of them. One of the busiest times of the year for migration, and this is one of the richest environs for them and not one single feather."

Marble nodded. "I've seen dead birds, or bits of them, all over town. What gives? Is there some kind of disease? It's eerie."

Her eyes filled with tears. "Don't you see? Can't you see? That's why you're here. To get back our…"

"What will you two kids have for dinner tonight?" Jackie appeared as if she had been hiding under the table.

A rapidly composed Jasmine looked at Marble. "Crab cakes?"

This was beginning to be a problem, he thought. Every time he tried to ask an important question about the birds, he was either interrupted or some unseen force pushed aside his words and inserted its own. Rather than tempt fate now, he simply nodded an affirmative.

"Two crab cake dinners, coleslaw, hushpuppies and veggie of the day, and I'll have a Heineken. Shooter, same for you?"

"Yuengling. Yuengling Lager." His mouth felt like sandpaper and a brew from the family-owned Pottsville, Pennsylvania brewery sounded mighty appetizing.

"Okey, dokey. Be back with your brewskies in a brief." Jackie swung away, her cute little butt in a sashay all the way to the kitchen. Marble snuck a brief glance at Jackie's tush and thought, yes, definitely a girl.

Marble looked back at Jasmine. "Wow. I don't quite

understand what I have to do with all of this. I've seen carnage all day and yet each time I tried to ask, something got in the way, almost like I wasn't supposed to know. OK, here goes, why are there no birds?"

"I think I can answer that." The voice came from one of the largest men Marble had ever seen. Popeye Worthington walked up to the table and introduced himself to Marble. He then proceeded to wedge himself into Marble's side of the booth.

Jackie returned with their beers, including an extra-large diet Coke for Popeye. Anna Smythe arrived next at the table, and to Marble's open-mouthed surprise, she slid next to Jasmine. It was apparent that they all knew each other because no further introductions were necessary. Behind him, he felt the seatback vibrate and he turned to see the bright smile of Callie as she leaned over their shoulders. Popeye started to sweat profusely, and his huge hands trembled. Marble could empathize because he began to feel very claustrophobic. The woman he'd had carnal knowledge of that afternoon now sat next to his current date. This had the wrath of a woman scorned written all over it.

"Shooter, there are no birds because of the actions of one man." Anna spoke and Marble still felt the warmth of their dalliance in his loins. "If we're right, and we believe we are, the balance of nature has been severely damaged, we think, because of one man. The cycle of life suffers because of him. And not one scientist in the world can diagnose or solve this problem. It is beyond their scope of reasoning. But it is also beyond our powers, for our energy derives from the cycle of nature, and that cycle is broken. You are our only hope. We need you, Shooter. Only you have the strength to rid this evil from our world."

He couldn't hold back the laugh. "What? You've got to be kidding me."

"We find none of this funny, I'm afraid. You have prescient abilities; you may be our best hope."

"What? I, uh, I mean, no, I'm nothing special, you got the wrong guy. I'm just plain old Larry Marble, nothing spectacular, the way I like it. I mean, I feel like I'm in a video game. Did you just really say 'rid this evil from our world'? I mean, that's crazy talk. Right?"

All eyes were upon him. Marble knew for a fact that no one in his life had ever said they needed him. Very few had ever taken the time to acknowledge him. Through all the trials and tribulations with Deelah, even the good times, she had never once expressed her hope in any of his abilities. *Boy, it sure felt good to be needed.* The tingle started somewhere deep within him, but it soon spread like wildfire all over his body. The clarity of the moment rang out loud and true in his mind: for the first time in his life, he felt alive. When nervous, he babbled.

"This is a bit out of pocket for me; weird, actually. I appreciate your words but I'm not sure what I have to do with all of this. I mean, what is it exactly that I can do?" *I've been having visions, that's it, honest, how can that help?*

Jasmine spoke in even softer tones, staring at him with unblinking eyes. "Shooter, you already know, don't you? You've seen his horror in your visions. Trust your instincts; they've been dormant, but now they're back. Trust your visions, learn from your sight."

Did she just read my mind?

Anna reached across the table and touched his hand. It was electric, just like before. "There is strength inside of you, Shooter. I felt it this afternoon. Honor that strength, honor your inner eye."

Yeah, that's right, honey, you felt my strength today, all right. He smacked the Bogart impersonator in his brain.

"Tr-tr-t-trust your p-p-p-power." Popeye stumbled over the words.

Gee, he's nervous? I'm the one with a boatload of memories and visions coursing through my head. Marble took a long swig from his beer and allowed the smooth lager to settle in his belly before he spoke. Clean as springtime rain shower was the realization of the moment. *So, the power from my youth has returned. Just what the crow lady said to me earlier.* Marble straightened his spine and glanced up at the ornamental fish net strung above him. On his horizon loomed another fun visit with Willem, the crazy sonofabitch who had threatened him earlier that afternoon. The same lunatic he'd seen on the stormy exit ramp the evening before. The same wild man he'd had a vision of baying at the moon on a stormy sea and throwing a black man overboard with cinder blocks strapped to his body, the one and only Hizzoner, Willem Clydesdale, the fourth. Oh yeah, and the spinning desk, major red flag warning there.

Marble's eyes panned back down but a commotion at the front door changed his focus. For the first time in his life, he finally knew the true meaning behind the phrase "you're not gonna fucking believe this." Shouldering her way past two extremely annoyed patrons, a frazzled Deelah Thayer crashed into Larry Marble's Grand Plan.

***

In the post-depression years of the 1930s, towns and cities across the country began expanding into rural areas. Along with this growth came the desire to capture bits of the wild and integrate them into human communities. Misguided souls decided how nice it would be to have Canada geese spend their winters adorning the lakes and ponds near the centers of their towns.

Across the northern states, this new touch of the wild right outside the back door became an instant hit. Unfortunately, for wild geese, they lost the need to forage because ground bounder food was abundant. Gaggles forgot their migratory paths and their migratory brothers, in fact, becoming a generation of fattened, domesticated geese that made a mess of bike paths, roadways, and backyards.

Silas, the recuperating goose on Ismelda's second floor, was not a member of the domestic clan, and the last thing he wanted was to become one of them. He and his kind were wild Canada geese, unfettered by the rolled-up balls of stale bread tossed by snotty-nosed ground bounders. His gaggle elders had warned him of the other side, never to venture near lest you be ensnared into the ground bounders' prisons.

Yet here he was, entombed inside a large wooden nest, cared for by a gentle, well-meaning female ground bounder. The food was foreign yet plentiful; the roof above him protected him from the elements and more importantly, the dangerous creatures that he could smell just outside the walls.

His body trembled at the memory of that fateful day: the site of his fellow gaggle family mangled in death, the burning smell of sulfur, and his excruciating fall into the bay. A ground bounder found him though, and he knew, that in some way, not all ground bounders were evil.

He stared through the window and longed to fly free once more for he wanted to exact revenge upon the creatures that had killed his family. His strength was not what it should be though, and he remained nestled in the bed of throw pillows, wistfully watching the day blend into the night.

"There you are, young warrior, staring outside at the

twilight. Not to worry, you shall soon return to your world. We are close… very close." Ismelda set down a fresh bowl of water and a dish of live earthworms and snails. She gently caressed the back of the goose, careful not to disturb his bandaged left wing.

"Soon, my friend, very soon your wing will be well enough for you to find a new family. Mr. Shooter will see to that, you'll see."

***

Marble didn't quite know how to behave. The blood had washed from his face and his shocked visage caused his booth mates to turn in unison toward the ruckus at the front door.

Iguana followed Deelah, squeezing through the doorway with his camera. Marble recognized the cameraman, having met him on several occasions in the past, and he remembered liking him. He instinctively raised a color-the-crabs place mat in front of his face.

After a second, he peeked over the top and saw that Deelah's back was to him. *Good, she hasn't seen me.* He noticed the all too familiar rear profile, and the icy breath memory of misery caused him to shiver. Marble felt other eyes on him, as his booth mates greeted him with quizzical expressions.

"Um, let's see, I should explain. The blond, that woman with the cameraman, well… that's my ex-wife. Never thought I'd see her again, that's for sure."

Jasmine glanced over her shoulder. "All I can say is that your taste in women is definitely improving, Shooter." She reached across and tickled his forearm.

"Let's see about getting your dinner out." Callie climbed out of the adjoined booth and whispered something to Jackie before

146

heading back into the kitchen.

"I must leave, also; you two enjoy your evening. We'll talk soon, Shooter." Anna stood and Marble could swear that she gave him a seductive wink. He had little time to reflect on it though because Popeye's massive hand squeezed his shoulder.

"Nice meeting you. Have a nice night, folks. But don't stay out too late. There's gonna be a red sky in the morning, that's for sure." Not a stutter in the sentence, thought Marble.

Jackie led Deelah and Iguana into a secluded corner of the restaurant, out of sight of Marble's booth.

Jasmine watched Marble carefully. "It's also obvious she's not a real blond."

Marble laughed out loud. It was the most honest reaction he'd had in years. "Hey, sorry, it was just a ghost, that's all. And ghosts can't harm me a bit. Come on, let's change the subject." His mind raged with questions. *What is she doing here? It can't be because of the car because she brought a cameraman. Wait a sec, I never told her my location. Is she here on work? And if so, what would bring her down here? The missing birds, of course, it must be a slow news season. Why in the world do I feel guilty?* He shook his head to rid the demons. He was determined to stay focused on Jasmine, his first official date of the Grand Plan.

"I saw remains of dead birds all day, lots of them. OK, OK, now some of this is starting to make sense. Birds eat insects and you guys sure have an abundance of those around here."

Jasmine nodded solemnly. "Bingo. Bats also help maintain a balance but they seem to have fallen victim to this blackness." She made a sweeping gesture over her shoulder. "They all have their theories; the Nile virus, avian botulism. But those afflictions leave whole dead carcasses. We have found bodies mangled almost beyond recognition. And all kinds, from sparrows to night raptors like owls and bats.”

“Mangled? You mean like being eaten?” Marble’s heart jumped when Jackie appeared with their dinners. She gave Marble an obvious wink before strutting away. He looked back to his date. “What’s your theory?”

Jasmine’s eyes sparkled with tears. “Nothing of this world, I’m afraid. But there’s no need to dwell on something we can’t address yet. We need you to gain nourishment first, to rediscover your soul, to become whole again. That’s where I come in; I’m one of your nurturers. The first step is to dive into these crab cakes while they’re still steaming and begging for our tongues.”

Marble was about to question her nurturer statement until his nose got a whiff of the food before him. Hunger overruled his mind, and he didn’t need further coaxing. One bite, and he joined the praise, because they were in fact the best crab cakes he’d ever eaten.

He gradually felt more relaxed as he kept his focus on Jasmine, and soon the beer and food helped him to forget about Deelah. This was, after all, part of his Grand Plan, and moving on without his ex by spending time with a lovely, much younger, female fit perfectly into his scheme. *Yeah, but why do feel like I’m cheating?*

Jasmine continued, in between bites, to bring him up to date with the mysterious disappearance of the birds.

“Every so-called learned mind has posited their speculations on the why. I’ve heard them all yet not one satisfies. Hundreds of victimized corpses have either washed up or been found throughout the county over the past two weeks. It’s not a predator of this world, I’m sure. Eagles, hawks, or owls don’t hunt in packs. And it’s not as if airplane engines or propellers could inflict such a wide swath of destruction. And pesticides or chemicals wouldn't account for the carnage. Fifteen miles away there's no damage, no dead birds. It's almost as if Clydesdale's skies are taboo, where nothing lives, that's what's driving us all crazy.

"No, I'm trained as a biologist but I'm afraid no earthly knowledge can answer this riddle. There are forces unseen by man and science that still play a crucial role in this era of humanity. Unfortunately, there are connective portals to dimensions not seen by humans for millenniums. And I'm afraid, just as are my sisters, that one of those portals has been reopened."

She gestured over her shoulder at a table of Environmental Protection Agency field operatives. "Yet these nerds continue to think it's some kind of chemical released into the air and water. They've been taking samples all day out in the marsh flats; heads up their butts, if you ask me."

For the first time in several minutes, Marble tore his gaze from the captivating spectacle that was Jasmine. He glanced around the room and saw the familiar back of Deelah's head, at a booth past the kitchen door, far enough from his table to keep the food down in his stomach. The restaurant was full with bustling sound. He made eye contact with Anna on the other side of the room, and for a fleeting moment, the now familiar surge down under caused his face to flush. She smiled coyly before she returned her attention to a conversation with Popeye.

Jasmine had followed his gaze. "Anna is one of my sisters, as are Callie and Ismelda."

Marble passed by all his other questions with the obvious. "Uh, by sisters, you mean exactly…?"

Jasmine set down her fork and stared quietly at Marble. She inhaled a deep breath of resolve and then continued.

"Sisters, yes, they are my coven of sisters. Well, I'm not a member officially yet, but my induction is next full moon. Then it's the real deal, a full-blown witch with a Wiccan family."

Her tone was reverent. Marble hurriedly gulped his beer. He had heard Willem call Ismelda a witch. Somewhere deep within his ever-expanding powers, he sensed that statement held a modicum of accuracy, too, and now Jasmine's revelation. Marble felt numb, as if all the feelings jumped from his body and stood next to the booth, wondering when they could return. His lack of sensation was the kind of chill that sneaks up on a person when something so outside the realm of normalcy is proposed. Come to think of it, he wondered, why shouldn't I have been numb all day? He could only muster a whisper. "You're a, a, um, witch, Ismelda? Anna, too?"

"Yep, Callie too and a few other sisters you've not met yet. Oh, don't look so shocked. We don't fly on brooms or build gingerbread houses to attract pudgy little kids so we can eat them." She smiled, a perfectly charming grin, and Marble wondered if he was under the influence of a spell. He tried to laugh with frolic, but it hacked out like a cough.

Jasmine laughed. "Oh, come on, it's no big deal. We are members of a Wiccan sisterhood that believes all living beings are intricate spokes in the wheel of life. That wheel also has spokes of earth, air, water, insect, animal, and fish. Take a spoke away and that wheel won't roll. That's what's happening here, Shooter. We are not rolling. All because Clydesdale has unleashed—"

She stopped mid-sentence and Marble followed her eyes. He swiveled to look over his shoulder. Callie stood there, covered in the trappings of a busy chef at dinner, and she leaned into their table.

"How was dinner? Mr. Shooter, looks like you enjoyed it; you cleaned your plate so well I won't even have to wash it. But next time, try and get it all in your mouth." She flicked off a morsel of crabmeat from his shirt.

While in close, she whispered instructions. "Jasmine, don't be talking about anything more in case any of these reporters or other nosy geeks got big ears. How's your head feeling, Mr. Shooter?"

Marble smiled. "Fine, just fine; dinner was superb, by the way."

Jasmine edged across the table, her cute butt in the air. "We should get out of here, Shooter, what do you think? Care to buy a girl a margarita?"

Marble agreed and pulled two twenties from his wallet and put them on the table. "Callie, does this cover our tab? Do you mind if we sneak out of here without any fanfare?"

Callie chuckled warmly. "Honey, first thing, your money ain't any good here. I, too, am a nurturer; my job is making sure you get all the energy you need in that belly." She stuffed the bills in his shirt pocket. "Secondly, there ain't any shame in getting your hand caught in the cookie jar after a divorce. Strut your stuff and show this young filly off."

All day Marble had wanted to talk to Deelah but now he just wanted to avoid confrontation at any cost. He also would never admit that a part of him still loved his ex-wife, despite the years of abuse and her annoying habits. Yet, even to Marble's taste, Deelha still had one of the hottest bodies he'd ever seen. Too many mixed emotions, though, are what drive men to well-stocked trout streams, live sporting events, backyard hammocks, golf courses, long hikes in the woods, and good Cuban cigars. Guys just can't handle too many jumbled emotions – they hurt the brain.

"Thanks for the advice but I think I'll save any strutting for another time."

Callie stepped back as he and Jasmine got up from the table. He fished a twenty from his pocket and set it on the table. "For Jackie, a tip." He picked up his bottle of beer and downed it in one long swig. "Hate to waste a good beer, too."

Callie laughed again. "Now that's the party spirit."

Jasmine knocked him for a loop as she came right into him and kissed him soundly, sensuously, warmly on his lips with just a hint of tongue. His blood rushed southward, and he guiltily glanced in Anna's direction. *What was in those crab cakes?*

"Come on, OC awaits our partying ways." Jasmine grabbed him by the hand and led him to the door.

Marble turned to look back at Deelah's table to see if he'd been spotted. Jasmine didn't give him much of a chance though as she pulled him toward the front door.

Callie thought, fanfare be damned. "Don't you two do anything I wouldn't do." Her rich laugh rang out above the din of diners.

***

Most Hollywood studios tape sitcoms and variety shows before live audiences with a "house laugher" in the crowd. The house laugher's mirth resonates above all others, ringing with infectious allure to join in the frivolity.

Iguana was a true trivia nut, and his specialty was old TV shows. The *Mary Tyler Moore Show*, *Dick Van Dyke Show*, *Lucy Show*, and *All in the Family* style genre. He couldn't help but take notice of Callie's laugh, such a pure example of a house laugher's melodic pipes. He pinpointed onto Callie but then followed her gaze to the couple at the door. A light bulb, albeit dim, crackled on in his head.

"Yo, Dee, isn't that, you know, that dude leaving over there, you know, yesterday's better half, you know, Larry, the former Mr. Dee?"

Deelah was engrossed in her iPhone, penning a report on the absurd theories of crop circles, alien abductions and a connection with the ancient Norse god Thor, anything, anything to keep her from having to engage in petty conversation with her moronic cameraman. The mention of Marble sparked her interest, though, and she twisted round to look at the front of the restaurant.

"You gotta be fucking kidding me." She arose, completely unaware that the back side of her purple Laura Ashley skirt was matted into the up position by a wayward smashed Tastykake Butterscotch Krimpet that had been errantly misplaced by Woody earlier in the day. The pastry held the skirt high enough to reveal two nicely toned butt cheeks, separated by a strand of black thong that disappeared into her netherworld. Of course, every diner in the restaurant who sat behind her, including Iguana, caught an eye full.

Deelah was unaware of her peep show. Her attention focused into laser beams. Directly in front of her was Larry Marble, one day from divorce, skipping out of the restaurant with Jasmine's hand strategically placed in a squeezing motion on his right butt cheek. Never, not even once, had Deelah ever doubted Marble's fidelity. In fact, she firmly believed that if it hadn't been for her bewitchingly seductive charms, Marble probably would have become a priest. Now, the vision of him prancing out of a restaurant with a hot-bodied younger woman who was practically spilling out of her excuse for a dress sent her common sense into temporary hiatus.

She made a beeline for the front door. Unfortunately, her path took her directly in front of the kitchen, a very dangerous place in any restaurant for the uninitiated. A feverishly engaged Pablo emerged from the kitchen at the precise moment of her passing, with an empty bus pan, eager to clear more tables.

Instead, he crashed into the butt-baring, intrepid small-town reporter with the fake boobs, smashing her directly in the nose with his hard rubber bus pan, sending her sprawling.

Marble never saw the damage done as Jasmine led him toward her Jeep. They strapped in and pointed the headlights southward toward the sparkling lights of Ocean City.

Back in the restaurant, a crowd began to gather around the prone reporter, and for the second time in one day, the new Clydesdale flyweight champion of the world, Pablo Escobar de Maria Consuelo, had successfully retained his belt by knocking out Ms. Deelah Thayer.

12

Willem thought he was slowly losing his mind. He imagined little streams of sanity twirl through his scalp and twist away into the abyss of space, which was a good thing, he surmised, because he'd read in some magazine that if you think you're going crazy, you aren't. Truly crazy people never think they're crazy and everything in print had to be God's Honest Truth, according to Patti.

Despite what the gossip rags purported, Willem's brain still felt squeezed, as if a thousand tiny anacondas tried to choke off his thoughts. His mind dragged toward the sulfur stink of the alien world that lay before him on his desk. He stared at the nest portal, in fact, he could almost see the snakelike tendrils, with tiny heads and forked tongues, whispering, "show us the way to your brain, mortal, we want to suck it dry". It was a comical hallucination brought on by another two-inch tumbler of Jack Daniels. A chuckle cackled forth as he slobbered the Tennessee whiskey between his waxy lips.

Ah, Jasper, if I'm going crazy, at least we might as well get drunk in the process. An attempt at another laugh erupted into a smoker's hack and his baldpate changed colors into a bright purple that would have made Patti double over in laughter.

Tennessee Sour Mash gold muscles urged him to swagger out of the marina's shack and physically confront Popeye Worthington and his illegally parked semi. *To boldly go where no Willem has gone before, to challenge that black nothinglessness for the rights to woo the widow Smythe, these are the synaptic travels of this Crazy Clydesdale.*

The "widow" part caused him to snort so loudly that snot oozed out of his nose. "Poor departed, holier-than-thou Captain Turner Smythe," he babbled while he wiped boogers with the back of his hand. "Dearly departed at the hands of one Willem Clydesdale the fourth, yours truly, here's to ya, Cap'n, he-he-he."

Certainly, it hadn't been premeditated. Although a competent prosecutor could plead intent because of the act of taking the mysteriously dangerous nest portal onboard for a simple and short fishing trip as an act of premeditation. But then the same prosecutor would have to convince the jury that the gnarly black lump of twigs opened a portal to another dimension. Willem poured JD drink *numero seis* into his glass and fired another Lucky. *Come on, insanity, let me taste your sweet molasses.*

Captain Smythe died because of his love for boats, especially the best-made crafts, and Willem owned one of the crème-de-la-crème vessels in the world, his only true luxury, paid in cash with the large inheritance he'd sat on for years.

After his retirement from naval service, Captain Turner Smythe spent every moment he could at the marina, admiring Willem's Rybovich. The mayor actually caught him drooling one time; it was a memory that again caused an even drunker Willem to laugh sloppily. The good captain had desired his boat and Willem desired the good Captain's smoking-hot wife. "A fair fucking trade if you ask me," he mumbled to no one in particular. As if on cue, echoing the fact it sucked to drink alone, a strange red glow slowly seeped from the gnarled top of the nest portal as it rested on Willem's massive desk.

Willem had first met Anna in person the previous spring

when the Captain had brought her to the marina to be enamored with the Rybovich. Willem, in turn, had been smitten at first sight; Anna was the one and only woman who'd ever had that kind of effect on him. To some civilized circles, it could be labeled obsession but for Willem, it hadn't waned, for he claimed it destiny, Anna was his soulmate, his pre-ordained partner for life.

"Nothinglessnesses, fucking nothinglessnesses." It was an original word, Willem Clydesdale the fourth's own word, no one else could have it, no one else could use it, and no one else could understand its true meaning. "My fucking word. Word."

Willem tried to raise his right hand in a gangsta motion but instead, he lost his balance and toppled out of his chair, hard onto the floor. He felt no pain though because another fit of laughter ensued when he realized he hadn't even spilled a drop of his beloved Jasper Jack Daniels.

Again, he dabbled in the memory of that fateful July day when the blues ran high in the canyons off the coast and Captain Turner Smythe gushed on the dock next to *Hizzoner*. Willem good naturedly invited the Captain on board for the morning fishing expedition.

"And you can even captain my vessel today, Captain. The blues are there for the taking, just my first mate Amos and me gonna set out about thirty clicks to Beggar's Canyon and drop six or seven lines. You game for some action?"

Willem reached for his chair in the marina office and missed. *"You can even captain the* Hizzoner, *Captain.* That's what I said to him, who-who-wee. Oh, the little boy behind the sailor's eyes bought that, hook, line, and sinker. That was a fucking classic moment, fucking classic."

Hizzoner couldn't stop giggling as he tried to climb back into the chair, oblivious to the nest portal's aura as it began to fill the room with an eerie mist.

The retired naval officer responded to Willem's offer as if he just found out that Santa really did exist. He called Anna to say he would be gone deep sea-fishing most of the day. His wife resisted because, in her estimation, all was not right in the world of one Willem Clydesdale the fourth, but her husband was so excited that she reluctantly granted assent and in doing so, lost her man forever.

Sour mash magic filled the now empty tumbler and became drink number seven, no ice, just nasty neat. Willem fought off the drunkard's spin as he attempted to stay focused on the memories.

Amos Campbell had been his first mate and yet *no nothinglessness had come inquiring about his disappearance*. No one had cared that he too had never returned from the same fishing trip. The only one who had seen the boat go out that day had been the old coot Doc Gilbert because his beaten old skiff had been returning from an early morning trip to the crab traps, as they passed each other at the inlet.

"Nobody saw your poor black ass, Amos, nobody. Here's to you, first mate. Dinner to the crabs. Sorry I had to let your black ass go. Sorry mate, sorry Mr. Crab Food Amos."

The top of the nest portal opened, and a burnt orange cloud of rotten egg stink seeped into the room. Willem finally noticed he wasn't alone in the marina office, and he slurred directly to the monster.

"You told me to take you on that fishing trip. You told me to bring you up on deck once we were thirty clicks out. You told me to place you on the captain's chair. I did as you asked, didn't I? Didn't I?" The nest portal made not a sound as the stinging mist swam above the desk and engulfed Willem, as if it had intelligent design. He didn't flinch at the stink because the bourbon had thoroughly desensitized him. "You remember that day, don't you?"

Once over Beggar's Canyon Captain Smythe had set the mighty engines into neutral. He climbed down from the captain's deck to help Amos bait and set the lines when Willem emerged from below decks with the nest portal in both hands. Neither of the men saw him approach from behind and set it on the center captain's chair.

A vessel is at the mercy of the swell of the ocean while rolling with the tide, and the swells that day were moderate, two to three feet. All three men were seasoned sailors though, and seasickness never called to them. Nevertheless, Willem remembered feeling strangely ill as he backed away from the nest portal.

"Yep, I set you there, prepped for din-din." Willem's eyes began to water, not tears of sorrow though, but tears from sulfur. His hand shook as he lifted the glass to his lips and drained it in one sloppy gulp. He reached for the bottle again, now bathed in a light that made it look evil. Willem didn't care, he'd drink evil anyway.

A low growl came from the image now revealed. It built in tremor, timbre, and tone. Willem didn't flinch, for this was not the first time he'd witnessed the power before him.

The first time had been at sea and the wailing cries from the nest had caused both Captain Turner and Amos to turn to the source. Willem's jaw dropped open now as then. That sound, that incredibly loud howling, whistling, screaming din that arose from the nest portal. As quickly as the noise escalated, it came to a screeching halt at the exact moment that Captain Turner Smythe vanished into thin air, scooped right out of this dimension.

Willem had begun to howl on the deck of the Rybovich; the memory spurred him to begin howling now in the marina's office.

On *Hizzoner*, Amos lived up to the expression of a man turned white as a ghost. As Captain Turner Smythe disappeared before his eyes, he'd fallen directly down onto his ass in fear and impaled himself through the kidneys with the grappling gaff, a wound dangerously close to fatal.

Willem had teetered with odd delight as he stared at his first mate. The decision popped into his head, and he went back into the galley and returned with rope and two cinder blocks that had been stored below. *Premeditation, your honor; why does a boat as luxurious as a Rybovich need two concrete cinder blocks on board? Ballast? I fear not. What conceivable purpose could they serve besides that of criminal intent?*

As he dumped the still breathing and frantically begging Amos overboard into the cold, deep ocean, the cinder blocks his death anchor, Willem again had begun to howl anew.

The memory faded as Willem stared at the monster pulsating before him. "I didn't know that you could, you would do that, and that you could read my mind and know I wanted Smythe out of the picture." Tears and snot streamed down his face. "I didn't know, I didn't know. Hot damn, that was so fucking cool, though. Hot fucking damn, that was so fucking cool."

***

Marble wet burped. The acidic tingle at the back of his throat was the warning acid reflux. Stress treats everyone a little differently and for Marble, the stomach took the brunt of the battle. Deelah's stress manifested itself in two ways: nasty knots between her shoulder blades that caused Marble to sweat like a draft horse when he played masseur, and nasty barbs zinged at her husband's weak-kneed approach to the world.

"What kind of man could I have been with all my doors opened?" he silently asked himself. *"The man who now rides with a sexy young woman in an open-topped jeep, heading for margaritas"* was a partial answer.

Deelah's presence in Clydesdale was a huge factor for his unease, but this time he handled it with different emotions. He tried to think of all the positives of the day, referring again to his well-practiced pro-and-con battle. It had been an incredibly eventful inauguration of the Grand Plan: his car pancaked, his head smashed, hot scx with Anna, on a date with Jasmine, Deelah showing up in Clydesdale, oh yeah, and the visions, memories, and dreams.

Jasmine's driving style didn't help his discomfort. She handled turns as if NASCAR was IVed into her arteries, upshifting into third gear and burying the accelerator to the floor on a hairpin curve, doing her best to cross Assawoman Bay in world record time.

Marble wished he had a Tums. He swallowed back the burp of spices and beer and tried to revel in his surroundings. As they made their way south of the town, the road dissected a huge marsh, now strangely silent without a bird in sight. Twilight shared another hour of light with the day, a time when birds socialized in a symphony of song, in search of their own suppers before nestling down. The marsh should have been a food court of activity, but now only morgue silence, forbidden, foreign, frightening solitude stared back.

Marble allowed his newly expanded senses to search the space in the hope of discovering what was killing the birds. Maybe he could garner some clue, some vision, some answer. He closed his eyes and tried to concentrate, to find his chi, his center, the chakra of inner peace and sight. Anna dubbed it his inner eye, but Jasmine unwittingly kept covering that eye with her personality.

The openness of the jeep made conversation difficult but, apparently, it didn't dissuade Jasmine. She babbled on even though Marble could barely hear her because of the buckets of air that whipped through the open-topped Jeep CJ-7, another great reason to wear a shoulder harness, as he held on for dear life when she took a turn on two wheels.

"…and it's absolutely amazing. I'm so glad you wound up in Clydesdale because I get to be the one to introduce you to perhaps the best nightspot on the East Coast, Seacrets, Ocean City's hottest location for fun. There's a stage for rock and roll, a space for reggae, a room for hip-hop, a bar for oldies. I have spent a whole evening just dancing to my heart's delight. Of course, we're in the downturn spiral toward the dreaded off-season so the venues are not as fruitful as other evenings. Would you look at the colors of the sky? Dear Good Mother, I miss the sight of birds settling in for the night. The skies should be teeming with life this time of day."

Marble tore his gaze away from her wonderfully muscled legs that moved in fluid fashion as they took turns pumping the clutch, brakes, and accelerator. His eyes now back on the sky, the horizon's clouds a pastel of red and purple shades, courtesy of the setting sun. Then it arrived, almost, *almost*, dare he say, by smell. They were out there, the glimpses of the invisible he'd seen earlier in the day as shadows, waiting, lurking; he inhaled deeply, hoping to catch a whiff of the unknown. Without warning, his head jerked to the right, and he stared off to the west where a line of loblolly pines, pin oaks and cypress trees framed the marsh.

Bam, wham, slam, kazzam, as the new vision smacked him in between the eyes. The impact was a crowbar to the face, swung with high velocity from a very short distance away, but without the pain, only revelation. His head rocked back into the headrest, bounced off the hard vinyl, and came back for more. *Hey there, inner eye, I see you.*

The creatures were indeed alien: cloudy yellow orbs, obsidian beaks lined with shark-like teeth, muscular bodies covered with matted purple feathers, shaggy black coarse hair, bat-ribbed wings that dispersed clouds of choking sulfur and smoke with every flap, and scimitar talons as razor sharp and black as the night, ready to tear the flesh from any living creature that dared take flight. Marble knew this wasn't a vision of something past; this was present tense, desperately alien and, dare he say, evil. He smelled them, sensed their thoughts: they were hungry, and the skies were empty. The bird kingdom must have gotten out word to avoid the spider's web of marshes around Clydesdale. The question leapt to the front of the line, and it startled him, especially since it wasn't his own: *now what can we eat?*

Marble swallowed but only dryness met his tongue. The Jeep sped east, away from the tree line and like a vintage antenna that loses signals, the images faded from his mind's view. I'll be back, he thought, I'll be back.

***

"Move aside, I'm a doctor. Lemme lift up this skirt to see if she's got any internal injuries."

"Do you think those are real? They just don't settle normal, you know?"

"I'll be shucked, those is some pretty nails on a woman. Who'd she say she was?"

"Doc, you keep your crab-stinking hands off of that woman's hoo-haw, you filthy old coot, do you hear?"

"Smashed into a back-flip loop and still not a hair outta place, how ya figure?"

"Doc Gilbert, I said behave. This isn't time for show and smell. Just let her get some air."

"I should have had the camera on. That was one helluva landing. Judges give it a ninety-five. And shit yeah, let's check for internal injuries."

"Jasmine was right, not a real blond, lookee at those roots. Whoo-hee."

"Think she needs an Aleve?"

"Hi there. Bitchin' camera and I love your goatee, sweet. I'm Jackie."

"Back away, this ought to wake her."

"Jiminy, Popeye, you went and soaked us all too."

Deelah floated above the room and the view below her was so frightening she didn't want to return. But a pitcher full of ice water thrown into the face of one's still living body will bring any soul back home. Her astral rope strained taut as she zipped back into her prone shell.

"HUUUHHHHH, what the fuck? Get your damn hands off of my legs." She kicked out and a Manolo Blahnik pump barely missed the grizzled chin of Doc Gilbert. "What the fuck happened to me? Which of you hicks hit me? Get the hell away from me, all of you. And how dare you fucking throw ice water at me, you big black oaf? To hell with all of you."

"Guess that knock sent all her personality to the cleaners."

"Behave that tongue, young lady, there are children in here."

Iguana snickered quietly. He wasn't just an ordinary cameraman, nosiree. No pretty, young waitress thing could distract him either because there had been a red flag issued in the land of camera guys and his calling came into the forefront. He adjusted the aperture of his camera's lens to capture the spectacle of Her Highness Bitch exposed for the second time that day. Of course, his between the ankles angle would please any red-blooded male.

Deelah tried to lift up from the sticky linoleum floor, conscious to keep her womanhood covered and yet so outraged her jilted efforts made her exposure worse, which brought an even wider smile to Iguana and Doc.

Ismelda had just arrived at Callie's and not a moment too soon. She and Anna came to the rescue and reached down to assist a fellow sister while simultaneously placing their back sides in front of Iguana's camera, thereby dashing any hopes of Iguana's amateur entry-level submissions to the "Assawoman gone wild, Clydesdale, MD." edition.

"Honey, you have to be careful walking in front of a kitchen door on a busy Friday night. We have to get some ice on that for you, too. Where you staying, sugar?"

Deelah tried to focus on Ismelda. Her words were strangely comforting and Deelah began to feel as if she were slipping back into unconsciousness. "I, I don't… I haven't had the… Marble… was that really—"

"We didn't check into any place yet, ma'am, any recommendations? I heard that all your motels are filled."

Ismelda turned to look at Iguana. "Are you with her?"

"Just professionally, ma'am, this is the closest I want to get to her, trust me."

Ismelda looked at Anna, who returned a knowing gaze. "I have a B&B, a little cozy place. But I only have one free room right now so how about I let our injured friend have a bed and you can bunk on my sitting room couch. Reasonable rates, breakfast at seven forty-five."

Jackie emerged carefully from the kitchen and handed Anna an ice-filled plastic bag, wrapped in a clean cloth. Anna held it to Deelah's nose where a quickly emerging swell began to tighten her skin.

"Uh, yeah, that sounds good. That OK with you, Dee?"

"Mmmph, oh, my nose, it hurts so bad."

"She's not in any state to complain right now I'm afraid. Doc, you and the boys help our sister to my car and then follow me over to the Paradise. Mr. …?"

"Iguana, that's what they call me, ma'am."

"Of course, they do, Iguana, right, should have guessed. Follow us, it's only a few blocks away. And you can turn off your camera now, there's not anything else newsworthy about to happen, I promise."

Jackie seductively slid over to Iguana's side and handed him an order slip scrawled upon with a smiley face and her cell number. "Call me. I get off at ten. I'll make it worth your effort, I promise."

"Jackie King, we're still open. Get your skinny butt back in here and run some food." Callie gave Iguana a stern look before bustling back into the kitchen, warming the place with another boisterous thunder of laughter.

***

"…It's amazing. My family would come here every summer

when I was a kid, and we would have a fantastic time. Memories are incredible, you know. Whenever I feel down, I just think of happy times. And Ocean City in the summer is that time for me.”

The wind churned her words into a swirling dervish as the open-aired Jeep barreled across the causeway bridge on Route 90, the northernmost avenue into Ocean City.

Marble twisted to look behind him, to the west, but the creatures he’d seen were no longer viewable. Either they were gone, or he was now out of reach. He suspected the latter, though. He tasted salt in the air. The dryness that had visited his mouth since the Deelah sighting in his Grand Plan had now turned into a sandstorm. Jasmine just kept on talking though, and Marble tried to pay better attention.

“Seacrets is a great place to hang. You’ll love it. Like I already said, and stop me if I repeat anything – sometimes that’s a problem I have – but this place has all these different rooms. Whatever kind of music, the venue is there. It’s great to watch the sunset in the summer, sipping a yummy concoction at the shell bar, checking out the people who shouldn’t wear spandex, and then dancing to the beat in front of live bands. It’s a blast. I’m craving a big, bad margarita. Whoo-hoo.”

She downshifted smoothly and the Jeep banked sharply into a cloverleaf turn. Marble leaned into it the best he could, battling the G-forces as the shoulder belt pressed against his chest. They approached the traffic light and before it flashed green, she leaned over and kissed him smack on the mouth. Marble was surprised, but he still kept an eye on the road as they sailed through the intersection.

“Whoo-hee, welcome to OC, MD.”

Billboards sailed past, touting the allure of a summer past. He was back, but the memory of that long-ago weekend was simply that, a memory. Bigger fish awaited his attention across the bay; despite his reawakened clairvoyance-inspired-bravado, he still had no clue as to what he could accomplish. But for now, he was in Ocean City and as they say, when in Rome. *Ah, the town that treated me so favorably many years before.* He leaned his head out and yelled his own whoop-de-doo into the night.

They sailed by high-rise hotels that bordered the beach side of Route 1, tepid chain restaurants and flashy package stores and bars. Then Jasmine made another signal-free turn into the huge parking lot of Seacrets.

September was quieter and the parking was easier, Jasmine commented as she skipped down the serpentine sidewalk, happily tugging Marble along. After a mini-maze of hallways, they settled at the shell bar, a cozy open-air watering station nestled right up to Assawoman Bay. Marble listened to Jasmine rattle on about her observations of the world, and after the second round of margaritas, he finally felt the stress stand aside and allow a more congenial version of a conversationalist to appear.

"Why did you major in marine biology? Does it give you any insight into the disappearance of birds around here? Is that why all those reporters, hell, my ex-wife even, are in Clydesdale? I've been having these, these, uh, sights, ideas, whatever, coming to me all day and it's driving me crazy."

For the first time on their date, Jasmine fell silent. She twirled her straw in her drink and avoided eye contact with Marble. She chose her words carefully and looked up at him.

"Yes, marine biology. Science tells me the birds have gone; my education tells me to search for logical causes. But academia doesn't hold all the answers. Especially when all they possess is based purely on conjecture, hypothesis, you know. There are greater mysteries that no scientist has ever postulated, successfully. Some turn to religion. I've turned to Wiccan. There I find answers my education never supplied."

Wow, now that's a response you don't hear every day. He searched his mental library for references. *Witch. Wizard of Oz. Wicked. Salem. Halloween.* Jasmine didn't fit any of those theaters. *Wing it, dude.*

"Wiccan? I guess my images are poisoned with the Hollywood versions. You don't look anything like the Wicked Witch of the West."

"Shooter." She clasped his hands.

Her skin was smooth, silky, and felt incredible. Marble wanted to touch more of her. *Wow, that's a quick reaction; what did they put in my tequila?*

"Shooter, yes, witches. There is a wonderfully blessed coven in Clydesdale. Tomorrow night is my initiation. I've waited three hundred and sixty-four days for acceptance into this sisterhood. Once the rapture is complete, I'm a witch.

"The preconceived notions are lies. We're not evil, we're not Satanists, we're not lesbians – well, not all of us – we don't build gingerbread houses just to eat little kids, we don't cast evil spells, we don't ride brooms. We do, however, promote healing and continuity between the forces that govern Mother Earth."

Another salty sip from her margarita and then her hands returned to motion. "Those forces are seriously fucked right now in Clydesdale. My sisters' powers derive from the blessing of earth, wind, fire, and water. When one or more of those are out of balance, so are our powers. So is Mother Earth." She let go of his hands and then placed them on either side of his temples. "In here, Shooter, in your mind, we pray, lies the answer to this riddle. We need you. We summoned you here to restore the balance to the cycle of life."

In the brain, well, in Marble's brain, beneath a plastic shield in the center of the control room main board lay the scary OH FUCK alert button. It's activated the first time you forget to set your alarm clock for a very important morning meeting. Once activated, you can never, ever again oversleep because the OH FUCK button becomes an automatic alert, waking you every fifteen minutes in the hour leading up to the set time. The OH FUCK alert button also works with the dreaded red flag beacons. Like when a beautiful woman tells you she's diagnosed situational bipolar, or she loves to hang out in biker bars, or her husband just came home, or she eats faster than you, or she pulls out her Steely Dan during sex and asks to use it on you, or when she claims that she's one day away from being a full-fledged Wiccan.

"That's a bit tough to swallow. I came here on my own accord." All Jasmine did was raise an eyebrow. "How did you know I'd make the wrong turn? This is all so fucked up. I wasn't summoned, get real. I mean my phone never rang, how could I be summoned? I know, I know, you did it on the astral plane network, right? Shit, Jasmine, this is so mind-blowing. I don't know what all of you expect from me." The clarity of the moment gave him an "awe, fuck me" response. All of it, from following the potato chip truck, the phantom in the middle of a stormy road, Ismelda's quirky B&B conveniently situated, and parking beneath a two-hundred-plus-year-old oak ready to bow toward the paper mill, all of it more than mere coincidence. He sipped his drink and the concerns disappeared into the mist over Assawoman Bay.

"We want you to trust your visions. Trust your inner eyesight. Trust your heart. But right now, drink up, dude. Another round and then we have to get back. I do value my driving license."

It was all the tequila's fault. That magical, wonderful juice distilled from the blue agave plant indigenous to Jalisco, Mexico. After his third Patron Silver margarita, Marble felt like he had a special blood brotherhood with Jimmy Buffet. It also felt like he was in the mood for more than just conversation as they stumbled through the hallway maze, pinballing off each other and a few other inebriated customers, back to the parking lot.

There is an urban myth that certain liquors, especially tequila, guarantee to kill inhibitions. Jasmine didn't disappoint. She joined the rhythm of the night as she unzipped his fly and dropped skillfully to her knees.

***

Across the bay, the beasts hungrily licked their chops. The birds were gone. Something else must now feed their craving for flesh, something else. Their eyes, the color of muddy sulfur, stared at the distant lights of Ocean City but that was much too far from the doorway to their homeland. This was a strange, new world for them, and the softened lights from nearby Clydesdale were a much closer potential feeding ground. In a silent explosion of acrid, biting dust, they rose to the sky, invisible to human eyes and senses, but not to the sharpened senses of the lone Canada goose in town.

Silas, still recuperating in the upstairs west room of Ismelda's Paradise B&B, awoke in frenzy and emitted a squawk that rattled the beveled glass windows of his ground bounder's home.

13

Deelah sat up so fast the room started to whirl. *What was that noise? It sounded like a goose. What would a goose be doing in my condo? Wait a second, this isn't my condo, what the hell?* Slowly, the reality set in and she pieced together the past couple of hours. Her head pounded, her mouth felt like sandpaper, and mini-anvils pressed on her eyelids.

She recalled her saviors. Ismelda and another woman named Anna had brought her here, helped her upstairs, and then she must have fallen asleep. The throbbing pain on her face reminded her of the accident with the busboy's pan and that scared the crap out of her. She raised her shaking hands to her nose and a gasp escaped her soul. The swelling had turned her nose into a snout, and into Dumbo the elephant size. *Oh my God, no, what the fuck do I look like?*

A lit lamp in the corner of the room granted adequate illumination as she inspected her surroundings: a paisley love seat in the corner, a dark-stained armoire along the wall, an antique sitting table with a burgundy stuffed high-back chair, a window, and a small night table by her bed, but not a single mirror.

She sat up a bit too hastily. The blood that rushed from her head made her eyes spin. Her breaths came in short spurts, and she steeled herself until her gaze steadied. *That a girl, yeah, you can do it, come on, Deelah, very, very slowly.*

With measured care, she swung her legs off of the quilted

bed, stood with gingered ease, and spotted her overnight bag on the floor. She pulled down her skirt and something sticky greeted her fingers. Her spine did the ewwyy jig as she pulled her hands away to examine the muck. A sugary hunk of butterscotch Krimpets was stuck to her right index finger. She shook it free as if it was a bug and the morsel took flight and plopped onto the antique armoire.

"I need a shower. Badly. And a shot of something strong." She bent over and it almost caused her to pass out from the pain, but she managed to snag the handle on her Gucci bag.

The goose in the room down the hall let out another honk of fear and this time she knew it wasn't delusional. She opened the door and a frazzled Ismelda met her in the hallway.

"Oh, you're up. Bathroom is right this way in case you'd care to wash up. Here, you should hold this against your, well, you might want to, the swelling…" She handed Deelah a bag of frozen baby peas.

Deelah turned her head away, fearful of seeing Ismelda's reaction to her face. "What… what time is it? I can't find my watch or my cell. Does Iguana have my cell? Where is he? And what the hell was that noise?"

"Now, now, don't you fret, it's just after ten p.m. Your cameraman isn't here. Would you like some help into the loo?"

"No, I don't need any… What was that noise? It sounded like a bird of some kind, and I thought they were all MIA." Her reporting skills, despite her ex's opinion, were actually online 24/7.

Ismelda was in a hurry, but she didn't want to alarm the bleached blond in front of her. She knew the mirrors in the bathroom would handle that task just fine. "We found a Canada goose that had been injured and I'm trying to nurse it back to health. When he gets hungry, well, sometimes it can get noisy."

Deelah felt her world start to spin again as she stared at Ismelda. "You better feed him then because I hope I don't have to hear that crap all night." She intended to sound diva-like but instead it came out so soft and whiny Ismelda thought she was going to cry. Deelah turned slowly to prevent any ricochet off the walls and shuffled down the hallway to the bathroom.

Ismelda decided to wait. It was catty, sure, but it's not often one can be live and in the front row to hear the satisfying sounds of a first-class bitch keen. She didn't have to wait long. Deelah's screams soon rivaled in decibels the frightened honks from the goose. With an impish smile, Ismelda turned and hurried toward the west room, aware all too vividly of the dangers that may lurk outside the windows, the true reason her avian guest was agitated.

A frantic Deelah rifled through her bag and found it; a 7.5-ounce silver flask, filled to the brim with 21-year-old single malt scotch from the highlands of Scotland. With a form that would make most fraternity brothers jump to their flip-flopped feet in applause, she drained half of the flask in 3.2 seconds. The fine whiskey began to work its magic almost instantly. It also gave Deelah the courage to look again at her swollen, discolored mug and her usually perfect hair now in horrific disarray. This time, no screams, just tears as she slowly slumped to the cool marble floor.

***

Ismelda entered the back room and saw the goose in a frantic state. As she rushed to him, the goosebumps rose on every inch of her skin. Although she couldn't see them, she could smell them. And she could definitely hear the scraping of their talons as they clamored at the thick-paned window only inches from the bird.

"Oh, this is not good for you, Mr. Goose, not good for you or for me." She moved quickly and pulled close the slatted wooden shutters to the window, hoping that the creatures might go away if they couldn't see the bird.

But the goose wouldn't calm because the stench, the smell of the murderers of his family were only feet from making him pâté. Ismelda carefully lifted up the bird, feeling his heartbeat pummeling against his downy breast, and hurried from the room.

"You'll stay downstairs with me tonight, just a change in scenery, that's all. And nothing will get to you, my dear, which I promise."

Ismelda slowed as she passed the bathroom and heard the showerheads turn on and she hoped that maybe, just maybe, Deelah had a good, wide pair of sunglasses.

***

As they crossed Assawoman Bay, Marble knew something was amiss. Though still influenced by the effects of Jasmine's nurturing, his newly awakened powers were on full alert. *Red flags Rover, red flags Rover, Rover, Rover, red flags Rover.*

"We're not in Kansas anymore, Toto." Marble whispered the words. His intuition paid attention to the sounds and sights, every shadow, every fleeting movement, as they made the turn toward Clydesdale. Again, saying it almost to himself, "Something is definitely going bump in this night."

Jasmine slowed almost to a stop and looked over at her passenger. His demeanor had changed, and she could almost see the rich, amber glow of energy that encompassed his head.

Tingles sprinkled up and down her arms.

"Ooh, baby, you've got the fire, I see it. Let it flow, let it flow. Ismelda was right; you needed a woman's taste, a woman's trust to open up your doors. I'm glad we could help. So, trust your powers. There are so many uncertainties that we can't explain by normal terms and my intuition is screaming to me that there's a whole boatload of more bizarre just around the corner."

Coincidence is one of the more underrated phenomena that occur on a vastly unnoticed regularity for humans. It's a barrel full of fun and yet rarely even acknowledged. Called serendipity in some circles, it is still a wonderfully played out chain of events that usually pays benefits.

***

Crosby Culp was sixty-three years young, a spry, petite widow who had lived year-round in Clydesdale for almost ten years. And by her side for the decade had been her faithful mutt, Connie, rescued from a shelter the same day she had buried her late philandering husband, Raleigh. Connie had been a treat of constant joy for Crosby. As near as Crosby could figure, Connie was a blend of at least four breeds of dog but the Husky in her blood explained her size, just shy of seventy-five pounds.

Like clockwork, every night, just before bed, Connie and Crosby took a leisurely stroll around the marsh perimeter, crossing Main Street as they looped back toward home. Without fail, ten p.m. to ten fifteen p.m., any other townie could find the two happily wagging their tales about the streets of Clydesdale. As with most retired folk, Crosby's daily routines were as rhythmic and predictable as breathing.

***

Jasmine made the turn onto Main Street just in time to fulfill her earlier prophecy. As the headlights illuminated the road ahead, they now became witnesses to a wildly bizarre sight. Jasmine slammed on her brakes and Marble was out of the CJ-7 before it came to a stop.

As Marble approached them, Crosby struggled to hold onto a levitating Connie. The dog floated ten feet off of Main Street and Crosby was on her tippy toes, with a two-hand grasp onto the pink leash for dear life. That's the picture that Jasmine had anyway.

Marble was privy to the whole macabre vision. Fifteen feet above the macadam he saw the hideously malformed shape of the flying black creature with the glowing yellow eyes, the same as his earlier vision, it's talons firmly a hold of a whimpering Connie's ornate collar.

Marble reached a frantic Crosby just as a second creature joined the tug of war and he wrapped his arms around her waist and pulled her back to terra firma.

"The leash, please, give it to me."

It wasn't really a request as he wrestled the looped end of the nylon cord from Crosby's hands and then ran toward the nearest lamppost, towing an extremely upset airborne Connie and hideous beasts behind.

He reached the post, looped the cord, tied it off, and then, with power that would make Samuel the Troll proud, he yanked with all his strength and brought Connie back to the pavement in a crunch. He looked up as the creatures escaped with just her pink collar, studded with rhinestones and an emblazoned nameplate for "Connie Culp, the Love of Crosby Culp's Life"

Crosby and Jasmine attended to a very distraught but healthy Connie as Marble tried to catch his breath, all the while observant of the two creatures that circled menacingly above, their stares not at the dog but directly at the odd ground bounder who had thwarted their supper.

They flapped their black spiked wings and vanished in a fart of smoky sulfur cloud that stank like rotten eggs. Marble searched the sky, unsure if he had heard their thoughts exactly right. What did "atlas, the props at sea run blue" mean, anyway? Still adjusting to his reawakened powers, he misinterpreted "alas, the prophecy is true," a fortuitous misinterpretation for the residents of Clydesdale because if Marble had translated the message correctly, it may have set him back a few notches of gumption and on the one road out of town. Gratefully, still confused, he let the adrenaline continue to surge through his body.

Jasmine wrapped her arms around his waist and pressed her face against his back. "My hero. I must admit, Shooter, you've given this girl one of the best dates she has ever had. Great dinner, great conversation, great margaritas, and great job saving a little old lady and her flying dog; wow, I mean, how can any guy ever top this one? If you don't marry me, right this minute, I'll never be able to date again."

She laughed and Marble turned around to face her. He delivered the next line in his best Robert Preston manner. "Jasmine, there is definitely trouble right here next to Ocean City. Those creatures, they were, well, they put the scare into scary, the fright into frightening, the heebie into the jeebie. Tell your sisters. Tell everyone. I *saw* them and the best thing for you right now is to get somewhere safe because…"

"Thank you, thank you, thank you, kind sir. What a

wonderful performance. Your timing, your bravery, my, my, you're cute, my knight in shining armor."

Crosby Culp, richly perfumed with a rancid eau de grandmother of lavender/mothball scent, made it a threesome, a *ménage a trois* sandwich hug where Marble was the meat. He felt his ribs collapsing. The seventy-five-pound mutt Connie soon joined the fray and humped Marble's leg.

That was the picture Sheriff Carl Heffley had, as he eased his police cruiser up to them, his rooftop lights on full flash.

"Mr. Marble, Larry, nice to see you again. Jasmine, hello, Ms. Culp, evening, hey there, Connie girl. You know, most folks do this kind of thing behind closed doors. But I'm surprised at your behavior, Connie. I thought you had better taste." Everyone in this town has a stand-up comedian fetish, thought Marble.

"You got it wrong, officer, because I didn't take enough vitamins for that kind of predicament." Marble broke free from the hug fest and addressed Carl directly. "Sheriff, uh, Carl, we just saved this lady and her dog from being carried off for a late-night snack. This isn't some fraternity prank, virus or whacked out Deliverance types. I know it sounds crazy, but there are some spooky killers on the loose tonight, and they are not, I repeat, they are not from this world." Will Smith couldn't have delivered the line better.

Carl returned a steely stare, without an ounce of humor or recognition. He opened his car and slowly peeled himself from the cruiser. He placed his arm around Marble and directed him away from the women and the lucky dog. "Mr. Marble, you're a guest in this town. Have you had maybe one too many this evening? Should I lock you up for your own safety?"

Marble bristled at the accusation and the tequila gave him huge cajones. "Listen, Carl, I can see them. That's what I'm trying to tell you. I have an inner eye, call it clairvoyance, prescience, whatever; it's been locked away for a long time in my head but now it's back and I can see these beasts, which means I can help clear the skies. You should want to help. These creatures, these things, I think they've killed all the birds and now they may be coming after our pets, maybe even after us. We have to go see Mayor Clydesdale. My intuition now confirms what everybody else has been saying: he may have something to do with all of this."

The sheriff put his hands to his head, pressed his scalp, and pushed back the brim of his hat. "That stupid son of a… listen, Mr. Marble, Clydesdale, he… well, he's a friend of mine, sort of, and I think he may have something to do with all this too, though I'm not right sure how. Believe me, he'd be my next stop tonight, if I had a lick of evidence."

Carl rubbed the bridge of his nose. This meant he was going to miss that evening's episode of *Law & Order*, homemade nachos and Arnold Palmer iced teas with just a hint of fresh mint leaves, snuggling with sweet Marylou Heffley on their new recliner sofa. The crap was hitting the fan, and even though Marble was an outsider, he sounded very believable. None of the news and government groupies in town bided well for the reputation of Clydesdale; besides, it would earn him a fine feather in his fedora if he had a hand in solving the mystery. The sheriff needed help and he needed it fast. He took a deep breath and opened up.

"I've gotten ten calls already tonight about pets that have gone missing. Old widow Annie Siegfried let her two poodles out her backyard tonight to do their biz and they never came back in for their treatie toots. I got a call from Vicky Butler that her Fluffy, some kind of big floppy-eared rabbit, got scooped right out of her pen on the front porch of the Butler trailer; her kids are going nuts. John and Wendy Rossman found the remains of their Siamese cats scattered all over their newly sealed driveway, catguts stuck in tar, freaking conniptions they're having, I tell ya. Sweet Marylou, I been getting calls just like that all night and they're not stopping." He took a moment and looked at Marble. "Ismelda calls you Shooter. Do you got any oomph to back up that handle? I mean, you really say you can see these things. Ever handle a shotgun?"

The vision hit Marble hard, and it knocked him to his knees. Did he ever handle a shotgun? Yeah, older bro Martin had shown him how. There it was, the vision from memory, finally, after thirty years. His brother, handcuffed and led away after his sentencing of five consecutive life terms in prison with no parole for the brutal slayings of his girlfriend Amy Green, her brother, Caleb, and parents Ebenezer and Mary Green; the unborn baby that Amy had in her womb made the count five – judge's decision.

For thirty years those images, those names, had remained imprisoned inside his head. Marble knew now, with certainty, that he couldn't allow his talents to foresee a danger without also providing a warning. He also couldn't let his abilities keep him from doing the right thing this time in his life. Badass ugly alien beasts from another world, well, they were front and center on the do-the-right-thing menu.

"You OK? Are you sure you didn't have too much to drink? You need to lie down?" Carl helped him to his feet.

"No, I'll be fine, sheriff, thanks, Carl. I just had a vision, an old memory that floored me. Sorry, I'm still getting used to this. And yes, I have handled a shotgun before. I had a good teacher, my older brother, Martin; Martin Aaron Marble."

"My brother taught me a lot of good stuff too while growing up. God rest his soul, I lost him to cancer about four years ago. It's tough to lose a loved one, especially blood, you know? But he's still with me, still here." The big man pounded his chest.

"Yeah, I lost my brother too. But not forever, that's for sure. He's in here too, finally." Marble did the same pound to his sternum. Then he took a deep breath and turned to look back at Jasmine, Crosby, and Connie, before addressing the sheriff once more.

"I have some kind of ability that I'm not even sure how to handle. But it's something we can use now so while I still have it, let's do it. Do I, you know, need to be deputized, or something?"

Before Carl could reply, his Motorola walkie-talkie begged for attention. "Heffley here… yeah… oh crap, now stay… Clarence, don't… Clarence, listen to me, leave your goats alone, I'll be right there." He looked at Marble. "And I'm bringing along the cavalry."

14

"Kooky old Clarence McDougal says poltergeists with scimitars are attacking his goats, reaching down from their invisible UFO. The ol' coot is over eighty, legally blind, a patch over one eye and the good one about cataracted over, so maybe he don't see nothing, you know. But, sweet Marylou, invisible things coming from the sky sounds right up your alley. Clarence's wife's been dead for nigh on five years, but he won't ask for no help from the church or any other do-gooder. He's a loner and a goat farmer, one of the last out these parts. Darn fine cheese too, I'll give him credit for that. But one helluva ornery ol' hound to boot."

Carl Heffley was tempted to turn on the siren, but Marble cautioned against it.

"If the beasts are still at the farm, I want to be able to get a shot off before they get wind of our arrival." Marble stared ahead, wearing his best Mr. Blonde face while cradling his weapon.

The shotgun, a Remington Model 870 pump action, sat across his lap, the barrel end resting out the open passenger window of the town's only police cruiser – a Chevrolet Impala with a 450 V-8 beneath the hood, the kind of muscle only police departments got to use legally to break the speed limit. Carl Heffley, town sheriff and diehard NASCAR fan, relished that perk as they careened down Main Street and banked into a two-wheel turn onto Buckwampum Drive, rubber-squealing yee-haws all the way.

With a free hand, the sheriff popped the glove box open. A

box of shotgun shells conveniently flopped out. "Go on, now, lock and load, Mr. Marble."

"I guess it's fitting now so feel free to call me Shooter, Carl. Now I know why they started calling me that. Funny, I never thought of myself as anything too special. Huh. I kind of wish my ex were here to see. On second thought, no, I don't."

"Divorce is one ugly scoundrel, that's why I cherish my Marylou with near every breath. No telling what tomorrow holds so I guess romance only lives in the here and now." Marble looked at the big man and marveled how simple it sounded, but then the Deelahs of the world blew Hallmark philosophies into the sewer. "That's it, right up ahead. His goats are usually penned out back."

Marble thought the McDougal residence looked like two piles of old wood that had been plopped onto one spot from some celestial wood-dumping trawler of the universe. Boards held together by old road signs, plastic milk crates, a mish-mash of cardboard boxes, and even an old shopping cart from the A&P, which, when the car's headlights shone upon it, appeared to form the alcove for the front door.

The headlights swung about, and Carl eased the car between the dump of a house and the pile of a barn. The lights now illuminated the goat pen where twelve tethered goats were in the process of being torn apart by over twenty beasts.

"Oh, sweet Marylou, sweet Marylou, what the heck do you make of this, Shooter? Do you see any of them things that's doing this?" The sherrif only saw the goats, some bleating cries of death with their bellies ripped apart, their bowels splattered on the ground, other goats cried in misery, a macabre parade float ten feet off of the ground.

Carl hadn't even noticed that Marble had left the cruiser. He now saw him approach the pen, cradling the shotgun in his left arm as he calmly loaded the pump action with shells.

The hovering creatures all stopped their feeding and lifted bloody fangs and gazes in the direction of Marble. Again, he heard their thoughts although this time there were too many at once and it sounded like gibberish.

He raised the shotgun to his shoulder, aimed and fired at the biggest, ugliest beast and the buckshot blew its head completely off. Marble's shoulder screamed for mercy but the adrenalin soaring through his body kept the scream to a whimper. The next message he received from the beasts was much clearer because the remaining creatures all said it at once, "Kill the prophet."

The old Marble would have run but the new Marble stood firm. There was no time for a pro and con debate, no time to be wasted, the pro side of his mind scolded. Regardless of how much his shoulder hurt, he cha-chunked the Remington, solid and smooth. One shot blew a black spiked wing in half, another imploded a beast's fangs into its gullet, and another ripped a chunk right through the gut. Two shots missed completely, and Marble now found himself in the middle of the pen as the beasts dropped the goats and rose to the air and circled him, countering his every move with lightening quick aerial acrobats. One beast dove at him and he turned in time to annihilate it in the face, but another one came from behind and a razor-sharp talon barely missed the back of his neck as someone else killed the beast in mid-dive.

"Take that, you ugly mudderfudder. Watch yerself, young feller, right above ya. Whoo-eee, I see you. I see you, mudderfudders. I ain't had this much fun since that pigeon shoot back in '79. Remember that one, Sheriff?"

Marble cautioned a quick glance at old man Clarence

McDougal. Sure enough, he had one eye patched and the other one the color of gray glass. Yet, there he was, eighty-years old if a day, wrinkled black skin with a greasy mop of gray hair, spittle flying from his mouth as he fired from his hips at the beasts with deadly accuracy, antique double-barrel shotguns in each of his leathery arms, a wizened old warrior, *Reservoir Dogs* senior citizen style. Marble felt like yelling, "Hey, aren't you supposed to be blind?" but the old guy's aim so far was dead on.

"Watch it, young feller. Lord a' mighty, I hope heaven is this much fun. Whoo-eee. Whoo-eee. Whoo-eee."

Marble instinctively ducked and rolled in his best Steve McQueen fashion. But, in reality, his impetus took him right into the carcass of a dead beast and the stench of acrid bodily fluids splashed all over his cotton rayon blend. He rolled away and fired from his back into the air. Five creatures turned to flee, and Marble hit one before it flew out of range. His ears rang, his clothes stunk, his arms trembled, and his chest heaved as he shakily stood. Adrenaline continued to pump hard into his heart, and he craved a cigarette so badly he could taste it.

"AHH, holy Toledo, sweet Marylou… they… they're… I can see them once you shoot them dead… ugly sons of bitches… holy Toledo… are they dragons?" Carl was shaking in his boots.

Marble wheeled about and the light bulb blazed in his head. "Not dragons or we'd be chicken-fried by now. No, they're something else, definitely not from earth's neck of the woods. They not only bleed, but they also stop being invisible when dead. So, others can see them then. I wonder what happens to their visibility if they're wounded, interesting."

"Shooter, are you OK? Are they gone? Oh, sweet Marylou, oh my Lord, would ya look at those beasts? If there's a Hell, then this is what spawned from there. Sweet, sweet, sweet Marylou."

Carl Heffley stood at the edge of the pen. His eyes were as wide as saucers as he pointed his Smith and Wesson .38 caliber revolver every which way.

"It's OK, Carl. They're gone. We got," he said, looking around at the beast carcasses, "about thirteen or fourteen, near as I can tell. Thank God that old Clarence here showed up with both barrels blasting. That was some damn fine shooting, sir… uh, Sheriff, I think we got a problem."

The goat farmer was dead on his feet, his spine straight as a rail, held up by a fence post, both shotguns still smoking in his clenched hands, his one eye wide open, and the biggest shit-eating grin of his life on his lips. Clarence McDougal, one of the last goat farmers in Worcester County and the only blind man who could help Marble get rid of the beasts, there he proudly stood, one extremely happy dead man.

"Dang, Clarence, you didn't have to go and die on us now. His heart must have conked out with all the excitement."

"That's what I call going out in a blaze of glory." Marble reverently reached up and closed Clarence's eye, then carefully removed the shotguns from his hands. "Thank you, kind sir, and have some fun wherever it is you're going."

"You can pry my guns from my cold hands when I'm dead and gone. Now I know what that looks like. Sweet Marylou, what a stink we got here, though."

Marble looked at Carl. "Yeah, they smell like sewer back up. I rolled right into one, too, not to mention goat guts and turds. Do you mind if we call this deputy thing off for the night? I stink and I'm tired. Besides, I don't know how many of these things are out there, but we just put a serious hurting on them tonight. Me and old Clarence, here, God rest his soul."

"Mr. Marble, uh, Shooter, listen, let's get a move on… I got a body bag in the trunk; never had to use it yet, though. I'll go get it and call LoBaido's Funeral Parlor so Bernie can come and get him. Nah, second thought, I don't wanna leave his body out here for those things to get at. And I don't want anybody else to see these carcasses. We'll take Clarence to the funeral home ourselves." Carl took hold of Clarence's body and gently laid him down to the ground.

"Sweet Marylou, Clarence, now who's gonna make your good cheese?"

***

"I ain't ever been in a news van before; been in vans, sure, but never a news van. What do all these buttons do?"

Jackie had just climbed into the WTTE-TV Mobile unit #4, and Iguana knew he'd just broken a couple of hundred company rules by allowing her in but then no one would know. Or so he thought.

"Now just keep your hands on me, pretty lady. Don't start messing with any of those instruments. That could get old Iguana here in one heap of cow's shit." He inhaled deeply and the marijuana joint flared at its end.

She moved in closer, her hands tickling his goatee. "I wouldn't want you to get in any trouble, sorry, baby. Why do they call you Iguana?" She pressed her lips to his and he shot-gunned his exhale, her tongue teasing his lightly.

"Couple of reasons, sweetness. Why don't you dribble off them Bobby Brooks and let me show you one of them?"

He pulled her close and buried his tongue deep inside her mouth. Several minutes later, they both came up for air.

"Whoa. Can that tongue do some other things besides

kissing my mouth? I am so very ready to feel it again.”

“Oh, you are one naughty little girl, aren’t you? Shimmy off that skirt and panties and let old Iguana work his magic.”

Jackie hesitated for a moment. She had talked about sex so much sometimes it felt as if she was an old pro. The truth of the matter was that she still had her virginity, and no matter how much experience she spouted, this was still a big deal. And she really, really, really had hoped her first time wouldn’t happen in a van, even if it was a news van. Besides, no one had ever pleased her orally and she knew that there would be no turning back if she allowed that to occur.

A knock on the driver’s door window saved her virtue for another night.

“Jiminy. What the fuck? That scared the crap outta me.” Iguana climbed back into the captain’s chair behind the wheel and rolled down the window.

Popeye Worthington filled his vision, and the big man came right to the point. “Not that it’s any of my business what you and that *underage* young lady do in your spare time, but I think you’re in this town to find the news and it’s not, I repeat, it’s not going to be found on Jackie’s *underage* body. What do you think I was supposed to do since you parked right next to my truck? And besides, if you have a camera handy, you’ll get a hankering real quick to have a gander at something truly newsworthy. I can guarantee you never filmed nothing like this before. Come on.”

It wasn’t a request. Popeye opened the driver’s door and grabbed a hold of Iguana’s left arm, pulling him out.

“Whoa, whoa, whoa, hold on, Sasquatch dude. I’m coming, I’m coming. Let me grab my gear.” He pulled his camera and bag off of the passenger chair and turned back to look at Jackie. “You mean you’re not eighteen?” She shrugged. “Shit, get out of my van, dude."

Iguana adjusted his beret. "Now where's this news you were talking about?"

Popeye leaned past him and looked into the van. "Jackie, you get on home now, you hear? And no funny stuff. No matter what you see, you drive right to your house and right into your garage, you hear me clear? The good Lord will be with you. I promise."

A large meaty paw landed on Iguana's shoulder. "Come on, Romeo, this way. Fire that picture-taker up."

Iguana shouldered his camera and mumbled, "The name is Iguana, not Romeo. We got a Romeo at the station and he's a real douche bag."

***

Sheriff Heffley and Marble had just delivered Clarence McDougal's body to LoBaido's Funeral Parlor when the radio squawked.

"This is gonna be one long night... Sheriff Heffley here... 10-4... no, don't go anywhere near it... you mean you can see it? No, Lou, no vigilante crap, you hear... Lou, have you seen Clydesdale anywhere... yeah, yeah, good... now you behave. I'll be there in a jiff.

"That was Lou Ottney. Apparently some really ugly creature that looks like a big shiny bear with wings just materialized on top of Clydesdale's marina office."

Marble's window was down, his head about as far out into the breeze as possible. He wistfully thought about how great a hot shower was going to feel. As the adrenaline faded from his system, fatigue crept in. He really didn't want to do anything else; his brain was on the point of total shut down and his shoulder was so numb he could barely raise his arm. This had been, without a doubt, the most bizarre day of his life since he was ten years old, and his brother Martin, committed mass murder.

"Did you say Lou could see it? Maybe, ah hell, I don't know…"

"What? Go on, we're all flying by the seat of our pants tonight. Any idea is worth hearing."

"Maybe it's one I shot but didn't kill. Maybe, wherever they come from, their powers to stay invisible diminish when wounded. We know they materialize when killed. You saw that for yourself." Marble reloaded the shotgun. "What the hell, I got a few ounces of spark left."

"Nope, you've done enough. I took an oath to serve and protect and if this thing can be seen, I'm gonna take it out. Sweet Marylou, would you look at that. What are those two a-holes doing?"

Heffley swung the cruiser into the spot in front of Clydesdale's and shone his spotlight's powerful beam onto the lurking creature perched on the roof of the marina office.

"Hey. Get outta there, now."

The sheriff hustled from the car and inched his way toward a very excited Iguana, camera locked and loaded and pointed at the beast. A visibly nervous Popeye stood behind him.

"Thanks for the extra light, officer. Oh baby, Emmy here I come; un-fucking believable, un-fucking believable." Excitement poured off Iguana.

"Back away, back away. These beasts are very, very dangerous." Carl Heffley had his Smith and Wesson .38 caliber pistol out and with a two-hand stance, zeroed in on the creature.

Marble quickly got out of the cruiser too and approached the marina office slowly. He glided to the opposite side of the other three men, his eyes never leaving the beast. As his guess proved right, the heavily panting creature had a damaged right wing and thick green/yellow ooze spurted out an open wound with every labored breath. Marble picked up the creature's thoughts when it turned cloud-yellow eyes in his direction. 'A nossa mae, a nossa mae, a nossa mae.'

"I don't understand. What do you mean?"

Marble didn't get the chance to receive a reply because Heffley fired his revolver, pop, pop, pop. The creature reared its hideous head back and wailed a long, eerie siren that resembled a train whistle. It then slid off the marina's slanted roof and splashed into Assawoman Bay.

The sound of an engine starting caused Marble to turn and he watched a very animated Iguana talking into a cell phone as he did a U-Turn with the news van and headed north up Main Street. Popeye and the sheriff crossed to Marble and stared into the water below the dock.

"Beware the hounds of Hell. Dear Jesus, my Savior, I hope this isn't the start of the Rapture. I haven't even had a chance to be with a woman yet."

"That ain't a hound, that's a bird of some kind, as if there is another world or dimension besides this one. Sweet Marylou, all of this is starting to hurt my head, geez, this is Clydesdale, we're supposed to be a sleepy, unpretentious little bay town."

An out of breath Lou Ottney ran up to them, wielding the largest wrench Marble had ever seen. "Oh baby, what a sight, what a sight. Come from one of them flying saucers, right? What kind of planet was it from? Anybody know?" He stank of the sixteen or so beers he had consumed that night, and his slurred words barely made any sense.

"Sweet Marylou, we gotta put this town to bed. Come on

folks, the show is over, move along, nothing else to see here. Lou, go to bed. Mr. Popeye, go to… well, wherever you want. Mr. Marble, let me get you back to the Paradise."

The creature's dying thoughts perplexed Marble. His head definitely hurt and not just because of the bruise from earlier in the day. This vision thing really drained his energy. He rubbed his neck as fatigue grabbed a hold of his body and he gladly walked back toward the police car.

They eased past Popeye as he climbed into his Peterbilt, and Marble couldn't help but marvel at this delayed reaction: *You mean Popeye's a virgin?*

<h1 style="text-align:center">15</h1>

As Popeye Worthington climbed into the cramped quarters at the rear of his Peterbilt cabin, he felt a shudder of fear when the unearthly cry reached his ears. It emanated from inside Willem's marina office, and the timbre, the decibel level and the haunting din caused every goose bump on his body to stand at full attention.

There was no need to peek out the passenger window to see what unearthly creature caused the noise. No, he was alone and safe in his cab for God was with him, he knew that to the very core of his being.

He also knew that God had delivered Larry Marble into Clydesdale for a reason that may very well help answer queries about the disappearance of his good friend, Captain Turner Smythe.

Popeye bowed his head and prayed, the Good Lord calmed him, and soon sleep came to his large body, good, sound slumber where he dreamed of Callie's laugh.

***

Marble trudged up the stairs of Ismelda's Paradise B&B, disrobing as he went. His clothes reeked of dead beast and goat shit. Once in the bathroom, he opened the small window above the toilet and threw them out onto the tiled roof below the dormer. He took a moment to look up into the dark sky, a blackness that held more of the beasts, somewhere out there. He had been witness to nightmares that evening and his childhood fear of trolls somehow lost a bit of its élan. Despite the mugginess of the evening, a chill ran up his spine and he closed the window, turned on the shower and climbed in.

Some of the simplest physical pleasures in life, Marble tiredly thought, were a deep shoulder massage, dropping a healthy deuce and a soothing, hot shower. And, of course, sex. *Oh crap, I never said goodnight to Jasmine.* Two hours had elapsed, and midnight was about to chime. He knew it was too late to call her, and besides, the water helped wash away the stink, and he let his mind close a few doors at the same time. He stuck his face into the pulsing beat of water, cleansing, soothing as the streams cascaded over his scalp, neck, and back. *Tomorrow... and what the hell did* "atlas, the props at sea run blue" *mean, and why was I called* "the prophet"? *And what the heck does* "nossa mae" *mean?*

Marble couldn't think further – it actually hurt, so he shut it down, turned off the shower, dried off, and then wrapped the towel around his torso and exited towards his room. There was enough illumination cast from a night light in the hallway to guide his way, and he dropped the towel by the side of the bed. He stretched, touching the sky and then his toes, grateful of the cracks as his spine realigned. He then slid beneath the covers buck naked, never once aware of the Gucci travel bag that hung on the foot of the canopied bed post.

***

The gnarly nest portal glowed with a blood-rich light, finally calm after the beast within its tangled portal had screamed for vengeance. The pulsing glow refracted through the nicotine-stained window of Willem's office, casting a blinking orb that reflected off the brackish waters of the marina, a buoy light from an alien land.

The wailing cry of the dying beast on the roof, the sound of gunshots, even the blood-curdling howls from the nest portal, none of them even caused the severely drunk Willem to awake from his stupor. He lay curled in a fetal position on the floor behind the desk, an empty bottle of Jack Daniel's cradled in his arms.

His snores shook the cheap paintings that hung on the walls and kept the rats at bay from their nightly scurries about the docks. As the nest portal settled, the world outside the marina office began to lick its wounds.

Carl Heffley finally pulled the cruiser into his driveway on Beresford Road and called it a night. He knew that the next day would be very busy indeed. Looking about to the night's sky, he shuddered thinking how many more of the beasts were still at large. Reassuringly, he patted his holstered revolver, entered his house, and kissed his wife, Marylou, as she lay asleep in bed.

He switched off his phone and said a prayer for Clarence, Marylou, and Shooter Marble. Witching hour was afoot, so Carl kept his Smith & Wesson on the nightstand. Sleep would come fitfully for the good lawman.

Several blocks away, bayside, a different serenade rang out over the crabgrass, petunias, and azaleas of town square.

If one stood in the middle of Main Street, with Callie's and Willem's marina on one side and Lou Ottney's Body Shop and the A&P on the other, somewhere around two a.m., an almost perfectly balanced duet of snoring drowned out the crickets and peepers of the marsh. Lou Ottney never made it past the first lift in an open garage bay and he lay flat on his back, snoring in perfect harmony with Willem across the street.

Silently, stealthily, a single figure of a woman, dressed in a long black cloak and hood with a huge black crow on her shoulder, glided through the snoring duet and headed north on Main Street toward Ismelda's Paradise B&B.

If not for invisible, horrifying beasts from another dimension, it was just another September night in Clydesdale, Maryland.

***

Marble effortlessly pushed away a heavy wooden door, made of randomly interlocked black twigs that opened into a world unlike any he'd ever seen. Muddled hues were the palette of this strange land: a stark, barren desert landscape, a sky the color of sulfur, and a few leafless trees petrified the color of soiled chalk. Scattered on the ground was a graveyard of bone shards, most baked to alabaster by an alien star. Marble knew this was a dream but still the place frightened him, and that fear heightened when he turned around to go back through the door and found no portal to be there.

He turned around again, and again, and again. As his breathing increased and his blood pressure rose, to his right he saw a figure approach. It moved much quicker than normal speed though, and in seconds he could see the face of his oncoming visitor. Aha, he thought, the woman on the porch swing, the woman hung at the old oak tree, the woman seen in a dream with bird's feathers growing out of her skin. This version of her was nothing short of breathtakingly beautiful.

She smiled coyly at Marble and extended her hand. As she

did, her cloak opened, revealing nothing but nakedness beneath. Marble's mind smiled because even in an alien world, he still got some candy in his dreams. He touched her hand and was instantly transported back to the confines of a room in a cottage filled with sunlight. A bed of goose down sat in a cozy corner, and Marble could hear birds singing through the open windows.

His beautiful guest lifted her cloak from her shoulders and let it fall to the floor. Marble was aware that he too was naked, and if this was only a dream, well, he was guaranteed to perform magnificently.

She led him to the bed and then lay down and turned her back to him. She pulled him down to lie behind her, the wonderfully classic spoon position. Marble marveled at how real she felt. His hands, his skin, his manhood, all felt alive and hungry for as much of her as she was willing to give. As he entered her from behind, she moaned, and it was the first time he'd heard her voice. Something about it was familiar, and he felt remarkably at peace. Their bodies moved in rhythm, his hands glided over her stomach, her breasts, and her neck. All of her, every motion, every curve, and every kiss felt so familiar, so right.

They came together and without further movement, fell asleep in the same spoon. Sometime later he awoke within his dream, and she was no longer in bed with him, but as he turned to look about the room, she sat on the floor before the fireplace; it was now night, and a gentle fire lit the room.

He came to her, and she pointed to the fire, then looked at Marble, and pointed again to the fire. Following her lead, he watched as a screen appeared in the middle of the flames and within that a picture of a room that looked so familiar. As the view of the room changed, a vision of a walled off fireplace appeared and above it a painting of a snowy egret in a marsh.

He knew this room, his dream mind told himself, he knew this room. Ismelda's. Yes. And then before his eyes, one of the beasts from the night before came into the painting and snatched the egret with its fangs, and blood spattered everywhere.

Marble awoke with a start. All a dream, he thought, this is reality, this place, this bed. The room was still dark, and he was on his right side, facing the window to the street. A soft glow emanated from a late rising moon, and he let his very heavy eyelids drift back toward sleep and hopefully, calmer, saner dreams.

***

Iguana awoke with a start and banged his shin on the underside of the news van. The alarm on his watch had chimed, and he fumbled to turn it off. Parked outside of Ismelda's, he looked around to see if anyone was out and about yet. It was six a.m. and he had to pee badly, but first he wanted to turn on the satellite computer to download the night's remarkable footage. He took the DVD from the chest pocket of his vest and placed it in the console's receiver. First stop of its journey, WTTE in Harrisburg, next stop ABC, next stop NY Times, next stop, stardom for moi, he thought, giggling like a schoolgirl.

The system lights powered on and while the warm-up and connections cycles were completing, Iguana skooched toward the aft side of the van and opened one of the swing doors.

A light mist arose from the bay on his left as he jumped down onto the pavement. Ahead of him sat the remains of the oak tree and Marble's car. "Whoa, cool, now that's a definition of crushed."

He took a glance up at Ismelda's and wondered what kind of mood Deelah, the news bitch, would be in today. "Probably her patented raging maniac mood," and for the second time that morning, he giggled. The video scoop he filmed the night before would quickly open doors for him at a network level, leaving bitchy Deelah in the boondocks. He crossed the street to the narrow strip of sand that rimmed the western side of the bay, unzipped his fly, and let the stream pour forth.

Across the bay, the rising sun had difficulty climbing over a stretch of low hanging clouds. The resultant effort had turned the whole morning horizon a rioja red.

What was that saying? Oh yeah, he thought, red sky at night, sailor's delight, red sky at morning, sailor's warning. Well, red sky at morning, Iguana is performing.

He did the obligatory shakes and was just about to zip it up when a squadron of mosquitoes, out on reconnaissance for a breakfast feast, descended on him, attacking every inch of exposed skin.

A man's penis is a sensitive barometer of pain, pleasure, and satisfaction. No teeth, please. No zippers, please. No crotch kicks or knee jerks, please. And now, as Iguana squealed like a puppy, he could add, no mosquito bites, please.

In the process of swatting the attackers away from his face, neck, hands, and exposed forearms, he not only caught his manhood in his zipper, but also inadvertently smacked himself hard in the family halupkis. Yes, Matilda, that will bring a man of any size to his knees.

In Iguana's case, it also brought him to his side, as he rolled with nausea. Which helped explained why he never saw the large black crow enter his open news van and then reemerge a minute later with a disc in its beak.

Stardom, alas, would have to wait for itchy, achy dick Iguana.

***

Deelah opened her eyes. It took a moment for her to adjust to the morning light and her strange surroundings. She was lying on her left side, facing a wall painted in a soft rose color.

The throbs in her head and nose were still present but the pain behind her eyes was greater. The whole flask of scotch, she silently scolded herself. She should know better. At least it helped her sleep soundly though. A warm rush washed through her, and she marveled at how she could still think about sex.

I'm naked in bed and feeling incredibly horny this morning. That hasn't happened since, well, since the early, good days with Marble. Then she remembered the events that led up to her knockout punch the night before. Marble… she thought she had seen her ex-husband.

Even a tough exterior can melt at times, and Deelah felt her eyes well up. *Oh Marble, baby, I'm so sad right now. So alone. I wish you were here…*

It was a queen-size bed, and when Marble rolled over, he found himself spooning a beautifully-built naked woman. This was no dream though. He scaled the ladder to consciousness. As he awoke he realized the rest of his body was already up and ready for action. But who was this woman in bed with him?

Marble opened his eyes at the same moment a surprised Deelah turned to face the naked man who pressed his woody into her ass.

No screams, no tirades, no curses, no words at all. Deelah's tough exterior, the raging bitch persona, was on hiatus. Her lips opened to his mouth, and they hungrily met. They rocked the squeaky, queen-size bed in hedonistic fervor, taking the sex to a level achieved by the lucky in life.

Closure sex, one time for memory's sake, one more for the Gipper, break-up sex, whatever the moniker, they rocked one day after divorce. The realization would hit him later in the day that Deelah had inadvertently entered the wrong room after her drunken shower and climbed into Marble's bed by mistake. There it was again, synchronicity. No problems, only solutions.

When they finished, Marble rolled to his back, catching his breath and marveling that he had come to the shore hoping to relive a distant memory of different sex partners in the same day, and sure enough, some memories were passable.

The real icing on his self-praised cake was the fact that the this woman was his ex-wife. Marble remembered his dream from the night before. The sex with the bird woman had felt so real, so familiar, so much like… o*h God. Deelah must have been in the bed when I had fallen asleep.* He had been too tired to even notice. And the very sexy dream had in fact been real sex with Deelah.

He turned to look at her. She was beautiful, that was never the issue. But he hadn't seen her like this in over six years. Her hair was down and sprawled all over her pillow. She had no makeup on and even the large red welt swelling out of each side of her nose was cute.

"What are you doing here? Did you know this was my room? I'm not complaining, not one bit. That was incredible, by the way."

Deelah hadn't enjoyed a rock-em, sock-em orgasm in far too long. And she had never had multiple ones, not even close. The wonderful sensations that soared through her body were new to her and it made her tongue work far too slowly, her voice was softer and sultry, and despite the little red flags in her head, she wanted this man, this Larry Marble, again. And again.

"I came here to check out a story about… missing birds… I saw you last night at some crab joint… had an accident… knocked out… Bradley left me… oh God… that was so good, baby… Marble, do it again… I never knew that… divorce would make you so hot… last night I came into the wrong room, I guess. I didn't know you were staying here, honest… I'm sorry… no, I'm not."

"Whew, this is tough for me, too, Deelah. Nice, but difficult. I can't stay; I have a job to do. The reason you're here, the reason I'm here, are somewhat the same. I've found out how the birds are dying, now I just need to find out why and how to stop it.

"I'll tell you what. You better get that nose looked at. And I have to go get some breakfast because I'm going to need all the energy I can muster today. But don't you worry, I'll make sure you get the exclusive on this. That much I can do for the woman I loved for the past eight years. By the way, you still are an absolutely incredible fuck."

Marble kissed her softly on the lips. He pulled back the covers on his side, stood up and grabbed a pair of wrinkled Dockers from his bag. Taking a glance out the window, he did a double take. Across the street, a disheveled Iguana rolled about in obvious discomfort, but the sight that caught his eye was the large black crow that flew from the back of the news van with a DVD in its beak.

He looked at his ex-wife with the well-laid look in her eyes. "You might want to rest a bit longer. I'm gonna shower, then head out. We'll catch up later. One more thing, don't listen to any medical advice from an old geezer named Doc Gilbert. Trust me on that one." Marble grabbed clean clothes and quietly left the room.

Deelah was in dopamine and testosterone shock. Overwhelmed, amazed, blown away, pick whatever adjective, she thought, that's how it felt. *Where is that bitch inside of me? Oh God, he fucked it out of me, could that be it? God, that was good.* For the first time in what seemed like eons, Deelah Thayer uttered a tearful prayer of thanks.

16

Willem awoke and immediately faced a warning that the rest of his body wasn't in a cheery mood. *At least I'm still on this side of the grass.* Before his eyes opened, he knew he was about to pay a heavy toll for the previous night's drunkenness. A Jack Daniel's hangover combined with lungs primed with enough tar and nicotine phlegm to fill a brass spittoon were magnified by arthritic stiffness brought on by his repose on the hardwood floor of the office.

He grunted heavily and tried to raise himself up, in the process knocking the empty bottle of whiskey under his desk. A few close encounters with heart failure later, relief now met his eyes as he spied the glass he'd used the night before still perched on the edge of the desk with half a finger's width of whiskey still intact. Hair of the dog that bit ya, he tried to chuckle, but it came out as a hacking cough.

His grimy, sausage-link fingers grabbed the glass. He raised it towards lips the color of fireplace ash. The brown whiskey was warm to his palate, and it worked its magic almost instantly, an alcoholic's Wheaties.

Willem struggled to his feet and stared at the gnarly nest portal on his desk.

"Howdy, partner, how the fuck did you sleep, huh? Jesus, I feel like shit; gotta get some coffee and some real food before this day gets any longer. I know ya want some action today, right? Let's see what old Willem can do for ya, OK?"

He knew he had to be careful because the monster could read

205

his thoughts and there was absolutely no way that he was going to reveal his true intentions. He silently coached himself. *A Clydesdale's mind is a mighty tool, able to block outsiders from gaining entry, even outsiders from another world. Able to leap tall buildings in a single bound.* This time the chuckle came out like a hoarse whisper as he stumbled for the bathroom.

Finished in the head, Willem shuffled out of his office. He paused a moment to glance at the cast-iron safe in the corner next to Patti's desk. It was an antique, manufactured late in the nineteenth century by Carry Safes, Buffalo, New York. The heavy door was open, the interior vacant. Next to the safe was a heavy-duty hand truck that had been placed there the day before by Sheriff Heffley, per *hizzoner's* request.

"Yes, siree, ya gotta get up awful early to fool a Clydesdale… not a nothinglessness alive can do the deed, he-he-he… able to leap tall buildings in a single bound." He cough-laughed again, bending over to pick up the Worcester County daily, *The Crabber*, from the mail slot.

Unfolding the script, the following headlines framed the front page:

Bird Mystery Deepens
>National Media & Scientists Invade Clydesdale
>Clarence McDougal Passes
>Gunshots or Fireworks?
>Crosby Culp Claims Attempted Alien Sexual Abduction

Willem snorted. *Fucking nothinglessnesses. Damn news media are going to make my plans that much harder to accomplish. Yes, well, no Clydesdale ever backed away from a challenge.* He snickered as he returned to the bathroom for round stinky-poo two.

***

Marble dressed quickly after toweling off, including an off-white Oxford that he rebelliously decided to leave untucked. Deelah would have a fit if she saw him… *wait a sec, I don't give a crap what she thinks about how I dress.* He looked in the mirror and smiled. This indeed was a new Larry Marble staring back. Maybe it was the reemergence of his extra sensory powers that contributed to this new swagger, his chiseled mojo, the sparkle in his eyes. He retrieved his stinking clothes from the dormer roof. *Whew, no you don't, outside for all of you again.* He extracted his wallet and cell phone and tossed the soiled duds back outside.

The bump on his head had progressed to a painter's spill of brown, black and purple. He brushed his hair with his hands and winced at the pain that the shotgun's kick-back had inflicted on his right shoulder.

"Suck it up, soldier. There's gonna be a few more rounds fired today." Crazy people talk out loud to themselves. But then, so do sane folk; he chuckled, because he knew he was sane, well, at least for the moment, although Deelah in his bed at Ismelda's Paradise B&B was one to strain the chains of lucidity to a breaking point.

Marble clomped his way down the stairs and then made a sharp turn to his left, down the hallway toward the kitchen at the back of the house. He smelled bacon and his stomach growled in anticipation. Food was needed; his inner eye required sustenance and hot bacon and steaming eggs would fill the coffers nicely.

Thomas Hardy wrote in 1871, "Though a good deal is too strange to be believed, nothing is too strange to have happened." Marble wondered if Hardy would feel the same if he was currently standing in the kitchen doorway of Ismelda's Paradise

B&B. The view that met his eyes as he walked into the brightly lit space definitely put a strain on whatever sanity he still clasped. Jasmine's words from the night before appeared in neon letters in his head: witches. One thing he knew for sure was that Salem, Massachusetts never got a load of this crew.

Anna Smythe was at the stove, dressed in a soft print pastel sundress, delicately highlighting every curve. Her hair was drawn back into a ponytail. Marble marveled at how beautiful it made her neck appear. She turned to smile and offer a greeting, but Marble's gaze had already drifted to Jasmine.

She was dressed in a pink halter top that left a deliciously sumptuous space of skin between her white shorts and chest. Her shapely legs were propped up on a stool, and Marble felt a familiar stir down below.

The real shocker sat at the kitchen table. The black crow woman from yesterday, the same one he remembered visiting him that fateful day in his youth, was delicately feeding a shoebox full of young sparrows and finches with an eye dropper. Sure enough, Marble noticed, she wore the same clothes he'd seen some thirty years before with several long, shiny black feathers askew in her tightly bunned salt-and-pepper hair.

Ismelda, dressed in a blue designer sweatsuit, was also at the table, feeding an obviously distraught Canada goose who was uncomfortably stuffed into a seventy's era high chair. Marble could just discern the faded Flintstones motif on the chair's weathered pleather backing, yabba-dabba-do-do. The color faded fast from Marble's face. The fight or flight switch leaned heavily toward the latter in his mind's control room.

Ismelda broke his fears with warm words. "Our hero arrives, welcome, dear Shooter. Breakfast is almost ready. Eggs and bacon are on the way, Anna Smythe style, which means a bit of spice this morning. Hope you're hungry. Come on, pull up a chair, I believe you know everyone."

Deelah had scolded Marble many times that he possessed one of the best stupid expressions and if an Oscar were ever to be given out for that reason alone, Marble would win hands down. He tried to smile and keep the stupid hidden.

"Uh, good morning to you, too, Ismelda." He looked at the crow woman. "Ma'am." Quickly he looked at Jasmine. "Morning, Jasmine, sorry I didn't get to say goodnight to you properly last evening. I had to, well, you know." Without waiting for a reply, he turned to a smiling Anna. "And good morning to you, Anna. I'd like to come by and look for the, uh, book again today if I may."

Marble felt the sweat start to bead on his forehead and the uncomfortable arrangement of two women he'd had sexual relations with positioned in the same room was a bit daunting. All he needed now was Deelah to waltz in and stupid face would be thanking the Academy.

"Oh, stop this drooling, mistuh Shooter. Sit yerself down on this chair, don't worry ya none… we don't bite." The crow woman laughed heartily, and it sounded more like a cawing than mirth. Marble pulled out a chair and promptly sat, the Looney Tunes bouncing his eyeballs around like super balls.

Jasmine hopped up and crossed to Marble, leaned down, and kissed him warmly on the lips. "Hey, Shooter, you're my hero. You were magnificent last night, baby. And you said goodnight to me in a wonderful fashion, trust me." She skipped playfully back to her stool and Anna approached Marble next. She too leaned down and kissed him. Her lips were wetter and softer than Jasmine's. She applied the subtlest flicker of tongue that titillated every inch of his yummies.

"You can come to my store whenever you want, Shooter. Whenever, for whatever. Now, breakfast is about to be served. Eat, we need you to have your energy." She glided back to the stove, her touch still warm on his body. Marble couldn't fight it off any longer, he let the frontal lobotomy look take over.

"Shooter, this is a Canada goose that Doc Gilbert found in the bay, nearly dead. He brought him to me, and I've been nursing him back to life. And protecting him from, well, I understand you know what I'm protecting him from. He's just about healthy enough to return to the wild."

Marble looked at the bird and the goose returned his gaze. A gentle click of channels changed the picture in his mind. The telepathic images that arrived were magnificent: huge, soaring spectacles from the eyes of a wild Canada bird. They soared over forests, lakes, and open fields. Banking to the left, he saw the rest of the gaggle, all flying in the form of a huge chevron, and he sensed the simple awe of freedom. The wind smelled of clouds and fresh breeze, gentle thermal shoots carried him above a misting glaze. The sun's rays warmed the back of his neck. It was a glorious snippet of freedom, of flight, of the magic of nature.

The connection with the goose snapped shut when Anna leaned in front with a cup of coffee but not before he heard the bird's thanks, the Canada goose's gratefulness at these ground bounders who cared for him. Marble relayed his thoughts of acknowledgement and with it, he knew that he'd touched the mystical side of life, a side only few get to experience: communication with a wild animal.

"Silas. The goose, his name is Silas. Very pleased to meet you, too, Silas."

"Hello, Silas. It's a joy to make your acquaintance." Anna placed a large oval dish on the table, piled high with bacon and steaming scrambled eggs, crab, and cheese. "A bit of fresh diced jalapeno makes this a wonderful way to start a day. And this smells like a huge day to me. Mangia, everyone!"

Marble was famished and he ate with gusto. Despite the genial conversation, he couldn't resist asking the most obvious question. "I never caught your name, ma'am." He had deliberately not looked at the crow woman across from him, but now the question required direct eye contact.

"That's a wonderful question, Shooter. Yes, it is. My name is Carlotta. I apologize for my lack of politeness in never telling you that. Ooh, looks like we got some lying to do, girls, forgive us Good Mother."

A visibly upset Iguana entered the kitchen, sand and gravel still pressed into his left side, and he was burdened with the gaze that most men wore after a shot to the nuts: pissed off with a healthy dose of nausea.

"Excuse me, but did anybody see a DVD that looks like this?" He held up a blank disc but only silence met his inquiry.

Marble turned to face Iguana. "What's up, Iguana? Long time no see."

Iguana was a bit startled. "Oh, uh, hey to you, dude, Mr. Dee. I'm in a bit of a bind, dude. Did you or any of the rest of you ladies see anything like this around? It was in my van, and I've scoured the whole freaking thing looking for that coverage from last night. Come on, anybody?"

"Guess not, Mr. Iguana," said a smiling Ismelda. "Now pull up a chair and have some breakfast. A day never starts off right without a good meal to stoke the fire."

Iguana just stared at everyone with an open-mouthed stupid look. Marble felt a bout of happy as he looked at Iguana. For once, someone else had a better stupid look than him. He was about to offer Oscar praise to the cameraman, but Iguana turned and stormed off down the hallway and out the front door, swearing four-letter bombs in Portuguese the whole way.

"Hmmm, I wonder what that was all about? This is delicious, Anna." Ismelda coyly looked at Marble and winked.

Marble decided to come clean with the witches. It couldn't hurt to keep them on his side, he thought. "Um, last night, back at the marina, Iguana filmed one of the injured beasts. Apparently, once maimed, they become visible. To everyone else, that is. Maybe that's what he's searching for because he seemed pretty excited about it all."

Anna put her left hand on Marble's thigh. "Shooter, we don't want this situation to reach the outside. Most of the world wouldn't comprehend this event. And Clydesdale doesn't want or need that kind of attention. Balance must be returned; the birds must return. Your abilities are essential if we're to deliver these creatures back to their realm. It was fate that brought you here and fate that will control what happens next."

Marble looked about at everyone's eyes. They stared back with an earnestness that he recognized. Red flag Rover waved in his head. *Wait just a halupkis, here*, his mind cautioned. *Am I just being used?* Indignation steamed the back of his neck, and he could feel his ears flush red. The remarkable sexual events of the past twenty-four hours, were they all a ruse to keep him here and happy? And if they were, what was the problem with that? He had come to the shore in hopes of reliving a day from his youth and sure enough, he'd exceeded that. But on the other hand, his car had been crushed. Yes, but that was an act of God. He never resolved the pro and con debate because fate came in the front door of the B&B.

"Excuse me, everyone, but, Mr. Shooter, we got us a, um,

well, a situation. I sure could use your talents again, please, sir."

Sheriff Carl Heffley looked like Rambo, armed to the teeth with two high-powered rifles equipped with scopes and four ammunition belts draped over his shoulders. The only thing missing, Marble thought, was the face paint and headband.

Marble shoved a few huge forkfuls of eggs into his mouth, downed a tumbler of orange juice, picked up a handful of bacon, and stood. "Help you want, help it is you get, ladies. I don't know how you finagled me to end up here, but now that I am, I plan on doing what I can with this gift of sight. In the meantime, keep giving me the same hospitality." Shakespeare wrote in *Julius Caesar*, "Cowards die many times before their deaths; the valiant never taste of death but once." Marble wasn't planning on dying soon but just to be sure, he bent over and valiantly planted a kiss on Anna's lips that should have been accompanied by a swell of violins and cellos.

"Shooter." Anna tried to catch her breath. Her cheeks flushed, her breasts pressed outward for more space, her lips glistened. "Oh my, oh my. There must be a portal for these beasts. I – we – don't know what form it's in. We do suspect that Clydesdale knows about it. Can you see anything? Have you seen anything? In your visions?"

Marble looked into her eyes and his pro/con debate was settled. Their affections had helped his powers to come out again and they, hell, this town, the birds, they all deserved his help.

"I'll do my best. And I will search for an answer about your late husband in the process. I promise you that. I promise all of you that. But I won't guarantee that this stuff won't leak out to the world. That's a bit selfish on your parts, ladies, you should know better. Far too many eyes have fallen upon this town now. I recommend just go with the flow. Oh, and I could use some clothes cleaned, Ismelda; if you have a washer handy, that would be swell. Good day, ladies." John Wayne would have nodded in classic Duke fashion with a tip of the ol' Stetson. Marble reached to tip his imaginary Stetson and then turned and walked down the hallway, his spurs clicking on the wood panels, his thumbs in the lips of his leather chaps, a wonderful direction on day two of the Grand Plan. He smiled to himself because he felt better than he had in years.

Outside, parked behind the police car, a very disconsolate Iguana sat on the rear bumper of the WTTE-TV news van, his head in his hands. The sheriff and Marble were about to climb into the police cruiser when Deelah came running from the Paradise front door.

"Marble. Wait for me. We'll follow you, honey. Thank you, thank you, thank you. Oh God, pull your shit together Iguana, and fire up this baby. We've got a fucking exclusive to work, boy."

Marble stared at his ex-wife with awe while sporting his award-winning stupid face. Deelah wore hip-hugger jeans, sneakers and a soft yellow middriff top. A black ABC News baseball cap covered her head, and her hair was back in a ponytail, a favored look he hadn't seen for almost seven years. Large black sunglasses hid some of the bruises, but Marble could still identify the swelling as she came up to him, kissed him warmly on the lips, and then ran back to the news van.

Anticipation of what was about to unfold for the day – that should have been the primary thought process in his mind. *Find some kind of portal, as Anna had described, look into my visions and search for clues. Blow away the beasts that are still out there, invisible and hidden in the trees. Figure out the strange messages from the night before.* All of these should have been foremost in his thoughts. Marble still hadn't made the connection between Ismelda's specially concocted beverages and his overly sensitive libido. Instead, as a stirring started to grow in his navy-blue Dockers, all he could think about was how great Deelah looked in her jeans.

17

"Shooter, I hope you slept well because I'm afraid we got some more of those devil's beasts on the prowl. Seems they ripped the shingles off of Tommie's Chicken Farm coops and made a real mess of things. Apparently, chickens aren't gonna be safe in these parts either. For me, dang, I had some awful nightmares. Sweet Marylou comforted me as best she could, God bless her precious heart, but still, those ugly creatures kept creeping back into my head every time I closed my eyes."

Carl Heffley sped north on Main Street with siren blaring, the same avenue that Marble had unwittingly used to enter Clydesdale two days earlier. The sheriff looked disheveled, a button missing on his khaki shirt and his face unshaven. Marble munched on bacon strips, shoving them into his mouth in one huge helping as Carl continued his briefing. "Want some bacon?"

"What? Nah, I'm good. Here's where it gets more complicated. Seems Tommie's coops extend a couple of hundred yards, south to north, as the crow flies. The south side of the coops got massacred but the north side has a boatload of scared pullets, squawking like maniacs. They only attacked the south side. There's nothing, no wall or nothing, stopping the beasts from killing the rest, but Tommie says only the birds in the southern section have been attacked; he's afraid the north side will all die of heart attacks. What do ya make of that?"

Bacon seemed to make all wrong right, or at least that's what his stomach relayed. Still, he knew focus was paramount, so

Marble thought about the events of the past twenty-four hours: the visions, the messages, the invisible beasts, and the irony of waking up in bed with his ex. He turned to look behind and saw the news van on their tail. Find the portal, those were Anna's instructions, and he set his inner eye in search for answers.

"Sheriff, I've a feeling this whole mess ties into your mayor, Clydesdale. These creatures aren't from our dimension, and I need to find the doorway to that world so I can send them back. Yesterday, when I stopped in to offer my apologies for denting the hood of his truck, the mayor's desk, which has to be a good five hundred pounds, levitated off the ground and started spinning. That's not normal behavior, not in this dimension. Do you have any idea what Clydesdale might be up to?"

Carl squirmed in his seat, reached over, and snagged a bacon strip from Marble, never once taking his eyes off the road. "Willem is an odd duck, that's for sure. He's been acting super strange the past couple of days, more so than usual; keeps carrying around this bundle with him. Don't rightly know what's wrapped up in that blanket but he's real secretive about it." He wiped the sweat from his brow. "Willem, we been friends, me and him, a long time; well, not the type of friend I invite over to my house – my bride, Marylou, won't allow him to set foot on our property. More of a careful friendship, you know what I mean? Me and him keep our distance, friendly like. Dang, this is good bacon.

"But yesterday he asked me to wheel over this old cast-iron safe from Lou's garage. Seems Lou's back couldn't handle the thing and Willem ain't never been one to do something physical, so I got the call. I wheeled this heavy old safe into his office, right next to Patti's desk. He wouldn't tell me what for, neither." Sweat poured heavily from his pores despite the air conditioner on full blast. Marble sensed it wasn't from the heat of the day.

"Listen, Sheriff, after we visit the chicken place, can we pay a visit to his office? I need to get some answers and I'd appreciate it if you were with me."

"Uh, sure, yeah, that's a plan. Not a problem." That was an understatement, Marble thought, because to his core he knew that Willem Clydesdale was a problem, a very big problem.

"Here we are, lock and load, Mr. Shooter."

The cruiser turned off onto a dusty driveway, past an old rusty sign that read, TOMMIE'S CHICKEN FARM… BEST TASTING PECKERS IN WORCESTER COUNTY.

Marble tried to laugh at the absurdity of the logo, but it was difficult to emit too much mirth when he was awarded a view of the land. The road led up to three long buildings made of metal, each with a weathered sign on the door: FEED STORE, CHICK STORE, and FRESH KILLED STORE, respectively. Marble felt a cold shudder run down his spine. *Fresh killed store*, now that held an ominous tenor for the day.

As they wound through the dirt parking lot, three football-field-sized chicken coops emerged to the north of them, and Marble saw a daylight version of the beasts. He couldn't get a count because they were crowded together, a mass of them in each coop, about halfway up. Something wasn't right though. The beasts seemed agitated, almost disoriented.

Marble eased out of the cruiser, a scoped .30 caliber Remington 710 rifle in his hands. His nose was punched with the stench of dust and chicken shit but that's not what affected his vision. The mangled thoughts of the creatures zeroed in on his brain and the shock of it made him stagger.

"Mr. Shooter, you OK? Sweet Marylou, do ya see 'em? Huh? Anything?"

"Yeah, they're even uglier in the daylight. I'm OK, really, just a whiff of dead chickens and those smelly beasts, not a welcome aroma so soon after breakfast, that's for sure." Marble steadied with Carl's aid. "They're communicating with me, or at least I'm hearing their thoughts. *Dios mío, besta de rapiñá mae; besta de rapiñá de Espantadas mae.* It's a, a boundary of some sort. This must be their wall, their limit. Something's keeping them from going after the rest of those birds. *'Nossa Mae'* won't let them. That's what they're telling me. *A nossa mae.*"

"What language is that, honey? Is that Spanish? Do you really see something we can't?" It was Deelah, microphone in hand with Iguana circling behind her, camera rolling. They had just appeared, eager for the opportunity.

"No, Dee, it's not Spanish. It's Portuguese. I know, my *avó*, my grandma, was born in the old country, Douro Valley, and she raised me speaking her native tongue. Geez, Mr. Dee, didn't know you were so bilingual."

Marble was confused. Where had those words come from? "I'm not, Iguana. I-I-I'm not sure where, or how I got that."

Iguana lowered his camera, and he carefully chose his words, especially since they made his skin crawl. "A nossa Mae, it means, to our mother, but also you said something like dear God, beasts of prey, the mother devil's beasts of prey. That's freaking—eh spooky, dude, cool in a Goth way, but spooky still."

"Now hold on there, you two. Miss, you and your cameraman get back; this is official police business here."

"It's OK, Carl. I offered them exclusive coverage. Besides, each one of those Tommie's Chicken Farm employees has a cell phone and pictures will hit YouTube before lunch, I guarantee it."

The sheriff looked like he'd seen a ghost. Sweat now seeped through his shirt. "Uh, Mr. Shooter, this ain't gonna go over well with the… with, uh, the powers; shoot, I mean… aw, sweet Marylou, let's get this over with."

Marble looked past the sheriff and saw a group of Tommie's employees huddled on the loading dock area of the FRESH KILLED STORE. Despite the stench and the rapidly escalating heat of the day, he took a deep breath and turned to Deelah. Something about her was different. Marble sensed it deeply. This was the woman he'd fallen in love with over eight years ago, the pre-bitch days. And yet, he knew right there on the dusty, dirt-covered yard that reeked of chicken shit, he knew that he could never go back to those days again. This time with Deelah was closure, no matter how good she looked in her jeans.

"Deelah, when I kill them, they become visible. I don't know anything about them except this: they are not from this world. Where they are from is also unknown. Just watch, oh and uh, cover your noses."

"Marble, when did you learn Portuguese?"

Marble shrugged and shouldered his weapon. Michael Madsen gave him a standing ovation, minimalist acting, baby, minimalist acting.

Deelah touched his arm. "Be careful, honey."

Marble pressed the stock into his sore right shoulder and sighted the first coop. He panned over the roofs and noticed the torn off tin shingles where the beasts had entered. He focused in on the first creature and marveled at the colors visible in daylight. Shades of indigo, black, and orange seemed to flow over their shiny matted feathers, like giant grackles. They had huge wings with razor sharp horns protruding from the ribs of the arms and long pointed heads, crowned by tufts of matted feathers, an alien version of a bad mullet. He steadied the crosshairs on a target.

The first shot tore through the beast and exploded into a

second one right behind it. That's when the cries of fear started. The beasts in all three coops clawed and crowded each other, ripping, and tearing at their peers to find the openings in each roof. Marble fired repeatedly. As each beast fell and became visible, the gasps escalated from the onlookers behind him. One of Tommie's employees screamed to high heaven, and it echoed the cries from the dying beasts.

There were over a hundred of the winged creatures in the coops and the realization spooked Marble. *Too many, far too many for one man, one gun.* "Sheriff, point your rifle below the opening in the roof of the coop on the far left. Aim four feet above the ground and pattern east to west. Shoot until I tell you to stop."

Carl knelt into a firing position, took aim, and fired. But even the two rifles were not enough as Marble watched the escaped beasts regroup into tight formation high above the yard. They formed a series of circles, smaller ones surrounded by larger and larger rings. Marble raised his rifle and fired into the inner circle. He had a hunch that this was where the leaders of the pack were. And he was right. He hit three of the inside loop, which caused the outer rings to disperse into panic and they flew off to the south, beyond his sight.

"Sheriff, that's enough, they're gone now." The beasts Marble had shot from above landed with huge smelly thuds only yards from Deelah and Iguana.

"Holy shit, how cool is this? Dee, we got us some beaucoup big press out of this footage, you and me going to the stars, who-eee." Iguana circled the carcasses, one hand over his nose as he zoomed in for close-ups.

Marble turned to Deelah. Her sunglasses were in her hand and the look on her face was complete astonishment. Bruised but astonished.

"We have to keep going, Deelah. I'll catch up with you later this morning, OK? Oh, and a word of advice. Don't send out any of this until I tell you. My business here isn't finished and the less notoriety, the better. Besides, as soon as you release this to the world, the world will be here looking for their own stories. And your exclusive will be gone, know what I mean?"

Deelah was speechless and Marble smiled to himself. There hadn't been many moments like this in the past eight years. He walked up to her and kissed her lightly on the cheek.

"See ya back at the Paradise in a couple of hours, OK?"

Deelah only nodded as Marble walked back to the police car. "Sheriff, we have an appointment with hizzoner, I believe."

Carl Heffley's color had faded to light green and his hands trembled. He nodded wordlessly to Marble, swallowed hard, clicked on the safety on his weapon, and got behind the wheel. The car rolled around the other astonished humans and sped down the dirt path, headed for another Clint Eastwood showdown.

Deelah stared hard at the dead carcasses of the beasts as Iguana positioned himself for a news byte presentation. She adjusted her sunglasses and faced the camera. *Bobby Kaster, you dumb sonofabitch, this one backfired on your fat ass, because I've got the story of the century right here, motherfucker.*

* * *

The Isle of Wight Wildlife Management Area sits five miles south of Clydesdale, at the intersection of St. Martins Neck Road and Route 90. A tidal marsh region, home to herons, geese, bufflehead ducks and a colorful, varied assortment of marsh birds, it is also hunting, trapping, and fishing locale. On the same warm September morning that Marble and gang were at

Tommie's Chicken Farm, a very different form of activity developed on the nearby bay.

A Coast Guard helicopter stationed out of Fenwick Island, Delaware, on routine patrol over the barrier island of Ocean City received a frantic call from a fisherman in one of the inlets off the Isle of Wight. Eddie Bierlitsky had been trolling for bottom dwelling flounder when the dying carcass of one of the beasts injured at Tommie's Chicken Farm dropped itself sloppily into the bow section of his skiff. The beast looked at Eddie and cried a final shrieking death wail as its cloud-yellow eyes faded rapidly to murky grey.

Eddie almost dropped his cell phone overboard as he scrambled backward toward the aft side of the boat. He dialed 911 and since he was on a body of water, the call was dispatched to Lt. Kerrie Peluso's headset.

She banked the Dauphin H-65A neatly over the hotels and condos of Ocean City and sped westward towards the Isle of Wight. A pilot with over two hundred hours under her belt, the lieutenant had little difficulty locating Eddie Bierlitsky's skiff. He was standing in his bay boat, waving his arms wildly. What really got her attention though was the huge, black, shiny carcass of the dead beast sprawled out over his bow. Its wing span had to be at least eight feet, she calculated.

Lt. Peluso brought the craft into a hover position above Eddie's boat and, in an instant, the world was made aware of tiny Clydesdale's plight, despite the witches' hopes. The pack of leaderless beasts that had fled to the southernmost boundary of their territory hysterically converged on the same spot as the helicopter and the mighty blades tore into over thirty of the invisible beasts, covering the copter and poor Eddie Bierlitsky in a visible hamburger hash of putrid alien muck.

***

Willem paid for his morning egg and cheese sandwich and coffee with a twenty but didn't wait for the change, a clear sign that all was not well in Mayor Prickface's penny-pinching world. Jackie wasn't certain if it was a tip, so she placed it in an envelope, just in case the sonofabitch remembered later.

Popeye Worthington opened the passenger door of his Peterbilt cab and stretched out his huge body on the outside step. Willem looked up from Callie's takeout window and scurried quickly back towards his office. The big black nothinglessness was not going to ruin his breakfast this morning, nosiree.

Willem burst in through the marina office's front door and a startled Patti jumped up and knocked a stack of papers onto the floor.

"Willem, you're not going to believe this. The governor of the state is on the phone for you. Can you believe it? The freaking-a governor."

Willem just stared at his former lover and processed the thought that the governor on the phone was obviously not going to be good news. Heat began to boil up his spine and turn his thick neck a purple red. He hadn't expected this predicament, no way; this one had snuck up on him. *Stupid. Stupid. Stupid.* He scolded himself silently.

"Transfer the mealy-mouthed bastard to my office phone. I can't wait to hear what this panty wearing nothinglessness has to say to me."

Patti couldn't resist the chuckles again as he slammed his door. "Mister Governor? Yes, that was the mayor's voice, yes, sir… yes, sir, he's always a bit surly in the morning… I'll transfer you to hizzoner now. Have a good day, sir." She hit the send button and laughed out loud as she reached for her thermos. *This deserves a drink*, she giggled, *because Mayor Prickface didn't even know that his insults were broadcast over speaker phone to the governor's office in Annapolis.* "Oh, this is gonna be a whopper of a morning," she said as the first sip of Southern Comfort coffee met her lips.

Willem set down his coffee and sandwich. He picked up his phone and hit the blinking "call waiting" light.

"Mr. Governor, to what do I owe this honor, sir?"

"Mr. Clydesdale, is it? I understand that you have yourself a dicey situation there in Clydesdale. I've heard some disturbing reports that something is killing all the birds in your area. You are aware of this, Mr. Mayor, are you not?"

Willem draped the old oilcloth over the resting nest portal. "Oh that, yes, I've been made aware of that dilemma. We have a number of scientists in town attempting to pinpoint this travesty." This is pure bullshit, he silently fumed as he took a huge bite from his sandwich.

"Excellent, Mister Clydesdale, but I'm afraid I must now commit a bit more firepower to this situation. In case you haven't been made aware of it yet, allow me to be the first to inform you.

"Approximately twenty minutes ago, a U.S. Coast Guard helicopter responding to an emergency call near the Isle of Wight encountered a huge flock of – what were they called – oh yes, a huge flock of invisible, unidentified raptors. Uh, is this right, Shirley? *Invisible* raptors? Whatever, it was a flock large enough to cause the helicopter to crash into the marshes off the Isle of Wight.

"Fortunately, none of the crew was injured badly. But this incident calls—no, it screams for direct support from the proud state of Maryland and specifically from my office. I shouldn't have to state the obvious, but the media has snagged this one by the nuts and that opens up a whole new ball-busting scenario."

Silence met the governor.

"Mister Mayor, are you with me still?"

Willem's chest felt like it was about to explode but he swallowed his mouthful anyway. He sat back heavily into his swivel chair and farted for a good ten seconds. *Ah good, not a heart attack after all.* The stench of flatulence, stale cigarettes and sour whiskey almost made him puke. He swallowed back the eruption.

"That's tragic. No, I haven't been apprised of this situation yet. Is there anything I can do, sir?" Dear God, he hated kissing this nothinglessness' ass, he steamed to himself.

"You just maintain the peace in your town, Mister Mayor. I've ordered in a regiment of the Maryland National Guard in the event I need to proclaim martial law. Their firepower will bring this issue to a head. I am certain of it. Your cooperation with the commanding officer is required, sir."

Willem knew that the governor was just being polite. He hated nothinglessnesses who couldn't say it like they meant it. His cooperation was *mandatory*, asshole. There, that's better. Willem had no choice but to be cooperative. *But the fucking National Guard coming into my town?* This was now past the point of his control. "Of course, Mister Governor. Complete compliance. Yes, sir." *You panty wearing ass wipe.*

"I'd like to say this has been a pleasure talking to you, Mister Mayor, but I'm afraid your previous insults will prevent me from extending that nicety. Hopefully, that's not too mealy-mouthed for you to understand. Good day, sir."

Willem hit the disconnect button. He looked at his hands, his desk, at the currently silent covered nest portal. It had all started so harmlessly – finding the mass of gnarled wood inside the surviving brick wall of his family's burnt-out mansion. But when it had come alive, his life had taken a series of bizarre twists and turns, and he knew that it had to end.

Willem reached for his coffee and sipped lightly, then shoved the remaining sandwich into his mouth. Yesiree, no change in routine, just think about the coffee and food, he schooled himself. Don't let on anything because he knew his strange bedfellow could read his thoughts. The one thought he did allow was the unanswered connection between the reason the National Guard was coming into his domain and the alien guest on his desk.

It was a temptation he couldn't resist, reaching out to him and controlling his will. He set down his coffee and uncovered the nest portal, pulling back the oily blanket. The mass of wood began to breathe, pulsing softly, slowly, undeniably alive, undeniably dangerous.

18

Danny, Ronny, and Woody turned off their chainsaws and removed their earmuffs. The final cuttings were completed, and they rolled the huge sections of oak to the shoulder of the road in front of Ismelda's Paradise B&B. They each picked a section to sit on, and then plopped onto the improvised stools and began their first Tastykake break of the day. Danny had butterscotch Krimpets, Ronny began sucking the cream out of the center of his chocolate cream-filled cupcakes and Woody smacked a toothless grin around the first of his peanut butter Kandy Kakes.

Just as they finished their repast, a visibly hungover Lou Ottney backed his flatbed tow truck up to the wrecked Ford. Amid the mechanic's expletive-filled rants, they helped Lou string the hook chains onto the car and then stood back as the hydraulics dragged the mass of metal onto the raked bed. Lou cringed and cursed his mother's sex life at every metallic clink and clunk, his head on the brink of explosion. Very few civil words were exchanged in the process. Lou drove away without even some thanks or a goodbye to the boys.

Sheriff Heffley and Marble slowed down as they approached Ismelda's. Marble noticed his Ford was gone and he felt a tinge of closure to all things of marriage past. Melancholy vanished quickly though. He laughed at the site of the three municipal employees who waved and smiled with jack-o'-lantern grins. Marble and Carl waved back, and Marble then glanced up at the B&B.

Rocking on the porch was the beautiful black princess from his dreams. She wore the same black cloak, and Marble felt her gaze bore into his head. *'Ave do Genio do Mal, besta de rapina do lair do Diablo, Senor Shooter. Boca do lair, boca do lair.'*

Marble swallowed dryly as the house and the message left his sight. Hopefully, he'd remember the lyrical tone of her voice, the message, in the right form when he saw Iguana again. One thing Marble did know without translation though: she not only was a princess, but a *princesa da bruxa,* a witch princess. He stared ahead as they drove toward the marina. A Portuguese witch princess who's a ghost – w*hat has my inner eye gotten me into?*

As if his guardian angel answered him, Marble let out a slow whistle when they passed Callie's and pulled in front of Willem's office. What indeed had he gotten himself into? Marble shuddered at the sight high above the marina. Over two hundred of the beasts of prey, *besta de rapiñá*, circled ominously. And one message came to him, the same one he'd heard at the chicken farm: *a nossa Mae* – to our mother.

"I'd say we hit pay dirt, sheriff. The sky above us is filled with these creatures, and they're all circling and crying for their mama. I've a hunch the good mayor may know who this bitch is."

"Sweet Marylou, are you serious? How many of 'em up there?" Carl looked nervously to the sky. "I figured we would go back to shotguns for this next excursion, is that OK?"

"We're going to need bigger firepower, I'm afraid. There are enough of these creatures to do some serious damage to the rest of the Chesapeake's natural reserves if they ever get out of Clydesdale. This is now taking on a whole new meaning of predator and prey. What's even more threatening is they seem to be growing in size. These guys are a lot bigger than the ones we've encountered. We don't have enough bullets to make much of a dent because I'm afraid it's only a matter of time before they start ganging up on humans." Marble didn't want to tell Carl of the brief vision he had just seen as it splashed on his mind's flat screen TV: beasts feeding on humans right in Clydesdale's center square.

"Oh great, Mister Shooter, thanks a lot. I really didn't need to hear that part."

"Come on, let's pay a visit to the mayor."

They exited the cruiser and Carl looked skyward, squinting as he vainly tried to catch a glimpse of what Marble had described.

Popeye Worthington emerged from behind the smiling potato chip trailer. The potato salesman had a stern guise of determination on his broad face and Marble was glad the gentle giant was on his side. "First of all, a good morning to you both; second of all, Mr. Marble, I've had some enlightening conversations with the Good Lord, and He has instructed me to stand by your side today."

"What about your conversations with me, sweet Bud? Dear me, I've heard it all now." Callie's laugh wake-trailed her as she appeared from the aft end of the Peterbilt's trailer. The mirth complemented the painted potato head with the shit-eating grin. Despite the corniness, it was infectious. Marble allowed a smile too, albeit briefly. More dangerous elements awaited, he sensed that to his core.

"Oh, and M-M-M-Miss C-C-C-Callie asked me, too." The large man stuttered it out, visibly uncomfortable in the presence of the restaurateur.

Marble smiled. "Whoever asked you, I accept, Popeye. Right now, I'm on my way to talk to the mayor. By the way, I'd love yours and the Good Lord's presence with me."

Marble checked to see the safety was on and then shouldered his shotgun. Carl popped out a magazine on his Smith & Wesson, examined the load, and then snapped it back home. The three men barely reached the marina office doors before they heard several sets of screeching tires behind them. Turning around, they saw the first of the multicolored news vans raise up a satellite dish. A flurry of doors, boom mikes, make-up checks, aperture adjustments, hairspray and cell phones converged on the trio. "Sheriff Heffley. Sheriff Heffley. Could you please answer some questions for us?"

Marble recognized the face behind the voice, but he couldn't place her name. He did know she was a prime-time reporter for ABC News. *So, the news media is rolling out its big guns for little ol' Clydesdale after all.* Four other reporters and their cameramen approached in hoarded mass. Marble recognized other nationally known faces, most on the Washington, D.C. beat. Must be a slow day at the capital, he mused. He also smiled because he knew that the only news reporter who was going to break the story was from a little affiliate in Harrisburg, PA. *Wow, since when did I decide to be nice to Deelah? It must be something in this beach air.*

The newsies pressed in toward the three men, jockeying for position with their microphones and boom mikes and Marble was glad claustrophobia didn't visit him often.

Carl raised his right hand. "That's close enough, folks. I'll, uh, well, I'll… Sweet Marylou," he turned to Marble and whispered, "What should I do?"

Marble thought for a second and then addressed the crowd. "The sheriff will hold a press conference this afternoon at three p.m. Please hold all questions until that time. We assure you, we hope to offer specific answers to you then." Taking the bull by the ball's diplomacy, Marble's delivery would have made Ronald Reagan proud.

"Who exactly are you, sir?" It was the cute Asian-American reporter from ABC.

Marble marveled at how perfectly shaped and white her teeth were. "I'm a friend of the sheriff's, that's all."

"Do you have a name, friend?"

"It's Marble. Shooter Marble." *Why is it when you tell news reporters that no questions would be entertained at this time do they completely ignore it and ask anyway? Part of the my-shit-don't-stink attitude of me first, me best; pure narcissists.*

"Shooter? Did you have anything to do with the rumors of gunshots last evening? Is that why you're carrying weapons?"

Gee, she is a bulldog, a bulldog with white sparkly teeth. "Like I said, miss, no questions now, perhaps you folks should turn up your hearing aids, three p.m. news conference, in front of Callie's next door. That will be all for now."

The three men turned in unison and entered the marina office and closed the door in the face of a barrage of questions. *Unbelievable.* Marble felt like a rock star, sort of.

Patti smiled and waved hello, her eyes and coordination already on the way to drunkenness, and it was only ten a.m. "Lemme guess, you gentlemen are here to see Willem. Howyadoing, Hef?"

"Good morning, Patti. Geez, hon, it's not even lunch yet. You should take it easy on that hooch of yours."

Patti sloppily giggled. Then Willem's office door swung open. "What the fuck is that racket outside? Tell those… oh shit." He composed his astonishment quickly. "Heffley, what the fuck is this? What's going on?"

Marble noticed that Carl had now sweated completely

through his khaki officer's shirt. "Willem, that's what we're here to ask you. What exactly is going on? I think you've got some explaining to do. This here is Shooter Marble and he'd like to ask ya a few questions."

Willem's face turned bright purple red and Marble could actually see the veins as they popped up on his sweaty bald head. "I know who the fuck he is. And I know you too, Worthington. You're parked illegally, by the way. And I don't have to answer any damn questions from any damn nothinglessness. I'm the fucking mayor, damn it."

Marble wasn't afraid of his histrionics as he roughly shouldered right past a startled Willem into his office.

"What the—? Hey, get outta there." Willem turned to face Marble with fists clenched. That's when Willem felt a huge, strong hand on his shoulder.

"Inside, Clydesdale. And don't even think about any funny stuff, you hear me, man?" Popeye refused to release the mayor, even though the thought of touching him was repulsive. He pushed Willem into his office, quickly followed by the sheriff who closed the door to a shocked Patti.

Marble looked about the room. It stank of stale liquor, shit, dirty ashtrays, spoiled eggs and rotting cigarette breath. What really caught his attention was the pulsating mass of twigs that sat directly in the center of Willem's desk. *Well, lookee here, just like in my dream.* He immediately sensed the incredible aura of the portal, its energy, its power, its evil.

Marble let out a soft, slow whistle. "What have we here? A nossa Mae? This… this thing has got to be it. I've seen this in a vision…" As happened the day before, the room changed in Marble's mind and he again watched the witch princess, covered in bird feathers, holding two glowing orbs over a large assemblage of… black, tangled, gnarled branches – a nest, a nest portal.

A jostle on his right shoulder shook the vision free. "Shooter, you OK? Ya slipped off again for a sec…"

"I'm fine sheriff, thanks." He directed his gaze at Willem who was obviously uncomfortable with Popeye's huge paw clamped down hard on his left deltoid.

"Where did you find this? And are you aware of its power?"

The color faded from Willem's face. "I don't have to answer any of your fucking questions. Get out of my office now or I'll have you arrested. Did you hear that this time, Heffley?"

Carl began to stutter but Marble cut him off. "What does this thing do? Is it a doorway of some sort? Is it a portal to some dimension or world? Are you aware it may have unleashed monsters? Answer me."

Marble saw the reaction first in Popeye's eyes, then Willem's, then Carl's. The tiny hairs on the back of Marble's neck began to tingle and he knew that something very unpleasant was happening behind his back. As the sheriff began to remove his weapon from its holster, Marble wheeled around.

His lungs went on hiatus. The nest portal had come alive. The gnarled twigs split apart and a cloud of orange and yellow, a fine mist that reeked of decaying maggot-infested flesh, seeped from the core. Marble felt like gagging but the noise that came next froze all his body functions. The hum started very low, as if it originated from a distant star, but it grew in intensity, the din of a thousand galloping hooves, a low, resonant rumble that grew louder and louder and louder. Marble finally took a breath and slowly backed away.

He couldn't "see" anything, but he didn't need extrasensory powers to deduce that the escalating noise was growing in intensity and something very bad was about to happen. He backed into Carl and the two of them, now with weapons ready, were pressed up against the wall to the left of the door. Popeye and Willem had also retreated to the wall to the right of the door. Marble cautioned a glance in their direction. Willem was losing his grip on reality as he coughed out a cackle and hooted like a crazed maniac.

The din now blasted their eardrums, and the room began to shake from the sonic vibrations that pulsated from the mass of vibrating twigs. Marble didn't foresee the next few seconds and it happened so quickly he barely had a chance to squeeze off a shot.

Willem's office door burst open and the cute little reporter from ABC barreled in, followed closely by her own cameraman version of Iguana. They entered the room with eyes wide just as a huge beaked head the size of a tank, eyes fire-yellow, with the same black and purple mullet haircut as the smaller beasts still circling the marina, emerged from the maelstrom of swirling mist. It snapped a razor-toothed beak and cleanly snatched the intrepid reporter and her cameraman in one sweeping plunge of a bite, gulping them down and then retreating back into the mist as fast as it had emerged. The clamor slammed to a halt, the nest portal snapped shut and the rattle of the walls instantly ceased.

"Sweet Marylou… what the… dear Jesus, where did they go, what did I just see, what the… Shooter, what just happened?"

Marble cautioned a glance at the other two men, and he saw a contrast of reactions. Popeye was plastered against the wall, his eyes the size of half dollars, his mouth wide open in astonishment and fear, mouthing a litany of Psalm 23. Willem, on the other hand, had a Cheshire cat smile that gurgled into a giggle, and Marble did sense that the good mayor showed signs of missing a boat that already sailed. Whack job, certifiable lunatic. Strait jacket time was not too far off for hizzoner, Marble dryly surmised. Marble's own hands were drenched, his own heart pounded in his chest, and he tried to make sense of the spectacle he had just witnessed.

"Sh… Sh… Shooter." Popeye's voice was weak. "Those two people… they just disappeared right in front of our eyes… dear Jesus, Joseph, and Mary… dear God, I've never…"

The light came on in Marble's head. None of them had seen the monster beast. They'd only seen the reporter and her cameraman disappear into thin air. Only he had seen the actual attack. To make certain, he quizzed Willem.

"Clydesdale. Clydesdale." Willem looked at Marble with a glazed stare. "Did you see anything? Did you?"

"I only seen two nothinglessnesses go poof. Just like before. Poof. Fucking cool, huh, don't ya think?"

A commotion in the outer office caused Marble to turn toward the open door. Patti yelled frantically. "Would one of you strong men help me hold this door shut? I got a slew of reporters trying to get in here."

Popeye came to her rescue, recomposing himself as he walked by Marble. "I got some serious praying to do today, Mr. Shooter. And I think we got the answers you were looking for. Now is also a good time to go ask Callie to marry me. Yep. That's what I'm gonna do."

Marble turned back into the office as Popeye opened the front door and pushed back the reporters with his huge frame.

Willem carefully placed the oilcloth over the nest portal, cooing to it as if it were a baby he was putting to sleep. Marble watched him carefully. *A portal, that's what that monstrosity is, and the huge beast, a nossa Mae. That's why Willem never knew he'd unleashed any of the beasts because he too couldn't see them.* It was also obvious he couldn't control the monster. Marble wondered if anyone could and once again, the black princess's words, her actions from his dreams, turned on yet another bulb in his head. Dark corners in his mind were now being bathed in a bright light.

"Sheriff Carl." The big lawman was having a bit more difficulty achieving composure. Marble placed a reassuring hand on his shoulder. "I need to get back to Ismelda's. Can you give me a ride? It's important." Marble then wheeled around to face Willem. "Don't you go anywhere, you hear me? I saw what came out of that monster. I think I know how to stop it from happening again. But you have to stay here. Don't, I mean it, don't let that beast out again. Clydesdale, do you hear me?"

Willem had drool extending from his lips to the nest portal. Marble didn't wait for a reply.

"Come on, Sheriff. On the way we need to stop and pick up a sledgehammer, too."

19

The WTTE news van squealed to a stop in front of Ismelda's Paradise B&B. Iguana fiddled with the shortwave receiver, trying to fine-tune in the chatter that squawked through the cab's speakers.

"There's some kind of hoopla down the street at the marina, Dee; sounds like a Coast Guard copter went down in the bay, ran into a flock of these devil beasts. We should hightail it there, don't ya think?"

Deelah felt like a huge weight had been lifted off of her back. Her shoulders were loose, her mind crystal clear pure, the color of a mountain lake fed by melting snow. She welcomed the lucidity and tears welled in her eyes, but the professional inside would not allow them to escape. She pulled the passenger visor down, lifted the mirror cover and looked at her visage. Her nose was twice its size and the telltale signs of black eyes already snaked across her orbital space: purple, orange, red, and beige, a medley of pain. She was shocked that she didn't feel more outraged. Where was that Deelah today? Had Marble's newfound persona really had that much of an effect on her? Was it a combination with Bradley being taken from her lair? Regardless of the reason, Deelah knew she had changed. This damaged goods look would play like gangbusters when she went on air with her exclusive: the embattled, intrepid reporter, down but not out, feisty yet professional, reporting with guts and glory. She blinked back the pool of tears.

"Listen, Iguana, we're to stay here. Marble asked us to. The rest of the pack is running toward shadows. We've got what we need so far, and he promised me that he'd deliver more. And the name is Deelah, fuckface, not Dee, got it?" OK, she thought, some of the old Deelah was still intact.

"Holy shit, chill woman, chill, just commenting on this whole bizarre stuff, that's all. Jesus, Dee... uh, Deelah... we got us a blockbuster, you know? Unbelievable shit, unbelievable."

"Come on, let's see if we can grab a coffee inside. Maybe they'll have a shot of something stronger I can put in it."

"Deelah, this footage, let me download this disc now, OK? This is gold. And I'm not letting *this* one out of my sight, no fucking way."

"OK. Let me do an intro first and then we can run with a polished feed."

"Dudette, of course, of course, I'm a professional, I know how to do my job."

They exited the van and as Iguana hoisted the camera to his shoulder, Deelah drew his attention. "We're in the big leagues now, grasshopper, check this parade out."

Iguana turned to look and sure enough, the world had come to Clydesdale. Direct from the highway, a cavalcade of green camouflaged military vehicles blustered down Main Street. "Iguana, quick..."

"Not a worry, not a worry, I'm all over this one, your highness." Iguana glided with precision and speed as he tossed Deelah a microphone. "Told ya, I'm a pro, baby, all pro. Come to Poppa, boys, smile big for the little dipshit news van from Harrisburg, fuckin' PA."

The convoy of military Humvees slowly approached, fifteen vehicles in all, with mostly young, fresh-scrubbed faces of the

Maryland National Guard staring out the open air windows with impish smiles.

"On me… in three, two, one…"

Iguana hesitated. "Uh, Deelah, you sure you don't wanna freshen up a bit? I mean, no offense, but you look like shit."

"Just film me, asshole. This is bigger than me, OK?" Had those words really escaped her mouth just now? She didn't take time to reflect. Instead, she raised the mike to her face and ran out into the street just as the first of the convoy's vehicles passed.

"The Maryland National Guard has been called into Clydesdale, Maryland, and the mystery of the missing birds has now reached martial law awareness. This is a beautiful early-fall day. Assawoman Bay sparkles, Ocean City lies across the water, welcoming beach lovers still. And yet this tiny town, surrounded by rich marshes and estuaries is strangely quiet. Local officials remain in the dark. Scientists have found no answers. But this reporter has uncovered the incredibly bizarre truth: an alien presence that will rock the beliefs of many. I will continue with an exclusive report on the very strange and very spooky events that have taken place in the last twenty-four hours. I do warn that the footage is not for the squeamish. For now, this is broken but unbowed Deelah Thayer of WTTE-TV, reporting live from alien-infested Clydesdale, MD."

Iguana slowly lowered his camera after finishing the report with a gentle pan of the sleepy bay to his left. "Deelah, you just gave me chills. You smoked that, girl. I always knew you had some real reporter chops in ya, honey."

Iguana clambered into the van's rear doors, ejected the disc from his camera, and snapped it into its slot, hit the download button, and the job was done. "God, that feels good. Yeah, java sounds great to me, too. And this time, I'm locking the van."

"There you go, Kaster, suck on this byte for a while." Deelah handed him her mike. Then she walked up toward the B&B. She couldn't help it, but the smile finally found its way to her lips. That did feel delicious. She didn't need a ton of makeup or hairspray to be good. There was something else too and she felt a warm rush of yummy roll through her. Why did she crave Marble between her legs again? "There must be some kind of aphrodisiac in the water down here, holy crap."

***

'Ave do Genio do Mal, besta de rapina do lair do Diablo, Senor Shooter. Boca do lair, boca do lair.'

Iguana crinkled his forehead and stroked his purple goatee. "Yeah, OK, it means, I think, uh, something like the beast from hell, the raptor of the devil. Mouth of the lair, mouth of the lair. Where are you picking this stuff up, Mr. Dee?"

Marble and Carl had passed the military convoy and had pulled up behind the news van. The question to Iguana was the first thing out of Marble's mouth.

"It's a message I've received, telepathically from these beasts. Thanks for the help, Iguana. Is Deelah inside?"

"Uh, yeah, sure; we were just heading in for coffee, you wanna join?"

Marble actually craved a huge glass of water because his mouth felt incredibly dry after the spectacle he'd just witnessed.

"Thanks, but I've got to talk to Deelah first. See you in a bit." Marble shouldered the heavy sledgehammer. It had been a donation from Paulie's Hardware Store, per the stern request of Sheriff Heffley.

"What do you need Thor's hammer for? Mr. Dee?"

241

Marble ignored his question and darted up the sidewalk and into the house.

The sheriff addressed Iguana. "He wouldn't tell me neither. This is making my blood pressure go through the roof, though. Sweet Marylou, I hope he puts this crap to rest soon, yesiree."

Sheriff Heffley's radio summoned him.

"Yeah, this is Hef… calm down, Patti, calm down, say again… Sweet Marylou… OK, OK, I'm on my way, be there in a jiff."

Carl leaned back out of the window to his cruiser. "Listen, tell Shooter that I have to get back downtown to meet with the commander of this group of boy scouts that just rolled into my town. Something tells me I should have stayed in bed this morning, not turned on the phone and just held my bride all day long. Sweet Marylou."

His voice trailed off as the police cruiser made a U-turn and sped toward the marina office, sirens blaring.

The sound of the police car made Marble stop in the hallway of the B&B and turn to look back out onto the street. The sheriff would be back, he thought, but Marble didn't need him around just now anyway. He entered the room to the right of the doorway and set down the sledgehammer, leaning it against the wainscoting of the wall. In front of him sat the walled-off fireplace and above it the mysterious egret painting.

He looked at the artwork and waited for something to happen again. All of the visions, all of the weird messages, all of it led to this moment, he was sure of it. The dream he'd had the day before, the same dream he'd awaken from to find crow-lady Carlotta perched on his bed railing, that vision where he'd seen the beautiful young witch princess kneeling in front of a fireplace, the same monstrosity of a beast before her and two glowing stones in her hands.

The mouth of the lair – she had controlled that portal with two stones. That was the message he was intended to hear. "I need to find those stones."

"What stones?" Marble jumped at the voice behind him. "Oh, sorry, didn't mean to startle you, honey."

He turned to look at his ex-wife, standing in the doorway with a large blue mug of steaming coffee.

"You look like shit, Dee."

"Thanks, I love you too. Besides, I've already heard that insult today, so you have to be a bit more original." She walked up to him and put her free hand on his chest. "Are we really a part of this? I must admit, I've never seen this side of you. Divorce definitely fits you, Marble. And I'd love to have you fit me in again if you'd like." She playfully winked. The old Deelah resurfaced. It was the same woman he'd fallen in love with once upon a time.

"Yeah, pretty wild, huh? Listen, about last night, this morning, that was beautiful but… ah, damn, I don't know what I'm talking about. Sure, I'd love to, you know, with you again too. But other fish need to be fried first." He kissed her lightly on the lips and tasted a hint of hazelnut from a shot of Frangelico in her coffee. "Deelah, I have some damage to inflict on Ismelda's wall. Is she in the kitchen?"

"Yeah, sure she is. Anything you'd like to tell me about that hullabaloo at the marina just now? We heard all the chatter on the airways, but you asked me to wait here for you." The mischievous lilt in her voice gave Marble a down-under stirring.

He looked into her swollen eyes. "There was a crew from ABC, I think. An Asian-American girl and her cameraman; she was real pretty, petite, seen her on the nightly news doing features before."

"Diana Wong? She's here? Jesus, Marble, this is big time. Thank you for giving me the edge, baby." She leaned up on tiptoes and kissed him warmly.

Marble accepted the buss and marveled to himself at how very different her lips now felt. A very good change because he couldn't recall the last time she'd kissed him like this. He gently pushed her away.

"Deelah, this… this between us, this is really bizarre and wonderful and weird. We'll definitely have to deal with this but not now. This reporter, Diana Wong, well, I just saw her and her cameraman get killed."

Shock caused Deelah to drop her coffee cup. Fortunately, Marble's hand caught it in midflight.

"We were in the mayor's office. They came bursting in and this monster, the mother, I think, of all of these invisible beasts, appeared and… shit, this sounds like a comic book story… well, it ate them. One huge gulp and they were gone." He snapped his fingers for emphasis. "Just like that."

Deelah quickly recovered. "Who else saw this?"

"The mayor – a real piece of work, trust me – the sheriff, and this guy, Popeye; well, they didn't see the beast. Apparently, only I can see these creatures, but they did see the two people just vanish into thin air. This thing, this monster has to be stopped. Now, this next part is something you've never known about me. I have an inner eye, Deelah, a clairvoyant power. I discovered it as a kid, but it's been covered up for a long time; I'd completely lost the memory. But now it's back, and I can see things, I can feel things. This town needs my help and you, my lovely ex-wife, you are going to be the one who brings this whole story to the world."

"None of the other news crews know?"

Marble chuckled. Say that fast three times in a row, he thought. "No one knows. Wong and her cameraman will be missed before long, so don't sit on this. Get this one out into the world right away."

"Holy shit, Marble, what should I say happened to them? I got it, they died in an accident… their bodies have not yet been recovered… at the marina, maybe drove off a bridge into the bay… but definitely something tied into the missing birds of this town. How's that sound?"

"My, my, what a criminal mind. You've got a second calling for mystery writing if reporting gets old." They shared a nervous chuckle, and then Marble asked for Deelah's phone, and after checking the Verizon directory on Ismelda's desk, he called Sheriff Carl and relayed the suggestion for the news van disposal. Carl was reluctant at first but then gave in when confronted with the option of having to explain the *real* reason the two news folk had disappeared.

Marble smiled at her. "Pretty creative, maybe you can be my ghostwriter someday. It's not like we're breaking any law, right? I saw Iguana outside, go do your stuff."

Deelah grabbed her coffee cup back and hurried toward the front door, stopping quickly to turn back to him. "You mean there's really a guy who calls himself Popeye?"

It caused Marble to laugh. "Oh, it gets a whole lot weirder than that, I assure you. Now go."

"How do I look?" She posed playfully in the doorway. "Don't answer that."

Marble watched her skip past the front window, down the porch steps and toward the news van.

"I guess the cat is out of the bag now. It's a shame, this town used to be so peaceful, so remote, so perfect for the likes of us."

Marble turned to face Ismelda. Also in the room were Jasmine, Anna and the old crow woman, Carlotta. Marble couldn't fight the urge, so he looked at Carlotta's feet and sure enough, his nightmare from the day before was confirmed: the feet were not human. This time, though, he maintained consciousness.

"We are Wiccan, Shooter, and not just we four. There are sixteen more sisters in this coven, a total of twenty. We are peaceful souls, each of us with interests and talents and each of us with limited powers. None of us, even all of us combined, come close to possessing your powers."

"We know that only you can end this. We can't stop the outside world from knowing anymore. That has already gotten much too big for us. We sisters are here to assist you in your trials, Shooter. Use us. Reach out to us for comfort, support, anything to help this evil disappear."

Marble had experienced so many new things in his Grand Plan. This revelation was going to rank right up there in the top ten of his "never seen anything like this before" list. He also felt like he didn't know how to respond. How often, he wondered, does someone explain a meeting with a coven of witches?

"That's not something a guy hears every day, I assure you. OK, I must admit, that does clear some things up.

"And yes, I have begun seeing things. Especially this pretty young ghost of a witch princess who was hung to death on that old oak some time ago – I don't know, maybe a hundred years or so ago – a *princesa da bruxa*." Marble noticed the visible recognition in Carlotta's eyes. "She's been appearing to me, giving me clues. And it's been a break of luck that not only has my ex-wife shown up this morning, but also her cameraman who happens to have been raised by a Portuguese grandmother, because this witch princess, she only communicates to me in that tongue, and I may be psychic but I'm not a linguist."

For someone who didn't know what to say, Marble developed diarrhea of the mouth. He continued on as he walked over to his sledgehammer and in true John Wayne fashion, deftly hoisted it to his shoulder.

"I've had to kill over fifty of these beasts from this mother devil. They're invisible to apparently everyone but me. Even to Clydesdale because he possesses their portal of entry into this world – some ghastly mass of twigs that opens up like a book. And I assure you, nobody wants to read what's in this tome.

"I believe, though seriously misguided, Clydesdale unwittingly released these flying creatures into our world. They've proceeded to decimate anything that flies within a fifteen or so mile radius of the nest portal, wherever it may be. And it's currently in his marina office.

"I know because I just witnessed the power of this portal. It explains why the creatures are circling above the marina, a couple hundred of them. They fear me and they want to go home to their mother. Who, incidentally, just made a guest appearance in Willem's office and promptly gobbled down a nationally known and overzealous reporter and her cameraman, in one bite. I saw it.

"And now I have to find the way to seal it in its hell forever. So, Ismelda, I apologize for the mess, but I need to get some aggression out because I refuse to let that thing take another life."

Marble swung the sledgehammer through the air, and it landed with a crash into the brick wall of the fireplace. Dust rose into the room as he landed hit after hit. The women had their mouths covered but none of them budged an inch.

Once the bricks started to loosen and fall away, the wall slowly revealed an open space. Sweating heavily, Marble dropped the hammer and pulled the loose bricks away. A large and very old tarp covered something on the floor of the old fireplace. He knew, without even revealing what lay beneath, that this was not the right location. Not for his purposes. But it was right for someone else's.

Panting heavily from the exertion, he wiped a dirty, sweaty brow and stood up. "Ismelda, I believe we found the remains of our dead witch princess. She can finally be put to proper rest and burial. Will you ladies be so kind as to attend to this?"

A tickle, a light fluttering of a touch caused Marble to turn and look up to the painting. Standing beside the egret was the young witch princess. She smiled, looked directly at Marble, and this time she actually spoke the words out loud.

"*As pedras nao estao aqui. Sentam-se ainda onde foram colocados para descansar. Procurare sua mente, voce sabera onde estao. Obrigado, Shooter, mim sera com voce sempre.*"

She smiled and he noticed tears rolling down her cheeks. She then walked out of the painting and into a realm not even Marble could see. The artwork returned to normal, a stationary egret in a marsh next to Assawoman Bay.

Behind him, Marble heard a man clear his throat. "Uh, Mr. Dee, um, I mean, Mr. Shooter, sorry to interrupt, but you might wanna know what she just said."

Marble turned around to find Deelah and Iguana in the doorway to the hallway, her mike still pointed in his direction. Iguana slowly lowered his camera.

"You mean you could hear that?" Marble looked about the room with his question.

"Not only could we hear it, but we also saw her in the

painting. She was beautiful. When did you first realize you could communicate with spirits?" Deelah tried hard not to sound too much like a reporter.

Marble ignored her. "Iguana, yes, please, translate for me."

"It may not be verbatim but here goes. The stones you're looking for aren't here. They are where they were laid to sleep, or maybe it was laid to rest. Yeah, *descansar*, laid to rest. Look into your head or mind because that's where you'll find the answers.

"Oh, and she said thank you, *obrigado*, and that she's always gonna be with ya. Sweet, sort of, don't ya think?"

Marble didn't get a chance to thank Iguana because a loud commotion erupted behind Deelah and the cameraman. A boisterous Callie squeezed into the Paradise, towing by the hand an embarrassed yet grinning Popeye Worthington.

"Sisters, great, great news. I'm getting hitched! Popeye done asked me to marry him."

A loud and joyous chattering ensued, accompanied by hugs, kisses, and whoops.

"Howdy, Mr. Shooter, you get a big hug cuz I think you've been a good influence in this town for more than just one reason." Callie grabbed him around the chest and squeezed him tight, realigning a few vertebrae in the process.

"Lordy, man, you did make a mess of Miss Ismelda's place though, didn't he, Izzy? Oh, and sisters, I have to tell you, I can't be in your coven no more. I not only got me one man in my life now, but I also got another. Jesus is now my other main man. Ain't that right, sweetie?" She turned and delivered a big sloppy kiss to Popeye, who was still obviously very uncomfortable with public displays of affection.

Marble looked about him at all the smiling faces. His eyes

finally rested on Deelah. "Congratulations, folks, I think you two will make a great couple. Now if you all will excuse me, I have to clean up a bit before I start my search for those stones. Sorry again for the mess, Ismelda, but…"

"Don't worry about a thing, Shooter. You go refresh and I'll have one of my special glasses of lemonade waiting for you when you come back down. Search your mind, your thoughts, and find those stones, and soon."

Marble eased past Deelah and Iguana, barely brushing his ex's chest with his, and he felt the surge of electricity race through him. Embarrassed, he sprinted up the stairs.

Deelah pushed Iguana out into the hallway and away from other ears. "Please tell me you got that on disc, please, please, please."

Iguana smiled. "Just remember to take me with you to the top, girl. Because this is gonna make you a star."

20

Doc Gilbert accepted the sheriff's call on his new cell phone. It took him a few seconds to remember how to answer an incoming call because he received so few of them. The phone had been a Father's Day present from Danny, just in case of an emergency. The call from Carl Heffley fit that bill perfectly.

Jackie walked back into the kitchen just as Doc stopped doing his prep work for the day. "Yo, Doc, did ya hear the news? Callie's getting hitched; isn't that the bomb? That big ol' hunk of a man came in and got down on one knee, right in the middle of the dining room and proposed. He was shaking like a leaf, but he didn't stutter one word. It was freaking romantic. God, I hope I get that kind of treatment someday. Hey, Doc, how did you propose to your bride, do ya remember?"

Doc Gilbert was somewhere between seventy-five and death but he didn't remember even where. And it had been an even longer time since anyone had asked about his wife, dead now for over twenty-five years. He also had a very short attention span. The question almost made him forget the sheriff's telephone request.

"Jackie, my bride said yes the moment I stepped off of the plane coming back from Korea. I was one of the few from my squadron who came back to the U.S. still standing on his own two legs. 'Course, back in the day, I was one of the few remaining who had his own two legs after the battle with the Gaels in Germania. Caesar Augustus himself praised me for my bravery.

I wonder where I put that medal he gave me…"

"Yeah, whatever, Doc, listen, I gotta run some food out; we're getting an early lunch rush. You should tell your stories to some of the customers out there. They're all news reporters and such, they could make you famous."

Old chandeliers rarely have bulbs that light up on their own, but Doc still had a few that twinkled. Dementia had not yet won the day. Jackie's mention of news folk brought back the phone call he'd just taken. "Darn, I almost forgot Sheriff Heffley."

He put down his oyster knife, wiped his hands on a grimy apron, and snuck out the service entrance at the back of Callie's Bistro. His attempt at a stealthy walk around the building looked more like a gimpy stork trying to find footing on a slippery slope. As he reached the side of Popeye's Peterbilt, he peered around the back end of the smiling potato chip trailer.

There it was, still parked ajar in front of the marina office: the ABC news van with the driver side door wide open. Most of the other news vans were across the street, parked haphazardly in front of the National Guard, who had parked their vehicles in a circle-the-wagons formation in front of the sheriff's office.

He crept up to the deserted van and was relieved to see the keys were still in the ignition. He climbed in, started it up, closed the door, eased out onto Main Street, and turned south towards the marshes. The sheriff had said to get rid of the ABC news van, make it look like an accident and Doc knew exactly the place. He passed Anna's bookstore and made a sharp left-hand turn onto Bolestridge Alley, a dead-end strip of pavement that led onto an old fishing dock that extended thirty feet out into Assawoman Bay.

He gunned the engine while in neutral, revved the rpms up high, slammed the transmission into drive, and with a smoking squeal of rubber, he drove the news van off the dock and nose first into the water. The only thing Doc Gilbert hadn't anticipated was how he was going to escape this maneuver. He was still contemplating this predicament as the van slowly slid beneath the water.

***

There is one cardinal rule in news reporting: everything, absolutely everything, stops for lunch. As Doc Gilbert had noticed, many of the news vans were across the street at the sheriff's office but no news crews were in sight. Even though eleven thirty was an early lunch start for most folks, the reporters and their cameramen took the early shift because feeding time held priority in their worlds.

Ranked in the top ten of all-time disgusting events are the sight of news media at an all-you-can-eat special. Callie's Bistro offered a selection of mixed greens, crab fries, fried calamari, and fried clams at lunchtime in the off-season, anything to get business in the door during the slowdown time of fall, winter, and spring. Newsies and fried food, a match made in cardio heaven; throw an 'all-you-can-eat' label over it and prepare to lose your financial shirt for that day's business. Pablo had been thrust into the role of head cook because of Callie's absence and he was in the weeds, an expression in the restaurant industry that describes the next step toward pure chaos. It didn't help that Doc had slipped off somewhere either. Pablo perspired like a pumped up boxer, shaking the fryer baskets onto a drip tray, splashed them with a healthy dose of seasoned salt, and reloaded them with handfuls of frozen seafood.

Jackie burst through the dining room doors, flustered to the max. "Damn animals. Pablo, *dos mas*, por favor. No wait, shit, *tres mas* sampler *platas*. Shit, where the fuck is everybody?"

Outside the restaurant, Danny, Ron, and Woody struggled with the heavy safe in Willem's office, guiding it onto the heavy-duty dolly. The three leaned into the handles and finally tilted it off the ground. Its weight still made the maneuvering difficult, and the boys made the process pure adventure. After a few deep gashes into the side of Patti's desk, they proceeded to take the molding strip off of the front door as the safe made it out onto the dock.

Willem watched from the doorway to his office. His color was Elmer glue pasty, his eyes had lost some brightness, and his demeanor was almost placid.

This scared Patti even more. She'd seen a ton of Willem's moods in her life but this one was brand new. She chided herself too because her Southern Comfort coffee thermos was now empty.

In an eerily calm voice, Willem directed the boys. "That's it, fellas, easy now, down the dock to my boat. Use the aft hydraulic lift to get it on board. Just leave it on the rear deck, near the aft opening. Good job, boys, good job. One man could move it yesterday, but it takes three of you girl scouts to handle it today. So be extra fucking careful."

An intrepid news reporter might have had an interest in three men moving a huge safe down a marina dock. After all, there were National Guardsmen in town, all the birds were still gone, there had been a crash of a Coast Guard copter, because of contact with alien creatures and an ABC reporter, cameraman and news van had mysteriously disappeared. Out-of-the-ordinary behavior should have created some hint of inquiry, but not when there was an all-you-can-eat buffet next door.

***

Danny's cell phone rang while the boys slowly moved toward Willem's Rybovich with the heavy cast-iron safe.

"Let's take a break, dudes." The wood whined heavily as the safe thudded to a rest. Woody had a fanny pack that contained three Tastykake peach pies, a perfect complement to moving an insanely heavy vault on a creaky wooden deck in September.

"Hello? Hello, Dad, you sound like you're under water… Oh… you are under water. Wow, this phone still gets good reception. What? You're where? Sugar tits a-wonder, we'll be right there."

***

Willem looked out his nicotine-stained window and with an incredulous, open-mouthed maw, wondered why the three municipal employees were now speeding out into the bay in an outboard-powered skiff, leaving the safe in the middle of the dock.

An all too familiar purpling of his pasty skin from the neck up and the beads of sweat on his scalp began to steam with the stink of alcohol and sweat.

"Is it too much to ask for some goddamn competent fucking help in this town? Fucking worthless nothinglessnesses."

***

Marble put his head under the stream of water and thought hard about the mysterious stones he'd seen in his dream. If the nest portal had been hidden all these years, it also must have been controlled by the stones. They had to be found. The resolve ran true with his intuition, a once again powerful version of his reawakened prescient abilities. He recalled the vision he'd seen of the witch princess hanging at the old oak tree. The old man with the beard, had he seen that man before? Who was he?

A knock came at the bathroom door as Marble began to towel off.

"Be done in a sec. Hope you can hold it a bit longer."

"Shooter, it's Anna. We need to talk."

He felt the familiar surge of heat that colored his chest and neck in red splotches, now evident as he wiped the steam from the bathroom's mirror. The rest of his stirring blood tweaked his Grand Plan buddy below.

"Be right there, Anna. Just a sec and let me get decent."

Marble did a quick brushing of his teeth with his finger and a dollop of toothpaste. He ran his fingers through his hair and wrapped the towel around his waist. He looked in the mirror. Decent enough, he judged. He opened the door and met Anna's gaze.

"Oh, uh, here, this is for you, Ismelda's lemonade." She smiled sadly, handing him the glass.

"Anna, I don't know… I mean… I do know… first let me get some clothes on."

He graciously accepted the lemonade and then walked past her and down the hallway, leaving his room's door open as he unashamedly dropped his towel in full view of the hallway. He leaned over and pulled on boxers, clean Dockers and a wrinkled polo shirt from his duffel bag. The Grand Plan held no shame, he smiled to himself. Besides, the witches had admitted that they had used him to help open up his powers. It also opened a cockiness that Marble wore just fine.

He turned to look at Anna, now standing in the doorway to his room. *If she's a witch, then she's a spectacular-looking witch, so much for the scary Hollywood version.* "I believe I know what happened to your husband. That creature is massive, deadly and has to be stopped before any others are killed. Anna, I'm sorry. Sorry for your loss. Willem may not be directly responsible but he's definitely an accessory."

Anna's eyes welled with tears. "I knew that… what I mean is, I felt… Turner hasn't come to me in the spirit world, but I knew… he was gone."

Marble wrapped his arms around her shaking body. She buried her head into his shoulder. He felt her warm tears on his neck, but he also felt quite a bit more. Her body, firm and supple, pressed against his… he had no control over it either… she responded by grinding her hips into his, molding her body tight.

Most men aren't equipped to handle the description of how amazing a beautiful woman feels when her body is pressed close to his. Too many synapses fire at once and the internal fireworks earn a dose of oohs and ahs and mms – not very eloquent tools.

Anna lifted her head from his shoulder. "Yesterday, our dalliance was not planned nor was it an act of manipulation. Your presence caressed me in a way I've not been touched in so very long. Touch me like that again, Shooter. Please."

They kissed warmly, sensuously and her lips, her tongue, sent Marble's firework display into heated frenzy; her body passionately wrapped closer to his beige polo shirt and navy blue Dockers.

Marble almost got lost in the moment; a hot, sexy woman, OK, a hot, sexy, grieving woman, wanting him, spontaneously, passionately… Wait.

"Anna… Anna… this isn't right… not right now, I mean… God, you turn me on, though." He reluctantly held her at arm's length. "There isn't time for this now. Believe me, I wish there was. Later, after this is done, rain check?"

She wiped the tears from her cheeks and feigned a slight pout. "I know. I'm sorry. Rain check it is, sweet Shooter Marble." She brushed a dark swath of hair from her eyes and straightened her dress with her hands, a marvelously sexy way of composing oneself. "How can I help? Can I… can I give you a ride anywhere?"

Marble couldn't resist the urge to touch her, so he reached up and carefully brushed her cheek, resting his hand against the warm tears that trickled down her skin. "Anna, are you going to be OK? I mean, with this news?"

She met his gaze and Marble felt strength and a resolve emanating from her. "I will survive this, Shooter. I will survive. Now, finish your lemonade and come down when you're ready. I have to get to my shop, so I'll drop you off wherever you'd like."

"Thanks. Maybe a lift to Sheriff Heffley would be helpful. I'm ready whenever you are."

For the second time that morning, Marble was faced again with an awkward moment of having two recent lovers in the same space. As he and Anna proceeded down the steps, Deelah walked in through the front door. *Make that three recent lovers.*

"Oh, uh, uh…"

Anna saved him. "Hi, I'm Anna Smythe, a friend of Ismelda's and an acquaintance of Mr. Marble. And you are the former Mrs. Marble, I understand?"

Marble saw the look in Deelah's eyes, and he recognized it as a precursor to one of her patented tirades. His mind ran through an array of possible responses: *The former? I never wanted to be the present Mrs. Marble. He's all yours, you trollop. Or... This piece of shit? You think I care about his sorry ass? Or... What are you doing coming downstairs with a man who fucked me this morning? Answer me, bitch.*

Deelah let the cloud pass though and she behaved civilly. Too nicely, Marble worried. "It's a pleasure to meet you, Anna. Call me Deelah. Do you mind if I have a moment alone with my ex-husband?"

Anna felt the underlying tension, primarily because she glanced at Marble and saw an award-winning stupid look on his face.

"Shooter, are you OK? You look a little green."

Marble wiped his brow. "What... what was in this... this lemonade?"

Anna chuckled. "Oh, that's just Ismelda's world-famous lemonade; just lemons, water, and sugar, and a few secret ingredients for your overall well-being." She winked at him, and then passed Deelah and went out the front door.

Deelah eased up to her ex-husband. "Oh, knock it off. We're not married anymore. I'm not allowed to rip you a new asshole because you just came down from your bedroom with a beautiful woman." She took a dangerous beat and Marble gulped for air, any air. But Deelah had indeed made an adjustment for the better. "I just patched into Harrisburg, and it was instantly picked up by the networks. They want me to do a live update at," she checked her watch, "twelve noon. I've got to get in the shower. You wouldn't have any time available to wash a lady's back, would you?"

Marble thought of all the Penthouse Forum letters and the Playboy Advisory letters he'd read over the years. All of those missives portrayed horny men detailing absolutely remarkable sexual conquests that rarely ever happened to the mere mortal man. Well, shucks, partner, this isn't any normal mortal man you're dealing with here, he said to himself in his best cowboy drawl.

"Deelah, I have to find a clue to controlling the monster I saw in Clydesdale's office. There's no time for anything besides that right now. But we'll connect later, I promise.

"Oh, and I told your peers that there would be a news conference at three p.m., just to get them off of our backs this morning." Deelah opened her mouth to protest but Marble leaned in and passionately kissed her. "But that's not going to happen. You get it all. Come find me after you do your noon update, OK? I have to fill you in on everything so you can do your job." He playfully squeezed her ass. "See ya later. Now go make yourself pretty."

Deelah looked at him. He remembered the first time he'd seen that look. Over eight years ago, the morning after the first night they'd spent together. She had wanted to do it again, and again.

Without a word, she turned and sprinted up the stairs, leaving Marble at the bottom of the steps, still stuck in a pleasurable memory. He recuperated quickly though and, smiling to himself, he set the empty lemonade glass on the small table in the hallway and headed outside to find Anna.

From the kitchen, he heard Silas' honk as he closed the door behind him. What do you know, he mused, a word of encouragement, Canada goose style.

***

Doc Gilbert squished his way through Callie's service entrance, pulling seaweed from his cap and his ears, his drenched clothes rich in the seeped odors of the brackish bay. His sneakers squeaked as he intercepted a plate pass from a very stressed out Pablo Escobar de Maria Consuelo.

"Take a break, amigo. The Centurion from Caesar's Twelfth Regiment has reported for duty; never fear, your Roman is here."

Outside the restaurant, an equally soaked Danny, Ron, and Woody resumed their quest with Willem's safe. Struggling mightily, they lifted it once more and began their three-man-pushing-really-heavy-shit dance down the rickety wood planks toward Willem's Rybovich, leaving a trail of soggy Tastykake peach pie crumbs in their wake.

21

Willem slinked warily from the marina office and squinted in the bright sunlight. It was an Indian summer day in late September, and he wondered why it was called that, though the warmth did nothing to relieve the clamminess he felt on his skin. The proverbial cat was out of the bag now, and he knew his goose was close to being cooked. Doomsday metaphors continued to bang on a door in his head, but he concentrated on vanilla thoughts. He didn't know how far the nest portal's telepathy reached so he didn't dare take a chance at revealing his true intentions. *Indian summer, I'll ponder that for a bit.*

A finality had to be achieved because the beast had now taken more human sacrifices and there had been witnesses, too many for Willem to dispose of himself. *Heffley, I can control, but that big, bad black bastard Popeye and that cocky-mouthed fucking nothinglessness from Pennsylvania all had seen the news crew disappear into thin air.* His skin gained some pink hue as anger bubbled within his gut.

Willem knew something was different with Marble though. The nothinglessness had seen what he and the others had not, something Willem had yet to experience. The result was the same with Captain Smythe, the Indian charlatan in Delaware and the news crew: vanished into the air. But the nothinglessness Marble's reaction had been one of pure terror because whatever came out of the book, he'd been privileged enough to witness. Willem schemed – *if Marble isn't careful, he'll meet the beast head on.*

The day had doom written all over it, but Willem's hangover prevented a clean read of that intuition. Crossing Main, he waddled toward Heffley's office and the group of Guardsmen who paraded in a tight circle around the sheriff.

Carl Heffley saw Willem's approach and mentioned it to the commanding officer. An officer who looked like he jumped from the pages of a GI Joe ad turned to face Willem and crisply saluted hizzoner. "Mr. Mayor, I wish the circumstances were different for our congregation but alas, that is not the case. Our governor has deployed my crack unit to your hamlet with orders of eradicating this, ahem, um, unidentifiable malady."

Willem looked at the name tag of the soldier who had his helmet under one arm and a hand stretched out to him with the other. He reluctantly shook the Major's paw. "Willem Clydesdale the fourth, mayor of Clydesdale, at your service."

"Pleased to meet you, sir. Major James Robins, Maryland National Guard at your service, also, sir. Sheriff Heffley informed us that these creatures, as he called them, only appear to our eyes once terminated. He also reports that there's one man in town who's been able to see them, a psychic, so to speak." The major said the last part with a sly smirk, the facial expression of "this is such bullshit."

"If that's what Carl says, it must be so. He's a straight shooter."

"Incidentally, that's what this feller's name is, Shooter. I forgot to tell you that part, Major." Carl barreled through two obviously bored guardsmen up to Willem's side.

Major Robins looked at both men and gauged his "I'm being fucked with here" meter. He'd seen quite a bit on tours of duty in Iraq, Kuwait, and Afghanistan to rate when someone tried to stretch his jockstrap into a thong.

"Gentlemen, this situation is directly related to the felled Coast Guard helicopter. Apparently, these creatures have also attacked livestock, in addition to birds. I am not present and accounted for to chase snippets in the dark. I'd like to meet this Shooter character and end this travesty once and for all. Believe me, I've got much loftier tasks to conquer than chasing windmills."

He slapped at a squadron of kamikaze mosquitoes that buzzed his forehead. The rest of the wave of bloodsuckers soon fell upon the guardsmen, hitting them at all exposed skin. "Great Caesar, you folks have a bug problem here, too."

One of his junior officers saddled up to his side and whispered in the major's ear.

"Oh, correct, thank you, Sergeant, I do believe this infestation is a direct result of the decimation of all the birds in this quadrant. Perhaps we might reconvene beneath the eaves of shelter?"

Willem was covered in bug spray. Carl had been taking a daily dose of Ismelda's lemonade, laced gently with enough secret ingredients to make his carbon dioxide taste like turpentine to the little flying needles. They both watched the swatting guardsmen and their major with amusement.

The sheriff stepped forward and gestured grandly. "In my office, Major; sorry about the bugs, you do get used to it in this town after a bit."

Willem reluctantly followed Carl and the major inside, turning around in time to see Anna's BMW pull up outside with the nothinglessness prick, Marble, in the passenger seat. Fuel on your fire, boy, fuel on your fire, he fumed. Reds and purples returned to mottled patterns on his skin; Marble seemed to have that effect on him. As the sheriff's door was slammed shut, Willem's hangover wailed to the rafters.

***

Marble leaned forward to examine the sky above the marina's office. Hundreds of the beasts were still evident; most of them now perched on every raised object in the marina, boat masts, rooftops, telephone wires, light poles, even the flagpole outside the marina's office. He swallowed dryly; he was still spooked by their sheer ugliness.

In the next instant, a huge squadron rose to the sky and flew northeast over Assawoman Bay. Marble knew their destination immediately. Another flock of birds on migratory paths had entered the forbidden zone and were soon to meet death. He thought about Silas, the Canada goose at Ismelda's, the wonderful visions he'd shared with the bird, and he felt sad for whatever species was about to meet its demise.

Within moments every other beast took to the skies, mostly heading northward in large packs, hungry for the migratory flocks that followed ancestral paths into Clydesdale, completely unaware of the menace awaiting them.

"Is it safe? Do you see them, any of them?" Anna put her hand on Marble's shoulder.

He turned to look at her. "They were just here. They've all flown off to hunt."

"Shooter, we have to stop this soon. I can sense the horror of the deaths these birds endure, and it's so very tragic."

Marble sat back in his seat. He looked outside at the guardsmen swatting themselves and running for cover, hiding in their Humvees. That's when his gaze fell upon the statue standing in the small-town square, just beyond a camouflaged vehicle.

The chiseled marble monument, its obdurate gaze pocked with acid rain over the past century and a half, bore a striking resemblance to the executioner he'd seen in his vision, the bearded man who hung the witch princess at the old blackjack oak.

"Anna, that statue, who is that man?"

"Ezekiel Clydesdale, reputed founder and benefactor of this town. It's a shame his descendant turned out to be such a madman."

The jigsaw puzzle began to take shape. The witch princess had been hung to death, her body entombed behind the fireplace in the room currently owned by Ismelda. The nest portal on Willem's desk had been discovered somewhere other than Ismelda's. It had to have been hidden, hopefully with the stones, at another location. One that Ezekiel Clydesdale's great-great-great-grandson would have access to.

The devil's portal, the lair of the beast, whatever its true name, and all access to the alien world was controlled by the stones he saw the witch princess wield in his dream. The energy of this portal gave the user powerful magic, powerful enough to have her hanged by Ezekiel Clydesdale. And now Willem possessed that power, and he obviously couldn't control it because he didn't have the stones.

The light went on, hell, the whole chandelier emblazoned, and Marble quickly turned to Anna. "Where does Clydesdale live? Is there an old building, a homestead, passed down through the generations? We need to get there and fast."

***

The din of laughter and conversation came to an immediate halt when someone noticed the television screen above the mini bar in Callie's Bistro. An Iguana clone turned up the volume all the way and a pall of silence instantly captured the atmosphere of Callie's.

Precisely at twelve noon, the ABC affiliate out of Baltimore switched to a New York newsroom where the extremely qualified Elizabeth Starr came on-screen, introducing a video of the real star of the moment, reporter Deelah Thayer…looking deliciously casual in sunglasses, a ponytail, a blouse open to the just the right button, tight jeans, and calf-high boots.

"This idyllic town, only miles inland from the barrier island of the world-famous shore resort, Ocean City, Maryland, this quaint, historic hamlet of Clydesdale, Maryland, is under attack." She swatted away at a swarm of biting flies. "Insects are feasting on the living because all the birds, every indigenous and every migrating bird, have vanished. They are gone because of this preposterously true event.

"This reporter never thought these words would be uttered but the evidence deems that impossibility extinct. Clydesdale, Maryland has been invaded by creatures from a different dimension, a different world."

She began to move to her right, Assawoman Bay still at her back. The move was perfectly timed, a few beats to allow the magnitude of her last statement to sink in. "Before I reveal pictures of some of these killed beasts, there is even greater tragedy to report."

Iguana zoomed in on Deelah. Her makeup was understated, the bruises were still evident around her eyes, and she now showed them to the world by removing her sunglasses.

"The last twelve hours have been dangerous for this reporter and her cameraman, but even more perilous for two of our colleagues. Elizabeth, it is my sad duty to report the disappearance of two of our own family, Diana Wong and her cameraman, Joey 'Bearcat' Winston. Apparently, in hot pursuit of a lead, the van made a wrong turn and drove into the Assawoman Bay, this gentle body of water behind me. Neither their bodies nor the van have yet to be recovered."

Iguana pulled away from her and settled on a pan of the bay. Deelah's voice carried over. "I am saddened by this event but not daunted by the task that lies ahead of me. For Diana, for Bearcat, for ABC, and for the world, this reporter will continue to bring first hand exclusive news of this bizarre and very strange phenomenon."

The earlier taped pictures of the dead beasts at the chicken farm soon found their way onto the world's TV screens. Deelah provided live commentary, including but not naming Marble, the only man able to see the creatures while they were alive, and when it had finished, she was back on the camera again.

"The governor of Maryland has called in the National Guard and a local division has only moments ago arrived in town. At the very next opportunity, I will report again on my findings. Until then, this is Deelah Thayer and Iguana Philips of ABC news affiliate WTTE in Harrisburg, PA, signing off and staying on combat alert in Clydesdale, Maryland."

Deelah waited and counted off ten seconds, the time needed to allow the satellite feeds to sign off. Iguana didn't care. He began whooping it up and dancing a jig. Deelah soon joined him in a spirited high-five.

***

All eyes were also glued to the small TV on Sheriff Carl Heffley's desk. Major Robins' face burned bright red as he wheeled away from Deelah's report to face Willem and Carl. "When the fuck almighty were you planning on briefing me about this sit-rep?"

The major's face began to rival Willem's for the purple-prickface crown, and he didn't wait for their reply. "A news crew drives into the bay, and you forget to tell me? Need I remind you, gentlemen, I have the authority to ask for martial law in this asshole of the world and then throw your two posteriors in the brig for subversive activities."

Willem had heard enough. "Shut the fuck up, dickhead. We just found out about this the same time as you. What arc you, a Patton wannabe? Give it a serious rest, major. This is as bizarre to us as to you. That's the first time I've seen footage of one of these creatures too. We're all in this together, OK? OK?" He had walked right up to the major, inches from his face.

"Willem, I mean, the mayor, is correct, Major." Carl swallowed with difficulty for the next lie. "That news crew, it, well, we didn't know… there are so many of them out there, I can't keep track of all of them." The sweat poured off his brow but the major only stood and walked to the front door, ignoring Carl's unease. *Sweet Marylou.*

Major Robins, unaccustomed to being rebuffed by a civilian, didn't know how to respond to the smelly mayor's outburst. He opened the door and before he stepped outside he addressed Willem and Carl. "Would you happen to know where this van went in the water? My troops will aid in its recovery. We have two certified divers in muster."

Carl picked up his radio. "I'll see if I can pinpoint that for you momentarily, Major. I'll be right out in a minute."

The sheriff feigned making a call and then set down the

Motorola when the door closed. "Sweet Marylou, that was hairy. I knew Shooter shouldn't have let that news reporter in on this. Sheesh… now, Willem, you behave, you hear? That-that-that whatever thing you have in your office, you leave it be until Shooter gets back here, you hear? That's an order, Willem."

Willem turned slowly to look at Carl. He smiled a Joker grimace. "So now you're giving me orders, Heffley? That's a fucking pisser, now, ain't it?" Willem fired up a Lucky, blew the smoke in Carl's direction, spat on his laminated NO SMOKING sign and then left his office. *No one, no one is ever going to order me around again.* The world now had an inkling of what was going on, and Willem knew no matter how hard he tried to spin it, the world would come crashing down on his doorstep if he didn't act soon.

He also had an idea what the beast that came from the nest portal looked like. A much bigger, much scarier version of the one he'd seen splayed out on Tommie's Chicken Farm on the sheriff's TV. A shiver ran down his spine. As he crossed Main Street, he veered to the right and walked down the main pier of his marina. Hopefully, he thought, the boys had loaded the safe safely onto his Rybovich. Safe safely, he chuckled dryly to himself, his skin slowly morphing back to cadaver gray.

***

As Willem entered his marina, the doors of Callie's burst open. Cameramen and news reporters, some in high heels and some in sneakers, all stuffing handfuls of fried seafood into their pockets, purses, and mouths, ran in mass mayhem across Main Street, towards the guardsmen, Sheriff Heffley, and their news vans. Not only were they leaving the feeding frenzy early, one of their own, a simpatico, a compadre, a teammate, had broken ranks and one-upped them, a serious breach of the unwritten news-folk etiquette laws. Usurped them mightily and she'd done it during lunch time. Egos were seriously bruised, and they were about to be damaged further. Angst, trauma, insecurity, inflated egos, withered fronts, and fetal fetishes, all surfaced with abandon. A slew of personal therapists across the mid-Atlantic region would be able to renew their Christmas club accounts for the next year before this damage could be amended.

In unison, the news vans, jockeying for position, network crews bullying top billing, of course, followed the caravan of military vehicles toward Carson Alley. Kept at a distance by the guardsmen, the news crews set up camp, each reporter gussying up in hand-held mirrors, picking pieces of fried clam and calamari from their chompers, readying themselves for up-to-the-second dramatic reporting on the missing ABC news crew.

It hadn't been difficult to spot the submerged van below the water. The depth of its demise was only twenty-four feet and Lou Ottney backed his tow truck gingerly up to the edge of the creaky old dock. Two eighteen-year-old guardsmen scuba divers dove into the bay and attached the cable to the rear tow bars of the submerged van.

It took a few minutes as the tow truck strained to pull the van from the bay's muck-covered bottom, but Assawoman finally released her muddy grip.

Cameramen jostled for position and zoomed in on the seaweed and silt-covered van. Alas, no bodies were found, as Major Robins sadly reported to the hovering cameras and microphones. The tides had probably already carried the bodies out to the sea, according to a local fisherman who was intimately familiar with the waters and just happened to show up in time to offer his sage advice. Doc Gilbert was disappointed though that none of the pretty reporters wanted to film him singing "The Battle Hymn of the Republic" in Italian.

On the other end of town, Anna's black BMW turned west onto Clydesdale Road as she and Marble drove toward what remained of the once prominent and magnificent Ezekiel Clydesdale estate.

22

Marble's new vision arrived as Anna eased into the long driveway that led to the charred, ivy and lichen-covered skeleton of the Clydesdale mansion. He was now an observer in a grand house colored in the same sepia tones as before. The room he saw in his mind was a library, stacked to the ceiling on two walls with leather-backed tomes hidden by floor to ceiling beveled glass doors. To Marble's left was an enormous teakwood desk with intricate carvings of ram's heads. Behind the desk, an inset window opened onto an outdoor patio paved with round river stones; the day was mid-morning, Marble guessed, summertime, because the country garden was in full bloom and butterflies danced among gladiola blossoms. He felt an astral tug that made him turn and face the primary interest of the room to his right.

Now in front of a six-foot-wide brick fireplace, he watched with bated breath as Ezekiel Willem Clydesdale entered the room carrying an object covered in an oilcloth. Masonry tools sat on the stone floor of the hearth, and Marble noticed an open hole in a space two feet above the mantle.

Clydesdale was dressed in the same long greatcoat and muddy boots that Marble recalled from the hanging scene. His beard was long, and his eyes held the same intensity the sculptor had successfully captured for his statue. Gingerly, with a reverence of handling a spiritual icon, Ezekiel placed the bundle into the open space. He then produced a smaller package, also wrapped in oilcloth, and set it on top of the larger one.

Marble gurgled with excitement as he surmised the smaller

273

package must be the stones. Ezekiel next proceeded to replace the bricks, expertly applying mortar, and in minutes he had sealed the hole. He then produced a Bible from inside his coat, and he began to pray in earnest, his body rocking in rhythmic cadence with Marble's breaths. After genuflecting, he made the sign of the cross over the entombed bundles. Ezekiel then pulled a brass crucifix from a deep pocket and nailed it into the mortar above the covered hole.

Marble's heart began to race because he felt the mystery had finally been solved. If the smaller package were indeed the stones used to control, to seal the portal, this whole nightmare could come to an end. His conscious mind wanted to return to the present, but he found it difficult to turn away. Ezekiel Clydesdale possessed a powerful demeanor, and even in prescient sight, his aura was captivating. Marble's delay proved to be costly.

Ezekiel wheeled about and faced the phantom Marble. His eyes blazed with anger, with wonder, with passion, with a sulfurous hint of insanity. Ezekiel reached again into his coat and as he pulled his hand free, a gasp of horror escaped from Marble's mouth. Ezekiel possessed a small stick with a shrunken head at one end and long beaded strands of human hair that spilled over his forearm. This tool was far from Christian, far from crosses, prayers, and genuflections. Ezekiel pinpointed Marble's position. *Had he heard me? No, that's, that's impossible, isn't it?* A wicked smile appeared on Willem's great-great-great-grandfather's face as he jabbed the talisman in Marble's direction. A jump back resulted in no movement – he was against a far wall. The panic consumed Marble and then the sensation of touch astoundingly seared into his chest.

His scream turned the vision black.

Anna's touch brought him back to the present, He entered

reality yelling at the top of his lungs. His hands were clutched to his chest and the searing pain he'd felt in his vision was real.

He frantically ripped open his shirt, the porcelain white buttons bouncing off the BMW's dash, and he delicately touched his chest. Looking down, he saw an emblazoned symbol, a raised welt colored blood red and seared directly over his sternum. It was a cross, a crude branding of the same crucifix he'd seen hung above the fireplace in his vision.

He panted hard and turned to look at Anna. She stared at his chest, her face painted in shock.

"I think I found it. And I think he, Ezekiel— no, I know, he sensed me in the past. In my vision, he swung a talisman, a pagan charm of some kind, a fucking shrunken head at me, hit my chest, and now… and this… this… this…"

"Black magic crossed with Christianity, practiced to this very day in Latino communities, called Santeriaism. It was a prevalent mix in his time, the ancient pagan beliefs partnered with Christian rituals and spells. But I've never seen anything like this. We must return to Ismelda. There are potions, salves that need to be applied. Are you OK to go on with this? Because you can stop it, Shooter; we have no hold over you, you may quit at any time."

Marble tried to settle his anxiety, tried to calm his rapid heartbeat, and think clearly. The storm delivered him to Clydesdale by mistake, or was it? The old oak in front of Ismelda's crushed his Ford, pure coincidence? He'd had sex three different times in the past twenty-four hours, with three different women. A wild goose communicated with him. Only he could see the hideous beasts that roamed the skies. He'd been front row witness to the deaths of two news folks. It had felt exhilarating to handle a firearm and get in touch with his inner macho. And, oh yeah, he thought again, he'd had sex with three different women in the past twenty-four hours. Deal sealed. He turned his head to the right, cracked his neck, and then pulled his shirt close. *Some super-duper Grand Plan, dude.*

"Anna, I'm not going anywhere. This attack confirms my beliefs that what I search for is somewhere on this property."

"Shooter, look outside, to your right. That's all that remains of the mansion. It burnt down over thirty years ago. I don't know how you'll find anything now."

"Willem found it; so can I." Marble twisted to his right and realized that he'd been so caught up in the vision that he'd not seen the reality of his situation. He opened the passenger door and walked toward the ruins.

The wall that Willem had pulled the nest portal from years before still stood and Marble carefully stepped over the shattered detritus of the former mansion. It was now covered in a carpet of weeds and small saplings. He cautiously approached the wall.

It was blanketed in ivy, hiding the brick beneath. Marble circled the wall and reached out with his inner eye to find the right location of the imprisoned stones. As he stepped to the south side of the wall, the vision of the library flashed in his mind, and he once again saw the room in the past.

On this visit, Ezekiel was not present, and Marble didn't care to dally any longer than necessary. His heart was practically bursting through his chest. The cross on his sternum raged with searing heat as he approached the crucifix that hung above the mantle. He reached out his hand.

Moss, cool and earthy, met his fingers as he found himself back in real time. He pushed his hand in further and searched the cavity beyond the ivy. Cool, damp stone came to his touch. He grabbed hold of the brick and pulled with all his might.

The ripping sound of vines reluctantly giving way to his pressure, the suction released from bricks no longer settled in centuries-old mortar, all came to him as he tugged.

A whoosh of air escaped the space as the mortar cracked free. Bricks and stone, cradled in the ivy's fingers, dangled free from the wall, and the cleared hole presented Marble with a small oil-clothed bundle. As his fingers encircled the package, another vision arrived.

He now witnessed a much younger and thinner Willem standing at the same wall, the steam and smoke of the burnt house encircling him. Marble watched as Willem reached in the same opening and retracted the larger bundle. Marble saw the smaller package, sitting atop the larger one, fall away as Willem, in his haste, pulled it free too quickly to notice.

Willem set the large bundle down on the ash-covered floor and opened the oilcloth. Marble moved to stand above him, and watched as the gnarled mass of twigs was revealed. It was the same deadly lair, the same nest portal.

The newly emblazoned crucifix on his chest began to throb and Marble turned completely away from the vision. The ivy-covered wall of present time met his eyes, and he opened his hand, which now grasped the small bundle.

He unfolded the old cloth, brittle at its creases, revealing two opaque stones. They were perfectly formed in the shape of large eggs, and he handled them gingerly, balancing one in each hand. Within seconds they began to glow with a light that did not heat, did not burn his skin. Marble backed away from the wall. He placed the stones in his pants pocket. It now was clear what had to be done. Though no vibration or temperature was released from the stones, he still felt their weight. Powerful magic indeed, he thought, powerful magic indeed.

As he turned to leave the mansion's remains, he sensed a presence. It began as a low whisper that seemed to come from all directions. He felt no fear though; if ghosts were around they could do him no harm. At least that's the message his mother had always told him and his brother when they were young children. Out of his mind's left field came the memory of his mother's soft smile and gentle voice. She had died when Marble was a teen. His father had said she passed because of a broken heart.

The cross tattoo on his chest began to flare and this time Marble clearly heard the whisper. It was a low "no" that grew in volume the closer he moved toward Anna's car. His trip down memory lane had prevented the warning from his inner eye.

"Shooter, behind you, look out." Anna was afraid and Marble sensed the imminent danger. He dove to the ground and rolled onto his back just as a heavy stone the size of a large pumpkin landed with a thud into the mud inches from his head. He quickly sat up and that's when he saw the specter. It was a manifestation of Ezekiel Clydesdale, long beard and greatcoat, fists raised in the air and fury blaring from his black as oil eyes.

The ghost began to fade rapidly from view. Whatever ethereal energy was needed to hurl a two-hundred-pound rock had apparently been spent. Marble stood slowly. He raised both middle fingers at the phantom and found a glorious satisfaction in Ezekiel's expression before he completely disappeared. His mom had been right after all – ghosts couldn't hurt him.

23

The cab of the Peterbilt was *a rocking, don't come a knocking*, a normal action at seventy miles per hour, but parked in between Callie's and the marina office, the motion of the ocean came from the speed of a couple of passion doors that had just swung open after two very long dry spells. Popeye and Callie commenced their union prematurely because, as they would later recount, they were moved by the passion of the Holy Spirit and that Essence told them, go for it, do the deed, rock the boat, chunk that junk in the trunk.

Willem didn't pay any heed to the animated semi for there were far greater tasks at hand, and he felt, no he knew, if his plan didn't unfold properly, it may be the last morning he would witness his miserable life unfold before him. Even the sound of Muddy Waters singing and picking to the "Pinetop's Boogie Woogie" that barreled out of Iguana's news van as it swung into a parking spot next to Willem's pickup failed to even register a raised eyebrow from hizzoner.

With an eye out for the National Guard, Willem scurried across Main Street and made a beeline for the dark cave of Lou Ottney's open service bay.

***

Jackie emerged from Callie's and frantically looked about while clutching a wad of order slips in her right hand. Ten tables had left without paying their tabs. Nothing is more infuriating and dangerous than a server who isn't tipped properly. To completely skip out on a tab was grounds for scofflaw genocide or at least crucial body parts removed by a rusty guillotine.

To add to her frustration, her boss was nowhere to be found. The last thing Callie had said before she bolted out of the kitchen after accepting Popeye's proposal was, "You got the house, Jackie girl, I'm gonna go get some of something big, black, and beautiful cuz this girl been crooning a lonely tune for too long." Jackie kind of knew what she meant, but right now her main concern was tracking down the other stiffs.

Iguana turned off the engine of the news van, thereby quieting the blaring stereo, much to Deelah's pleasure.

"Deelah, we have to find your husband, um, ex, Mr. Shooter Man. With this story smoking, let's stay on his trail. Can you believe our luck? Unbelievable. Effing awesome. Come on, wanna grab some grub first?"

Deelah hesitated at the sight of Callie's again in daylight. Last night's painful encounter with Pablo still ached on her face. But the thought of food reminded her of how long it had been since she'd eaten anything at all. Good reporting needed healthy reporters and nourishment overrode her willies.

"Food, mmm, that sounds good. Let's do this but let's do this fast. Marble should be around here somewhere, and I want to stay visible."

With a whoop of hunger spurred adrenaline, Iguana bounded up the steps, slyly acknowledging a very perturbed Jackie, while holding the door for the talent, all the while balancing his camera on his left hip.

"Now don't you two try and leave without paying too." Jackie said as she reluctantly followed them in.

Willem scanned the black macadam of Main Street through Lou's grimy window. To the south, he saw the leading Humvee as it led a contingent of vehicles back toward town square.

Before he could even swear, Anna's BMW appeared from the other direction and pulled neatly into an open parking spot in front of Callie's restaurant. *What is this, déjà vu?* The sight of Marble still in the car with his amour caused the bile to once again churn in his gullet, but he chose to stay focused on the more important task at hand.

"I'll deal with your worthless Pennsylvania nothinglessness ass soon enough, tough guy. If I have my way, you're all mine. All mine."

"What's that you say, Willem?"

Willem continued to talk to the window as he watched Anna and Marble exit from her car. "They're back. The fucking National Guard. And all those nothinglessness reporters. This has got to end. This has got to fucking end."

Lou had just returned with the ABC news van trailing from his tow truck, the remaining drops of Assawoman Bay pooling the concrete in bay number three.

Continuing to ignore Lou, Willem watched the horde of news people swarm back into town and proceed to pile into the marina office. "He's not here. He's not in. Don't know where the mayor is." He mimicked Patti answering all the requests for an interview with his person.

"Willem, you OK? Jesus, man, you're starting to spook me."

"Shut the fuck up, asshole. I'll be out of your face in a jiff. Stop being such a panty wipe." Willem scratched himself in the area most young boys learn early in life not to touch in public.

"You're in a typically sunny mood today. Shit on you then, I don't give a whelk's ass about your fucking problems, Clydesdale." Lou nervously rattled his toolbox, a set of ratchets clattering to the floor as he disappeared deeper into his cave.

Willem looked to the skies and wondered if the ghastly beasts were still out there. He felt their eyes, those hideous, yellow eyes, staring at him now, licking their chops at the chance to catch him in the open. Movement across the street earned his attention again as the horde of news folk emerged from the marina office and, like a flock of starlings evading a black-tailed hawk, turned in mass toward Callie's, hoping beyond hope that the all-you-can-eat-special was still special.

"Lou, my miserable existence of a living being friend, my time with you is now done. Go play with your tools and drool. Bigger fish to fry, bigger fish to fry." He lit a Lucky and dangerously tossed the lit match in the direction of flammable spills that made Lou's garage floor look like a bad modernist painting. Another peek for clear sailing and Willem scuffled out the open bay door and did his best imitation of a sprint across Main Street.

***

"Now there's something you never get to see too much of, sugar. Whoo-eee, that has got to be the ugliest piece of humanity I ever seen jiggling all over the street like that." She had come up for air in the hopes of allowing it to cool away her sweat. Callie's laugh took on new levels of angelic melodies in the closed compartment of the Peterbilt's cabin.

Popeye joined her in the driver's side window, both of them

sporting that age-old expression of the well-laid look, and he joined in her laugh as Willem jelly-bopped across the street, panting heavily as he collapsed into the doorway of the marina office.

***

Bruce Willis, thought Marble, the character of John McLean in the first *Diehard*, the cocky, street-smart toughness. Marble tried on the persona as he and Anna walked into Callie's and his ex-wife caught his eye. Without a hitch, he sidled up to her booth as she took a bite from a crab cake sandwich.

"Hey. I'm back and I'm ready to roll. Go ahead and finish up first, though. What's up, Iguana? How about you two meet me at the marina office door in fifteen." He consulted a watch-less wrist. "I've a feeling this thing is going to come to a head pretty quickly so be sharp. I've got to find Popeye first. I'm going to need some muscle."

Deelah reached up and touched his chest, the Diehard-imitation-ripped-open-shirt look revealing his new chest brand. "Honey, oh my God. What happened? Are you all right?"

The Willis smirk. "Nah, it's nothing, just a scratch, a sidecar to this whole fubar day. Fifteen minutes, don't be late." *Yippie-kai-ohs, mudderfudders.*

Anna squeezed his elbow. "Oh crap, this can't be good. Shooter, we better go through the kitchen. The reporter hordes are returning. Sorry, folks, present company excluded."

Marble leaned over the linoleum table and saw the swarm rapidly approaching. Anna grabbed his hand and began to pull him towards the kitchen doors. Deelah called out something, but Marble didn't catch it as his ears were masked with the sound of the ice-crushing machine at work. Pablo was doing a knock-out on a bucket of ice, turning it into a bed of crushed snow for the salad bar's seafood array.

"All hail Caesar Augustus, emperor extraordinaire. Doc Gilbert Octavius, humble liege and fervent centurion of the Roman Empire, at your beck and call, your majesty."

Doc Gilbert saluted Marble and Anna in the right hand across his chest fashion, a large ladle of lobster bisque carelessly splashing across his left side.

"Hi, Doc. Have you seen Popeye? Do you know where we could find him? And could you please do something to keep all these news people occupied for an hour or so?" Anna was accustomed to Doc's antics and never enabled the old coot by laughing.

"Fair maiden, he's in betrothal in his carriage. And never fear, the challenge you present to me is accepted and will be completed without fail."

Jackie burst in through the swinging doors. "Ms. Anna, Mr. Shooter, I mean, Larry. Table five wants to follow you in here too before the cheap bastards come back in. Iguana and your ex, you know, table five. You know?"

"Jackie, tell them to hurry. I don't want them followed by the rest. Anna, let's keep moving. Doc, carry on, Tribune." He returned the chest salute.

"*Vada con Il Dio, senore, vada con Il Dio,*" Doc sang the words.

The stones began to vibrate in Marble's pockets as they emerged onto the wooden deck at the rear of Callie's Bistro. He reached in and cradled them in his palms, pocket pool, magic style. They were getting warmer.

As they rounded the corner into the alley between the marina and the office, they were met by Danny, Ron, and Woody. The boys were perched on wooden slatted crab and whelk pots, bare feet splayed out onto the deck with wet shoes and socks between them, pant legs rolled up to their knees, bare-chested with wet T-shirts drying on their heads.

When they saw Anna, they made a feeble expression of modesty as they tried to hide their bony chests with opened packages of Tastykake peanut butter Kandy Kakes.

"Gentlemen, at ease. Danny, your father needs your assistance. Get dressed and go to his aid."

Anna gave the command with the authority of one who learned it from a captain of the seas. Still holding Marble's hand, she interlocked their fingers as they ran towards the front of the marina office. Popeye's truck blocked their view of Main Street and the town square, and for now that proved advantageous.

They stopped and Marble called out. "Ahoy there, mate. Trouble is afoot and your pirate strengths are requested."

Anna looked at him with a mischievous smile. "Don't tell me. You're a fan of Johnny Depp in the *Pirates of the Caribbean?*"

Marble returned her smile. That was much too close to be reading his mind for his comfort. "Actually, I always wanted to be a pirate when I was a little kid. And part of me feels like this is a pirate's adventure. Besides, Errol Flynn's pirate in *Captain Blood* is more like it." *Duh.*

The passenger door of the Peterbilt swung open and the space was soon filled with Popeye's mass. He hopped down and created a sandstorm of mini dust waves as his feet hit the wooden planks. In his best impersonation of a pirate, ersatz British accent and all, he said, "Aye, me captain. Nary is a day when the good sea doesn't beckon for a grand fight to meet with her enjoyment.

Petty Officer 2nd Class Quartermaster Bud 'Popeye' Worthington, Retired, at your humble service."

"Oh great, another man in touch with the little boy inside of him." Anna smiled at them both.

Ah yes, I do like this woman's sense of humor. He squeezed her hand harder. "Popeye, I need to get that mass of twigs, nest portal, door of the devil, whatever name it's called, I have to get it away from that nutcase Clydesdale. It's a doorway into an alien world, and I believe I now possess the powers to seal that door, hopefully forever. I could sorely use your aid."

Marble felt them before he smelled or saw them. Looking upward, the first of the beasts, a giant, menacing creature, filled the sky above the alley, its wingspan ten feet across. The vision initially startled him but then it gave Marble impetus because this beast was much larger than any he'd seen yet. The next thought made him shudder. This meant that they were growing fast and the bigger they got, the bigger the appetite. And the huge head that had emerged from the portal earlier that morning had a taste for human flesh.

"The Lord is my shepherd. We are with you. What's your plan then, Mr. Shooter? You can count on me."

With hair disheveled and eyes so dreamy, Callie appeared in the doorway of the cab. "Now don't you go do nothing that might hurt my man, Mr. Shooter. Ya hear, child?"

A commotion arose on the other side of the Peterbilt after Danny's voice had called out over a megaphone, "Callie's is now offering a FREE seafood buffet for the next hour. COME AND GET IT."

Callie lost the dreamy look in a heartbeat. "Oh no you don't, mister. This ain't no soup kitchen. This is my *honor*, my life. Help me down, sugar man of mine. I have to knock some noggins together."

As Popeye helped his lover down, Anna asked Callie for some generosity aid in keeping the news crew busy. Callie gave an exasperated look and then laughed heartily.

"For the good Mother Earth, the sky, the water, and all of us other folk, then. But only an hour and they're paying for condiments and beverages." She gave Popeye a huge, wet kiss and then hustled down the alley.

From the direction of the marina office, a very out of breath Sheriff Heffley approached them quickly.

"Mr. Shooter. You're OK. Sweet Marylou, thank the good Lord. That soldier guy wants to meet you ASAP. He says he's gotten martial law declared per the governor's office. And that I work for him now. I wonder, can he do that?"

"Quite true, Sheriff. Martial law dictates absolute control. May we obtain this declaration on camera?" A very composed Deelah nudged by Marble and Anna, Iguana in tow. Iguana balanced a huge hushpuppy in his mouth while he hoisted the camera to his shoulder.

Sheriff Heffley looked a bit stunned and turned his gaze to Marble for guidance. Popeye eased behind Iguana. Cameras made him stutter too, and he didn't want to quite lose his composure at this junction of his life. The scent of lovemaking still lingered in his nostrils, and he wanted to savor it for all its worth.

"Anyone know what time it is?"

Anna raised her wrist and Marble caught the hour.

"One forty-five. Deelah, the sheriff will speak with you on camera but make it snappy because we have an agenda and I want you to catch it all." They exchanged glances and Marble saw the woman he'd first fallen in love with in her eyes, that long ago day in Maxie's seemed to be as fresh and new as if it happened yesterday.

Deelah had noticed the change in her ex-husband, too. It was almost miraculous how he'd come alive. His normally pasty skin now had vibrancy and color and his eyes contained a passion and spirit she'd never seen in any man.

The snowball was rolling downhill though, and she set the longing thoughts aside and turned true pro. "Marble, we're right with you, all the way, honey. Sheriff, let's take this from the top again."

As Deelah raised her microphone toward the sheriff, Callie's voice could be heard bellowing behind them.

"Lord Almighty Blessed Mother of Jesus. What hurricane just hit my kitchen?"

<h1 style="text-align:center">24</h1>

Willem leaned heavily against the inside of the marina office door and tried to catch his breath. Forty years of two packs a day had turned his lungs into tar pits, and he could feel his heart pleading, begging, imploring for sustenance from his clogged arteries and veins. Sweat stung his eyes as he stared hard at Patti. There had been a time, he thought, oh such a time long gone, me and her, one fine piece of nookie, back in the fucking day.

Patti wilted under his gaze and feebly attempted to shuffle pink message slips on her desk, afraid of hizzoner and the temper that usually accompanied this kind of look.

"You have messages. A doctor or something, he called himself a bird forensic scientist detective, Peter Pumkineiter, such a funny name, don't you think? Oh, and the major from the army called sixteen times. The governor's office called seventeen times. And here are the business cards from the news reporters. They all want an interview with you."

Willem had the diversion planned. Patti was just another tool to use. He shook his head violently, the proximity of the nest portal now reaching out its deadly tendrils into his mind. "Not this Clydesdale, either. Saturn has rings. Jupiter has a moon with a climate. Pluto isn't even a planet. No fucking nothinglessness can get up earlier than me. Not a chance, Neptune, not a chance."

Patti badly needed a hit from her Southern Comfort thermos. Willem wasn't making any sense, and she feared unfettered psychosis the most of all. Instead, she held out the stack of messages and her hand shook so violently it looked like she was swatting at flies. Willem took a careful step away from the sanctuary of the door. He discovered his heart would allow him to take a few more steps in this life. He approached Patti's desk as she closed her eyes, turning her head to the side, cringing in fear of the beating to come.

Willem stopped in shock. *Now this is a new development.* He looked down but his Buddha belly blocked his view, so he touched it with a meaty left hand. Sure enough, a woody, a boner, a pudgy little phallic cry for attention. *How long has it been since I had one of these? And why the fuck now?* Someone somewhere was having a particularly demented laugh at this situation. Another thought that shocked Willem. He was agnostic and an atheist; not only didn't he believe, he also didn't give a fuck, and yet here he was wondering what deity poked fun at his expense.

"Fucking nothinglessnesses. ALL OF THEM." With his right hand, he swatted away the pink message slips from her hand. He squeezed hard little Willy tighter with his left hand and thought, the play is about to begin.

"Patti, this place is a pig's sty. Clean it the fuck up. How am I supposed to have the respect I deserve when we live in such a shit hole? Before you do another fucking thing today," the office phone rang. Patti opened her eyes and looked at the caller ID. "Before you do another fucking thing…" Willem reached out with both hands and ripped the phone from its connection, hurling it over his shoulder. It crashed into the water cooler, exploding the glass canister, and sending a tsunami of water across the worn, AstroTurf carpeting.

Willem took a beat and then continued, returning his left hand to his crotch, copping another feel. "Before you do another fucking thing, clean this dump up. And start with my office. Stern to aft, starboard to port. Peter Pumkineiter can chomp on this. Hop the fuck to it, woman."

Patti looked up at Willem. Never, not once in the twenty-two years she'd worked for him, had he ever asked her to clean his office. And now he wanted her to go into the same room in which a reporter and her cameraman had never come out of again. Patti was no dummy; she'd counted who'd gone in and who'd come out and heard the noise that had made her huddle below her desk. *Hit me hard, wherever you want, but don't make me go in there. Please.*

"I'm leaving. And I'm taking my friend with me; we're going for a walk. You have nothing to worry about. We won't be in your way. So snap to it, employee of mine. I'm not paying you to sit on your ass all day and look pretty. Get Uranus in gear, girl."

He walked to his office door and swung it open. The nest portal was quiet, sitting on his desk. "Start cleaning in here, please. Any surface that a hand, a foot, a butt could touch, wipe it clean. No fingerprints, you hear? Dust every surface, wash these fucking blinds, sweep the floors and for damn sake, open some windows and clear this room of its stench. Mars and Venus have a truce, whoopee. We have a reputation to uphold as the pinnacle of government in this fair town."

Patti slowly stood. Mayor Prickface, she thought, and realized that maybe, just maybe she was about to see the final phase of hizzoner truly gone mad. He pinballed about his office and grunted and groaned while he cranked open windows that hadn't been released from their locks in years. The salty scent of the bay wafted in on a gentle, warm zephyr. And the nest portal stirred from its rest.

A subtle movement washed across the surface of the twigs, and they undulated with animation as if they were worms intertwined together. Papers swirled on his desk, dust deviled into spirals, cigarette ashes swirled into mini clouds as a chilled air swept through the room. It encompassed Willem and he stepped back, aware of the sudden sensation he wasn't alone in the room. He shook it off as paranoia and then gently covered the nest portal with its old oilcloth, hefted the package with both hands, and rested it on the shelf of his belly. *Much heavier than ever before or is it just my heart warning me I can only do so much more?*

He turned casually toward Patti who now stood in the doorway with a Windex bottle and a roll of paper towels. "Ah, good, you may begin, Patti. Thank you for your kindness. We are going to get out of your Milky Way and go for a walk, maybe even a boat ride out into the bay; it's a beautiful morning to find the Big Dipper, don't you think? It's a stellar day and I believe I could use some sun. Vitamin D, don't you agree?"

Patti tried to recall that movie, the one where aliens from another world came here in pods and infected humans, turning them into robots. Her memory was cloudy, an alcoholic's bane. Either that or Mayor Prickface had clearly lost his marbles. The giggles started deep within, and she struggled to stifle them.

"Certainly, Willem, your mayorship, certainly, whatever you say. Enjoy your jaunt through the universe today, sir, you and your, uh…enjoy." She carefully circled Willem, allowing him free passage out.

Willem wished he could touch his hard-on again because it had felt so good to feel his old friend after so many years. Instead, he walked as casually as he could, past Patti's desk, past the defeated water cooler that now sported an upside-down phone as its hat, past the indentations in the green AstroTurf where the safe had perched.

He balanced his package carefully, opened the door, and walked into the afternoon sun, its warmth surprisingly refreshing. People were to his right, but he ignored them and instead strode purposefully to his left. He progressed twenty feet and was just about to enter the wooden plankway of the marina when he heard the call.

"Hey, fatso, yeah, you, scumbag. That's right, I'm talking to your lard ass."

Willem twirled an unsteady 360 degrees. That voice, he knew that voice, but it couldn't be, that was impossible. It was a balmy Indian summer afternoon and the temperature had just reached 75 degrees, but the sweat poured off Willem's skin in troughs.

With added incentive now, he hurried down the plankway just this side of briskly. "No, no, no, no voices, Willem, no voices, that's just your imagination, there are eight planets, a dimension so vast and yet so near." He mumbled the words, afraid to waken anything that should still be deeply, permanently asleep.

"Meester Big Shot, who do you think you are? Huh? Meester Big Shot? Dat is you I be talking about like this, yes, you fuckhead doodle dandy, Meester."

A different voice now, but just as familiar as the first, and this one came from beneath the wooden planks. Willem began to put the puzzle together as he reached the T of the pier. He turned right and baby stepped towardhis Rybovich.

"Hey, Mr. Manatee, nice fucking boat, asshole. Come on, take me for a ride again. Please, please, pretty, pretty please."

Willem stopped dead in his tracks because ahead of him, propped on the teak-trimmed bulkhead of his boat, were the ghosts of one Captain Turner Smythe and the Indian shaman/convenience store owner from Seaford, Delaware. A whiff of curry and seaweed reached his nostrils, and the stench sent his stomach into a double jackknife dive towards nausea.

"This can't be. This can't be. You, you, you're…" The ABSURD neon light began to flash in his mind. Willem bent back his head and cackled one loud laugh-cough. *So, this is how it's supposed to end, eh? Seeing ghosts, hallucinating, hearing voices of the dead?* He leered at the spirits perched on his vessel's bulkhead, mocking him with dead, smartass smiles. *So, nothinglessnesses make it into the spirit world too.* He chuckled to himself. *Happy Ebenezer Scrooge to you too.*

"What's so funny, fatso? Hmmm? Bird got your tongue? That's right, we're dead, both of us, me and Raj here. And both at your hand thanks to that evil little doorway to hell you're cradling like a baby. Things are happening now, fatso, and happening fast. Thanks for prying open the windows in your cesspool of an office. Raj here smelled the fresh ocean breeze first, and thankfully, he led us to a portal. It opened up a doorway big enough for us to escape from that hell."

The ghost of Captain Smythe maintained a steady grin. "Now we have to move on to the portals of this world's crossings. But before we go, we've some cleaning up to do around these fatso parts. Oh yeah, we brought along some help."

Just then the galley door opened on *Hizzoner* and two very ticked-off ghosts appeared. Willem recognized the recently deceased ABC reporter and her cameraman as they stalked out onto the deck. Ms. Wong was doubly pissed too because her hair looked like shit.

***

Major Robins stood up so quickly his coffee spilt onto his

clipboard of notes, and quickly congealed into a puddle over the names under the heading of "suspicious characters" the good major had identified in Clydesdale. His reason for clumsiness came from the simultaneous observation of Willem waddling down the walkway of the marina just as suspicious character number 2, one Larry "Shooter" Marble, appeared from behind the Peterbilt's trailer.

"Sergeant Balent, front and center, on the double, soldier. Follow that buffoon of a mayor and reconnoiter with him ASAP. Take two men with you and order him to retreat immediately to my position, if not sooner, and inform that elected official that I expect not a single ounce of civilian horse shit in return. You copy Sergeant Balent?"

"Yeah, no horse shit, I copy, sir." The National Guardsman sergeant, Terry Balent, a tax accountant in the civilian world, a life that would appear for him again in sixteen hours and twenty-three minutes, acknowledged his commanding officer with a limp salute.

The major shook off his clipboard and then wiped it on the back shoulder of his sergeant's blouse. He then twisted at the waist and cracked his back while he unclipped the snap on his leather holster that housed his Springfield .45 caliber pistol. He rotated his neck, a series of pops came from vertebrae realigning as he worked up the impetus to address Marble and his band of conspirators. He cupped his hands together, remembered to breathe from his diaphragm for optimal voice strength and then bellowed.

"I say there. Yes, you, Mr. Shooter, sir. Front and center, young man, I require your audience at once."

Marble glanced across the street toward town square and noticed what appeared to be a military officer waving his arms animatedly in his direction. But Marble couldn't hear the soldier because in his ears was a repeated wail of *'a nossa mae, a nossa mae, a nossa mae'*.

He looked skyward and the flock of creatures had returned. They alighted onto the roofs of the buildings that surrounded the town square, and it seemed as if every creature sent out the same thought, a wavelength that only Marble could decipher. What concerned him the most was their size. The largest one he'd seen moments before was now perched atop Ezekiel Clydesdale's pigeon shit statue in the middle of the park.

Marble sensed it before he saw it. The large beast eyeballed the military officer, still in histrionic cavorting. The creature twisted its huge ugly head and cocked a raptor's incisor-lined beak in that direction.

"Oh shit, oh shit. Oh no. Oh no." Marble didn't hesitate any longer. Without a weapon, though he wasn't sure what effect he might have, he ran anyway, as hard as he could toward the man in fatigues.

Deelah couldn't see what had spurred her ex, but she didn't wait to ask for directions. "Iguana. Camera. Let's move."

"Way ahead of you. I don't know what's about to happen, but nothing would surprise me with your old man running this show. Whoo-eee." Iguana passed Deelah, his camera perched atop his shoulder, and he slid into a kneeling position on the opposite side of Main, oblivious to the gravel shoulder that scraped his knees. "Battle stations."

Marble could now hear the major, but he tried to yell even louder. "GET DOWN. GET DOWN."

Major Robins didn't quite know how to react to this civilian who charged him screaming. This was no way to approach a military officer, especially one in charge of such an important mission. The good major was a high school theater arts teacher, and though he could never get his students or faculty to support the production of Shakespeare's plays, he nevertheless felt as though King Richard or Lear or Macbeth would never, ever, bow to the request of a mere civilian, a peasant, a commoner.

Marble was ten feet away, but his eyes were now on the beast that lurched from the statue, it's pointed, razor-sharp wings and talons stretched before its mass, on a direct path for the frustrated thespian's head.

The major wished he could remember a quote because it would be a wonderful twist to his future memoirs, as he reminisced of the moment the crazy civilian dove to the ground at his feet. A furtive glance at Marble's eyes changed his thinking though as he saw that the man's gaze lay somewhere above his own head.

A more accurate memoir would be that the major instinctively ducked as he saw the horror in Marble's eyes and saved his own head from being snatched from his neck by the deadly talons of the invisible beast as it swooped low for a snack.

Marble tackled the major by his ankles and rolled with him, borrowing his .45 from its holster in the process. With the major straddling him in a not very PG13 pose, Marble raised the pistol and emptied the clip into the beast that hovered directly above, poised to grab its prey again. The huge head exploded, and the creature fell heavily to the earth, splashing the ground with its body, its blood, and brain matter, and now visibile.

A gasp arose from the National Guardsmen who remained cloistered about their vehicles. Deelah made a beeline for Marble while Iguana circled their position. "Pulitzer, Emmy, fucking-A-Oscar. You're the talent, Deelah, so talent away. Let's see you shine."

"Marble. Marble. Honey, are you hurt?"

Major Robins rolled off Marble, stared with horror at the carcass of the beast that had almost made him its bitch, and then threw up his lunch onto the grass. And Iguana got every chunk of chum on tape.

Marble stood up, brushed himself of grass clippings and a Tastykake jelly Krimpet wrapper that had somehow managed to attach itself to his arm. He looked at the twitching carcass and appraised his actions as perhaps those of a Will Smith in *Bad Boys* – drop, roll, and come up shooting. A brief urge to blow the smoke from the barrel was resisted as he set the pistol down next to the major who was in the process of the dry heaves, something not even Shakespeare could have penned to sound poetic.

Deelah rushed into his arms and squeezed him so tight he felt his back crack. "Whoa, easy there, girl. I'm fine, Deelah, I'm fine. And I was just lucky enough to reach this man in time before something worse could happen."

With her microphone now in place and Iguana zooming in for a close-up, Deelah asked her ex-husband, "Luck had nothing to do with it. And where did you learn to shoot like that?" Brushing back a few stray hairs that had fallen into her face, Marble almost forgot the situation on hand and wanted to instantly kiss his somewhat disheveled ex-wife because it just made her look so cute. Deelah sensed the look in his eye and quickly became reporter, placing her microphone between their faces.

"You can see these creatures and no one else can. You just saved this officer's life and in the process killed his attacker with the major's own weapon. I can see now that the new nickname Shooter fits you like a T."

Marble jumped back to the moment with her. "Thanks,

Deelah, but I've no time to get into this further because like my father used to say, 'you kill one mosquito and a hundred come to its funeral' may actually hold true for these beasts because now I've riled them up good." Indeed, Marble had feared the truth for he sensed the agitation of the beasts that congregated onto the roofs and into the sky above the town.

"You can see them, of course. How many more are out there?" Deelah also looked upward. Iguana panned the skyline as Marble answered.

"It's tough to count them because many are now taking flight but suffice to say, everybody better get indoors. And quickly."

The creatures' wailing thoughts increased and Marble's ears began to hurt. As the word spread to every onlooker to find cover indoors, an arm reached out to Iguana.

"Come on, man, a dead cameraman can't reap the rewards of fame. Let's move it." Marble tugged on Iguana's sleeve that interrupted a sweeping pan of the National Guardsmen running into their Humvees as if the devil was on their tails.

"Do you see that? Our sworn civil servants, here to protect with weaponry that could blow these things out of the sky, and yet they run, run, run. So glad I cheat on my taxes." Iguana focused in on the frightened young faces.

Marble got him moving toward the sheriff's office as Deelah joined his other side. A somewhat demure version of his former self, the major limped in after them. Once safely inside, Marble turned to Iguana.

"What does 'a nossa mae' mean? It's all I hear from these beasts."

"Our mama. Our mother. Is that what they're saying now?"

"They're thinking it. I can hear their thoughts. I'm betting that Clydesdale's nest of evil might just be what they're referring to.”

"I think I can help you there.” The major wiped a sleeve across his chin as they all turned to him. “It’s the mayor, that Clydesdale character. I saw him heading down the marina’s gangplanks. He was carrying a big bundle of something in his arms.”

Sheriff Heffley burst in through the door, sweat staining his armpits and chest, giving his khaki shirt a dark brown patina. “Shooter, good, you’re here. Sweet Marylou, I don’t remember seeing one that big out at the ol’ man’s farm last night or this morning at the chicken farm. Sweet Jesus, Shooter, are they really getting bigger?”

"Yeah, and hungrier. But I need to get to Clydesdale. The major here says he saw the mayor on the marina dock, carrying something heavy. I think I have the clue to solving this riddle before any more of us get killed. But I need to reach him.” Marble’s hands went into his pockets as a reassurance that the stones were still there. A reassurance also that he hoped they would work.

"You saw him carrying something down to the marina? Sweet Marylou, he’s got one big-ass boat down there.” The light went on simultaneously for all of them. “Oh dang, this means we have to run again, don’t it?”

25

"Sheriff, nobody else has to leave; it's not worth the risk. Only I can see them, so I'll do this alone. Oh, I'll need another weapon, please."

As soon as the words left his lips, he knew Deelah would balk. Her tone was the same belittling one he'd heard for the past eight years but even she sensed it and a lighter, yet still forceful end came to her sentence. "No way, Marble. This is my fucking story and, well, if you can protect me, I want to see it through to the end. Honey, please." A roller coaster of eight years spun into a few words, Marble was amazed.

Iguana cocked his head in appraisal of Deelah, the kind of head posturing that would have made his namesake lizard cousins proud. Sure, he wanted to follow the story to the end too, but he also wanted to live to reap the benefits. But they were a team so as a team goes, so goes its players. Play-ah, step up, he chided himself. "Uh, Deelah? I gotta make a pit stop at the van to get a new battery pack first. Don't worry, I'll be fast."

The sheriff unlocked his armory cabinet and swung the doors open to reveal four neatly stacked Mossberg 835 Ulti-Mag pump-action shotguns. Major Robins whistled softly in awe.

"They're waterfowl rifles, twelve shells per housing, I'm loading them with 3-inch shot shells. I've got four of them because me and my cousins do some duck hunting every fall, down south of Ocean Pines. We got blinds that hide us better than dirt, and these babies will knock anything that flies out of the sky.

My cousins got a barge full of kids between them though, so their women folk don't take kindly to weapons lying around the trailers, but they've got no problem with eating roast goose and duck every winter. So, I keep the guns safely here." During his speech, Carl deftly loaded all four shotguns. "Shooter, there ain't no way you're going alone. We're all in this together. No sense arguing. You just tell me a clock position to fire at and bam, I'm pumping lead into the sky."

"Now that's what I call a good coming-out party. Hey, Sheriff, raise a gun in both arms and give me a good Rambo cry." Iguana focused in on a close-up of Carl.

Marble took a shotgun, but Sylvester Stallone was not in his demeanor, rather a subdued Gary Cooper from *High Noon*. Carl handed one to the Major and Marble was careful to watch and learn as the National Guardsman and full-time theater man smoothly cocked the pump action, smiling in its fluid machinations.

"This is one fine piece of gunsmith artistry. Now we shall see what we shall see." He one handed the pump slide, cha-chink, as a shell slipped into firing position. "What will be, will be." Major Robins had regained his swagger and he smiled a mischievous grin. "*To be or not to be: that is the question. Whether 'tis nobler in the mind to suffer the slings and arrows of outrageous fortune, or to take arms against a sea of troubles, and by opposing end them? To die, to sleep...*"

"*To sleep? Perchance to dream. Ay, there's the rub.*" The major gawked at Iguana who lifted his face from behind the camera and returned a wink. "Portuguese mother who read Shakespeare to us as our bedtime stories. Surefire way to get a kid to fall asleep."

"Hamlet will have to wait for fairer days, I'm afraid. Right now, I want everyone to get ready to hightail it. We'll head for the marina office first. The biggest creatures are still circling high above, and only smaller ones are perched on the buildings so we should reach there safely. Run ahead and I'll bring up the rear. If I give a clock position to you, fire into the air in that direction. Clear?"

Sheriff Carl appeared over Marble's shoulder. "Locked and loaded, ready to roll." He held a Mossberg in each hand and pump-cocked them both at the same time. With a little boy smile, he sheepishly admitted to Marble, "Gee, I always wanted to do that. Cool, huh?"

Marble smiled in return, but it was brief. Gary Cooper took over and the stern appraisal of their situation followed. "OK, let's go everyone."

Iguana went first as he muscled through Marble and Carl and darted out, whooping and hollering like a madman, running ahead of them for the angle that would film their flight from the sheriff's office to the marina; he safely crossed Main Street and dove into the news van.

Marble looked skyward and deduced that Iguana's movement had caused several of the beasts to take notice. They circled closer and closer toward the earth. Marble felt the feed me, feed me, feed me urge for the big buttski again, and he cursed his former addiction as the craving grabbed him by the aorta and shook him hard.

Carl didn't give him a chance to dwell on it though. "OK, Shooter, let's go." He ran out the door, followed by Deelah. The major followed and Marble went last, his shotgun raised across his chest, wary of any beast that attempted another attack. What he'd forgotten to do was to check his six. Flash pictures popped before his eyes, and everyone was bright red: danger.

The talons strafed his left shoulder just as his instincts told him to duck. The huge beast had waited out of sight on the roof of the sheriff's office, ready to pounce and it was selective, not targeting anyone else but Marble.

The blow felled him to his knees, and he rolled head over heels and banged hard into the back legs of Major Robins. A warm stickiness matted his shoulder, and he knew it was his blood but at least for the moment, there was little pain. What hurt more was that his shotgun had flown from his hands and landed ten feet ahead.

The major halted and crouched, wheeled around and shouted back to Marble, "WHERE? WHERE?"

Marble rolled over and looked upward. Directly overhead was a beast even larger than the dead one that now lay nearby. It had circled to a hover and was now in a dive-bomb position twenty feet above. "Twelve o'clock. Twelve o'clock. Twenty feet and closing."

The major fired into the afternoon sun, tracing his path downward in as close to a twelve o'clock pattern as he could discern. The last four shells found their mark and Marble rolled to his left, barely freeing himself from the dying body of the creature as it exploded onto the ground, materializing for all to see just inches from his head.

Deelah ran to her ex and took his face into her hands. "Shit, you're bleeding. That monster hit you; we need to get you medical attention. And fast. Hold on, honey."

Marble sat up, assessed his situation, and then stood, using Deelah as a crutch. "Have to get to shelter, Deelah. Quickly. Thank you, Major, it looks as if we're even now."

"The feeling is mutual, Mr. Shooter. I'm just glad I can tell time." He stepped around the fallen beast and fired another round into the beast's head. This time Major Robins didn't puke. Instead, he was buoyed by his own troops who leaned out of their Humvee windows and whooped and screamed in honor of their commander's valor on the field of battle. In true warrior style, the major ignored the hoopla, retrieved Marble's weapon, and turned and helped lead Marble across the hot pavement of Main Street and into the marina office safely.

Popeye and Anna welcomed the group but the most attention went to Marble's shoulder. Patti supplied a dusty first-aid kit that hadn't been opened in thirty years, so Major Robins again came to the rescue.

He radioed his corpsman. Seconds later the medic arrived via a tire-screeching Humvee as it crashed into the tight spot next to Willem's pickup, knocking the truck over the six-inch concrete embankment that lined the perimeter of the harbor. The old pickup teetered on two wheels as gravity had a senior moment as to which way it was going to reclaim the full weight of the Chevy. The bay side won, and the pickup flopped onto its roof in the brackish black water next to the marina office, gurgling with escaped air and gasses as it sank to a watery grave.

***

Sgt. Balent heard the report of gunshots. He and his two men stopped in their tracks and turned back toward the sound. Balent performed the tennis match dance between Willem and the town square, and then looked to his men, not knowing them beyond their left-breasted name tags, both inferior in rank and time served, and asked, "What do you think we should do?" A clear representation of why some officers are shot by their own troops.

Fortunately for Sgt. Balent, an accountant from Princess

Anne, Corporals Benny Velasquez and Armando Nomalaro, both back waiters at a posh premium steakhouse in Baltimore, were more fascinated by the sight of Willem Clydesdale IV. Ahead of them, the man was apparently involved in an animated conversation with his huge, luxurious boat. But of more interest was the pile of twigs that rested on the deck beside Willem, for an eerie yellow glow emanated from the nest portal, sending out a beam of light that carried well into the soft blue sky above Assawoman Bay.

"Yo, Holmes. Check out this sight. That's some crazy fucking *mierda* going down. Come on, sarge, dude, pull your shit together." Velasquez spoke good English, and he physically turned the accountant/sergeant toward the Rybovich. "Let's rock, Sgt. Dude, do your thing, hombre."

Sgt. Balent took a deep breath and called out to Willem, now only thirty feet away. "You there, sir. Uh, ahoy, or hello. I mean, stay put, sir. Major Robins requests you accompany us, please. We're to escort you back, sir. Please."

Corporals Velasquez and Nomalaro looked at each other and rolled their eyes. Their thoughts were similar: *Holy gringo shit, we could use a few hits of Yucatan red right about now.*

***

"Ha! Ha! Ha! Will you look at that? The cavalry has arrived. Easy there, Willem, you don't want to go and get yourself shot."

"You are not real. You are a figment of my imagination. That's all. Now disperse, get the fuck out, whatever you do to just be gone."

"Oh, we be good friends to you, Meester Big Shot. Slurpee you down, mofo, gangsta man. How's that fit for some shit in your face smack 'em down?"

Even in the spirit world, the former Captain Turner Smythe gave the former convenience store shaman a funny look. "What kind of horse manure is that you're shoveling, sahib?"

"The kind that rocks him up, up, and away in his beautiful balloon, oh yeah, Meester Big Shot, time to trip the light fantastico, beeatch."

Willem just stared for a moment. Time was of the essence, and these ghosts could not dissuade him from his task. He picked up the nest portal and set it on the deck. "Come to papa, boys and girls. You got out but daddy wants you back home." He looked down at the pulsing mass of twigs. "They're all yours, amigo. Go get them."

The voice of Sgt. Balent made Willem twirl around, the kind of movement that sent his head spinning. When his eyes returned to focus, he saw the three National Guardsmen standing nervously out of reach.

"What's that I hear, boys? Come a little closer so we can hear you better."

"Oh no you don't, gringo. I ain't getting anywhere close to that glowing thing. No fucking way."

More gunfire erupted from behind, and Balent turned sharply towards the sound. This gave Willem the chance he needed, the unplanned diversion that convinced him his task at hand was the one-and-only avenue of choice.

The ghosts on board *Hizzoner* saw the activity from the nest portal and didn't hesitate to vamoose. The doorway to their demise, which had recently sprung them into the astral plane of this world, was not a welcome sight.

Willem noticed their absence and carefully picked up the nest portal, its warmth and light bathing him in a ghostly glow.

He set it on the starboard bulkhead's shelf and then mightily struggled to lift one foot after another over the six-step ladder that led onto his vessel. The effort caused him to stop at the top of the bulkhead, trying to catch a breath of air that would silence his pounding heart.

Ahead of him on the port side of the aft deck, sat the large cast-iron safe, inches from the stalwart panel that would release it to the ocean depths. Willem was careful not to concentrate too heavily on this thought, so he turned his mind toward the visions of the ghosts. "Fucking… fucking… worthless pieces of shit… nothinglessnesses, no-good mother… fucking nothinglessnesses."

He lifted the nest portal and set it on the deck, directly in front of the safe's open door. His breath returned to an even-paced wheeze now. He moved as a man on a mission and released the lines that moored the boat to the dock. The physical effort was eased by a shot of adrenaline because he noticed that the National Guardsman had redirected their attention towards him.

Sgt. Balent yelled when he saw Willem releasing the mooring lines, but Willem ignored the warnings and climbed to the top of the captain's cell where he fired up the powerful twin diesel engines.

Corporals Velasquez and Nomalaro drew their M-16s, released the safeties and aimed at the Rybovich. Sgt. Balent nervously pulled his rifle from his shoulder and in the process of releasing the safety, dropped the weapon onto the deck. The corporals just shook their heads in disgust and moved forward cautiously, unsure of exactly what their mission called for in this situation.

The powerful engines sent a gurgling maelstrom of Assawoman Bay churning out the aft discharge pipes as the boat began to slowly ease from the dock, its fluidity in movement evident as Willem captained it masterfully through the watery avenues of his marina.

Sgt. Balent was on the verge of panic because he wasn't sure how to proceed so he radioed his commander. Major Robins' response was quick. "Shoot the engines."

Velasquez, Nomalaro, and Balent raised their rifles and fired at the aft end of the boat, their .30 caliber shells punching holes into the fiberglass and teak wood of the boat, sending chips flying into the air. Their fusillade was short because Willem made a quick turn into the bay, separating his boat from the shooters with a line of moored vessels.

Damage had been inflicted to one of the engines as Willem soon discovered. The tachometer for the starboard diesel quickly reflected zero rpm and Willem turned to watch the thick black smoke that now poured from the engine hatchway. The other massive diesel still churned out power. Willem pushed the throttle down, slowly picking up speed as he headed south toward the Atlantic Ocean's open waters.

26

Marble ran outside the marina office upon hearing Sgt. Balent's transmission to Major Robins. The pop, pop, pop reports of rifle fire echoed off the news vans parked out front, but Marble kept his eyes pinned to the sky. The beasts had alighted from their perches surrounding Clydesdale's town square and now moved in mass eastward, out into the bay. Marble cleared the corner just in time to see the smoking trail of the Rybovich as it rounded the small peninsula of sandbar that harbored the marina.

"I'll be a… now it makes sense. The creatures are following their 'nossa mae,' that nest portal. Aw shit, I hate boats." Marble mumbled the words as Anna came to his side.

"Doc's skiff is nearby. With luck, we may be able to catch him. Are the creatures moving?"

"Yeah, it's what I suspected. Their perimeter has that nest portal as its axis. When it moves, so do they. Maybe Clydesdale will do us all a favor and take it out to deep waters and then sink the damn thing. I've had a glimpse of their world. I'll wager those beasts aren't good swimmers."

Marble directed his gaze at Anna. Her skin's creaminess was a perfect palette for the subtle ruby of her lips, her sparkling hazel eyes. *Why can't I stay focused, damnit? It must be the air at the shore that makes me so horny.* He steeled his thought process toward the task at hand. *That a boy.* "Anna, a boat is what we need, and fast. Damn Clydesdale, somehow he opened a doorway to an alien world, a desolate, frightening landscape of death. And these… these creatures, beasts, whatever, escaped to here. And they were hungry. That's where your birds have gone. I've got to catch that boat and close the portal." He lifted the stones from his pockets. "These are the sealers of that doorway. Willem took the nest from its bricked coffin and left these stones behind. I may be able to end this if we can catch that boat."

"Holy Cow, Shooter, that's some story. Holy freaking A." Marble turned to see a camera lens in his face, wielded by a wide-eyed Iguana who smiled at him with a look of sheer awe.

Anna grabbed Marble's elbow. "Come on, Shooter, let's catch that sonofabitch."

They ran past the marina office, Anna leading the way and holding Marble's hand. Popeye, Deelah, Iguana and Major Robins followed. Moored to the dock behind Callie's sat Doc Gilbert's rust-colored fishing skiff, its 2-cycle Evinrude outboard motor tilted out of the water.

"I'll captain this craft, Shooter. Hop in." Popeye dropped onto the deck of the skiff and the boat rocked as if a tsunami had just hit. Quickly reacquiring his sea legs, he steadied the vessel enough to aid Marble in a safer, saner boarding. Next on board were Deelah and Iguana. "That's the max I can carry with this horsepower, Anna, Major. Sorry, sir."

Major Robins replied in stoic fashion. "Heard, sailor, I hail from a long line of landlubbers, nevertheless. Carry on and Godspeed."

Anna leaned down and touched both Marble and Popeye. "Please, please, end this. Safely. And come back, both of you." Tears welled in her eyes and Marble turned away just as Deelah placed a hand on his arm.

"Marble. I'm scared. I don't want you to get hurt, I don't want to lose…"

Marble placed an index finger on her lips. Thirty-six hours ago, he had walked away and yet it now felt like weeks. His Grand Plan had begun in a mind-boggling blitzkrieg of reawakened prescient powers. Doorways had swung open, and the overpowering influx of memories and visions had expanded his heart into a fuller, wider man. This time, he knew, there would be no going back, to any of the past.

The whining mini roar of the Evinrude and subsequent blue cloud of oily smoke caught everyone's attention. A flustered Doc Gilbert rushed out of the restaurant's kitchen door, followed by Callie, Jackie, and Ismelda. Marble did a double take when he spotted the large black crow that sat on Ismelda's shoulder. He could have sworn that Carlotta winked at him.

"Hold onto the bulkheads for balance, folks. We're underway and may God guide us safely." Deelah lurched back into Marble's chest as the skiff pulled away quickly and Marble stretched his hands out and grabbed the oversized vessel's sides.

Marble glanced back at the dock as Doc Gilbert did his across the chest salute. There was no way Marble was going to release his grip, so he just nodded in return. *Take that as my salutation, centurion.*

Iguana seemed to have the same sea legs as Popeye as he deftly maneuvered his body, stepping over Marble's right arm, past Deelah and into the bow of the skiff, all the time not missing a single f-stop adjustment. He captured the faces of his boat mates, the attention to every detail in Deelah's eyes, the stern resolve and stoically set chin of Marble, the bright smile and happy visage of Popeye Worthington who prayed out loud with open eyes.

Marble's body bounced in rhythm with the skiff as it sped across the bay, blessed by the fact that the water was calm and relatively free of waves. He cautiously moved his hands from the bulkheads and pulled the smooth round stones from his pockets. They had been vibrating for several minutes and he held them in his lap and stared at the kaleidoscope of colors that rainbowed across their spheres. In his hands, their vibration ceased, and tingling warmth began to radiate up his arms.

"Ahoy. Ahead of us. Do you see it?" Iguana pointed at a stream of black smoke that spiraled into the sky. They were about a half click away as they watched the Rybovich sail underneath the concrete abutments of the Route 90 bridge overpass. "Do you see it, Popeye?" Iguana barked out a laugh, the great equalizer to tension. "I mean, shit, how fuckin' funny is it that I'm on a boat piloted by a guy called Popeye? Cartoon kooky classic."

"I see him, Iguana, and you can laugh at my nickname all you want but please refrain from the profanities. I'm captaining this vessel and I say we keep the language clean. Or it's walking the plank for you, mate." Both men laughed and Marble just shook his head silently. Something weird was happening to his body. He wasn't sure if he should stray from the attention of the visions that now entered his mind.

Deelah sensed a change and turned back to face Marble. She placed her hands on his thighs and leaned into him and kissed him softly on the lips. "Ooh, baby, you're warm." She reached up and rested her hand on his forehead. Then she touched the bandage on his back shoulder. "That gash isn't too deep but it's still bleeding; you sure you want to go through with this?"

"I'm all right, Deelah, honest. This is about to come to a head though, and I pray I don't screw it up."

"Thank you, Marble, for this opportunity. We still make a great team, eh? Who'd a thunk?" She kissed him lightly again and turned back around.

At another time, he would have asked how Bradley Jr. was. It would have been in a tone that would have instigated another battle. Marble was so tired of drama, and the surrealism of the past two days hadn't given him too much time to reflect on the fact that not only was his ex in cahoots with this escapade but that he'd also had sex with her. He looked at the sensuous shape of her back, blending smoothly to her waist and downward toward her—no, he told himself, look away. More pressing activities required his full attention. But one thought kept returning, *why am I so freaking horny?*

Marble closed his eyes and his mind soared to the heavens. The vision of the earth far below leapt into his mind. He flew high above a coastline, soaring on the currents. The sensation was incredible, exhilarating, amazing. Turning his vision to his right, he noticed the feathered companions of his gander in formation behind him. Silas, he thought, this is a hopeful vision of that brave soldier I met in Ismelda's kitchen.

The vision came to a halt as Popeye shook his shoulder. "Shooter. Shooter. You OK?"

Marble turned back to him. The large man seemed too big for the tiny skiff. "I'm good, I'm good. Just a bit nervous."

Popeye smiled. "That smoke coming out of the engine compartment is black. That means an oil leak or fire, or both. Which means we'll catch those monster engines pretty soon. I was wondering, Shooter, what's the game plan?"

Ah, Grasshopper, no warrior engages battle without a plan, without preparation, without the proper spirit. Marble smiled at the memory of David Carradine in the old *Kung Fu* television series from his youth. He still held the stones in his hands, and he concentrated on a message, any message, but all he received in return was an overwhelming sense of calm. He twisted to face

Popeye.

"I don't have a clue, I'm afraid. Just get us as close as possible." He glanced upward and the vision was captivatingly horrid. Close to two hundred of the beasts, varying in size but all with one single thought: *a nossa mae, a nossa mae*, circled high above the smoking Rybovich.

Marble's throat felt desert dry. "Just get us as close as possible. And Popeye? Keep praying."

The truck driver laughed loud enough to be heard over the roar of the outboard motor. "Already on board with that, Mr. Shooter. The Good Lord is with us, and He's got our backs, believe me. Believe in Him and you shall be set free."

Marble squeezed out a smile as they sailed underneath the Route 90 bridge and into the Isle of Wight Bay. "Oh, I believe, my friend, I believe."

27

Willem ignored the flashing digital lights on the dash of the helm that warned of serious malfunctions afoot. A shift in the wind from inland sent a choking cloud of black smoke into the cabin and he coughed, bending low to try and grab a pocket of clean air. This can't be happening, not to me, not to me, he thought in between mucous filled hacks.

"Yes, that's right, breathe in deep. It's good for you, Clydesdale. You know how refreshing it is to be out on the bay. Especially on a perfectly glorious September afternoon. It is still September, isn't it? I've been unable to determine the time but by the looks of the sun and sky, my memory tells me it's September, an Indian summer day. Do you know why they call it that? I sure don't but it's no matter because I do know I loved the fall, Willem. And I loved my wife, Anna. You remember her, don't you, Willem? She told me after meeting you the first time that she thought you were a perfect definition for the word *disgusting*. Did you know that, Willem?"

Willem didn't want to face the ghost of Captain Turner Smythe, so he kept his head down. It was bad enough he had to hear him. One hand was still on the joystick throttle, and he ignored the now metal on metal clank, clunk, clang sounds that clamored from the aft engine compartment. Willem dragged an arm over his eyes and tried to wipe away the tears. They weren't from the smoke as much as the thought that his beloved dream girl, Anna Smythe, had disrespected him in such a harsh fashion.

"Fuck you. She would never say that, not about me, just not true."

"Willem, you're mumbling. Come on, suck it up, asshole, breathe in good and deep. What's that you say? Speak up, sailor."

Willem looked up into the empty space that held the shape of the former Captain Turner Smythe. The black smoke faded any distinguishing characteristics, but the voice remained strong. "You're a fucking liar. A dead fucking nothinglessness liar… she never would say those things… you'll get yours."

"You can't do a thing to me anymore, you sonofabitch. Your time is nigh, you sorry excuse for a human being. Soon, you'll receive the payment you deserve."

The sound of a diesel engine blowing a piston is loud enough to shake the spirits from many a grave within miles. It succeeded in dispersing Captain Smythe and pals while a new wind change from the Atlantic Ocean quickly cleared the cabin.

Willem stood shakily and viewed his position. *Hizzoner* was now down to 2 knots and the ear-shattering sound of magnesium screeching on titanium was evident on his tachometer: one of the two mighty diesels had blown. Audible alarms garnered his attention elsewhere. There was a fire down below, and Willem grabbed an extinguisher from its bulkhead brace. The aft deck below was awash in a plume of black, thick smoke that poured from the fringes of the engine compartment hatch. It kept Willem from getting a clean look at the nest portal near the safe. He carefully slid down the outer rails of the deck ladder, the extinguisher squeezed between his fat thighs.

Owning a quarter of a million-dollar vessel doesn't mean that an owner is automatically skilled to handle every situation that arises from sailing a ship upon the open water. Captain Turner Smythe would have known not to stand directly over a hatch while opening it to a possible fire below. The incredible pressure created by a maelstrom in an airtight compartment is a dangerous explosion ready to pop at the slightest hint of fresh oxygen.

Willem bent over at the waist and released the engine compartment door. It exploded upward and the newly fed fire gobbled up the fresh intake of air, neatly singing every single remaining hair from Willem's face and chest. He only remained alive by simultaneously not inhaling at the exact moment of the accident, sparing his lungs from immolation. The impact of the blown hatch threw his three-hundred-pound slab of flesh back into the galley's outer bulkhead, denting the aluminum bulkhead, breaking all his ribs, dislocating a shoulder, and knocking him unconscious.

The ghosts of Captain Smythe, Raj, Diana Wong and her cameraman, Bearcat, materialized around the fallen mayor, waiting to greet Willem's damned soul to the astral light. They also kept a wary eye on the portal of their demise, for there was not a chance in their ethereal world that they ever wanted to return to that hell.

***

Iguana shouldered his camera and focused in on *Hizzoner* as the smoke billowed from its aft. The vessel had come to a halt, its engines seizing up as the diesel fuel line leaked into the bay. They were only minutes from an imminent explosion, but Popeye didn't let up on the outboard's throttle. It was Deelah's scream that made both Iguana and Popeye change their focus.

She had reached back to touch Marble's arm, but her hand recoiled when she felt the feathers that covered his skin. Turning on her seat, the vision was even more bizarre.

Marble's exposed skin on his arms was covered in a beautiful array of silver feathers, each 3 inches long, layered atop each other in downy symmetry. His eyes were closed and his breathing shallow, but she didn't sense alarm as longer, silky silver feathers grew from his scalp. She yelled his name and shook his shoulders, but Marble was far, far away.

***

The witch princess glided toward him. Her dress, long and rough-hewn, was open at the breasts, exposing her chest to the air. What delightful air it is, thought Marble. *It's almost as if I'm on a cloud.* Looking down, the view caused an alarm to clang in his head, but he felt no fear. Far below lay the landscape of the Assawoman and Isle of Wight Bays.

He identified the barrier island that housed the long strip of buildings of Ocean City. The eastern side of the bay revealed the gentle indentations of the marshes and waterways, the vital sanctuary for birds. Directly below, he spied the billowing black smoke from Willem's boat and the circling beasts that swirled above in the shape of a giant, moving storm. An alien maelstrom that does not belong in this world, he thought.

The princess touched his arm, and he lifted his eyes to hers and in the reflection of her corneas he saw his own visage, the feathers pluming out of his head. He then looked at his arms, covered also in the wings of a bird.

She lifted his hands and the stones spread an orb of visible energy that extended up her bare arms, its power sprouting feathers on her body. The dream, Marble remembered, the dream where I saw you, naked on your knees, holding out these stones.

She smiled and he heard the message, unspoken by her

tongue but clear as a wind chime in his mind. *"Feche o portal. Acalme a besta. Sele seu fate."*

***

"Marble. Marble. Wake up. Where are you?"

He opened his ears before his eyes and the sound of the Evinrude's straining prowess, the whipping of wind, the whump, whump, whump of the skiff as it skipped over the swells of the bay, all came to him as he returned from his vision. Opening his eyes, he met the concerned gaze of Deelah, leaning into him with teary eyes.

"Oh, my God, you're alive, I mean, with us again, I mean… oh shit, Marble, I don't know what I mean." She leaned into him and hugged him hard.

"Easy now, ma'am, we can't rock this boat too much so careful with any sudden movements, please. It's obvious to me that a power higher and mightier than any of us has ever seen is at play here. Dear God, guide my hand."

"Feche o portal. Acalme a besta. Sele seu fate. That's what I must do."

Iguana's eyes were the size of saucers as he looked out from behind the camera's eyepiece. "Whoa, momma, this so freaking cool, better than any drug I've ever had, that's a certainty. Uh, Mr. Shooter, birdman dude, channeling the spirit world… you just said, close the portal, calm the beast, and seal her fate. Pretty cool, pretty fucking a cool. Oh, shit, I mean, sorry, Captain Popeye."

Marble squeezed the stones tighter as they began to vibrate in his hands. He looked upward and thoughts of the flying beasts filled his mind: our mother, our mother, our home.

"Mr. Shooter, this is going to be dicey. She may blow before we can get there in time and that could be real bad."

Marble turned to face the helmsman. "Pull up along the windward side. I may require help putting out the fire before I can seal the portal. We'll have to board her. Are you OK with this?"

Popeye laughed although Marble could see the concern in his big brown eyes. "I've traveled this far in life with the good Lord as my shepherd. There ain't no turning back now, sir, no turning back. Incredible, by the way, incredible. Praise Him. You got your own angel wings. Praise the Lord."

Marble smiled and looked down at his downy arms. *Oh yeah, this Grand Plan is one kick ass adventure, that's for sure.*

The skiff reached the heavily smoking yacht, and Popeye guided the boat to the windward side. Per Popeye's instructions, Deelah stood and grabbed the copper rail of the aft space of the boat as Popeye idled the outboard engine. He tossed roped crab buoys over the side for buffering between the two hulls and then threw a nylon line across the railing, expertly tying a bosun's knot in seconds that allowed for a secure mooring.

"OK, Shooter, let's do this. Ma'am, you and the cameraman stay here; we have to make quick work of this." Popeye helped Marble on board and then he swung his big body up the side of the Rybovich, climbing over the railing. Once on board he untied the line and leaned over, pushing the skiff away.

Deelah yelled in protest but Popeye raised a hand as if to stop her words. "If we blow, you'd best be away. Otherwise, how will the world know about what takes place here today?"

He directed his gaze towards Marble, who now stood over the unconscious slab of Willem. Popeye crossed the deck quickly and picked up the fire extinguisher that rolled in between Willem and the galley hatch. Moving carefully, he approached the open engine hatch and fired steady blasts of CO_2 into its belly. Inching ever closer as the flames subsided, he opened the second door of the hatch, allowing a wider-angle spraying of the engine compartment.

Marble now saw the nest portal, glowing red and pulsating as it sat on the bottom of the open cast-iron safe. It was clear now as to Willem's intentions. He was trying to seal the portal himself, dumping it at sea, locked in a safe.

Marble looked at Willem, knocked out cold and covered in black soot. In this condition, he would be no problem, Marble thought, as he approached the nest portal. The dream had shown the witch princess sealing the portal. Marble now understood why the witches had called him Shooter. It was a common-sense conclusion to him as he raised his feathered arms skyward, pointing the glowing, vibrating orbs in his hands, pointing them at the swirl of frenzied beasts now circling ever closer to the boat.

"Shooter, I'm climbing up to the helm. I've stopped the flames but I've got to turn off the other engine before the pistons freeze up too. You do what needs to be done; I'll get out of your way." He walked past Marble, patted him on his feathered shoulder and said, "God is with you, brother." Then the big potato chip salesman stepped over Willem, climbed up the ladder and disappeared from Marble's sight.

With his concentration returned, Marble brought both hands together, touching the stones, and a blast of laser like energy erupted. It was powerful and his arms shook under the force. It took a few seconds for him to steady his arms enough to control the beam. As it fell onto the closest beast, it grabbed the creature, freezing its massive bat wings in mid-flight. Marble thought of William Shatner, Captain Kirk of the Starship Enterprise, as he used his very own version of a Star Trek tractor beam, dragging the screaming beast down to the portal, watching in amazement as the nest opened and accepted the offering, sucking the creature through its gnarly mass of pulsating twigs.

Looking skyward, he used the beam to capture five beasts this time. The results were equally amazing as physics not of this world reduced the beasts in size, squeezing them with a pop through the nest portal.

It took another twenty minutes to rid the skies of the invisible creatures that had wreaked havoc on the tiny hamlet of Clydesdale, Maryland. Marble's arms felt heavy as he pulled the stones apart, ceasing the powerful beam. His body sagged from the effort, and he stumbled to the starboard side of the Rybovich to catch his breath. *Yeah, let's see Samuel the Troll add this exercise to his torture regimen.*

The sound of a distant rumbling locomotive halted his brief musings and sent them packing. It came from the nest portal, and it was the same ear-shattering din they'd heard earlier in Willem's office. The stones vibrated violently in his hands and Marble knew he had to seal the portal before that hideous head appeared again. Inhaling deeply, he spread his legs to help balance a sudden swell in the bay that rocked the boat.

"Out of my way, you fucking nothinglessness. This is my boat, my duty, my fucking world. You hear that? You piece of whelk shit, waste of human sperm." Marble was hit from behind and sent sprawling next to the open engine room hatchway.

Willem had awakened to see Marble covered in bird feathers making wild gestations over his head, holding two glowing stones together, acting as if he were making weird incantations toward the nest portal.

The back of Willem's head was sticky from coagulated blood

and a searing pain in his chest stabbed him as he struggled to rise. It took a few moments for him to catch his breath as he watched Marble lower his arms and move to the railing. The sound of impending doom spurred his weakened heart to move, *for this is my plan, my fucking idea and no charlatan from Pennsylvania will steal my thunder, not while a Clydesdale still walks this earth.*

***

Popeye knelt in prayer on the helm when he heard the loud din of alien thunder approach. Then the screams of Willem reached his ears, and he opened his eyes but the sight before him shook him to its core. In front of him stood the ghost of his dead friend, Captain Turner Smythe, holding out a spectral hand to the large man.

"Need some assistance in dragging that fat butt off the deck, sailor?" Smythe laughed and then held his palm out to Popeye. "Be still, my angelic son, for what will be has no need for your intervention. We will meet again someday in a different setting. My time is short.

"I and my new friends have been liberated of that hellish land where we met our deaths. We are now free to cross over to whatever wonders the portals of the astral lands hold for us. Please, continue to be a friend to my precious Anna. And tell her I will walk with her again someday, and we will watch the birds of nirvana together. Goodbye, Popeye, may heaven continue to bless you, my friend."

The ghost melted into nothingness before Popeye's eyes. The wonder of the visitation left him with heavy tears that rolled down his brown cheeks. If he wasn't to intervene, then at least he could watch. With a few more steps, he now saw the sprawled body of Marble, moving slowly, his feathered arms struggling into a push-up. Then he noticed the manatee of the man Willem, who swayed above the cast-iron safe, reaching for its heavy steel door.

The sound from the nest portal became louder: a thousand locomotives, a hundred jet airplane engines, the wails of a million tortured souls, the incessant dripping of a faucet onto a forehead locked into a vise, a hundred thousand versions of any Yanni song, all hellish, all splitting apart the serenity of the bay with alien, hell-bound din.

Popeye screamed to Shooter, but it was as if his voice held no power. Below him, the vista played itself out.

***

Marble's arms felt so very, very heavy. His rough landing on the deck had also knocked the wind from his diaphragm. He gasped trying to catch his breath. Standing would take too much effort so he took option number two. The decibel shattering din from the nest portal spurred him to roll onto his back to face the oncoming beast.

Willem blocked his view of the nest portal. Marble yelled for him to move, to get away, to run for his life. His voice fell silent amidst the dirge of alien cries.

It happened so quickly, Marble barely had the time to bring both stones together. The huge head of the mother beast exploded from the nest portal, sending Willem flying through the air for a second time, crashing into and breaking the galley hatch.

Saliva dripped from the beast's jaws and Marble smelled its hot, sulfuric breath. Huge, cloud-yellow eyes cast their gaze upon his feathered features. Marble saw the recognition as the beast recoiled slightly, as if surprised to see this new priest before it, splayed out in such fortuitous fashion, exposing the vulnerable belly to the dominant predator. Never in its long life had the beast had such an opportunity, not from any of the portals to any of the worlds it had visited. With added zeal, it reached back its long black neck, coiling like a serpent to strike at Marble.

Willem didn't see the beast, but he knew the nest portal had thrown him back, fighting for its own life. Every cell in his body screamed for him not to move, but the adrenaline of living with this alien creature for so long won the argument and his limbs straightened, lifting his heavy frame. Another swell aided his cause as the Rybovich pitched to the aft, allowing Willem a downhill run.

Marble brought the stones together as Willem burst into view, bearing the full brunt of the mother beast's gaping, razor sharp jaws. The beast recoiled slightly, unaware of the prey in its jaws, thereby snapping Willem in half.

Willem's lower torso, spouting bile, intestine, and blood, kept running, the wide ass, thighs, and legs waddled on, right past the cast-iron safe, and splashed into the waters of the bay. The remains of Hizzoner, the mayor of Clydesdale, sank beneath the surface, as the dinner bell rang for the scavengers of the deep.

Marble viewed the spectacle of Willem's lower half run into the bay and it was a delay that almost cost him his life. The huge head attacked quickly, shaking off the interruption of the Willem upper torso meal. Marble's stone beam pointed off to the side and before he could swing it back onto the beast, a black leviathan appeared from his left, swinging a grappling hook above its head, burying it between the beast's yellow eyes.

Popeye couldn't see the beast, but he saw Willem's demise

and he acted on instinct, grabbing the grappling hook in the same motion as he leapt the ten feet to the deck below, swinging the pole in what he hoped was the right direction.

The beast wailed and twisted its head in pain. Popeye hadn't let go quick enough though and he was cast heavily overboard with a splash that would send a tiny tsunami toward the Clydesdale marina in about an hour.

The diversion was enough for Marble to refocus the beam upon the beast, and it froze the head in place, saliva and the blood and guts of Willem frozen in time around the bloody jaws. Marble's winged arms began to shake violently, but adrenaline aided muscles on the verge of collapse. He climbed to his feet and pushed with all his might as he guided the huge head backwards with the beam, stuffing it downward into the nest portal.

Snap. It closed, the colors faded to charcoal gray and Marble now staggered to the open safe. Kneeling, he placed both of the glowing stones above the nest, turning his palms downward. They began to vibrate and then shook free of his hands and floated downward onto opposite sides of the nest portal. As they touched the twigs a parting occurred and the stones settled as if alive, nestling among the twigs, then fading from sight.

Marble stood as quickly as possible and pulled the heavy steel door of the safe, swinging it around and slamming it closed. He gave the combination dial a spin, and then leaned heavily into the mass. Praying for a favorable swell, he was soon awarded a cresting tilt as the bay accommodated his lean. With a groan of cast-iron metal on the teak deck, a final grunt and push sent the safe heavily into the bay. It disappeared almost instantly, the dark gray water accepting this burial without a murmur save the air bubbles that escaped to the surface. Marble stared at the water and the image before his eyes began to lose focus. This wasn't his inner eye but his outward orbs that carried the signal of system shutdown from his brain. He fell heavily into a sitting position, his breathing rapid and weak. With a final exhale of conscious air, Marble leaned back onto the deck, now covered in Clydesdale blood, and passed out.

Popeye pulled himself onto the aft deck just as Deelah piloted the skiff to the same spot. With Iguana standing to get a better camera angle, they all watched as Marble's feathers mysteriously disappeared before their eyes. Even more amazing was the sight of the four ghosts, who leaned over to touch his scalp before vanishing into thin air themselves.

28

Marble heard the voices of birds in his dream, cardinals, bluebirds, ducks, even crows and Canada geese. Melodic, varied, soothing, the whistles, hoots, barks, and chirps carried him from slumber to wakefulness. It was true then, he thought, as his eyes adjusted to the early morning light that streamed in through the window. The songs were not a dream; the birds had returned, and the balance of nature had been restored.

He focused on his surroundings and felt a slight concern because they were unknown to his memory. Soft pastel yellow walls and white lace curtains whispered gently with the early morning breeze that sailed in through open patio doors. Marble pulled down the soft flowered quilt and noticed that he was naked. He sat up slowly and the stiffness and soreness in his body screamed for mercy.

I feel like I've slept for a year. Now with a different perspective, he looked about the room as his blood readjusted to gravity. It was furnished with matching dark cherry armoire, dresser, and mirror. A photograph of a beautiful sunset sat above the wall to his right. None of his personal items like clothing or shoes were in sight. He rubbed his face with his hands and a couple days of growth met his fingers. He tried to remember the last time he shaved. With that search, the dust blew away and the remainder of his recent adventures gushed forth.

The bay, the stones, the feathers, the safe, Willem's legs running into the bay. The memories returned in a foggy mist – birds, alien beasts, and the nest portal. He groaned as he swung his legs from the high mattress, bare feet now on a hardwood floor. At the foot of the bed was a terry cloth bathrobe, big enough to cover a man, and he draped it over his shoulders, intent on discovering some history to these foreign walls.

French-style patio doors extended out onto a deck that overlooked a marsh and Marble walked out into the early morning light. The sun had risen in the east, and he shaded his eyes as he looked across the vast expanse of marsh that melted into Assawoman Bay.

He saw them in flight, a pair of widgeons, gliding over the salicorna grass and settling down to a morning meal. A squawk high above caught his attention. He gazed northward as the high-flying chevron appeared, pointed southward. Canada geese, elegant and free from invisible predators, unrestricted to roam the skies once more.

The vision was a live feed and Marble didn't even budge when the picture changed in his mind. He floated high above on thermal channels, inland breezes parried with ocean zephyrs, slight moisture on his face as the sun began to reveal the bountiful riches of the marshes below. *Thank you, kind ground bounder, thank you for blessing us once again with the heavens.*

Marble's vision returned to the earth, and he smiled. It was Silas, the bird from Ismelda's B&B, finally healed and released to join a new gaggle of friends.

"You're welcome, Silas. You're welcome."

"Should I say thank you or wasn't that directed toward me?"

Marble turned quickly and embarrassment joined the party as he was instantly aware that he hadn't closed the front of his robe. Anna stood in the doorway, her long brown hair pulled back into a ponytail, a thigh length silk robe covering her shapely body, and open just enough to show Marble a hint of what was yet to come.

"Not unless your name is Silas. Um, good morning. I must say, this is a pleasant surprise. This is your place?" She nodded. "How long have I been out? My body feels like I've slept for ages."

Anna laughed lightly and the sound was magical to his ears. "No, not ages, but you have been asleep for three days, I'm afraid. I've never seen anyone so completely out of it. We even had a doctor look at you, but we were reassured that you were only deeply asleep. If you hadn't awakened after a couple of more days, that's when medical attention may have been initiated. Doc Gilbert was already sharpening his rusty scalpels." She laughed again. "Welcome to my home, Shooter."

"Three days? Wow." He sniffed his pits. "Any chance a man could get some clean and scrub?"

"Only if you let your host wash your back."

Marble agreed to take a shower to try and wake up the rest of his body. His morning continued to turn out wonderfully as Anna graciously joined him in the shower to ensure, in her words, that all of his body once again was in working condition. After a thorough cleansing, she opened her closet where his freshly laundered clothes hung on hangers.

The fogginess in his noggin had cleared and he rejoined Anna on her deck where she handed him a steaming mug of tea. A plate of pastry sat on a small round glass table and Marble ate his first meal in three days. The sustenance gave him instant energy and he sat back, allowing the morning sun to warm his face while he appraised his hostess.

Anna was radiant, a classic, sensual beauty, and he wondered if the two of them had a chance for something more, something deeper. But questions remained and answers were still unknown.

"My ex, Deelah, is she OK?"

Anna smiled. "Oh, I'd say her calendar is quite full. She and her cameraman, Iguana, have been all over the news and talk shows. They were even on *The Tonight Show*, *GMA*, *Nightly News*, real celebrities now. As are you too, Shooter, a genuine American hero."

Marble cringed. That kind of label was not something he craved, like a square peg being forced into a round hole. "Yeah, well, I'm no hero, just a man in the right place at the right time with the right talents. It's really weird too, how you guys tricked me into getting stuck here. That tree falling must have been some powerful magic."

Anna laughed again. "We 'guys' had nothing to do with that. Greater powers than ours kept you here in Clydesdale."

"Speaking of angels, how's Popeye? Is he OK? I don't completely remember…"

"Popeye survived unscathed, and he remains definitely deeper into his religion. Apparently, there were some strongly clarifying experiences out there on the bay. We all agreed that he should take possession of Clydesdale's Rybovich, it only seemed fitting. So now he's living on it and restoring the engines while he and Callie plan their wedding. Oh, and Patti, Willem's secretary? Well, apparently, Willem had a will that left the marina to her and Jackie. Some good finally done by a man who never seemed capable of good. Irony, the stuff that makes life so interesting, don't you think?"

Marble stared off into the horizon and allowed his prescience full access. The images that arrived were colored in adventure, excitement and laughter, the perfect background for the Grand Plan. It was a peaceful decision then, though twinged with bittersweet. "Anna, thank you for your hospitality, you've been aces. Thank you for everything. This has been a crazy, crazy experience. There's a new man inside of me that I have to learn to control. There are still things for me to accomplish, new trails to walk. I'd love to stay but I've much—"

She stopped him by leaning in and kissing him deeply. "You can leave at any time. A brand-new Ford Bronco is parked out front, courtesy of your ex-wife. The keys are on the kitchen counter. All of your belongings are in the back seat. Ismelda put them there." She kissed him again and this time her tongue touched him in a way that opened up all of the happy genes in his body.

"But before you go, I want some more of you. I want you to remember me in a way that will bring you back again someday. What do you say, sailor? Up for the challenge?"

Birds frolicked in the early morning mist that hugged Assawoman Bay. Their songs filled the air with life. Anna's hand glided up his thigh and rested on his manhood, already eager and hungry for play time. *That's it, Assawoman Bay sure smells horny.* Especially during Indian summer, a much-used expression with an origin unknown even to the *Farmers' Almanac.*

THE END

Printed in the USA
CPSIA information can be obtained
at www.ICGtesting.com
LVHW041218080823
754338LV00001B/83